Five AUTOBIOGRAPHIES and a *Fiction*

Five AUTOBIOGRAPHIES and a *Fiction*

Lucius Shepard

Subterranean Press 2013

First Edition

ISBN
978-1-59606-555-0

Subterranean Press
PO Box 190106
Burton, MI 48519

www.subterraneanpress.com

Table of Contents

INTRODUCTION

Before I got kicked out of school I briefly played tight end/linebacker for the Seabreeze High Sandcrabs in Daytona Beach, Florida. The team was commonly known as the Crabs, inspiring newspaper leads such as Crabs Nip 'Cudas. Because "crabs" was also a word used in conjunction with pubic lice, the name sparked a number of brawls, both during and after games, and this attracted me to the sport—though I wasn't an especially talented athlete, my enthusiasm for hitting people was off the charts. I was a big, angry kid, 6'2" in the ninth grade, eager for the opportunity to unleash my anger, whether within the bounds of the game or outside of it, and I was as violent with my teammates when we practiced as I ever was when we played Edgewater Orlando or Sanford or South Broward. Eventually my football career was cut short by my penchant for skipping afternoon classes and practice, instead heading down to Beach News on Main Street to shoot snooker and nine ball, trying to hustle the old men who patronized that establishment, a practice that ultimately led to a physical confrontation with Seabreeze High's vice-principal and my subsequent expulsion—but for as long as my glory days lasted, a few months, football made me happy.

When I had the idea of doing a fantasy story set in the milieu of high school football, as all writers do I drew upon experience...and, in doing so, I discovered that the two central characters of "The Flock," Andy and Doyle, stood in for the two halves of my personality that had not fully integrated during my teenage years: one a vicious, near-sociopath and the other an immature manchild. While working on the story, I realized how easily I might have wound up being one or the other of the two. All it would have taken was an inciting incident, a sudden shift in circumstance, and there I would have been, working at a sawmill and busting heads in some bar at night, or finding a niche that would support the weaker, less aggressive soul I had become, insulating me from excesses of pain and joy. Thinking this led me to consider other alternatives and for the next year or so I found myself writing stories that contemplated various potential outcomes for the narrative of my life. The most obvious of these alternate realities, "Dog-Eared Paperback of My Life," derives its inspiration from some editorial advice I was given early in my career on how to become a commercially successful writer, advice that I ignored either because I had too much integrity or else was too bullheaded to accept. A secondary inspiration was the trip I made to Southeast Asia in 1994 during which I traveled from the upper Mekong from Laos to the delta region of Vietnam, a trip achieved in considerably less luxurious circumstances than my protagonist's—I was sick about half the time, mirroring the experience of my protagonist's alter-ego.

It's interesting, at least to me, how in both the above-mentioned story and "The Flock" I examined my personality from the standpoint of an essential divide, sensing perhaps that some mental health issues remain unresolved. If so, I'm certain they had their genesis one October evening when, at the age of fourteen, I returned home to find my parents and my family doctor in my living room, there ostensibly to give me a flu shot. I remember the shot, but nothing else until later that night I woke in a sleeping compartment of a train, a male nurse in hospital whites sitting beside me. He gave me another shot. When next I woke I found myself in a straight jacket, in an ambulance, in Westchester, Pennsylvania, on the final leg of my journey to the hopeless ward of the Devereaux Instititute, a private mental facility where I would sleep each night for the next seven months in a bed between that belonging to a hydrocephalic idiot and that of an old man named Louie with a penchant for eating cigarette butts. The reason I had been sent to Devereaux was ostensibly that after years of physical abuse I had decked my father when he came at me with his fists, secondarily because I got in an inordinate number of fights with other kids—my parents deemed me uncontrollable and thought a spot of therapy and the company of madmen would straighten me out. Naturally my time at Devereaux had precisely the opposite effect. Once I had recovered from the trauma of essentially being kidnapped and imprisoned, I hunkered down and went into survival mode, armoring myself with anger, building up a store of resentment and malice. Several times a week I was conveyed to an office where a psychiatrist waited. He would ask how I was doing, what was on my mind, and so forth, and to each and every question I would respond, "Fuck you!" Whereupon I would be led back to the ward to rejoin the medicated, shuffling, muttering herd of my fellow inmates.

My only friends at Deveraux, the only people I felt comfortable talking to (indeed, the only people on the ward capable of carrying on a coherent conversation), were the two Afro-American orderlies in charge of the night shift. I developed a relationship with them over the period of a couple of months, playing cards and telling them about Florida, trying to establish myself as a normal kid who had been victimized and did not belong at Devereaux. Through barred windows, they pointed out the town's attractions and anomalies, foremost among them the presence of a distinguished elderly man with a cane, clad in an overcoat with a velvet collar, who walked past the Institute every evening—this was, they said, the actor Claude Rains, best known for his roles in *Casablanca* and *The Invisible Man*. He owned a farm nearby and was living in town while undergoing tests at the local hospital. I took to watching with regularity his evening strolls past the window. Something about his solitude and halting progress resonated with me and I came to look upon the Invisible Man's presence in my life as somehow omenical.

I was well on the way to proving my normalcy to the orderlies, forging a bond between us that might, I hoped, give them a reason to trust me and perhaps even help me get the hell out of Deveraux—but then I made the mistake of telling them about the water-skiing elephant at Cypress Gardens in Florida and their attitude toward me underwent a sea change. They thought I was delusional, they didn't believe me. I was flabbergasted. Images of the elephant could be seen on every post card rack and brochure display in Florida. I had known about the water-skiing elephant since I was old enough to shoplift (my reason for frequenting gift shops) and had thought its existence was common knowledge—but apparently not. It was a baby elephant, I told them, wanting to clarify, to explain. Its skis were pontoons. Still they refused to believe me and began keeping their distance, treating me with diffidence and poorly masked disdain as they did the other inmates. Desperate to regain their trust, I wrote my mother, asking her to send me a post card with a photograph of the elephant water-skiing. Each day I anticipated receiving the post card, but she did not respond. She had basically abandoned ship, taking refuge in canasta games and bridge tournaments, and told me years later that she thought I had been joking about the post card, but didn't bother to explain why she never answered my letters.

It seems odd that so much could turn upon something as deeply inconsequential and absurd as a water-skiing elephant, but such was the case. Unable to repair my relationship with the orderlies, devoid then of any meaningful human contact, I spent the remainder of my time at Devereaux plotting my escape. Once a month a group of less-afflicted patients were taken for an outing into Philadelphia, treated to movies and hamburgers and so on. I had previously rejected participating in this field trip because the idea of being lashed together with a bunch of over-medicated droolers, like pre-school kids who could not be trusted to cross the street...it was too humiliating. But on this occasion I chose to accompany the group and, when the opportunity arose, I used a knife I'd liberated from the kitchen to saw through the twine linking me with a Downs Syndrome guy named Donnie and ran off, losing myself among the pedestrians crowding a Philadelphia street. To make a long story short, I was picked up by the cops the next afternoon while attempting to sell some 45s I had stolen from a record store to a group of schoolgirls, trying to raise enough money for a bus ticket to New York.

Back at Devereaux, realizing I would never be let outside again. I began a letter-writing campaign, begging my relatives, all of them, to rescue me. I described the Institute's hopeless ward in detail for them—petty squabbles between patients often ending in screams and ineffectual violence, soul-deadening meds, TV permanently tuned to channels showing cartoons and quiz shows, long winter days so devoid of incident or interest that when a fly became trapped in the drapes, buzzing crazily, that alone could provide sufficient entertainment to keep a patient watching it for hours. If someone didn't break me out of that place, I said, I was going to lose it, a prophecy that proved self-fulfilling, because by the time one of them (an uncle) came to my rescue, moving me into his home in Alexandria, Virginia, and enrolling me in school there, I was completely batshit crazy. To demonstrate the extent of my unsoundness—on my first day of school I sat in the back of the class during home room, staring out the window directly into the low sun, while girls peered at me, giggling and whispering behind their hands, and boys tried to injure me with glares and scowls. I figured there would be some serious assault and battery if I stuck around and when the teacher introduced me as a new student and asked me to stand, I walked out into the hall and out the main entrance and made my way to my uncle's house and hung out in the vacant lot across the street until my aunt spotted me and came outside and asked why I wasn't in school?

"I didn't much like it," I said mildly. "If Ben Irving tries to make me go back there, I'm afraid I'm going to have to kill him."

As I recall, I favored her with a tight little smile, wanting to convey both my seriousness and my regret over possibly having to harm her husband. Always be polite when you threaten someone's life, a lesson learned from my father.

That same evening I was sent off to the home of another relative, the first in a series of moves that wound up with me residing on a farm belonging to a distant cousin, attending school in the farming community of Goochland, Virgina, a blue collar environment less volatile than the charged atmosphere of Alexandria. At Goochland High the kids were generally affable and not predisposed to make snap judgments—they seemed to understand that I would not be there for long and thus treated me as an exotic event rather than as a person who might threaten them. Though we had little in common, I fit in just fine with guys who had to skip football practice to clear brush from a field and girls who had to forego the prom committee meeting to nursemaid a sick calf. My father's abuse had been directed toward a training program, cultivating in me an appreciation for the finer things in life, molding me into a writer, an ambition at which he himself had failed, and my comfort with the environment at Goochland, allied with my desire to thwart my father's wishes, steered me farther down a path I had already gone some distance along—a path of anti-intellectualism that caused me to embrace the unrefined, to value boxing over ballet, cheesy movies over museums, beer and chips over champagne and crudités. For the next twenty years I traveled aimlessly, engaged in bar fights, street fights, insulated myself from the possibility of self-examination with drugs, played in a number of rock bands, married twice without giving the matter much thought, dabbled in low-level criminality, drug dealing, burglary, etc., and eschewed anything that smacked remotely of the cerebral. I could have easily become an amoral street person with a glib rap, a minor league hustler like the protagonist of "Ditch Witch," or a blue-collar bon vivant like the protagonist of "Halloween Town," hiding his intelligence beneath a rough-edged surface—in fact, I was very nearly there on several occasions. And it's even easier for me to picture myself as Cliff, the protagonist of "Vacancy," trading upon a minor celebrity, drifting along in some undemanding, unchallenging life, a circumstance I tend to slide into whenever my finances permit.

So that is why I refer to these five stories as "autobiographies," "near-autobiographies" being too unwieldy a term. They embody alternate versions of myself that are really not so alternate, they flicker on and off like light bulbs with failing connections, occasionally achieving brilliance, obscuring the lesser beacon of my ordinary self, then fading into obscurity. As for the sixth story, "Rose Street Attractors," the "fiction," well, time has taught me that it, too, may be an autobiography, not in the sense that it's a past life, a memory of my passage through the Nineteenth Century, but in that it has every bit as much reality as the fiction I am living, a narrative that becomes less real second by second, receding into the past, becoming itself a creation of nostalgia and self-delusion, of poetry and gesture, of shadows and madness and desire.

DITCH WITCH

Late in the day Michael kept passing little towns with deserted streets and winking caution signals, paper trash swirling in the gutters, places that reminded him of movies in which mankind had been destroyed and computers continued to operate stoplights and sprinklers, and house pets feasted on the rotting flesh of their owners. Beyond them, sun-browned hills conveyed the interstate north toward Oregon—traffic was sparse and he boosted his speed, letting the Cadillac drift wide on the turns, driving with his neck turtled and his shoulders hunched. He felt that he was burning with indefinable brilliance and menace, that he had inhabited some nihilistic fantasy and become its outlaw Jesus. Every half an hour or so the girl beside him, a skinny bottle blonde in a tank top and cut-offs, would break into his baggie of coke, taking a few hits for herself, then loading the tip of her nail file and holding it beneath his nose, smiling and making meaningful eye contact as he sniffed and blinked. She had milky skin, nice legs and sharp features that reminded him of photographs from Depression-era Appalachia and matched her hick accent. She might, he thought, remain pretty for three or four years before she began to look dried up and waspish, and that would most likely be fine with her. Three or four good years would be about what she expected.

He had picked her up in a rest area near Sacramento and she had jumped in, abubble with false conviviality, saying Hi, I'm Tracy, where you heading? Seattle? Me, too! She talked a mile a minute about her travels in Europe, the ex-boyfriend who had become a rock star, an affair with an older man. If she had done half what she claimed, she would have been older than he was, and he figured her for seven or eight years younger. Seventeen, maybe. He had told similar lies during his days on the streets and knew her story was not designed to be believed; it was like a prostitute's make-up, both a statement of availability and a cheap disguise. She was frightened, probably broke, hoping to hook up with somebody who would take care of her. He wondered if he would let himself be hooked. It would be the stupid thing to do, the careless, impractical thing. The allure might be too much to resist.

"I might not go all the way to Seattle," he said after driving for an hour through the empty golden afternoon. "I might head east. Hell, I might even head back to LA."

He thought about Charlie. One kiss, he said to himself. A pathetic little kiss, that's all it had been. Charlie wasn't trying to seduce you, he was just fucking up the same as he did with everything else. Punishing himself for playing in a different key. And it's not as if you were cherry, un-uh, yet here you go running through the world, fuming with outrage and clutching your torn bodice like a goddamn nineteenth century virgin.

"This car really yours?" the girl asked.

"You think I stole it? I'm not the kind of guy who can afford a Caddy?"

"Naw, I..."

"You got me. I stole it from this old fag I lived with in LA."

A pause. "Yeah. Right."

"No joke," he said. "He was like my perv uncle, you know. My pretend daddy. Don't sweat it. He'll be too twisted up by me leaving to call the cops. Time he gets around to thinking about the car...the guy owns a dealership. He'll find a way to put it on his insurance."

She stared at him, horrified.

"I told you it's cool," he said.

Her voice quavered as though from strong emotion. "You're gay?"

He restrained a laugh. "I like girls, but I've done a few tricks. You know how it is."

He looked sharply at her, forcing her to acknowledge the comment—she lowered her head and responded with a frail-as-sugar noise.

Satisfied, he swerved around a slow-moving piece of Jap trash and leaned on the horn.

He could still turn back, he thought. Things could be mended. Charlie would fall all over himself trying to apologize, and life at home might be better than ever.

Too realistic, he decided; too humiliating, too logical and kind.

The sky grayed, rinsing the girl's hair of its sheen—it showed the old yellow of flat ginger ale. Her breasts looked tiny, juiceless. Mouse breasts. She caught his eye and flashed one of her Runaway Poster Child smiles, rife with daffy trust and precocious sexuality. He was offended by her presumption that he would be taken in by it.

"We going to drive straight through?" she asked.

"I don't know."

"Might be better to stop somewhere, you know, than hitting Seattle all wore out."

She said this with studied diffidence, fishing in the glove compartment for the coke, making a production of unearthing the vial from among road maps and candy wrappers, as if that, and not the idea of cementing the relationship, were foremost on her mind.

He said, "I'll see how the driving goes."

"Well, if I got a vote it'd be great to catch a shower."

As if in sympathy with her, his skin began to feel oily, itchy, in need of a wash.

She sat sulking, toying with the vial; after a mile or two she began to sing, a frail wordless tune, something the Lady Ophelia might have essayed during the last stages of distraction. Suddenly vivacious, she waved the vial under his nose and said, "Want to hurt yourself?"

After they had done the coke, she fiddled with the radio, trying to bring in a rock station from the background static, and Michael settled back to enjoy the Cadillac feeling in his head, the Cadillac richness of the afternoon, the richness of a stolen car, cocaine, another man's money in his pocket and a strange woman at his side.

"You look sick," said the girl. "Want me to drive?"

"I'm okay."

"Know what's the best thing when you're sick from coke? Milk. And not just milk. Cheese, ice cream. Dairy products, you know. Maybe you should stop somewheres and get some milk." She crossed her legs, jiggled her foot. "I could go for an ice cream myself. I mean I ain't sick, you know. I got a thing for ice cream is all. Especially the kind with the polar bears on the wrapper. Ever had one of them?"

"Oh, yeah! They're terrific." His grin tightened the packs of muscle at the corners of his mouth.

"I could eat 'em all night long," she said with immense satisfaction. "'Course I wouldn't want to lose my shape." She twisted about to face him. "I do a hunnerd sit-ups every morning and every night. I jog, too. You like to jog?"

"You bet."

"I'm serious. You should take care of yourself."

"Why?"

"You just should," she said defensively.

"I'd need a better reason than that to waste my time."

"It ain't a waste, it makes good sense."

"Why?"

"Because…" Flustered, she shifted away from him, plucked at the hem of her cut-offs. "You want to live a long time, don'tcha?"

"I'm fucking with you," he said. "Okay?"

She tried another tack, working hard to establish what a fine traveling companion she'd make, but he tuned her out. Mount Shasta loomed against a twilight sky—the huge white cone with a single golden star sparkling off to the side had the graphic simplicity of a banner. In his mind he pushed ahead to Seattle, imagining whale worshippers and lumberjack sex cults, but those thoughts found no traction and he found himself thinking about LA. He was back on Sunset with the mutant carbon breathers and death's head bikers and tweaking whores and the little black kids with their little guns and little crack rocks, with the runaways he had lived among before Charlie took him in. Kids who came on with a mixture of paranoia and hard-boiled defiance, yet proved by their deaths to have been innocents with a few sly tricks. Most of them dead now, the rest just swallowed up. His memories of them were as oppressive as family memories, which was what they had been—a screwed-up family with no parents, no home, no future, no visible means of support, cooking stolen hamburger over oil drum fires and selling bad dope and getting infections. He tried to escape the memories, to find a place in his head where they hadn't established squatter's rights, and wound up in a hotly lit, cluttered space that seemed familiar, but that he couldn't identify. It must be, he thought, partly a real place and partly some pathological view he'd had of it...Oncoming headlights blinded him and he swerved into the left lane, angrily punching on his brights, leaving them on until the other driver dimmed his. He felt wrecked, wired. It had gotten dark and Shasta lay far behind.

The girl made a weak noise; for a second he was not sure how she had come to be there.

"Where are we?" he asked, and she said, "Wha..." and sat up straight, as if she were in a classroom, trying to give the impression that she had been paying attention.

"We in Oregon yet?" he asked.

"Uh...I don't know. Maybe. There was a sign back a ways."

He fingered a cigarette from a crumpled pack and lit up. The smoke tasted stale, but cleared his head. The radio with its crackle of static and glowing green dial seemed like an instrument for measuring background radiation.

"I remember now," said the girl with sober assurance. "We been in Oregon a long time."

Curls of mist trailed across the road and towering into a starless sky a group of neon signs ahead was haloed by a doubled ring of shining air. Apart from the rank grasses along the shoulder, Michael could see nothing of the land. A road sign shot past. 113 to Portland, 12 to Whidby Bay. On the left a pancake house with glaring picture windows looked as bright and isolated as an orbital station. The mist was thickening and it tired him to peer through it.

"Break out the coke," he told the girl.

Dutifully, she fed his nose. His heart raced, the skin on his forehead tightened, but there was no sharpness, no shrugging off of fatigue. His skull was impacted with something that prevented all but the most rudimentary thought. He was exhausted, he stank, his fingernails were rimmed with black. At the last possible moment he swung off the interstate and sent the Cadillac squealing along the curving access road that led to Whidby Bay.

"Where we going?" the girl asked.

His mouth was so dry he could barely speak and, when he did, the word he spoke sounded guttural and unfamiliar, like troll language.

"Motel."

—

Set at the end of the main street, capping off a row of muffin shops, gift shops, restaurants that resembled cabins and had cutesy names, and a closed-up Boron station, the Elfland Lodge appeared to be too much motel for a town the size of Whidby Bay, a three-story green and white structure with a wing at one end and no more than a half-dozen cars in a huge parking lot bordered by a chest-high hedge. Michael supposed that the town must have a booming tourist season, a time for macramé festivals and Vegan-paloozas, and this was not that time—either that or someone was using the place to launder money. An electrified sign featuring a leprechaun-like figure in a green suit doing a jig was mounted on a pole out front. Stick-on letters applied to its facing promised free cable and welcomed the Whidby Bay HS Class of '87 for their 25th Year Reunion—dates showed this glorious event was scheduled to begin and end the week previous.

The night man was a plump thirty-ish guy with frizzy hair and a beer gut, wearing Mother Goose glasses and a t-shirt that read ORYCON 26 and sported the cartoon of a chubby rocket put-putting through the void, propelled by little poots of smoke. He was kicked back in a swivel chair behind the reception desk when Michael entered, listening to an Ipod, his head nodding as if to a sprightly rhythm. The lights in the office were dim, there was a strong scent of air freshener, and a stubbed-out roach lay in an ashtray back of the desk.

"One-twenty...it's out back," the night man said, handing over a key card. Then as Michael was about to leave, he called, "Dude! Check out the elves."

This roused a mild paranoia in Michael. "Elves?"

The night man adopted a fatuous air and a fruity tone of voice. "Those from which our establishment derives its name. The owner brought them back from the Black Forest. Believe me, they are not to be missed."

"What are you talking about?"

"The Black Forest. In Germany, you know," the night man said defensively. "Elves...little statues of elves."

"Why the fuck should I care about some dumb-ass statues?"

"They're artifacts. Relics. I guess some old Nazi guy owned them."

Michael continued to glare at him, unsure whether or not he was being played in some way.

"Hey, forget it," said the night man. "I simply thought you'd find them amusing."

Michael parked in front of One-twenty, a few slots away from a brown Dodge minivan, the only other vehicle on the seaward side of the motel. Heavy surf pounded close by. Salty air. Orange light bulbs ranging the breezeway illuminated a wide stretch of lawn bounded by a waist-high flagstone wall; beyond the wall, the darkness was absolute. He saw no elves.

There were, however, what looked to be a bunch of oddly shaped, painted rocks standing at the far end of the property. With the girl in tow, he strolled across the lawn toward the rocks and soon realized that these were the elves of which the night man had spoken. There were twenty of them, each about three, three and a half feet tall, carved from wood, disturbingly lifelike, and they had been arranged into groups of five, distinct within the larger grouping. They had dark brown faces, floppy caps like Santa hats but green, shirts with embroidered buttonholes and seven-league boots with sagging tops. Their laminated surfaces held a sticky-looking gloss.

"Lord help us," said the girl. "Those things are wicked."

Michael was inclined to agree. These were not the benign creatures of heroic fantasy, but the corrupt denizens of Grimm fairy tales. More like dwarves than elves. Their faces were those of long-chinned, hook-nosed, cadaverous old men with Mormon beards and hideous rouge spots dappling their cheeks. About half of them brandished axes and long knives and warty cudgels. Their gnarled hands and thick limbs gave the impression of unnatural strength. Some were hunched over, appearing to have been struck wooden and inanimate in the midst of a furious assault, while others leered at their companions as though anticipating a bloody result. In motion, Michael supposed, they would lurch and caper, tilt and wobble, but fast, they would be as fast as wolverines, clumsy yet facile, ripping bellies, slashing throats, then tripping over their victims' bodies. He questioned the sensibilities of the man who had stationed them in such an untroubled spot.

The girl tried to drag him away. "I got to pee!"

"I'll be in in a minute." He handed her the key card.

"C'mon with me."

She plucked at his arm and he shook her off, saying, "You need help to pee?"

Her lips thinned. "You stay out here, I can't be responsible."

He chuckled and shook out a cigarette from his pack. "I wasn't counting on you being responsible."

"They got evil in 'em. You're just stirring 'em up, standing here and all. They'll hurt you. Or maybe worse."

"The elves?"

"Whatever you want to call 'em."

"And you know this how? You have these amazing powers, right? Your mama's a witch back in West Virginny and she passed them onto you."

"Tennessee! I'm from Tennessee! And it don't have nothing to do with my mama!"

"So you are a witch? You whup up potions out of possum guts and a pinch of geechee root? You cure warts and love troubles? How'd you get to be a witch if you mama didn't teach you?"

She fixed him with a hateful stare.

"I bet I know." He lit up and adopted a hick drawl. "You was standing on a corner over to Taterville one evening, waiting on the bus to Hog Jowl, when this here beam of light pierced down from heaven…"

She stalked off toward the motel.

"Or maybe you was in Hog Jowl! Waiting on the bus to Taterville!" he called after her. "I get them two places confused!"

She whirled about and said venomously, "You think you're so damn smart! Well, go on! Stay there and see what happens!"

Startled by her defiance, he watched after her until she vanished inside the room. Little Missy, he thought, could serve up a side of mean. He returned his attention to the elves. He gave some of them names—Groper, Sleazy, Ratfuck, Spongehead—but became bored, distracted by the booming surf. Peering over the flagstone wall, he could see nothing, but it was apparent that the motel stood atop a cliff, a high cliff if his spider senses were reliable. The darkness beneath wanted him, drew him down, and he had a fleeting impulse to vault over the wall. Not a good sign. Almost as not-good as no longer being able to amuse oneself with one's own wit.

Turning away from the drop, he could have sworn one of the elves had moved closer. Moved and stopped the moment he turned, once again counterfeiting the inanimate. The elf was weaponless, crouching, its swarthy, snarling face visible between upraised hands, poised to deliver a push…

"Wily little bastard," he said. "You want some of me?"

The elf appeared to quiver with eagerness, the light trembling on its surfaces, glinting from its eyes.

"Fuck you!"

Michael flipped his cigarette at the elf, showering it with sparks. As he crossed the lawn he tried not to glance behind him, but he looked back twice.

—

Once inside One-twenty, he stripped off his shirt, switched off the lights and lay down, listening to the shower hissing, the shuddery hum of the air conditioner. Glare from the breezeway penetrated the drapes, spreading a sickly murk throughout the room. The blond production line furniture and the mirror bolted above the writing desk wavered like fixtures in a mirage. He felt that he was floating off the bed. Nerves jumped in his cheek. Phosphenes drifted and flared in the dimness. Something was lumped up under his ass and he remembered Charlie's money. He sat up, pulled the wad from his hip pocket and counted it. Seven thousand dollars and change. The bills were cool and slick, like strange skins.

He wondered if he should give Charlie a call. It would be painful, but Charlie might feel better afterward. He would be guilty, morose. The first thing he'd say would be not to worry about the money or the car, and he hoped Michael could forgive him. He hadn't meant it, the kiss. For four years he'd been straight with Michael, and he had fucked up once. It would never happen again. And then, he, Michael, would say…maybe nothing. Maybe he'd just hang on the phone, knowing that if he opened his mouth he would indict himself, because it had been his fuck-up, too. Or maybe he'd get angry with Charlie for making him feel guilty and call him a spunk-muncher, a pole-smoker, an aging drag queen with a ring in his dick. But Charlie wouldn't let him off so easily. If you're determined to run, he'd say, all right, but don't pretend it was casual, don't pretend you're not feeling anything. They'd trade back and forth like that for awhile, and finally Michael would say he had to go, and Charlie would say, okay, but once you've had time to think things over, please, please, get in touch, and so what was the point in calling when he knew everything that would be said…and, hell, Charlie would know he was going through this process and wouldn't expect a call, so what was the goddamn point?

"I am going to hell," he said, anticipating a demonic chuckle in response.

The girl came out of the bathroom, toweling her hair, still wearing tank top and panties. He thought it was extremely demure of her to be clothed at this juncture—such restraint and modesty well might be considered a touch of class in their circle.

"It's so cold in here!" she said.

"I like it cold."

"Well." She toweled briskly. "I guess it's just my hair's still wet."

He let out a sigh and saw a shadow pour from his mouth; a sensation of calm stole over him, like the calm after the passing of a fever.

The girl pulled off the tank top; beneath a tan line, her pale breasts were luminous in the half-light, the nipples pink and childlike. She burrowed beneath the covers, drawing them up to her chin.

"You coming in?" she asked.

He skinned out of his jeans and shorts. The sheets were cold and once he had drawn them up, he could no longer feel anything below his waist. The girl's thigh nudged his and he felt that—a patch of skin warming to life. Strands of damp hair tickled his shoulder.

"Hey," she said softly. "You pretty whacked out, huh?"

"That's me…whacked out."

"You had a tiring day." Her hand spidered across his abdomen. "All that driving and hardly ever stopping. You must be wore right down."

He touched one of her breasts, let its weight nestle in his palm. It was a fine thing to hold, but he felt not even a glint of arousal. "I don't think it's going to work," he said.

"All that coke's numbing you out," she whispered, her mouth brushing his ear, her fingers caressing, molding his limp cock. "You lie back now and let me take care of you."

He became immersed in her fresh soapy smell, in her breathy voice and the mastering cleverness of her hand.

"I wish it was just the two of us," she said.

"Is somebody else here?"

"I mean, you know. Like even when you're alone, how you can feel other people pressing in on you. People in the vicinity."

"Uh-huh."

She took to singing distractedly again, an aimless, wordless, off-key tune of the sort a child might sing while concentrating on a toy. She gripped him more tightly and increased her rhythm. "You ain't still mad, are you?"

"Not so much."

She gave a husky laugh and it seemed there was a note of triumph in it. "You're a funny fella. I don't know why you strike me funny, but you sure do. Maybe it's 'cause you like pretending you ain't serious about nothing when you serious about 'most everything."

"Seriously funny," he said. "That's me."

"That don't mean a blessed thing," she said, making it sound seductive. "You can talk like that all you want, 'cause I'm onto you."

The planes of her cheeks, her lidded eyes and half-smile…they were so close to him, they no longer appeared to be elements of a face, but features on a map that he couldn't read.

"Yeah? How's that?"

"I been watching you all day. I can tell when you're easy, when you're worried. When you're lying." She peeled back the covers, checking to see what her hand had wrought. "Look at that! 'Pears it's gonna work after all."

She scooted lower in the bed, teased him with her lips, then slipped half his length into her mouth; he brushed the hair back from her face so he could watch her cheeks hollow. After a minute she wriggled back up beside him. Her tongue darted out, flirting with his, and her hand moved slowly, insistently.

"You keep that up, I'm going to come," he said.

"Be all right with me," she said. "I think that'd be kinda nice."

He laughed, happy with her.

"Know what else I know about you?" she asked after a pause.

"What?"

"You know all about me…'least more than you think you know. But you're so busy being funny, you ain't noticed."

He felt a delicate shift in attitude that he hadn't felt for a long time, that perhaps he had only told himself he could feel. The silky lengths of her wet hair gave her face a cunning sweetness like that of a nymph, a dryad, and he had the idea that her expression—rapt, yet with a trace of uncertainty—was a mirror image of his own.

"We're the same people," she said. "You might be older than me, and you think you're smarter. But we been the same places, we had the same trouble. We understand each other."

Though he had reached this conclusion on his own, he wanted to deny it now, but could not—he recognized her from some foul adit of experience, a dead end, a still-life alley with full moon and heaped garbage bags glistening like fat black boulders, and while she gave a blow job to some middle-aged douche he would wait in the zebra-striped island of light and shadow beneath a fire escape, her agent, her mystic protector, counting the cash, watching her shade kneel and merge with the flaps of a raincoat, and afterward she would hurry over to him, wiping off her lips, and ask, "We got enough?" Enough for the joys of modern chemistry, enough to transform an abandoned house into the Beverly Hilton, cockroaches into glittering brown jewels, life into a death-trip with pretty colors, hunger into a cool side-effect, love into a blue movie with a warped sound track and junk food.

"Bet you don't believe me," she said.

"You might be wrong."

As if saying this bridged some vital distance between them, he felt close to her, shrouded in a thick, honeyed sexuality, and believed he knew her completely.

"Am I?" she said.

"Can't you tell? I thought you were onto me."

"Quit teasing!"

"I'm not teasing," he said. "Can't you tell?"

He pulled her atop him, nuzzled her breasts. He thought he could taste her resilience, her fragility, the lesser hopelessness she might call hope, all braided together in the chewy plugs of her nipples.

"It's me you want?" she asked, tremulous, a virgin asking for proofs. "It's really me and not just…things?"

"You," he said with such a wealth of solemnity that his mood was broken, but then she pushed his hand between her legs, saying, "See… see how much I want you, see…" and he was with her again, nearly breathless, easing two fingers inside her. Her ass churned, her tongue was in his mouth and she moaned at the same time. They rolled and tossed, the dim mirror filling with their thrashing shadows, the walls billowing, fiery specks jiggling in mid-air, all locked into the rhythm of the tumbling bed. He had a feeling of liberation and unfamiliarity, as if this were something more powerful and involving than the sex he remembered, but when he sat up, braced on one hand, preparing to enter her, he froze, a cocaine freeze that left him dead and empty, like a machine whose current had been stopped. He felt isolated, embedded in miles of darkness, and he thought if he were to shift his head an inch, the wires holding it in place would snap. His elbow ached from the strain of supporting his weight, and his forearm began to tremble.

"What's wrong?" she said, urgency burring her voice, trying to guide him between her legs.

Thoughts poured from his head like dirty water down a drain. He was poisoned, out of his element, unable to speak. His erection wilted. The girl took him in her mouth again and that did the trick, that sent a jolt of current flowing through the dead machine. But when he entered her, when she lifted her legs, her heels digging into his calves, and she cried out, "Oh God, God...ahh God," her speech had the rushed monotonous cadence and impersonal fervor of somebody calling a horse race, and he remained distant, never losing himself in the turns of her body, fucking her with mechanical ferocity and never once speaking her name.

—

Years before, a couple of years after he ran away from home, he and a girl named Chess had fled LA, planning to live as one in some lush, secret paradise, to produce children and art, and think the eloquent thoughts of the Awakened. Instead, they wandered around Mexico, stealing and fucking other people for drugs and food. He had believed he loved her and in a sense he had. The problem had been that they, too, were the same people and he had loved her with the same malignant intensity with which he loved himself. In the end he pimped her to a prosperous middle-aged German for a quantity of Mexican mud and Chess and the German guy flew off together for what was supposed to be a week in Valparaiso, never to be heard from again.

He talked about Chess a great deal over the ensuing years, he told their story of squandered love to friends, to marks, to Charlie. The story became his big ticket item, the heartbreakingly honest confessional he used to impress people with his depth, his soulfulness, convincing them to let him get close enough so he could take advantage of them in some way; but the more he talked, the less he remembered of what he had felt, as if each word was carrying off a fragment of experience, until he could no longer recall how it had actually been between them. He could summon up her face, but it was a dead face, a police sketch of a face, devoid of nuance, of energy.

This girl now, lying with her pale back to him, dozy from sex…no way he felt about her as he had about Chess. That is, if what he recalled wasn't total bullshit. But this girl…What was her fucking name? Tammy, Trudy…Something like that. Tracy. He couldn't deny she had a certain appeal. Maybe it was her ignorance, the sheer doggedness of it—maybe that bespoke a measure of innocence. Innocence was a quality he could use to delude himself into believing there was more to the relationship. He ran a hand along the curve of her waist and hip, and she stirred to the touch. No, he decided. He didn't need any complications.

"Hey, Tracy."

He nudged her and she made a complaining noise. He flicked on the bedside lamp and said again, "Tracy!"

"Oh, Lord! I forgot." She squinted up at him. "When I hitchhike I never use my real name. It makes me feel safer out there. I know it's silly. I meant to tell you, but…" She flashed a lopsided grin. "We got a little busy."

She scooted up to a sitting position and gave him a peck on the cheek and said, "Sorry."

He caught a whiff of Elfland Hospitality Pak Shampoo.

"My name's Carole," she said. "Carole with E on the end."

For some reason it seemed harder to dump a Carole than a Tracy, and he was tempted to relent. Then she began to prattle like she had in the car, wondering if there was a place open where they could get some food, probably not, it must be two o'clock already, and she couldn't hardly wait to hit Seattle, she bet the sea food there was awesome…

"Listen, Carole," he said. "I don't think we should travel together."

Uncomprehending, she gaped at him.

"I'll give you money for the bus," he said. "And enough so you can get situated in Seattle. But that's it."

She made a weak, half-completed gesture toward her brow. "What do you mean?" she asked. "I thought..."

"I don't want to argue," he said.

She seemed prettier than she had earlier, the sharpness of her face less evident. "But we were..."

"And don't be telling me how wonderful it can be," he went on. "If we stay together, all that'll happen is one of us will rip the other off."

She started to object and he said, "I'll give you a thousand dollars," seeing this as a stroke of moral genius, charity abolishing the sin of theft, saving himself grief and at the same time giving the girl a shot. He would still have six thousand left.

"I don't give a damn about your money!" she said tearfully. "I want to be with you!"

"It's not going to happen."

She let out a thin cry and clasped her hands to the side of her head.

"It's for the best," he said. "If you stay calm and think about it, you'll see that."

She hugged her knees, rocking back and forth, doing her mad girl impression, singing tunelessly, breathily, the song of a fly buzzing in an asylum window, drunk on sunlight.

"Stop that!" he said.

Her keening rose in pitch.

"What are you...fucking nuts? Talk to me."

He expected her to start blubbering, but she didn't leak a single tear and kept on with her broken teakettle noise.

"That's not going to get it," he said. "Acting all crazy and shit. I've seen crazy, I *know* crazy. You can't sell that shit here."

Her eyelids drooped so that slits of white were visible beneath them.

Fed up with her, he pulled on his pants, shrugged into his shirt and stepped out into the breezeway, slamming the door behind him.

The Dodge minivan he had parked beside was gone. He wished that he hadn't left his car keys in the room. He could have booked. A thousand dollars? Christ, what was he thinking? She was likely used to selling her ass for fifty, a hundred tops. The cool air soothed him, tuned his anger lower. He dug the loose change from his pocket and went padding barefoot along the breezeway toward the vending machines next to the office. If he got her something to eat, that might placate her. It might be worth driving somewhere—that pancake house back on the interstate might still be serving. Once she was loaded with carbs and sugar he could talk her down from hysteria, open a dialogue, reason with her, and in the end they would share a hug, a semi-chaste kiss, alas, alack, adios, adieu, we'll always have the Elfland.

He selected a bag of chips and a Snickers from the vending machines, and then noticed particles of glass on the sidewalk in front of the office—the door had been blown inward and glass shards strewn across the carpeting, as if something had struck it with explosive force. The lights were on, but the night man was nowhere in sight. Michael stuck his head inside and called out. No reply. He picked his way across the carpet, walking on his toes, and peered behind the desk, half-expecting to find the night man's bullet-riddled corpse, but saw only an overturned office chair and what might have been a dusting of Dorito crumbs on the counter. Going back outside, he surveyed the parking lot, an acreage of blacktop divided by concrete islands and the occasional patch of shrubbery, slots demarked by diagonal white lines, luminous under the arc lights. His sense of unease spiked. There had been at least six or seven cars in the lot, not counting the minivan, and now there were none. What were the odds that their owners had all checked out between midnight and two AM? Not inconceivable, he told himself. The Elfland might be a no-tell motel. He scanned the façade of the building. Yellow lights sprayed from the open door of a second floor room, silhouetting a short, squat figure no larger than a child. Whoever it was didn't move a muscle. Michael waved, but the wave was not returned. The figure might have been stone...or wood. It looked to be wearing some sort of hat. Like a Santa hat.

Oh, no you don't, he said to himself.

You're not going there, you are definitely not buying into the Carole-induced premise that magical Nazi elves have taken over a motel in Bumfuck, Oregon.

"Hey!" he shouted at the motionless figure. "What's going on?"

Silence.

"Somebody broke into the office! Did you see anything?"

A clattering sounded behind him—like someone running in wooden shoes.

He spun about. Something darted behind a shrub about fifty feet away. Something quick and approximately elf-sized. He couldn't be certain of it—he would have liked third-party corroboration. He was exhausted, coming down from a coke binge, and his eyes were playing tricks.

"Is anybody there?" he called in a shaky voice.

The shrub quivered, as if being shaken. He shot a glance toward the second floor room. The figure in the doorway was gone.

Michael's balls tightened. He eased toward the parking lot exit, choosing a path that led well away from the suspicious shrub, intending to put some distance between himself and the motel, cross the road to the Boron station and take stock. Let his nerves settle and then head back to One-twenty, because it had become clear he was under the influence of the coke and of that nutbag Carole with an E on the end, and he needed to gain perspective. That was all. He'd pull it together, return to the room, grab his keys, and drive. Thinking this made him feel steadier. He'd go as far as Portland and find a motel not named the Elfland, a Comfort Inn, a TraveLodge or Best Western, a good old American franchise free of Black Forest statuary and street meat…

The lights went out.

Not just the lights of the motel and the parking lot, but also those of the Boron station, the shops, and the winking traffic signal. The darkness was unrelieved. It was as if a dense black cloud had lowered over the town, reducing visibility to almost zero. Power failure. He waited for the lights to come back. When they did not he moved forward, groping, shuffling along, making for the exit, determined to follow through on his plan of taking stock, pulling it together.

He heard the clattering again. It was louder, closer, issuing from every direction—lots of diminutive wooden feet darting near. As he turned this way and that, tracking the noise, something snagged his shirttail and nearly succeeded in dragging him down. Panic put a charge in him and he ran blindly, his arms pumping. Pieces of gravel stuck in the soles of his feet. He ignored the discomfort and kept running until he crashed into the hedge bordering the lot. Twigs tore at his sides, dug into his chest. He fought to break through the hedge, tearing away handfuls of leaves, but it was impenetrable—he hung there, supported by the bushes. The clattering had stopped and, but for the wheezing of his breath, the silence was absolute. No semis grinding on the interstate, no barking dogs, no ambient noise whatsoever. He pictured the town cut off from the universe of light and life, adrift on an infinite ocean of nothingness, monsters with mile-wide mouths rising toward the surface, lured by this tasty morsel, and panic took him a second time. He struggled free of the hedge, lost his balance, and fell backward, smacking his head on the asphalt. Splinters of white light lanced through his skull. Dazed, he rolled over onto his side, preparing to sit up.

Overhead, the Elfland's sign switched on, humming, buzzing, painting on the asphalt a ragged island of illumination upon which he was marooned. The leprechaun on the sign mocked him with a knowing leer. Michael's instincts prompted him to flee, but he was too enfeebled to do other than scrabble at the pavement. He waited for the leprechaun to leap down from the sign, for whatever form the next shock might take.

"Who's there?" he shouted, and then: "Quit fucking with me!"

Darkness swallowed his words.

He remained lying there, alert for the least sound and hearing none. Moths came to whirl whitely like windblown snowflakes about the sign and this emblem of normalcy helped restore his capacity for thought. No other lights showed, either in the motel or the town, and that did not make sense, that the sign was the sole source of radiance, unless he were to believe in a reality he wanted to reject…and yet he couldn't reject it. The girl, Carole, she'd never denied being a witch. She must be orchestrating this somehow. That funky singing she did now and again, it could be part of a spell, a retarded Tennessee mantra that helped her focus. She was the only person who had reason to screw with him. Except for Charlie, maybe. Except for Chess. Except for damn near every fucking person he had ever met, everyone he had used and abused while working out his parental issues. Perhaps that's what was happening here: karmic retribution.

He laughed off the possibility and then had the urge to cry out for help; but even if things were normal, if everyone was safe in their beds and the town was not the empty, abandoned-by-God place he envisioned, there was nobody within earshot. And if help arrived what would he say then? This redneck bitch I picked up hitchhiking, goes about a hundred-five, hundred-ten pounds, IQ of a snail, she's a freak, man, she's tripping me out, animating the elf population of Whidby Bay. Sure, son, the cops would say. Let's put you into the nice holding tank where you'll be protected from her unnatural power. Hey, where'd you get the seven grand? You suppose this white powder might be an illegal substance? Got a pink slip for the Caddy?

At length he got to his feet, feeling stronger for the effort, and began walking toward the motel, its unlit façade melting up from the dark. He was in rotten shape, his head throbbing, vision fluttering, feet and torso bleeding, but bottom line, he had to get the keys. Arguments occurred to him as he went. Explanations. The Elfland's sign must be on some weird separate circuit. The night man had blundered into the door, shattered the glass and run away. Vandals had set the elf in the second floor doorway, or else it was a kid wearing a funny hat. He had been unsteady on his feet and imagined the tug on his shirttail. The clattering...well, he'd have to work on that one. None of this held water, but neither did any less rational explanation, and he allowed it to satisfy a need for some logical ground, however flimsy, on which to stand.

On reaching the rear of the motel he was blind again, and virtually deaf. The breezeway lights had not come back on and the crash of the surf drowned out lesser sounds. He moved out onto the grass, cool, dewy, and easier on his feet, and shuffled along, waving an arm before him to feel for obstructions. His instep came down on some hard, sharp thing. He yelped and sprawled on the ground, squeezing his foot to stifle the pain. Once the pain had subsided he groped about in the grass and found a sprinkler head. He twisted the thing angrily, trying in vain to uproot it, and then clutched at his foot again, rubbing away the soreness. Suddenly weary, he hung his head and closed his eyes. He could have nodded off, no problem, but he remembered that this sort of sleepiness was a symptom of concussion and forced himself to stand. His thoughts narrowed to keys, car, drive.

He must have gotten turned around, because after a couple of steps he came up against the wall at the edge of the cliff. He clung to it for an instant, getting his bearings, and made a beeline for the breezeway—he estimated that no more than fifteen or twenty steps would carry him there. But he took twenty-five steps, then thirty, and still was walking on grass. Thinking he might have gone off on a diagonal, he altered his path by a few degrees and continued. He went another twenty steps. The lawn hadn't been this extensive—he should have hit concrete by now. He decided to return to the wall, get his bearings again, and start over; but he walked until, by his reckoning, he was somewhere out over the Pacific and did not encounter the wall. He tamped down his anxiety, telling himself to stay calm…and then he saw that the character of the darkness had changed. Whereas before it had been dead black, now the air had acquired a distinct shine, a gloss that reminded him of obsidian or polished ebony, and appeared to be circulating around him, as if he were at the center of a slow whirlpool. Behind the currents of the whirlpool he could see the elves. Not clearly and not for long, but they were gathered around him, cutting off every avenue of escape, fading out and reappearing closer to hand and in different postures—like watching a streaming video with gaps in the continuity. Fear seeped into the corners of his mind, but did not flood and overflow it. It was fear tempered by doubt and disbelief, by a degree of acceptance, and by one thing more. He wanted the elves to be real. Death at their hands would be preferable to the ignominy of an overdose, hepatitis, any of the protracted stand-ins for suicide toward which he was inexorably bound. This would be death by punch line. Suicide by elf.

"Bring it, bitches," he said, slurring the words.

On Sleazy, on Spongehead, on Ratfuck and Groper.

He gave an amused grunt. Now this was some funny shit. I mean, really. Elves. They were almost in striking distance, cudgels lifted, knives at ready, their scowling faces knotted in fury. In their original context they might have been seen as brave and resolute, the defenders of a helpless village. Rambos among elves. Forest guerillas. Hardy little fuckers. Here they could only be misunderstood.

At the last second fear eroded his intention to meet death head-on and he made a panic move, stumbling forward in an attempt to break through their defenses. Something cracked the top of the head and he found himself gazing into the depths of the whirlpool, into a funnel of blackness at whose blacker-than-black bottom a convulsed flower revolved, a bloom with a thousand petals that rippled and undulated like those of some vast and complicated sea creature sucking him down into its nothing-colored maw.

—

An orange glow penetrated his lids and his first thought was that the breezeway lights had come back on; but on opening his eyes he realized it was the early sun. He lay at the base of the wall and everything ached, especially his head. His clothes were soaked with dew. Laboriously, he made it to his knees and saw over the top of the wall other cliffs, stratifications of reddish sediment towering above the ocean. Beneath the shadows of high cumulus the water was dark purple and among the cloud shadows lay swatches of glittering orange. The soft crush of the surf was constant and serene. He touched the crown of his head and couldn't tell whether he felt his scalp or the pads of his fingers.

"Thank goodness," said the girl's voice behind him. "I thought I was going to have to call 911. What happened?"

Her hand fell to his shoulder and in a reflex of fright he knocked it away and scrambled to his feet. She retreated, bewilderment plain on her face. At her rear, a couple of yards distant, stood the elves—an evil

Walt Disney platoon prepared to follow their hillbilly Snow White ditsy queen into battle. He was fairly certain they were grouped and posed differently from when he had initially seen them. Dizzy, he sank down in the grass and leaned against the wall.

"You got blood all over you," she said, and held out a packet of tissues. "I bought you some wipes."

If she were a witch, if she had almost killed him and was gaming him now, she had a smooth fucking act.

"Did you know the office door's busted out?" she said. "That have anything to do with how you got bloody?"

"You tell me."

She took to running her mouth, saying there was so many criminals these days, why even in a piddly place like her home town, people were always breaking into Coulters, this big old department store, and robbing the Dairy Queen and all. His paranoia ebbed and, though with half his mind he believed that her asinine rap was designed to put him at ease, make him let down his guard, he permitted her to kneel beside him and dab at his injuries with the wipes. The astringent stung, but it felt better than it hurt. He kept an eye on the elves. Sunlight glistened on their caved-in faces, charged the tips of their weapons. Their scowls seemed diminished. They approved of this union between Magic Girl and Action Lad. What the fuck, Michael said to himself. If you believe what you think you believe, you should render her ass unconscious and beat it—but he wasn't sure he could drive.

"You're wrong to be doing this," said the girl as she finished her clean-up.

"Doing what?"

"Breaking up with me."

"I don't think so."

"Well, if you don't think so, there's nothing to say, 'cause when you go and think something you're bound to believe it. I may not know much about you, but I know that."

He rested his head on his knees. "I don't want to talk."

After a while the girl said, "I'm sorry."

He cocked an eye toward her. "What for? Did you do something to me?"

"That wasn't my meaning. I'm just sorry about everything."

The wind gusted, flattening the grass; a thin tide of light raced across the lawn and from somewhere below the rim of the cliff came the crying of gulls. Michael felt weak and lazy in the sun.

"You really going to give me a thousand dollars?" she asked.

"I meant it when I said it."

She plucked a handful of grass and let the wind take it from her palm. "I been trying to think how to convince you we'd be good together. I know what I was feeling last night. It was just a start—I understand that. But it was real and if you can't remember how it was, if it got knocked out of you or whatever, maybe you should hunt up what you felt and take a chance on it. 'Cause that's all feelings are—things you catch and ride as far as they'll take you. It's sorta like hitchhiking."

That Tennessee mountain homily, pure as moonshine trickling from a rock.

I hear you, Sonnet darling, but things got a tad too freaky for me.

"That's not the point," he said. "I…"

"Let me talk, all right? I ain't asking for nothing."

She tugged at the crotch of her cut-offs; her face was calm.

"When you said you'd give me a thousand dollars," she went on, "I was angry. I thought you was treating me like a whore. Then I got to wondering why you're giving me so much."

Impatient with analysis, he said, "You don't have to explain this shit."

"It won't take a minute." She peered at him. "You feeling okay? You don't look too good."

The time has come for solicitude, he thought. After passion, after anger and despair, after the fear and the trembling, a little friendly concern: the cheese tray of the romantic supper.

"I'll live," he said.

Actually, lover, I'm in tiptop shape. I'm sitting here communing with my peeps, the Mojo Demon Elves, the Kamikaze Hellfighter Elves, while you and I discuss, among other subjects, Sexual Politics in the Theater of the Real.

"I told myself, he can't be giving me all that money just to make hisself feel better," she went on. "I guess that showed me you wasn't trying to deny that something happened. And it made me see things your way. Like maybe you were right about us."

"Uh-huh, yeah," he said listlessly.

"I don't understand why it's okay to split up," she said. "But I guess it is. I never thought I'd say that after last night. I suppose the money helps make it okay. I ain't a total fool—I know that's part of it. But I keep wanting to say for us to give it a try. And I keep thinking it's me who's right."

She looked him straight in the eye, a strong look, something certain behind it. The wind strayed a few strands of hair across her cheek, touching the corner of her mouth—she didn't bother to brush them aside.

"It's funny how when you're surest about things, at the same time you're scaredest that you're fooling yourself," she said.

She poked a finger into the black dirt beneath the grass, digging up a clump. Michael was enthralled. There was a new tension in her delivery and he believed she was building toward something important, something that would punctuate or define.

"It may not make sense," she said. "But the way I see it, maybe we're both wrong."

Disappointed, his thoughts shifted miles and hours ahead to Seattle in the rain, new night streets, new opportunities for failure, for fuck-up.

"Know what I'm saying?" she asked.

"Yeah, well," said Michael. "It'd be sort of hard not to know."

—

The girl drove past the shattered office door and the empty parking lot, past the shops, none of them open, no one in the streets, not a stray cat or a loose dog. Sitting beside her, Michael was spooked but too wasted to react. They had seen only one person in Whidby Bay and now even he was gone. Someone should be up and about, putting out the trash, opening for business.

"I don't see a hospital," the girl said.

"I don't want a hospital. Drive."

"You should get yourself checked out!"

"There'd be too many questions. They might call the cops. All manner of shit could go wrong. Just drive. I'll get myself checked out later."

"You want me to drive anywhere special? Some other hospital?"

"Seattle."

"That mean we're sticking together?" she asked in a chirpy tone.

It might add some zest to his latest downward spiral to hang with a chick who possibly could animate elves or transform him into a lizard, and herself as well, and they'd go scampering along the ditches and make scaly, tail-lashing love underneath a yucca plant…or she'd set a fire with her eyes in a trash alley and they'd lean out a window with a cardboard flap for a curtain and toast marshmallows, until one day she got super-pissed and crushed underfoot the teensy spider into which she'd implanted his soul. Not knowing about her would be exhilarating. Inspiring. And how could this bizarre uncertainty be worse than what he'd been through already? Or worse than where he was ultimately headed. It was a tough call. Regular Death or Premium? Two blocks slid by before he said, "I don't care."

She slowed the car. "What you mean, you don't care? I don't know what that means."

"Don't worry about it. It's all good," he said. "Just keep driving… and make sure I don't go to sleep."

She stepped on the gas and after another block she said, "How am I supposed to do that?"

"Talk. Engage me in conversation."

She pulled out onto the interstate. It too was empty, devoid of traffic. "What you want I should talk about?"

"Fuck, I don't know! Tell me why there's no people around, no cars. Where the fuck are we? Limbo? You're a goddamn motormouth—it should be easy."

"Limbo? That some place in Oregon?"

Naw, it's over in Moontana, Suzi Belle.

"Well, is it? Say."

"Never mind."

She sang her tuneless tune and before long a car passed, traveling in the opposite direction.

"See," she said. "There's a car."

"Yeah. Quite a coincidence." He shifted in the seat, half-turned toward her. "What's that singing thing about?"

She gave him a quizzical look and he did a poor imitation of her.

"Oh, that!" she said. "It's just something I do, you know, when I'm concentrating on stuff…or when I get emotional. 'Bout half the time I don't know I'm doing it." She punched him playfully on the shoulder. "But I don't sound nothing like that. You make me sound awful!"

Gray clouds obscured the sun and the world grew increasingly gloomy as they drove. Traffic picked up, but he didn't see people moving about in the food marts and gas stations along the highway. The sun was a tinny glare without apparent vitality or warmth that leached the evergreens and billboard images of color. The girl began to sing again and Michael noticed that she had an erratic glowing silhouette—the light dimming and brightening around her ever so slightly with the rhythm of the tune. His vision still wasn't right, flickering at the edges, but he chose to accept that what he'd noticed was not the product of a concussion. That's my girl, he thought. My special Jesus groupie, my Mary Magdalene. He settled into the ride, stretching out his legs, un-kinking his neck, and said, "This country's deader than shit. I hope Seattle's got some fucking people in it."

The girl's singing trailed off—she kept her eyes straight ahead and said, "It's a big city, dummy. There's bound to be people." She hadn't spoken to him this way before, flat and disaffected, like a woman disappointed in a man she had once held high hopes for. Then, with a lilt in her voice, a distinct hint of sly merriment, she added, "'Course you just can't never predict what kind of people they'll be."

THE FLOCK

Doyle Mixon and I were hanging out beneath the bleachers at the Crescent Creek High football field, passing a joint, zoning on the katydids and the soft Indian summer air, when a school bus carrying the Taunton Warriors pulled up at the curb. Doyle was holding in a toke, his eyes closed and face lifted to the sky; with his long sideburns, he looked like a hillbilly saint at prayer. When he caught sight of the team piling off the bus, he tried to suppress a chuckle and coughed up smoke. The cause of his amusement—Taunton had three monstrously fat linemen, and as their uniforms were purple with black stripes and numerals, they resembled giant plums with feet.

One lineman waddled over, his pod-brothers following close behind. "You guys got a problem?" he asked.

Doyle was too stoned to straighten out and he kind of laughed when he said, "We're fine, dog."

Standing in a row, staring down at us, they made a bulging purple fence that sealed us off from the rest of the world. Their hair had been buzzed down to stubble, and their faces were three lumpy helpings of sunburned vanilla pudding. Tiny round heads poked up between their shoulder pads. They might have been some weird fatboy rap act like that old MTV guy, Bubba Sparxxx.

"What's so fucking funny?" a second one asked, and Doyle and I both said, "Nothing," at about the same time.

"We got a couple of stoners, is what we got," the first one said, showing Doyle a fist the size of a Monster Burger. "Want to trip on this, freak?"

I kept my mouth shut, but Doyle, I guess he figured we were safe on neutral ground or else he simply didn't give a damn. "You guys," he said. "If beer farts were people, they'd look like you guys. All bloated and purple and shit."

The third lineman hadn't said a thing—for all I knew, he might not have possessed the power of speech; but he could hear well enough. He yanked Doyle upright and slammed an elbow into the side of his jaw. All three of them went to beating on us. It couldn't have been more than ten seconds before their coach dragged them off us; but they had done a job in that short time. Doyle's eyelid was cut and his lip was bleeding. They hadn't gotten me nearly as bad, but my cheekbone ached and my shirt was ripped.

The coach, Coach Cunliffe, was a dumpy little guy with a torso shaped like a frog's and a weak comb-over hidden beneath a purple cap. "Son-of-a-buck!" he kept saying, and pounded on their chests. They didn't even quiver when he hit them. One said something I was too groggy to catch and the coach calmed down all of a sudden. He took a stand over us, his hands on hips, and said, "You boys intend to make a report about this, I expect we got something to report on ourselves. Don't we?"

Doyle was busy nursing his eye, and I didn't have a clue what Cunliffe was going on about.

"I was to search your pockets, what you reckon I'd find?" Cunliffe asked. "Think it might be an illegal substance?"

"You lay a hand on me," Doyle said, "I'll tell the cops you grabbed my johnson."

Cunliffe whipped out a cell phone. "No need for me to search. I'll just call down to the sheriff and get him on the case. How about that?" When neither of us responded, he pocketed the phone. "Well, then. Supposing we call it even, all right?"

Doyle muttered something.

"Is that a no?" Cunliffe reached for his phone again.

"Naw, man. Just keep these fuckwits out of my face."

The fuckwits surged forward. Cunliffe spread his arms to restrain them. "You're number twenty-two for the Pirates," he said to Doyle. "I remember you from last year. Cornerback, right?" He gave us both the eye. "You boys down here doing a little scouting?"

Doyle spat redly, and I said, "Uh-huh."

"That's gonna help!" one of the linemen said, and his buds laughed thickly.

Cunliffe shushed them and locked onto Doyle. "You played some damn good ball against us last year, Twenty-two. You figger marijuana's gonna enhance your performance next month?"

"Not as much as the juice made these assholes' nuts fall off," said Doyle.

The linemen rumbled—Cunliffe pushed them toward the field, and they moved away through the purpling air. "Better get that eye took care of," he said. "Get it all healed up by next month. My boys are like sharks once they get the smell of blood."

"Those are some fat god damn sharks," Doyle said.

—

The towns of Taunton, Crescent Creek, and Edenburg are laid out in a triangle in the northeast corner of Culliver County, none more than fifteen miles apart. My mama calls the area "the Bermuda Triangle of South Carolina," because of the weird things that happened there, ghosts and mysterious lights in the sky and such. Now I've done some traveling, I understand weirdness is a vein that cuts all through the world, but I cling to the belief that it cuts deeper than normal through Culliver County, and I do so in large part because of the chain of events whose first link was forged that evening in Crescent Creek.

Doyle and I hadn't gone to the game to scout Taunton—we knew we had no chance against them. Only ninety-six boys at Edenburg High were eligible for football. Most of our team were the sons of tobacco farmers, many of whom couldn't make half the practices because of responsibilities at home. Taunton, on the other hand, drew its student body from a population of factory workers, and they were a machine. Every year they went to the regional finals, and they'd come close to winning State on a couple of occasions. It was considered a moral victory if we held them to thirty points or under, something we hadn't managed to do for the better part of a decade. So what we were up to, Doyle and I, was looking for two girls we'd met at a party in Crescent Creek the week before. We were only halfheartedly looking—I had a girlfriend, and Doyle was unofficially engaged—and after what the linemen had done to us, with our clothes bloody and faces bruised, we decided to go drinking instead.

We picked up a couple of twelve-packs at Snade's Corners, a general store out on State Road 271 where they never checked ID, and drove along a dead-end dirt road to Warnoch's Pond, a scummy eye of water set among scrub pine and brush, with a leafless live oak that clawed up from the bank beside it like a skeletal three-fingered hand. There was a considerable patch of bare ground between the pond and the brush, littered with flattened beer cans and condom wrappers and busted bottles with sun-bleached labels. Half a dozen stained, chewed-up sofas and easy chairs lined the bank. The black sofa on the far left was a new addition, I thought—at least it looked in better shape than the others.

The pond was where a lot of Edenburg girls, not to mention girls from Taunton and Crescent Creek, lost their cherry, but it was too early for couples to be showing up, and we had the place to ourselves. We sat on the black sofa and drank Blue Ribbon and talked about women and football and getting the hell out of Edenburg, the things we always talked about, the only things there *were* to talk about if you were a teenager in that region, except maybe for tobacco and TV. Doyle fumed over the fight for a time, swearing vengeance, but didn't dwell on it—we'd had our butts kicked before. I told him that big as those linemen were, vengeance might require an elephant gun.

"I hate they kill us every year," Doyle said. "I'd like to win one, you know."

I cracked a beer and chugged down half. "Not gonna happen."

"What the hell do you care? Only reason you play so's you can get a better class of woman."

I belched. "You know I'd lay me down and die for the ol' scarlet and silver."

Annoyed, he gave me a shove. "Well, I would for real. Just one win. That's all I'm asking."

"I'm getting a special feeling here," I said.

"Shut up!"

"I'm getting all tingly and shit...like God's listening in. He's heard your voice and even now..."

He chucked one of his empties at me.

"...universal forces are gathering, preparing to weave your heartfelt prayer into His Glorious Design."

"I wish," said Doyle.

Darkness folded down around us, hiding the scrub pine. Though it had been overcast all day, the stars were out in force. Doyle twisted up a joint and we smoked, we drank, we smoked some more, and by the time we'd finished the first twelve-pack, the dead live oak appeared more witchy than ever, the stars close enough to snatch down from the sky, and the pond, serene and shimmering with reflected light, might have been an illustration in a book of fairy tales. I thought about pointing this out to Doyle, but I restrained myself—he would have told me to quit talking like a homo.

Clouds blew in from the east, covering the stars, and we fell silent. All I could hear were dogs barking in the distance and that ambient hum that seems to run throughout the American night. I asked what he was thinking and he said, "Taunton."

"Jesus, Doyle. Here." I flipped him a fresh beer. "Get over it, okay?"

He turned the can over in his hands. "It ticks me off."

"Look, man. The only way we'll ever beat them is if their bus breaks down on the way to the game."

"What do you mean?"

"If they show up late, they'll have to forfeit."

"Oh...yeah," he said glumly, as if the notion didn't satisfy him.

"So get over it."

He started to respond but was cut off by a shrill *jee-eep*, a sound like a rusty gate opening; this was followed by a rustling, as of many wings.

I jumped up. "What was that?"

"Just a grackle," Doyle said.

I peered into the darkness. Though it was likely my imagination, the night air looked to have taken on the glossiness of a grackle's wing. I didn't much like grackles. They were nest robbers and often ate fledglings. And there were stories...A droplet of ice formed at the tip of my spine.

"City boy," said Doyle disparagingly, referring to the fact that I had spent my first decade in Aiken, which was a city compared to Edenburg. "Is Andy scared of the birdies?"

There came a series of *jee-eeps*, more rustling. I thought I detected almost invisible movement in every direction I turned.

"Let's get out of here," I said.

"Want me to hold your hand?"

"Come on! We can drive over to Dawn's and see if she wants to do something."

Doyle made a disgusted noise and stood. "Something's about to poke a hole in my ass, anyway." He touched the back of his jeans and then inspected his finger. "Christ, I'm bleeding. I think something bit me." He kicked at the sofa. "I could get an infection off this damn thing!"

"I bet you can get Dawn to suck out the poison," I said, hurrying toward the car.

As I backed up, the headlights swept across the bank, revealing the row of thrown-away sofas and chairs. I could have sworn one of them was missing, and as I went fishtailing off along the dirt road, the more I thought about it, the more certain I became that it was the one we had been sitting on.

—

If it hadn't been for football, I would have been an outsider in high school, angry and fucked-up, a loner whom everyone would have voted the Most Likely to Go Columbine. People said I took after my mama—I had her prominent cheekbones and straight black hair and hazel eyes. She was one-quarter Cherokee, still a beauty as she entered her forties, and she had a clever mind and a sharp tongue that could slice you down to size in no time flat. She was a lot quicker than my daddy (a stoic, uncommunicative sort), way too quick to be stuck in a backwater like Edenburg. Some nights she drank too much and Daddy would have to help her upstairs, and some afternoons she went out alone and didn't return until I was in bed, and I would hear them fighting, arguments in which she always got the last word. When I was in the eighth grade I discovered that she had a reputation. According to gossip, she was often seen in the bars and had slept with half the men in Taunton. I got into a bunch of school-yard fights that usually were started by a comment about her. I felt betrayed, and for a while we didn't have much of a relationship. Then Daddy sat me down and we had a talk, the only real talk we'd had to that point.

"I knew what I was getting when I married your mama," he said. "She's got a wild streak in her, and sometimes it's bound to come out."

"People laughing behind your back and calling her a slag…how do you put up with that?"

"Because she loves us," he said. "She loves us more than anyone. People are gonna say what they gonna say. Your mama's had a few flings, and it hurts—don't get me wrong. But she has to put up with me and with the town, so it all evens out. She don't belong in Edenburg. These women around here don't have nothing to offer her, talking about county fairs and recipes. You're the only person she can talk to, and that's because she raised you to be her friend. The two of you can gab about books and art, stuff that goes right over my head. Now with you giving her the cold shoulder, she's got no outlet for that side of things."

I asked straight out if he had slept with other women, and he told me there was a time he did, but that was just vengeful behavior.

"I never wanted anybody but your mama," he said solemnly, as if taking a vow. "She's the only woman I ever gave a damn about. Took me a while to realize it, is all."

I didn't entirely understand him and kept on fighting until he pushed me into football at the beginning of the ninth grade; though it didn't help me understand any better, the game provided a release for my aggression, and things gradually got easier between me and Mama.

By our senior year, Doyle and I were the best players on the team and football had become for me both a means of attracting girls and a way of distracting attention from the fact that I read poetry for fun and effortlessly received As, while the majority of my class watched *American Idol* and struggled with the concepts of basic algebra. My gangly frame had filled out, and I was a better than adequate wide receiver. Not good enough for college ball, probably not good enough to start for Taunton, but I didn't care about that. I loved the feeling of leaping high, the ball settling into my hands, while faceless midgets clawed ineffectually at it, and then breaking free, running along the sideline—it didn't happen all that often, yet when it did, it was the closest thing I knew to satori.

Doyle was undersized, but he was fast and a vicious tackler. Several colleges had shown interest in him, including the University of South Carolina. Steve Spurrier, the Old Ball Coach himself, had attended one of our games and shook Doyle's hand afterward, saying he was going to keep an eye on him. For his part, Doyle wasn't sure he wanted to go to college.

When he told me this, I said, "Are you insane?"

He shot me a bitter glance but said nothing.

"Damn, Doyle!" I said. "You got a chance to play in the SEC and you're going to turn it down? Football's your way out of this shithole."

"I ain't never getting out of here."

He said this so matter-of-factly, for a moment I believed him; but I told him he was the best corner in our conference and to stop talking shit.

"You don't know your ass!" He chested me, his face cinched into a scowl. "You think you do. You think all those books you read make you smart, but you don't have a clue."

I thought he was going to start throwing, but instead he walked away, shoulders hunched, head down, and his hands shoved in the pockets of his letterman's jacket. The next day he was back to normal, grinning and offering sarcastic comments.

Doyle was a moody kid. He was ashamed of his family—everyone in town looked down on them, and whenever I went to pick him up I'd find him waiting at the end of the driveway, as if hoping I wouldn't notice the meager particulars of his life: a dilapidated house with a tar paper roof; a pack of dogs running free across the untended property; one or another of his sisters pregnant by persons unknown; an old man whose breath reeked of fortified wine. I assumed that his defeatist attitude reflected this circumstance, but I didn't realize how deep it cut, how important trivial victories were to him.

—

The big news in Culliver County that fall had to do with the disappearance of a three-week-old infant, Sally Carlysle. The police arrested the mother, Amy, for murder because the story she told made no sense—she claimed that grackles had carried off her child while she was hanging out the wash to dry, but she had also been reported as having said that she hadn't wanted the baby. People shook their heads and blamed postpartum depression and said things like Amy had always been flighty and she should never have had kids in the first place and weren't her two older kids lucky to survive? I saw her picture in the paper—a drab, pudgy little woman, handcuffed and shackled—but I couldn't recall ever having seen her before, even though she lived a couple of miles outside of town.

During the following week, grackle stories of another sort surfaced. A Crescent Creek man told of seeing an enormous flock crossing the morning sky, taking four or five minutes to pass overhead; three teenage girls said grackles had surrounded their car, blanketing it so thickly that they'd been forced to use a flashlight to see each other.

There were other stories put forward by more unreliable witnesses, the most spectacular and unreliable of them being the testimony of a drunk who'd been sleeping it off in a ditch near Edenburg. He passed out near an old roofless barn, and when he woke, he discovered the barn had miraculously acquired a roof of shiny black shingles. As he scratched his head over this development, the roof disintegrated and went flapping up, separating into thousands upon thousands of black birds, with more coming all the time—the entire volume of the barn must have been filled with them, he said. They formed into a column, thick and dark as a tornado, that ascended into the sky and vanished. The farmer who owned the property testified to finding dozens of dead birds inside the barn, and some appeared to have been crushed; but he sneered at the notion that thousands of grackles had been packed into it. This made me think of the sofa at Warnoch's Pond, but I dismissed what I had seen as the product of too much beer and dope. Other people, however, continued to speculate.

In our corner of South Carolina, grackles were called the Devil's Bird, and not simply because they were nest robbers. They were large birds, about a foot long, with glossy purplish black feathers, lemon-colored eyes, and cruel beaks, and were often mistaken at a distance for crows. A mighty flock was rumored to shelter on one of the Barrier Islands, biding their time until called to do the devil's bidding, and it was said that they had been attracted to the region by Blackbeard and his pirates. According to the legend, Blackbeard himself, Satan's earthly emissary, had controlled the flock, and when he died, they had been each infused with a scrap of his immortal spirit and thus embodied in diluted form his malicious ways. No longer under his direction, the mischief they did was erratic, appearing to follow no rational pattern of cause and effect.

Some claimed they had poison beaks and could imitate human speech and do even more arcane imitations. A librarian sent a letter to the paper citing an eighteenth-century account that spoke of a traveler who had come upon an ancient mill where none had stood before and watched it erode and disappear, dissolving into a flock of grackles that somehow "had contrived its likeness from the resource of their myriad bodies, as though shaped and given the hue of weathered wood by a Great Sculptor." Her account was debunked by a college professor who presented evidence that the author of the piece had been a notorious opium addict.

Jason Coombs's daddy—Jason was our strong-side tackle, a huge African-American kid almost as imposing as the Taunton linemen—preached at the stomp-and-shout church over near Nellie's West Side Café, and each year he delivered a sermon using the Devil's Bird as a metaphor, punctuating it with whoops and grunts, saying that evil was always lurking, waiting for its opportunity to strike, to swoop down like an avenging host and punish the innocent for the failures of the weak, suggesting that evil was a by-product of society's moral laxity, a stratagem frequently employed by evangelists but given an inadvertent Marxist spin by the Reverend Coombs, who halfway through the sermon took to substituting the word "comrade" for "brother" and "sister." He had a field day with the Carlysle murder. Jason broke us up after practice one afternoon with an imitation of his old man ("Satan's got his flock, huh, and Jesus got his angels! Praise Jesus!"), an entertainment that caused Coach Tuttle, a gung-ho Christian fitness freak in his thirties, to rebuke us sharply for making fun of a God-fearing man such as the Reverend. He ordered us to run extra laps and generally worked us like mules thereafter.

"You boys better flush everything out of your heads but football," he told us. "This team has a chance to achieve great things and I'm prepared to kick your tails six ways from Sunday to see that you get the job done."

I wasn't fool enough to believe that we could achieve great things, but it was a heady time for Pirate football. We were assured of having our first winning season in four years. Our record was 6-2 going into the Crescent Creek game, and if we won that, our game with Taunton would actually mean something: win that one and we'd play in the regionals up in Charleston.

I did my best to focus on football, but I was experiencing my first real dose of woman trouble. My girlfriend, Carol Ann Bechtol, was making me crazy, saying that she didn't know anymore if we had a future and, to put it delicately, was withholding her affections. She wanted more of a commitment from me. I envied those city kids who had friends with benefits, who could hang out and have sex and stay commitment free, because in Edenburg we still did things the old-fashioned way—we dated, we went steady, we got all messed up over one girl or one boy. Mama warned me not to let myself get trapped.

"You know that's what Carol Ann's doing," she said. "She knows you'll be off to college next year, and she wants to catch onto your coattails and go with you."

"That's not such a bad thing," I said.

"No, not if you love her. Do you?"

"I don't know."

She sighed. "You can't tell anybody what to do, and I'm not going to try and tell you. You have to work it out on your own. But you should ask yourself how Carol Ann is going to fare away from Edenburg, and whether she's going to be a burden or a partner. Will she try and pull you back home or will she be glad to put this sorry place behind her?"

I knew the answers to her questions but kept silent, not wanting to hear myself speak them. We were sitting at the kitchen table. A steady rain fell and the lights were on and the radio played quietly and I felt distant from the gray light and the barren town outside.

"She's a sweet girl," Mama said. "She loves you, and that's why she's manipulating you. It's not just a matter of desperation. She's convinced you'll be better off here in the long run. Maybe she's right. But you're bound to try your wings and you have to decide if you can get off the ground with Carol Ann along."

"Is that what happened to you?" I asked. "With Daddy, I mean."

"It's some of it. I've had regrets, but I've lived past them and learned to make do."

She flattened her long-fingered hands on the table and stared down at them as if they were evidence of regret and love and something less definable, and I saw for an instant what a wild and lovely creature it was that my daddy had gentled. Then the radio crackled and she was just my mama once again.

"What I wonder, Andy," she said, "is if making do's a lesson you need to learn this early on."

—

I broke up with Carol Ann the Wednesday before the Crescent Creek game, at lunchtime in a corner of the practice field. She accused me of using her for sex, of ruining her life. I didn't trust myself to speak and stood with my head down, my face hot, taking her abuse, wanting to say something that would make her stop and throw her arms around me and draw me into a kiss that would set a seal on our lives; but I couldn't pull the trigger. She ran off crying, looking for her friends, and I went off to American history, where I listened to Mrs. Kemp tell lies about South Carolina's glorious past and doodled pictures of explosions in my notebook.

Friday night, I played the best game of my career. I played with hate and self-loathing in my heart, throwing my body around, slamming into the Crescent City corners with vicious abandon, screaming at them while they lay on the ground—I scored three times, twice on short passes and once on a fumbled kickoff, threading my way through tacklers and plowing under the last man between me and the goal with a lowered shoulder. In the locker room afterward, Coach Tuttle was inspired to curse, something he rarely did.

"Did you see Andy out there tonight?" he asked the gathered team. "That boy played some damn football! He wanted to win and he did something about it!"

The team roared their approval, sounding like dogs with their mouths full of meat, and pounded me on my pads, doing no good to my bruised and aching shoulder.

"You know what next week is?" he asked, and the team responded on cue, "Taunton Week!"

"If y'all play like Andy did tonight, and I know you can"—he paused for effect—"their mamas are gonna be wiping those Taunton boys' asses for a month!"

Doyle and the others wanted me to party with them, but I begged off, saying I needed to ice my shoulder. At home, I told my parents that we'd won and I'd done all right.

Daddy gave me a funny look. "We listened to the game, son."

"Okay," I said angrily. "So I was the goddamn hero. So what?"

His face clouded, but Mama laid a hand on his arm and said I seemed tired and suggested I get some rest.

I burrowed into my room, clamped on the headphones, and listened to some of the new Green Day album, but it wasn't mean enough to suit my mood, so I got on my computer, intending to check my e-mail—all I did was sit and stare at the blank screen. I understood that I hadn't truly broken up with Carol Ann until that night, and the game, my show of ultra-violence, had been a severing act, a repudiation of sorts. If my shoulder hadn't been sore, I might have hit something. I finally turned on the computer and played video games until the dregs of my anger were exhausted from splattering the blood of giant bugs across the walls of a ruined city.

—

The next morning I received a call from Dawn Cupertino, Doyle's fiancée. She said she was worried about Doyle and wanted to talk. Could I come over? Dawn had been in the class ahead of ours and dropped out at sixteen to have a baby, which she lost during her first trimester. She had never returned to school, instead taking a waitress job at Frederick's Lounge and an apartment in Crescent City, the second floor of an old frame house. She was thin and blue-eyed, a dirty blonde two years older than Doyle, almost three older than me, and had milky skin, nice legs, and a sharp mountain face that might remain pretty for three or four more years before starting to look dried-up and waspish. That would likely be fine with Dawn. Three or four good years would be about what she expected.

Though Doyle bragged on having an older woman with her own place, I thought the real reason he stuck with her was that she shared his low expectations of life but was cheerful about them. She was given to saying things like, "You better be enjoying this, babe, 'cause it's all we're gonna get," and accompanying her comment with a grin, as if even the pleasure of having a beer or watching a movie was more than she could have hoped for.

That morning she met me at the door in jeans and an old sweatshirt three or four sizes too big; her hair was pulled back into a ponytail. She sat on the living room sofa with her knees tucked under her, while I sat beside her, looking around at her collection of glass and porcelain trinkets, a display of old football pennants on the walls, pictures of cute kittens and cuddly dragons, her high school annual on the coffee table. It was a museum of her life up to the point that the baby had come along. Apparently nothing of note had happened since. I felt ungainly, like I was all elbows and knees, and any move I made would shatter the illusion.

Dawn put on a pot of coffee, we chatted about this and that. She said it was too bad about Carol Ann and asked how she was doing.

"She hates me," I said. "I expect she's finding some strength in that."

Dawn giggled nervously, as if she didn't get my meaning.

"What?" I said.

"It just was funny…the way you said it." She brushed loose strands of hair back from her brow, then briefly rested her fingers on my arm and asked with exaggerated concern. "And how're you doing?"

"Fine. What's this about Doyle?"

She heaved a sigh. "I don't know what's got into him. He's been acting all weird and…" Her chin quivered. "You think he's getting ready to break up with me?"

"Why would you think that?"

"He don't seem real interested anymore." She knuckled one eye, wiping away a trace of moisture from beside it. "Seeing how you broke up with Carol Ann, I figured he might follow suit. Doyle loves you, Andy. Sometimes I think more than he ever loved me."

"That's bullshit," I said.

"It's true. He's always talking about Andy this and Andy that. If you started putting on lipstick and wearing a dress, I swear he'd do it, too." She squared her shoulders. "Maybe we should break up. I'm almost twenty. It's about time I stopped going out with a kid."

"Is that how you see him?"

"Don't you? In a lot of ways Doyle's the same ten-year-old runt who was always trying to lift up my skirt with a stick. Even after he got it lifted up proper, he treated sex like it was something neat he found behind the barn and he's just busting to tell his friends about."

The coffee was ready, and Dawn brought in a tray with the pot and two cups, cream and sugar. When she bent to set it on the table, the neck of her sweatshirt belled and I could see her breasts. I'd seen them plenty of times before whenever a group of us would go skinny-dipping in Crescent

Creek, but they hadn't stirred me like they did now. It had been three weeks since I'd been with Carol Ann, and I was way past horny.

I asked Dawn to fill me in on how Doyle was acting weird. She said he'd been spacey, easy to anger, and I told her it had more to do with the Taunton game than her, how he had been obsessed with Taunton ever since the linemen kicked our butts, and how it had made him extra-depressed. That appeared to ease her mind, and she turned the conversation back to Carol Ann and me. I opened up to her and told her everything I'd been feeling. She took my hand and commiserated. I knew what was happening, but I didn't allow myself to know it fully—I kept on talking and talking, confessing my fears and weaknesses, thinking about her breasts, her fresh smell, until she leaned over and kissed my cheek, at the same time guiding my hand up under her sweatshirt. She pulled back an inch or two, letting me decide, her eyes holding mine; but there was really no decision to be made.

Afterward, in her bed, she clung to me, not saying anything. I recalled Doyle's stories about her ways. She was a talker, he said. Being with her, it was like making it with a radio play-by-play announcer. Oh, you're doing that, she'd say, and now you're doing this, as if she were describing things for a nationwide audience who couldn't see the field. But with me Dawn had scarcely said a word—she was fiercely concentrated, and when we had done, there was no game summary, no mention of great moves or big plays. She caressed my face and kissed my neck. This made me feel guilty, but that didn't stop us from compounding the felony and doing it a second time. Only after that, as I sat on the edge of the bed buttoning my shirt, did Dawn speak.

"I suppose you're blaming me for this," she said.

"What gives you that idea?"

"You just sitting there, not talking."

"No," I said. "It was mutual."

"Well, that's refreshing."

She padded into the bathroom. I heard the toilet flush, and she came out belting a robe that bore a design of French words and phrases: *Ooh La La* and *Vive la Difference* and such.

"Don't go whipping yourself for this. Okay?" she said, sitting beside me.

"I'm not."

"Sure you are. You're fretting about what Doyle's gonna say. Don't worry. I won't tell him. Me and him are over…mostly, anyway."

I glanced at her and began pulling on my socks. She looked neither happy nor sad, but stoic.

"It was my fault, kinda," she said. "I needed to be close with someone. Doyle hardly ever lets me in close, but I thought you would…even though it's a one-time thing." She angled her eyes toward me, awaiting a response; then she nudged me in the ribs. "Cheer up, why don'tcha?"

"I'm all right. I was thinking about my mama. About how I used to scorn her when I was in junior high for sneaking around behind my daddy."

The seconds limped past and she said, "I don't reckon we're much smarter than when we were in junior high, but we're for sure less likely to be judging folks."

She offered to fix me lunch, and not being urged in any direction, I accepted. We sat in her kitchen and ate. It was dead gray out the window. Four or five grackles were perched in a leafless myrtle at the corner of her front yard, flying up and resettling. No pedestrians passed. No cars. It was like after an apocalypse that only grackles had survived. I polished off two BLTs and Dawn fixed me another, humming as she turned the strips of bacon, like a young wife doing for her man. I suddenly, desperately wished that I could fit into her life, that we could sustain the fantasy that had failed my parents.

She slipped the sandwich onto the table and handed me a clean napkin, and sat watching me eat and swill down Coke, smiling in pretty reflex when I glanced up. I asked what she was thinking and she said, "Oh, you know. Stuff."

"What kind of stuff?"

I half-hoped she would mention what was in the air and we could embark on a deluded romance that would of course be a major mistake. I was for the moment in love with the idea of making such a mistake. Getting involved with Dawn was the easy way out. Not the easy way out of Edenburg, not out of anywhere, really; but with Dawn and a couple of squalling kids in a double-wide parked on my folks' acreage, at least my problems would be completely defined. Dawn, however, was too smart for that.

She flashed her cheesy waitress grin, the same one she served with an order of chicken-fried steak and biscuits at Frederick's, and said, "Can't a girl keep none of her thoughts private?"

—

Sundays in Edenburg were deader than Saturday mornings. There was one car in the Piggly Wiggly lot that must have been left overnight, and the store windows gave back dull reflections of parking meters and empty sidewalks. Kids had managed to sling several pairs of sneakers over the cable supporting the traffic light at the corner of Ash and Main—a stiff wind blew, and the shoes kicked and heeled in a spooky gallows dance. It reminded me of a zombie movie where things looked normal, but half-eaten citizens lay on the floors inside the feed store and Walgreens.

Somebody with a strong arm could have heaved a baseball from one end of town to the other in maybe three throws, but it took me a long time to drive from my house on the east side to Doyle's, which lay to the west, a mile beyond the city limits sign. I sat idling at the light by the Sunoco station. Wind snapped the blue-and-yellow flags strung between the pumps, scattering paper trash and grit across the concrete apron. I tried once again to resolve the problem I'd wrestled with most of the night. Sooner or later Dawn or one of her friends would tell Doyle, I figured. If I didn't beat them to the punch, I'd lose his friendship. Yet telling him would be a betrayal of Dawn. The whole mess was so fucking high school, it made me want to puke. The light changed. I gunned the engine but didn't put the car in gear and let it drop back down to an idle, resting my head on the seat and closing my eyes. *Screw Doyle*, I thought. I wasn't going to tell him. We'd drive on over to Snade's and sit on the front stoop with a couple of Buds and talk football.

THE FLOCK

A dairy van pulled up behind me and I rolled down the window and motioned for it to go around; but it just sat there. I peered back at the van. Its windshield was streaked with bird mess. I couldn't make out the driver, though I detected movement inside the cab. I motioned again, and the van didn't stir. It began to piss me off. I climbed out of the car and gestured like one of those guys who guide planes up to the terminal. Nothing. I was inclined to walk back and pound on the door, but the van looked to have acquired an air of menace. Beneath the streaks and gobs of bird shit, its windows were dark, as if they had been blacked out, and I had again a sense of agitated movement within. Horror movies about haunted vehicles flickered through my head. I got back into the car and peeled out, leaving the van stuck at a red light.

Doyle was standing atop a hillock in the field that adjoined his father's property, wearing his letterman jacket, waist deep in brown weeds and grasses; grackles were circling above his head, a half dozen or so. I pulled onto the shoulder and got out and called to him, but he was facing in the opposite direction from me and the wind snatched my words away. I was about to cross the highway when the dairy van came whispering over the hill, going at a fair rate of speed. I flattened against the car, my heart doing a jab-step, and it rolled past me, continuing toward Taunton, disappearing over the next rise. Shaken, I walked to the edge of the field and called to Doyle again. One by one, the grackles dropped from the leaden sky, secreting themselves among the tall grasses, but Doyle gave no sign of having heard. I found a gap in the rusty wire fencing and went twenty or thirty feet into the field. There I stopped, made uneasy by the birds.

"Doyle!" I yelled.

He turned, his face expressionless and pale, and stared—it was like he didn't recognize me for a second or two. Then he signaled me to come up to where he stood. I took pains to avoid places where I thought the grackles had gone to ground.

"Let's go," I said.

He surveyed the empty field with what seemed a measure of satisfaction, like a man contemplating the big house and swimming pool that he planned to build thereon. "Ain't no rush," he said. "Snade's ain't going nowhere."

We stood for nearly a minute without speaking and then he said, "Think we might get some rain?"

"Who the fuck cares? Let's go!"

"We can go. I just thought you might have something you wanted to get off your chest."

I wasn't afraid of Doyle—I had five inches and thirty pounds on him—but I expected he'd come at me hard. I backed off a pace and set myself. He chuckled and looked out over the field.

Perplexed by this behavior, I said, "What the hell's wrong with you?"

He smiled thinly. "That's a fine question, coming from a guy who poked my girlfriend."

"Did she tell you?"

"It don't matter who told me. You got other business to worry about."

He aimed a punch at my head but pulled it back the last second and laughed as, in avoiding the blow, I tripped on the uneven ground and went sprawling. He bent down, hands on his knees, grinning in my face.

"She's a slut, man," he said. "She puts on a real sweet act, but I'm surprised she hasn't jumped you before now."

I stared at him.

"Seriously," he said.

"I thought you two were getting married?"

He snorted. "I'd sooner marry a toilet seat. All she's ever been to me is a hump."

A storm of grackles whirled above the hill behind which the dairy van had vanished, and that confusion in the sky reflected the confusion in my mind. I remembered how needy and tender Dawn had been. After what Doyle had said, I wanted to doubt her, to accept his view of her... and I did doubt her on and off for a while; but his lack of regard for her rubbed me the wrong way. For the first time I realized that we might not be friends forever, and I wondered if all my relationships would be so fragile.

THE FLOCK

—

Against my better judgment, I got caught up in the frenzy of Taunton Week. It was hard not to, what with the entire population of Edenburg telling us that we could win and offering tactical advice. GO PIRATES GO signs were in every shop window. Pep rallies were exercises in hysteria—one cheerleader broke an ankle going for an unprecedented triple somersault and was carted from the gym, still shaking her pompoms and exhorting the crowd. Even Carol, who'd been spreading lies about me all over school, kissed me on the mouth and told me to kill 'em. But along about midweek, reality set in when I watched a tape on Taunton's All-State outside linebacker, a kid named Simpkins, number fifty-five. Coach Tuttle planned to use me on pass patterns going across the middle of the field, where Fifty-five would be waiting to saw me in half. My shoulder hadn't completely healed, and I actually gave consideration to ramming it into a wall or a door, and knocking myself out of the game. On Thursday, after practice, I took a nap and dreamed about Fifty-five. He was standing over me, wearing a black uniform (Taunton wore special black unis for the Edenburg game), and was holding aloft my bloody left shoulder, arm attached, like a trophy.

After my nap I went downtown, trying to walk off the effects of the dream, and ran into Justin Mayhew, our quarterback, a compact, muscular kid with shoulder-length brown hair. He was sitting on the curb out front of the Tastee-Freeze, looking glum. I joined him and he told me that he was worried about the offensive line holding up.

"That number eighty-seven liked to have killed me last year," he said.

"Tell me about it," I said, and mentioned my concerns about Fifty-five. "If you see him lining me up, throw the ball away…because I'm going to protect myself first and think about catching it second."

"If I can see around those fat bastards they got on defense, I will." He hawked and spat. "Tuttle's a damn idiot. He can't game plan for shit."

Conversation lagged and Justin was making noises about going out to Snade's, when Mr. Pepper, the ancient school janitor, came shuffling along. He was moving slower than usual and looked somewhat ragged around the edges. We said, "Hey, how you doing?" Normally a garrulous sort, he kept walking. "Hey!" I said, louder this time. Without turning, in a small, raspy voice, he said, "Go to blazes."

We watched him round the corner.

"Did he say, 'Go to blazes?'" I asked.

"He must be drinking again." Justin got to his feet. "Want to run out to Snade's with me?"

"What the hell," I said.

—

The arc lights were on and the bleachers at Pirate Field were half-full when I arrived for the game. The crowd was mainly Taunton boosters, and they were celebrating early, hooting and carrying on; they were cordoned off from Edenburg supporters by a chain that didn't serve much purpose when passions started to run high. They always brought more people than the bleachers could hold, the overflow spilling onto the sideline behind the Warrior bench. It was like a home game for them. The image of a black-bearded pirate brandishing a saber adorned the scoreboard, and following each victory, they would paint over his jolly grin with an expression of comical fright.

We dressed in a bunkerlike structure in back of the bleachers and the atmosphere inside it was similar, I imagined, to the mood on death row prior to an execution: guys sitting in front of their lockers, wearing doomed expressions. Only Doyle seemed in good spirits, whistling under his breath and briskly strapping on his pads. His locker was next to mine, and when I asked what made him so cheerful, he leaned over and whispered, "I did what you said to."

I looked at him, bewildered, "Huh?"

He glanced around the room, as if checking for eavesdroppers, and said, "I fixed their bus."

I had a vision of bodies scattered across a highway and Doyle in handcuffs telling the police, "I just did what Andy told me." I pushed him against the locker and asked what exactly he had done.

"Ease off, dog!" He barred his elbow under my chin and slipped away. "I nicked their fuel line, okay?"

"They'll just call for another bus."

"They can call," he said. "But all their backups got their tires slashed…or so I hear." He winked broadly. "Relax, man. It's in the bag."

It was like someone spiked my paranoia with relief, and I began to feel pretty good. We went out for warm-ups. Taunton had not yet arrived, and an uneasy buzz issued from the bleachers. Coach Tuttle conferred with the game officials while we did our stretches. I ran a few patterns, caught some of Justin's wobbly passes. The field was a brilliant green under the lights; the grass was soft and smelled new mown, the chalked lines glowed white and precise; the specter of Number Fifty-five diminished. The chirpy voices of our cheerleaders sounded distant:… *the Edenburg Pirates are hard to beat. They got pads on their shoulders and wings on their feet.* Tuttle sent us back inside and went to talk more with the officials.

In the locker room guys were asking, *What happened? They gonna forfeit?* Doyle just smiled. An air of hopeful expectation possessed the team as it dawned on everyone that we might be going to regionals. Then Tuttle came back in, put his hands on his hips, and said, "They're here." That let the air out of things.

"They're here," Tuttle repeated grimly. "And they don't want no warm-up. Do you hear that? They think they can beat us without even warming up." He searched our faces. "Prove 'em wrong."

I suppose he was going for a General Patton effect, trying to motivate with a few well-chosen words in place of his typical rant; but it fell flat. Everybody was stunned—Doyle, in particular—and we could have used some exhortation. The locker room prayer was especially fervent. As we jogged onto the field, Taunton jeers drowned out the Edenburg cheers and dominated the puny sound of our pep band. The Taunton bus was parked behind the west end zone, and their tri-captains waited at midfield with the referee. In their black uniforms and helmets, they looked like massive chunks of shadow. Justin Coombs and I walked out to meet them for the coin toss. Number Fifty-five centered the Taunton quarterback and one of the linemen, Eighty-seven, who had jumped us in Crescent Creek. He appeared to have grown uglier since last year.

"Gentlemen," the ref said to the tri-captains. "You're the visitors. Call it in the air."

He flipped the silver dollar and Fifty-five said in a feeble, raspy voice, "Tails."

"Tails it is," said the ref, scooping up the coin.

"We'll kii-iick." Fifty-five barely got the words out.

They didn't shake our hands—Edenburg and Taunton never shook hands.

"Did Fifty-five seem weird to you?" I asked Jason as we headed to the sideline.

"I don't know," Jason said, absorbed in his own thoughts.

Things moved quickly after that, the way they always did in the last minutes before the game whistle blew. I knew Daddy and Mama would be home listening to the game—watching me play made Mama anxious—but I searched the crowd for them anyway. Noise and color blurred together. I smelled an odd sourness on the heavy air. Tuttle ran up and down the sideline, slapping us on the ass; then he gathered the return team, yelling, "Right return! Right return!" They trotted out to their positions.

Taunton was already lined up along the forty-yard line, a string of eleven black monsters. I expected them to operate with their characteristic machinelike efficiency, but the kicker approached the tee with a herky-jerky step and the ball dribbled off his foot; the others just stood there. One of our guys recovered the onside kick at the Taunton forty-six.

"They're pissing in our faces!" Coach Tuttle said, incensed. "Disrespecting us!"

He told Justin to run a short-passing series, but when Justin got us huddled up, he called for a long pass to me off a flea-flicker.

"That ain't what Coach called," said Tick Robbins, our tailback.

"Fuck him!" Justin said. "This is my last game and I'm calling what I want. That retard's done telling me what to do."

Tick complained and Justin said, "We throw short passes over the middle, it's gonna get Andy dead. Now run the damn play! On two."

THE FLOCK

We broke the huddle and I lined up opposite a Taunton cornerback. He was looking up into the sky, like he was receiving instruction from God. On two, I faked toward the center of the field and then took off along the sideline. Nobody covered me, and as the ball descended out of the lights, I thought this might be a satori moment. I made the catch, but the pass was a little overthrown and my momentum carried me stumbling out of bounds inside the twenty, where I fell.

That didn't stop the Taunton defenders. They had scarcely moved a muscle when the ball was snapped, yet now they came at what seemed an impossibly fast clip. Their outlines blurred, and it looked as if they weren't running but were skimming over the grass. Three of them piled onto me, but the impact didn't have much effect. I felt something jabbing at me and fought to get clear. As I did, I thought I saw a lemony eye open in the chest of the guy lying atop me—just a flicker, then it was gone—and heard above the noise of the crowd a single, unmistakable *jee-eep*. I scrambled up, confused and frightened. My jersey was covered with tiny rips.

The ref had thrown a flag for unnecessary roughness, and he was chewing out the Taunton players, threatening ejections. They appeared unconcerned, picking themselves up and walking stiffly, laboriously away. I showed the ref my jersey, but he was mad at the world and told me to shut up and play football. In the huddle I said that something funny was going on, but Justin was all afire to score and paid no attention. After the penalty, we had possession on the Taunton nine-yard line—he dismissed the play Tuttle had sent in and called a quarterback draw. And then Tony Budgen, our right tackle, said "Holy shit!"

The Taunton Warriors, the players on the field and on the sideline, were disintegrating, dissolving into flights of grackles. Their uniforms, their bodies...their every particular had been composed of birds, compressed into ungainly shapes, and now those shapes were breaking apart. A helmet appeared to open into a bloom of glossy wings; the numbers 3 and 6 lifted from a jersey, assuming plumper forms, becoming two birds that flew at me, creating a gap from which others emerged; a headless Warrior winnowed to nothing, deconstructing from the neck down like one of those speeded-up time-lapse films detailing the building of a skyscraper, only this one ran backward; the defensive front four exploded into a shrapnel of birds.

Alarmed yet fascinated by the display, we backed toward midfield as the grackles flapped up from the last remaining relics of our opponents, some to perch on the Taunton bus, lining its fenders and roof, a row of hunched, silent spectators, while the rest ascended beyond the lights to join a vast, indistinct disturbance in the sky. Screams issued from the bleachers. Portions of the crowd were disintegrating, too, leaving patches of empty seats, and people pushed and clawed at one another, desperately trying to flee. I had in mind to do the same but was rooted to the spot, staring up into the toiling darkness above the field. It began to get close, stuffy, like when you pull a blanket over your head, and the reason for this soon came clear.

The disturbance above the field was a host of grackles, an unthinkable tonnage of feathers and hollow bones and stringy flesh—as they descended to the level of the lights, the air thickened with their sour smell. They descended farther, whirling and whirling, obscuring the lights so that they showed as dim, flickering suns through a water of black wings.

I could no longer see the sign on the Toddle House beyond the east end of the field, and this led me to believe that the flock had sealed us off from the world. Everyone in the bleachers had poured onto the grass. The pep band's instruments were scattered about. Somebody had stepped on a French horn, crushing the bell. A cheerleader, Beth Pugh, crawled past, black hair striping her face, encaging her demented eyes—when I tried to help her, she slapped my arm away and screamed. People were on their knees, weeping and praying; some shielded their eyes and mouths against the droppings that fell, intermittently peeking at the grackles.

There must have been millions. They must have been stacked to the top of the sky in order to bring such a stench, such an oppressive presence. The great seething of their wings and the rusty chaos of their cries reduced the sounds of human terror to barely audible interruptions in an ocean of white noise. They descended lower yet, roofing the field with their swarming, swirling bodies, darkening the light, and I lay flat, my face buried in the grass, certain that I would be torn apart or crushed or carried off like Amy Carlysle's daughter and dropped from a height.

But when I looked again—after no more than a minute or two, I think—the flock had retreated beyond the tops of the light poles, and they continued their retreat, going beyond the range of sight and hearing until a mere handful were left swooping and curvetting overhead, and those few still perched atop the Taunton bus. Then the bus itself exploded, vanishing in a flurry of the purplish black wings and lemony eyes and cruel beaks that had composed its shape, and we were alone, less than a thousand of us, splattered with bird shit, terrified, wandering the field and searching for our loved ones. I had no one to look for other than Doyle, but I could find him nowhere.

—

We won the game by way of forfeit and lost in the regionals the week after by the same means. No one wanted to play, and despite some *blah blah blah* spouted by Coach Tuttle about how the dead would want us to soldier on in the face of tragedy, how events like this could define our lives, the team voted unanimously to accept a painless defeat.

Actually, our losses were not so severe as they had been at first assessed. Coach Cunliffe and the entire Taunton team were found unharmed, albeit bewildered, in a field three miles from Edenburg, their bus intact, and those missing—fourteen, when all was said and done—were peripheral figures like Mr. Pepper and Sally Carlysle, the aged and the unwanted.

And Doyle. I attended his funeral, received a sloppy kiss from one of his gravid sisters and a hug from his daddy, who had made of his death a newly righteous excuse for his drinking; yet I was not terribly surprised some months later when I heard he had been spotted in Crawford, a mill town less than a hundred miles away. I drove over there one evening, intending to question him about his involvement with the flock, whether it had been conscious, coerced, or otherwise—I knew he must have had something to do with them or else he wouldn't have run away.

I tracked him down in a roadhouse on the outskirts of Crawford and stood watching him from a noisy corner. He had his arm around a depressed-looking blonde—she was perhaps a decade older than him—and the meanness that now and then had come into his face seemed to have settled in permanently. I left without confronting him, doubting that he would have anything to tell me and realizing that I wouldn't believe him even if he did.

Football, as Coach Tuttle and others of his mentality are fond of saying, is a lot like life. By this I take them to mean that the game seeks to order chaos by means of a system of rules and demarcations. Even if you accept the metaphor as true, it begs the question, what is life like?

In the weeks following the Taunton game, those who could afford to leave Edenburg did so. Dawn Cupertino, for instance, hooked up with a paper towel salesman, and after a whirlwind courtship, they got engaged and moved to his home in Falls Church, Virginia. Most people, my parents included, could not afford to leave and thus suffered through the fumblings of the police, an FBI investigation, an inquiry conducted by the State Bureau of Wildlife and Fisheries, and questioning by countless investigators of the paranormal (they continue to trickle through town). None of this yielded a result that could explain the advent of the flock, but talking and talking about it, and then talking more, it helped dial down our temperature and we began settling into our old routines, both good and bad.

School started up again. Carol Ann and I made a stab at getting back together, but the fizz had gone out of that bottle and we drifted apart. Mama had another of her flings and fought with Daddy until all hours. When you think about it, with its lack of plan or purpose, its stretches of sameness and boredom, its explosive griefs and joys that either last too long or abandon us too quickly, life's not a thing like football, not as Coach Tuttle meant it, anyway...though maybe it's a little bit like Edenburg football.

One morning in April, I got a call from Dawn. She had been daydreaming about home and couldn't think of anyone she wanted to talk to except me. I told her I'd received early acceptance into the University of Virginia and that I was doing okay after, you know, all the weirdness. She asked if there had been any grackle sightings, and I said that Culliver County was basically a grackle-free zone, what with everyone declaring open season on the Devil's Bird, blowing them away on sight.

The conversation began to drag and Dawn said she should probably be going, yet showed no real inclination to hang up. I asked what she was doing, and she said that Jim, the salesman, wanted her to have a baby.

"It's a big thing with him," she said. "I'm scared if I don't go along, he's gonna kick me out. I'm not ready to have babies. I don't know as I'll ever be ready."

"I'm not going to be much help with this one, Dawn."

"I know. It's just...Oh, hell!"

I thought she might be crying.

After a spell of silence, she said, "Remember when you and me and Doyle and Carol Ann drove up to the Outer Banks that time, and we were dancing to the car radio on top of the dunes?"

"Uh-huh, yeah."

"I wish I was there now." She sighed. "It all seems so damn ordinary, but when you think back on it, you see it's really not."

"I was thinking just the opposite. You know. How things that seem great, they turn out to be nothing in the long run."

"Yeah," she said. "That, too."

VACANCY

Chapter 1

Cliff Coria has been sitting in a lawn chair out front of the office of Ridgewood Motors for the better part of five years, four nights a week, from mid-afternoon until whenever he decides it's not worth staying open any longer, and during that time he's spent, he estimates, between five and six hundred hours staring toward the Celeste Motel across the street. That's how long it's taken him to realize that something funny may be going on. He might never have noticed anything if he hadn't become fascinated by the sign in the office window of the Celeste. It's a No Vacancy sign, but the No is infrequently lit. Foot-high letters written in a cool blue neon script: they glow with a faint aura in the humid Florida dark:

VACANCY

That cool, blue, halated word, then…that's what Cliff sees as he sits in a solitude that smells of asphalt and gasoline, staring through four lanes of traffic or no traffic at all, plastic pennons stirring above his head, a paperback on his knee (lately he's been into Scott Turow), at the center of gleaming SUVs, muscle cars, minivans, the high-end section where sit the aristocrats of the lot, a BMW, a silver Jag, a couple of Hummers, and the lesser hierarchies of reconditioned Toyotas, family sedans with suspect frames that sell for a thousand dollars and are called Drive-Away

Specials. He's become so sensitized to the word, the sign, it's as if he's developed a relationship with it. When he's reading, he'll glance toward the sign now and again, because seeing it satisfies something in him. At closing time, leaving the night watchman alone in the office with his cheese sandwiches and his boxing magazines, he'll snatch a last look at it before he pulls out into traffic and heads for the Port Orange Bridge and home. Sometimes when he's falling asleep, the sign will switch on in his mind's eye and glow briefly, bluely, fading as he fades.

Cliff's no fool. Used car salesman may be the final stop on his employment track, but it's lack of ambition, not a lack of intellect, that's responsible for his station in life. He understands what's happening with the sign. He's letting it stand for something other than an empty motel room, letting it second the way he feels about himself. That's all right, he thinks. Maybe the fixation will goad him into making a change or two, though the safe bet is, he won't change. Things have come too easily for him. Ever since his glory days as a high school jock (wide receiver, shooting guard), friends, women, and money haven't been a serious problem. Even now, more than thirty years later, his looks still get him by. He's got the sort of unremarkably handsome, rumpled face that you might run across in a Pendleton catalog, and he dyes his hair ash brown, leaves a touch of gray at the temples, and wears it the same as he did when he was in Hollywood. That's where he headed after his stint in the army (he was stationed in Germany near the end of the Vietnam War). He figured to use the knowledge he gained with a demolition unit to get work blowing up stuff in the movies, but wound up acting instead, for the most part in B-pictures.

People will come onto the lot and say, "Hey! You're that guy, right?" Usually they're referring to a series of commercials he shot in the Nineties, but occasionally they're talking about his movies, his name fifth- or sixth-billed, in which he played good guys who were burned alive, exploded, eaten by monstrous creatures, or otherwise horribly dispatched during the first hour. He often sells a car to the people who recognize him and tosses in an autographed headshot to sweeten the deal. And then he'll go home to his beach cottage, a rugged old thing of boards and a screened-in porch, built in the forties, that he bought with residual money; he'll sleep with one of the women whom he sees on a non-exclusive basis, or else he'll stroll over to the Surfside Grill, an upscale watering hole close by his house, where he'll drink and watch sports. It's the most satisfying of dissatisfying lives. He knows he doesn't have it in him to make a mark, but maybe it's like in the movies, he thinks. In the movies, everything happens for a reason, and maybe there's a reason he's here, some minor plot function he's destined to perform. Nothing essential, mind you. Just a part with some arc to the character, a little meat on its bones.

—

The Celeste Motel is a relic of Daytona Beach as it was back in the Sixties: fifteen pale blue stucco bungalows, vaguely Spanish in style, hunkered down amidst a scrap of Florida jungle—live oaks, shrimp plants, palmettos, Indian palms, and hibiscus. Everything's run to seed, the grounds so overgrown that the lights above the bungalow doors (blue like the Vacancy sign) are filtered through sprays of leaves, giving them a mysterious air. Spanish moss fallen from the oaks collects on the tile roofs; the branches of unpruned shrubs tangle with the mesh of screen doors; weeds choke the flagstone path. The office has the same basic design and color as the bungalows, but it's two stories with an upstairs apartment, set closer to the street. Supported by a tall metal pole that stands in front of the office is an illuminated square plastic sign bearing the name of the motel and the sketch of a woman's face, a minimalist, stylized rendering like those faces on matchbook covers accompanied by a challenge to Draw This Face and discover whether you have sufficient talent to enroll in the Famous Artist's School. Halfway down the pole, another, smaller sign to which stick-on letters can be affixed. Tonight it reads:

WELCOME SPRING B EAKERS
SNGL/DBL 29.95
FREE HBO

The Celeste is almost never full, but whenever Number Eleven is rented, the No on the No Vacancy sign lights up and stays lit for about an hour; then it flickers and goes dark. Once Cliff realized this was a reoccurring phenomenon, it struck him as odd, but no big deal. Then about a month ago, around six o'clock in the evening, just as he was getting comfortable with Turow's *Presumed Guilty*, Number Eleven was rented by a college-age girl driving a Corvette, the twin of a car that Cliff sold the day before, which is the reason he noticed. She parked at the rear (the lot is out of sight from the street, behind a hedge of bamboo), entered eleven, and the No switched on. A couple of hours later, after the No had switched back off, a family of three driving a new Ford Escape—portly dad, portly mom, skinny kid—checked in and, though most of the cabins were vacant, they, too, entered eleven. The girl must be part of the family, Cliff thought, and they had planned to meet at the motel. But at a quarter past ten, a guy with a beard and biker colors, riding a chopped Harley Sportster, also checked into eleven and the No switched on again.

It's conceivable, Cliff tells himself, that a massive kink is being indulged within the bungalow. Those blue lights might signal more than an ill-considered decorating touch. Whatever. It's not his business. But after three further incidents of multiple occupancies, his curiosity has been fully aroused and he's begun to study the Celeste through a pair of binoculars that he picked up at an army surplus store. Since he can detect nothing anomalous about Number Eleven, other than the fact that the shades are always drawn, he has turned his attention to the office.

For the past four years or thereabouts, the motel has been owned and operated by a Malaysian family. The Palaniappans. The father, Bazit, is a lean, fastidious type with skin the color of a worn penny, black hair, and a skimpy mustache that might be a single line drawn with a fine pencil. Every so often, he brings a stack of business cards for Jerry Muntz, the owner of the used car lot, to distribute. Jerry speaks well of him, says that he's a real nice guy, a straight shooter. Cliff has never been closer to the other Palaniappans than across a four-lane highway, but through his binoculars he has gained a sense of their daily routines. Bazit runs the office during the morning hours, and his wife, a pale Chinese woman, also thin, who might be pretty if not for her perpetually dour expression, handles the afternoons. Their daughter, a teenager with a nice figure and a complexion like Bazit's, but with a rosy cast, returns home from school at about four pm, dropped off by a female classmate driving a Honda. She either hangs about the office or cleans the bungalows—Cliff thinks she looks familiar and wonders where he might have seen her. Bazit comes back on duty at six pm and his wife brings a tray downstairs around eight. They and their daughter dine together while watching TV. The daughter appears to dominate the dinner conversation, speaking animatedly, whereas the parents offer minimal responses. On occasion they argue, and the girl will flounce off upstairs. At ten o'clock the night man arrives. He's in his early twenties, his features a mingling of Chinese and Malaysian. Cliff supposes him to be the Palaniappan's son, old enough to have his own place.

And that's it. That's the sum of his observations. Their schedules vary, of course. Errands, trips to Costco, and such. Bazit and his wife spend the occasional evening out, as does the daughter, somewhat more frequently. In every regard, they appear to be an ordinary immigrant family. Cliff has worked hard to simplify his life, though the result isn't everything he hoped, and he would prefer to think of the Palaniappans as normal and wishes that he had never noticed the Vacancy sign; but the mystery of Number Eleven is an itch he can't scratch. He's certain that there's a rational explanation, but has the sneaking suspicion that his idea of what's rational might be expanded if he were to find the solution.

Chapter 2

When Cliff was eighteen, a week after his high school graduation, he and some friends, walking on the beach after an early morning swim, came upon a green sea turtle, a big one with a carapace four feet long. Cliff mounted the turtle, whereupon she (it was a female who, misguidedly, had chosen a populated stretch of beach as the spot to lay her eggs) began trundling toward the ocean. His friends warned Cliff to dismount, but he was having too much fun playing cowboy to listen. Shortly after the turtle entered the water, apparently more flexible in her natural medium, or feeling more at home, she extended her neck and snapped off Cliff's big toe.

He wonders what might have happened had not he and the turtle crossed paths, if he kept his athletic scholarship and, instead of going to Hollywood, attended college. Now that he's contemplating another foolhardy move—and he thinks taking his investigation to a new level is potentially foolhardy—he views the turtle incident as a cautionary tale. The difference is that no pertinent mystery was attached to the turtle, yet he's unsure whether that's a significant difference. When he gets right down to it, he can't understand how the Celeste Motel relates to his life any more than did the turtle.

Cliff's scheduled for an afternoon shift the following Saturday. Jerry thinks it'll be an exceptionally high-traffic weekend, what with the holiday, and he wants his best salesman working the lot. This irritates the rest of the sales staff—they know having Cliff around will cut into their money—but as Jerry likes to say, Life's a bitch, and she's on the rag. He says this somewhat less often since hiring a female salesperson, the lovely Stacey Gerone, and he's taken down the placard bearing this bromide and an inappropriate cartoon from inside the door of the employee washroom...Anyway, Cliff comes in early on Saturday, at quarter to eleven, and, instead of pulling into Ridgewood Motors, parks in the driveway of the Celeste Motel. He pushes into the office, the room he's been viewing through his binoculars. The decor all works together—rattan chairs, blond desk, TV, potted ferns, bamboo frames holding images of green volcanoes and perfect beaches—canceling the disjointed impression he's gained from a distance.

"Good morning," says Bazit Palaniappan, standing straight as if for inspection, wearing a freshly ironed shirt. "How may I help you?"

Cliff's about to tell him, when Bazit's pleasant expression is washed away by one of awed delight.

"You are Dak Windsor!" Bazit hurries out from behind his desk and pumps Cliff's hand. "I have seen all your movies! How wonderful to have you here!"

It takes Cliff a second or two to react to the name, Dak Windsor, and then he remembers the series of fantasy action pictures he did under that name in the Philippines. Six of them, all shot during a three-month period. He recalls cheesy sets, lousy FX, incredible heat, a villain called Lizardo, women made-up as blue-skinned witches, and an Indonesian director who yelled at everyone, spoke neither Tagalog nor English, and had insane bad breath. Cliff has never watched the movies, but his agent told him they did big business in the Southeast Asian markets. Not that their popularity mattered to Cliff—he was paid a flat fee for his work. His most salient memory of the experience is of a bothersome STD he caught from one of the blue-skinned witches.

"Au-Yong!" Bazit shouts. "Will you bring some tea?"

Cliff allows Bazit to maneuver him into a chair and for the next several minutes he listens while the man extols the virtues of *Forbidden Tiger Treasure*, *Sword of the Black Demon*, and the rest of the series, citing plot points, asking questions Cliff cannot possibly answer because he has no idea of the films' continuity or logic—it's a jumble of crocodile men, cannibal queens, wizards shooting lurid lightning from their fingertips, and lame dialog sequences that made no sense at the time and, he assumes, would likely make none if he were to watch the pictures now.

"To think," says Bazit, wonderment in his voice. "All this time, you've been working right across the street. I must have seen you a dozen times, but never closely enough to make the connection. You must come for dinner some night and tell us all about the movies."

Mrs. Palaniappan brings tea, listens as Bazit provides an ornate introduction to the marvel that is Dak Windsor ("Cliff Coria," Cliff interjects. "That's my real name."). It turns out that Bazit, who's some ten-twelve years younger than Cliff, watched the series of movies when he was an impressionable teenager and, thanks to Dak/Cliff's sterling performance as the mentor and sidekick of the film's hero, Ricky Sintara, he was inspired to make emigration to the United States a goal, thus leading to the realization of his golden dream, a smallish empire consisting of the Celeste and several rental properties.

"You know George Clooney?" she asks Cliff. That's her sole reaction to Bazit's fervent testimony.

"No," says Cliff, and starts to explain his lowly place in hierarchy of celebrity; but a no is all Mrs. Palaniappan needs to confirm her judgment of his worth. She excuses herself, says she has chores to do, and takes her grim, neutral-smelling self back upstairs.

Among the reasons that Cliff failed in Hollywood is that he was not enough of a narcissist to endure the amount of stroking that accompanies the slightest success; but nothing he has encountered prepares him for the hand job that Bazit lovingly offers. At several points during the conversation, Cliff attempts to get down to cases, but on each occasion Bazit recalls another highlight from the Dak Windsor films that needs to be memorialized, shared, dissected, and when Cliff checks his watch he finds it's after eleven-thirty. There's no way he'll have time to get into the subject of Number Eleven. And then, further complicating the situation, the Palaniappan's daughter, Shalin, returns home—her school had a half-day. Bazit once again performs the introductions, albeit less lavishly, and Shalin, half-kneeling on the cushion of her father's chair, one hand on her hip and the other, forefinger extended, resting on her cheek, says, "Hello," and smiles.

That pose nails it for Cliff—it's the same pose the Malaysian actress (he knows she had a funny name, but he can't recall it) who gave him the STD struck the first time he noticed her, and Shalin, though ten-fifteen years younger, bears a strong resemblance to her, down to the beauty mark at the corner of her mouth; even the mildness of her smile is identical. It's such a peculiar hit coming at that moment, one mystery hard upon the heels of another, Cliff doesn't know whether the similarity between the women is something he should be amazed by or take in stride, perceive as an oddity, a little freaky but nothing out of the ordinary. It might be that he doesn't remember the actress clearly, that he's glossing over some vital distinction between the two women.

After Shalin runs off upstairs, Bazit finally asks the reason for Cliff's visit, and, fumbling for an excuse, Cliff explains that some nights after work he doesn't want to drive home, he has an engagement this side of the river, he's tired or he's had a couple of drinks, and he wonders if he can get a room on a semi-regular basis at the Celeste.

"For tonight? It would be an honor!" says Bazit. "I think we have something available."

Suddenly leery, Cliff says, "No, I'm talking down the road, you know. Next weekend or sometime."

Bazit assures him that Dak Windsor will have no problem obtaining a room. They shake hands and Cliff's almost out the door when he hears a shout in a foreign language at his back. *"Showazzat Bompar!"* or something of the sort. He turns and finds that Bazit has dropped into a half-crouch, his left fist extended in a Roman salute, his right hand held beside his head, palm open, as if he's about to take a pledge, and Cliff recalls that Ricky Sintara performed a similar salute at the end of each movie. He goes out into the driveway and stands beside his car, an '06 dark blue Miata X-5 convertible, clean and fully loaded. The April heat is a shock after the air-conditioned office, the sunlight makes him squint, and he has a sneaking suspicion that somehow, for whatever reason, he's just been played.

Chapter 3

Sunday morning, Cliff puts on a bathing suit, flip-flops, and a Muntz Mazda World T-shirt, and takes his coffee and OJ into his Florida room, where he stands and watches, through a fringe of dune grass and Spanish bayonet, heavy surf piling in onto a strip of beach, the sand pinkish from crushed coquina shells. The jade-colored waves are milky with silt; they tumble into one another, bash the shore with concussive slaps. Out beyond the bar, a pelican splashes down into calmer, bluer water. Puffs of pastel cloud flock the lower sky.

Cliff steps into his office, goes online and checks the news, then searches the film geek sites and finds a copy of *Sword of the Black Demon*, which he orders. It's listed under the category, Camp Classics. Still sleepy, he lies down on the sofa and dreams he's in a movie jungle with two blue-skinned witches and monkeys wearing grenadier uniforms and smoking clove cigarettes. He wakes to the sight of Stacey Gerone standing over him, looking peeved.

"Did you forget I was coming over?" she asks.

"Of course not." He gets to his feet, not the easiest of moves these days, given the condition of his back, but he masks his discomfort with a yawn. "You want some coffee?"

"For God's sake, take off that T-shirt. Don't you get enough of Muntz World during the week?"

Stacey drops her handbag on the sofa. She's a redhead with creamy skin that she nourishes with expensive lotions and a sun blocker with special cancer-eating bacteria or some shit, dressed in a designer tank top and white slacks. Her body's a touch zaftig, but she is still, at thirty-eight, a babe. At the lot, she does a sultry Desperate Housewife act that absolutely kills middle-aged men and college boys alike. If the wife or girlfriend tag along, she changes her act or lets somebody else mother the sale. Jerry plans to move her over to his candy store (the new car portion of his business) in Ormond Beach, where there's real money to be made. For more than a year, he's tried to move Cliff to Ormond as well, but Cliff refuses to budge. His reluctance to change is inertial, partly, but he doesn't need the money and the young couples and high school kids and working class folk who frequent Ridgewood Motors are more to his taste than the geriatric types who do their car-shopping at Muntz Mazda World.

As Cliff makes a fresh pot, Stacey sits at the kitchen table and talks a blue streak, mostly about Jerry. "You should see his latest," she says. "He's got a design program on his computer, and he spends every spare minute creating cartoons. You know, cartoons of himself. Little tubby, cute Jerrys. Each one has a slogan with it. Every word starts with an M. What do you call that? When every word starts with the same letter?"

"Alliteration," says Cliff.

"So he's doing this alliteration. Most of it's business stuff. Muntz Millennium Mazda Make-out. Muntz Mazda Moments. Trying to find some combination of M-words that make a snappy saying, you know. But then he's got these ones that have different cartoons with them. Muntz Munches Muff. MILF-hunting Muntz. He took great pains to show them to me."

"He's probably hoping to get lucky."

Stacey gives him a pitying look.

"You did it with Jerry?" he says, unable to keep incredulity out of his voice.

"How many women do you see in this business? Grow up! I needed the job, so I slept with him." Stacey waggles two fingers. "Twice. Believe me, sleep was the operative word. Once I started selling…" She makes a brooming gesture with her hand. "Does it tick you off I had sex with him?"

"Is that how you want me to feel?"

"How do I want you to feel? That's a toughie." She crosses her legs, taps her chin. "Studied indifference would be good. Some undertones of resentment and jealousy. That would suit me fine."

"I can work with that."

"That's what I love most about you, Cliff." She stands and puts her arms about his waist from behind. "You take direction so well."

"I am a professional," he says.

Later, lying in bed with Stacey, he tells her about the Celeste and Number Eleven, about Shalin Palaniappan, expecting her reaction to be one of indifference—she'll tell him to give it a rest, forget about it, he's making a mountain out of a molehill, and just who does he think he is, anyway? Tony Shaloub or somebody? But instead she says, "I'd call the cops if I was you."

"Really?" he says.

"That stuff about the girl…I don't know. But obviously something hinkey's happening over there. Unless you've lost your mind and are making the whole thing up."

"I'm not making it up." Cliff locks his hands behind his head and stares up at the sandpainted ceiling.

"Then you should call the cops."

"They won't do anything," he says. "Best case, they'll ask stupid questions that'll make the Palaniappans shut down whatever's going on. As soon as the pressure's off, they'll start up again."

"Then you should forget it."

"How come?"

"You're a smart guy, Cliff, but sometimes you space. You go off somewhere else for a couple hours...or a couple of days. That isn't such a great quality for a detective. It's not even a great quality for a salesman."

Slitting his eyes, Cliff turns the myriad bumps of paint on the ceiling into snowflake patterns; once, when he was smoking some excellent Thai stick, he managed to transform them into a medieval street scene, but he hasn't ever been able to get it back. "Maybe you're right," he says.

—

After a therapy day with Stacey, Cliff thinks he might be ready to put *l'affaire* Celeste behind him. She's convinced him that he isn't qualified to deal with the situation, if there is a situation, and for a few days he eschews the binoculars, gets back into Scott Turow, and avoids looking at the Vacancy sign, though when his concentration lapses, he feels its letters branding their cool blue shapes on his brain. On Thursday evening, he closes early, before nine, and drives straight home, thinking he'll jump into a pair of shorts and walk over to the Surfside, but on reaching his house he finds a slender package stuck inside the screen door. *Sword of the Black Demon* has arrived from Arcane Films. A Camp Classic. He tosses it on the sofa, showers, changes, and, on his way out, decides to throw the movie in the player and watch a little before heading to the bar—refreshing his memory of the picture will give him something to talk about with his friends.

It's worse than he remembers. Beyond lame. Gallons of stage blood spewing from Monty-Pythonesque wounds; the cannibal queen's chunky, naked retinue; a wizard who travels around on a flying rock; the forging of a sword from a meteorite rendered pyrotechnically by lots of sparklers; the blue witches, also naked and chunky, except for one...He hits the pause button, kneels beside the TV, and examines the lissome shape of, it appears, Shalin Palaniappan, wishing he could check if the current incarnation of the blue witch has a mole on her left breast, though to do so would likely net him five-to-ten in the slammer. He makes for the Surfside, a concrete block structure overlooking the beach, walking the dunetops along A1A, hoping that a couple of vodkas will banish his feeling of unease, but once he's sitting at the bar under dim track lighting, a vodka rocks in hand, deliciously chilled by the AC, embedded in an atmosphere of jazz and soft, cluttered talk, gazing through the picture window at the illuminated night ocean (the beach, at this hour, is barely ten yards wide and the waves seem perilously close), he's still uneasy and he turns his attention to the Marlins on the big screen, an abstract clutter of scurrying white-clad figures on a bright green field.

"Hey, Cliffie," says a woman's voice, and Marley, a diminutive package of frizzy, dirty blond hair and blue eyes, a cute sun-browned face and jeans tight as a sausage skin, lands in the chair beside his and gives him a quick hug. She's young enough to be his daughter, old enough to be his lover. He's played both roles, but prefers that of father. She's feisty, good-hearted, and too valuable as a friend to risk losing over rumpled bed sheets.

"Hey, you," he says. "I thought this was your night off."

"All my nights are off." She grins. "My new goal—becoming a barfly like you."

"What about...you know. Tyler, Taylor..."

She pretends to rap her knuckles on his forehead. "Tucker, he's gone."

"I thought that was working out."

"Me, too," she says. "And then, oops, an impediment. He was wanted for fraud in South Carolina."

"Fraud? My God!"

"That's what I said...except I cussed more." She neatly tears off a strip of cocktail napkin. "Cops came by the place three weeks ago. Guns drawn. Spotlights. The whole schmear. He waived extradition."

"Why didn't you tell me sooner?"

She shrugs. "You know how I hate people crying in their beer."

"God. Let me buy you a drink."

"You bet." She pounds the counter. "Tequila!"

They drink, talk about Tucker, about what a lousy spring it's been. Two tequilas along, she asks if he's all right, he seems a little off. He wants to tell her, but it's too complicated, too demented, and she doesn't need to hear his problems, so he tells her about the movies he did in the Philippines, making her laugh with anecdotes about and impersonations of the director. Five tequilas down and she's hanging on him, giggly, teasing, laughing at everything he says, whether it's funny or not. It's obvious she won't be able to drive. He invites her to use his couch—he'd give her the bed, but the couch is murder on his back—and she says, suddenly tearful, "You're so sweet to me."

After one for the road, they start out along the dunes toward home, going with their heads down—a wind has kicked up and blows grit in their faces. The surf munches the shore, sounding like a giant chewing his food with relish; a rotting scent intermittently overrides the smell of brine. No moon, no stars, but porch lights from the scattered houses show the way. Marley keeps slipping in the soft sand and Cliff has to put an arm around her to prevent her from falling. The tall grasses tickle his calves. They're twenty yards from his front step, when he hears the sound of a boomerang in flight—he identifies it instantly, it's that distinct. A helicopter-ish sound, but higher-pitched, almost a whistling, passing overhead. He stops walking, listening for it, and Marley seizes the opportunity to rub her breasts against him, her head tipped back, waiting to be kissed.

"Is this going to be one of those nights?" she asks teasingly.

"Did you hear that?"

"Hear what?"

"A boomerang, I think. Somebody threw a boomerang."

Bewildered, she says, "A boomerang?"

"Shh! Listen!"

Confused, she shelters beneath his arm as he reacts to variations in the wind's pitch, to a passing car whose high beams sweep over the dune grass, lighting the cottage, growing a shadow from its side that lengthens and then appears to reach with a skinny black arm across the rumpled ground the instant before it vanishes. He hears no repetition of the sound, and its absence unsettles him. He's positive that he heard it, that somewhere out in the night, a snaky-jointed figure is poised to throw. He hustles Marley toward the cottage and hears, as they ascend the porch steps, a skirling music, whiny reed instruments, and a clattery percussion, like kids beating with sticks on a picket fence, just a snatch of it borne on the wind. He shoves Marley inside, bolts the door, and switches on the porch lights, thinking that little brown men with neat mustaches will bloom from the dark, because that's what sort of music it is, Manila taxicab music, the music played by the older drivers who kept their radios tuned to an ethnic station—but he sees nothing except rippling dune grass, pale sand, and the black gulf beyond, a landscape menacing for its lack of human form.

He bolts the inner door, too. Resisting Marley's attempts to get amorous, he opens out the couch bed, makes her lie down and take a couple of aspirin with a glass of water. He sits in a chair by the couch as she falls asleep, his anxiety subsiding. She looks like a kid in her T-shirt and diaphanous green panties, drowsing on her belly, face half-concealed by strings of hair, and he thinks what a fuck-up he is. The thought is bred by no particular chain of logic. It may have something to do with Marley, with his deepened sense of the relationship's inappropriateness, a woman more than twenty years his junior (though, God knows, he's championed the other side of that argument), and she's younger than that in her head, a girl, really...It may bear upon that, but the thought has been on heavy rotation in his brain for years and seems to have relevance to every situation. He's pissed away countless chances for marriage, for success, and he can't remember what he was thinking, why he treated these opportunities with such casual disregard. He recalls getting a third callback to test for the Bruce Willis role in *Die Hard*. Word was that the studio was leaning toward him, because Willis had pissed off one of the execs, so on the night before the callback he did acid at some Topanga cliff dwelling and came in looking bleary and dissolute.

Looking at Marley's ass, he has a flicker of arousal, and that worries him, that it's only a flicker, that perhaps his new sense of morality is merely a byproduct of growing older, of a reduced sex drive. He has the sudden urge to prove himself wrong, to wake her up and fuck her until dawn, but he sits there, depressed, letting his emotions bleed out into the sound of windowpanes shuddering from constant slaps of wind. Eventually he goes to the door and switches off the lights. Seconds later, he switches them back on, hoping that he won't discover some mutant shape sneaking toward the porch, yet feeling stupid and a little disappointed when nothing of the sort manifests.

Chapter 4

He's waked by something banging. He tries to sleep through it, but each time he thinks it's quit and relaxes, it starts up again, so he flings off the covers and shuffles into the living room, pauses on finding the couch unoccupied, scratches his head, trying to digest Marley's absence, then shuffles onto the porch and discovers it's the screen door that's banging. Thickheaded, he shuts it, registering that it's still dark outside. He walks through the house, calling out to Marley; he checks the bathroom. Alarm sets in. She would have left a note, she would have shut the front door. He dresses, shaking out the cobwebs, and goes out onto the porch steps, switching on the exterior lights. Beyond the half-circle of illumination, the shore is a winded confusion, black sky merging with black earth and sea, the surf still heavy. The wind comes in a steady pour off the water, plastering his shorts and shirt against his body.

"Marley!"

No response.

With this much wind, he thinks, his voice won't carry fifty feet.

He grabs the flashlight from inside the door, deciding that he'll walk down to the Surfside and make sure her car's gone from the lot. She probably went home, he tells himself. Woke up and was sober enough to drive. But leaving the door open...that's just not Marley.

He strikes out along A1A, keeping to the shoulder, made a bit anxious by the music he heard earlier that evening, by the boomerang sound, though he's attributed that to the booze, and by the time he reaches the turn-off into the lot, his thoughts have brightened, he's planning the day ahead; but on seeing Marley's shitbox parked all by its lonesome, a dented brown Hyundai nosed up to the door of the Surfside, his worries are rekindled. He shines the flashlight through the windows of the Hyundai. Fast-food litter, a Big Gulp cup, a crumpled Kleenex box. He bangs on the door of the bar, thinking that Marley might have changed her mind, realized she was too drunk to drive and bedded down in the Surfside. He shouts, bangs some more. Maybe she called a cab from his house. She must have felt guilty about coming on to him. If that's the case, he'll have to have a talk with her, assure her that it's not that she isn't desirable, it's got nothing to do with her, it's him, it's all about how he's begun to feel in intimate situations with her, and then she'll say he's being stupid, she doesn't think of him as a dirty old man, not at all. It's like the kids say, they're friends with benefits. No big deal. And Cliff, being a guy, will go along with that—sooner or later they'll wind up sleeping together and there they'll be, stuck once again amid the confusions of a May-September relationship.

As he walks home, swinging the flashlight side-to-side, he wonders if the reason he put some distance between him and Marley had less to do with her age than with the fact that he was getting too attached to her. The way he felt when she popped up at the Surfside last night—energized, happy, really happy to see her—is markedly different from the way he felt when Stacey Gerone came over the other morning. He's been in love a couple of times, and he seems to recall that falling in love was preceded on each occasion by a similar reaction on his part, a pushing away of the woman concerned for one reason or another. That, he concludes, would be disastrous. If now he perceives himself to be an aging roué, just imagine how contemptible he'd feel filling out Medicare forms while Marley is still a relatively young woman—like a decrepit vampire draining her youth.

His cottage in view, he picks up the pace, striding along briskly. He'll go back to bed for an hour or two, call Marley when he wakes.

And if she wants to start things up again…It's occurred to him that he's being an idiot, practicing a form of denial that serves no purpose. In Asia, in Europe, relationships between older men and young women—between older women and young men, for that matter—aren't perceived as unusual. All he may be doing by his denial is obeying a bourgeoisie convention. He gnaws at the problem, kicking at tufts of high grass, thinking that his notion of morality must be hardening along with his arteries, and, as he approaches the cottage, verging on the arc of radiance spilling from the porch, he notices a smear of red to the left of the door. It's an extensive mark, a wide, wavy streak a couple of feet long that looks very much like blood.

Coming up to the porch, he touches a forefinger to the redness. It's tacky, definitely blood. He's bewildered, dully regarding the dab of color on his fingertip, his mind muddled with questions, and then the wrongness of it, the idea that someone has marked his house with blood, and it's for sure an intentional mark, because no one would inadvertently leave a two-foot-long smear…the wrongness of it hits home and he's afraid. He whirls about. Beyond the range of the porch lights, the darkness bristles, vegetation seething in the wind, palmetto tops tossing, making it appear that the world is solidifying into a big, angry animal with briny breath, and it's shaking itself, preparing to charge.

He edges toward the steps, alert to every movement, and starts to hear music again, not the whiny racket he heard earlier, but strings and trumpets, a prolonged fanfare like the signature of a cheesy film score, growing louder, and he sees something taking shape from the darkness, something a shade blacker than the sky, rising to tower above the dunes. The coalsack figure of a horned giant, a sword held over its head. He gapes at the thing, the apparition—he assumes it's an apparition. What else could it be? He hasn't been prone to hallucinations for twenty years, and the figure, taller now than the tallest of the condominiums that line the beach along South Atlantic Avenue, is a known quantity, the spitting image of the Black Demon from his movie. Somebody is gaslighting him. They're out in the dunes with some kind of projector, casting a movie image against the clouds. Having established a rational explanation, albeit a flimsy one, Cliff tries to react rationally. He considers searching the dunes, finding the culprit, but when the giant cocks the sword, drawing it back behind its head, preparing to swing a blade that, by Cliff's estimate, is easily long enough to reach him, his dedication to reason breaks and he bolts for the steps, slams and locks the inner door, and stands in the center of his darkened living room, breathing hard, on the brink of full-blown panic.

The music has reverted to rackety percussion and skirling reeds, and it's grown louder, so loud that Cliff can't think, can't get a handle on the situation.

Many-colored lights flash in the windows, pale rose and purple and green and white, reminding him of the lights in a Manila disco created by cellophane panels on a wheel revolving past a bright bulb. He has a glimpse of something or someone darting past outside. A shadowy form, vaguely anthropomorphic, running back and forth, a few steps forward, slipping out of sight, then racing in the opposite direction, as if maddened by the music, and, his pulse accelerated by the dervish reeds and clattering percussion, music that might accompany the flight of a panicked moth, Cliff begins to feel light-headed, unsteady on his feet. There's too much movement, too much noise. It seems that the sound-and-light show is having an effect on his brain, like those video games that trigger epileptic seizures, and he can't get his bearings. The floor shifts beneath him, the window frame appears to have made a quarter-turn sideways in the wall. The furniture is dancing, the Mexican throw rug fronting the couch ripples like the surface of a rectangular pond. And then it stops. Abruptly. The music is cut off, the lights quit flashing...but there's still too much light for a moonless, starless night, and he has the impression that someone's aiming a yellow-white spot at the window beside the couch. Cliff waits for the next torment. His heart rate slows, he catches his breath, but he remains still, braced against the shock he knows is coming. Almost a full minute ticks by, and nothing's happened. The shadows in the room have deepened and solidified. He's uncertain what to do. Call the police and barricade himself in the house. Run like hell. Those seem the best options. Maybe whoever was doing this has fled and left a single spotlight behind. He sees his cell phone lying on an end table. "Okay," he says, the way you'd speak to a spooked horse. "Okay." He eases over to the table and picks up the phone. Activated, its cool blue glow soothes him. He punches in Marley's number and reaches her voicemail. "Marley," he says. "Call me when you get this." Before calling the police, he thinks about what might be in the house—he's out of pot, but did he finish those mushrooms in the freezer? Where did he put that bottle of oxycodone that Stacey gave him?

A tremendous bang shakes the cottage. Cliff squawks and drops the phone. Something scrabbles on the outside wall and then a woman's face, bright blue, reminiscent of those Indian posters of Kali you used to be able to buy in head shops, her white teeth bared, her long black hair disheveled and hanging down, appears in the window, coming into view from the side, as if she's clinging to the wall like a lizard. Her expression is so inhuman, so distorting of her features, that it yields no clue as to her identity; but when she swings down to the center of the window, gripping the molding, revealing her naked body, he recognizes her to be what's-her-name, the witch who gave him the STD. The mole on her left breast, directly below the nipple gives it away. As does her pubic hair, shaved into a unique pattern redolent of exotic vegetation. Even without those telltales, he'd know that body. She loved to dance for him before they fucked, rippling the muscles of her inner thighs, shaking her breasts. But she's not dancing now, and there's nothing arousing about her presence. She just hangs outside the window, glaring, a voluptuous blue bug. Her teeth and skin and red lips are a disguise. Rip it away, and you would see a horrid face with a proboscis and snapping jaws. Only the eyes would remain of her human semblance. Huge and dark, empty except for a greedy, lustful quality that manifests as a gleam embedded deep within them. It's that quality that compels Cliff, that roots him to the floorboards. He's certain if he makes a move to run, she'll come through the window, employing some magic that leaves the glass intact, and what she'll do then...His imagination fails him, or perhaps it does not, for he feels her stare on his skin, licking at him as might a cold flame, tasting him, coating his flesh with a slimy residue that isn't tangible, yet seems actual, a kind of saliva that, he thinks, will allow her to digest him more readily. And then it's over. The witch's body deflates, shrivels like a leathery balloon, losing its shape, crumpling, folding in on itself, dwindling in a matter of four or five seconds to a point of light that—he realizes the instant before it winks out, before the spotlight, too, winks out—is the same exact shade of blue as the Vacancy sign at the Celeste Motel.

It's a trick, a false ending, Cliff tells himself—she's trying to get his hopes up, to let him relax, and then she'll materialize behind him, close enough to touch. But time stretches out and she does not reappear. The sounds of wind and surf come to him. Still afraid, but beginning to feel foolish, he picks up his cell phone, half-expecting her to seize the opportunity and pounce. He cracks the door, then opens it and steps out into the soft night air. Something has sliced through the porch screen, halving it neatly. He imagines that the amount of torque required to do such a clean job would be considerable—it would be commensurate with, say, the arc of an enormous sword swung by a giant and catching the screen with the tip of its blade. He retreats inside the house, locks and bolts the door, realizing that it's possible he's being haunted by a movie. Thoughts spring up to assail the idea, but none serve to dismiss it. Understanding that he won't be believed, yet having nowhere else to turn, he dials 911.

Chapter 5

Detective Sergeant Todd Ashford of the Port Orange Police Department and Cliff have a history, though it qualifies as ancient history. They were in the same class at Seabreeze High and both raised a lot of hell, some of it together, but they were never friends, a circumstance validated several years after graduation when Ashford, then a patrolman with the Daytona Beach PD, displayed unseemly delight in busting Cliff on a charge of Drunk and Disorderly outside Cactus Jack's, a biker bar on Main Street. Cliff was home for a couple of weeks from Hollywood, flushed with the promise of imminent stardom, and Ashford did not attempt to hide the fact that he deeply resented his success. Nor does he attempt to hide his resentment now. Watching him pace about the interrogation room, a brightly lit space with black compound walls, a metal table and four chairs, Cliff recognizes that although Ashford may no longer resent his success, he has new reason for bitterness. He's a far cry from the buzz-cut young cop who hauled Cliff off to the drunk tank, presenting the image of a bulbous old man with receding gray hair, dark, squinty eyes, a soupstrainer mustache, and jowls, wearing an off-the-rack sport coat and jeans, his gun and badge half-hidden by the overhang of his belly. Cliff looks almost young enough to be his son.

"Why don't you tell me where her body is?" Ashford asks for perhaps the tenth time in the space of two hours. "We're going to find her eventually, so you might as well give it up."

Cliff has blown up a balloon, peed in a cup, given his DNA. He's fatigued, and now he's fed up with Ashford's impersonation of a homicide detective. His take on the man is that while he may drink his whiskey neat and smoke cigars (their stale, pungent stench hangs about him, heavy as the scent of wet dog) and do all manner of grown-up things, Ashford remains the same fifteen-year-old punk who, drunk on Orbit Beer (six bucks a case), helped him trash the junior class float the night before homecoming, the sort of guy no one remembers at class reunions, whose one notable characteristic was a talent for mind-fucking, who has spent his entire adult life exacting a petty revenge on the world for his various failures, failures that continue to this day, failures with women (no wedding ring), career, self-image...Another loser. There's nothing remarkable about that. It is, as far as Cliff can tell, a world of six billion losers. Six billion and one if you're counting God. But Ashford's incarnation of the classic loser is so seedy and thin-souled, Cliff is having trouble holding his temper.

"I want to call my lawyer," he says.

Ashford adopts a knowing look. "You think you need one?"

"Damn right I do! You're going to pick away at me all day, because this doesn't have anything to do with my guilt or innocence. This is all about high school."

Ashford grunts, as though disgusted. "You're a real asshole! A fucking egomaniac. We got a woman missing, maybe dead, and it's all about high school." He pulls back a chair and sits facing Cliff. "Let's say I believe someone's trying to set you up."

"The Palaniappans. It has to be them! They're the only ones who know about the movie."

"The movie. Right." Ashford takes a notebook from his inside breast pocket and flips through it. "*Sword of the Black Demon.*" He gives the title a sardonic reading, closes the notebook. "So you had one conversation with the Planappans..."

"Palaniappans!"

"Whatever. You had the one conversation and now you think they're out to get you, because the daughter looks like a woman you caught the clap from back in the day."

"It wasn't the clap, it was some kind of...I don't know. Some kind of Filipino gunge. And that's not why they're doing this. It's because, I think, I started sniffing around, trying to figure out what's going on with Bungalow eleven."

Ashford grunts again, this time in amusement. "Man, I can't wait to get your drug screen back."

"You're going to be disappointed," Cliff says. "I'm not high; I'm not drunk. I'm not even fucking dizzy."

Ashford attempts to stare him down, doubtless seeking to find a chink in the armor. He makes a clicking noise with his tongue. "So tell me again what happened after you and Marley left the Surfside."

"I want a lawyer."

"You go that way, you're not doing yourself any good."

"How much good am I doing myself sitting here, letting you nitpick my answers, trying to find inconsistencies that don't exist? Fuck you, Ashford. I want a lawyer."

Ashford turtles his neck, glowers at Cliff and says, "You think you're back in Hollywood? The cops out there, they let you talk to them that way?"

Cliff gays up his delivery. "They're lovely people. The LAPD is renowned for its hospitality. As for where I think I am, I trust I'm among guardians of the public safety."

Ashford's breathing heavies and Cliff, interpreting this as a sign of extreme anger, says, "Look, man. I know what I told you sounds freaky, but you're not even giving it a chance. You've made up your mind that I did something to Marley, and nothing I say's going to talk you out of it. Lawyering up's my only option."

Ashford settles back in his chair, calmer now. "All right. I'll listen. What do you think I should do about the Palnappians?"

"That's Palaniappans."

Ashford shrugs.

"If it were me," says Cliff, "I'd have a look round Bungalow Eleven. I'd ask some questions, find out what's happening in there."

"What do you think is happening?"

"Jesus Christ!" Cliff throws up his hands in frustration, and closes his eyes.

"Seriously," says Ashford. "I want to know, because from what you've told me, I don't have a clue."

"I don't know, okay?" says Cliff. "But I don't think it's anything good."

"Do you allow for the possibility that nothing's going on? That given everything you've said, the multiple occupancies, the sign, the vehicles disappearing…" Ashford pauses. "Can you remember any of the vehicles that disappeared? The makes and models?"

"I'm not sure they've disappeared. I haven't been able to check. But if not, they must be piling up back there. But yeah, I remember most of them."

Ashford tears a clean page from his notebook, shoves it and a pen across the table. "Write them down. The model, the color…the year if you know it."

Cliff scribbles a list, considers it, makes an addition, then passes the sheet of paper to Ashford, who looks it over.

"This is a pretty precise list," he says.

"It's the job. I tend to notice what people drive."

Ashford continues to study the list. "These are expensive cars. The Ford Escape, that's one of those hybrids, right?"

"Uh-huh. New this year."

Ashford folds the paper, sticks it in his notebook. "So. What I was saying, do you think there could be a reasonable explanation for all this? Something that has nothing to do with a witch and a movie? Something that makes sense in terms someone like me could accept?"

This touch of self-deprecation fuels the idea that Ashford may be smarter than Cliff has assumed. "It's possible," he says, but after a pause he adds, "No. Fuck, no. You had…"

A peremptory knocking on the door interrupts Cliff. With a disgruntled expression, Ashford heaves up to his feet and pokes his head out into the corridor. After a prolonged, muttering exchange with someone Cliff can't see, Ashford throws the door open wide and says flatly, "You can go for now, Coria. We'll be in touch."

Baffled, Cliff asks, "What is it? What happened?"

"Your girlfriend's alive. She's out by the front desk."

Cliff's relief is diluted by his annoyance over Ashford's refusal to accept that he and Marley are not lovers, but before he can once again deny the assertion, Ashford says, "Your house is still a crime scene. You might want to hang out somewhere for a few hours until we've finished processing."

Cliff gives him a what-the-fuck look, and Ashford, with more than a hint of the malicious in his voice, says, "We have to find out who that blood belongs to, don't we?"

Chapter 6

In the entryway of the police station, Marley mothers Cliff, hugging and fussing over him, attentions that he welcomes, but once in the car she waxes outraged, railing at the cops and their rush to judgment. Christ

Almighty! She woke up and couldn't get back to sleep, so she went to a diner and did some brooding. You'd think the cops would have more sense. You'd think they would look before they leaped.

"It's my fault," Cliff says. "I called them."

She shoots him a puzzled glance. "Why'd you do that?"

He remembers that she knows nothing about the Black Demon, the blood, the slit porch screen.

"You left the door open," he says. "I was worried."

"I did not! And even if I did, that's no reason to call the cops."

"Yeah, well. There was weird shit going on last night. I got hit by vandals, and that made me nervous."

They stop at a 7-11 so Cliff can buy a clean t-shirt—it's a tough choice between a white one with a cartoon decal and the words Surf Naked, and a gray one imprinted with a fake college seal and the words Screw U. He settles on the gray, deciding it makes a more age-appropriate statement. They go for breakfast at a restaurant on North Atlantic, and then to Marley's studio apartment, which is close by. The Lu-Ray Apartments, a brown stucco building overlooking the ocean and the boardwalk—with the windows open, Cliff can hear faint digital squeals and roars from a video arcade that has a miniature golf course atop its roof. It's a drizzly, overcast morning and, with its patched greens and dilapidated obstacles, a King Kong, a troll, a dragon that spits sparks whenever someone makes a hole-in-one, etcetera, the course has an air of post-apocalyptic decay. The dead Ferris wheel beside it emphasizes the effect.

Marley's place is tomboyishly Spartan, a couple of surfboards on the wall, a Ramones poster, a wicker throne with a green cushion, a small TV with some Mardi Gras beads draped over it, a queen-size box spring and mattress covered by a dark blue spread. The only sign of femininity is that the apartment is scrupulously clean, not a speck of dust, the stove and refrigerator in the kitchenette gleaming. Marley tells Cliff to take the bed, she has to do some stuff, and sits cross-legged in the wicker chair, pecking at her laptop. He closes his eyes, surrendering to fatigue, fading toward sleep; but his thoughts start to race and sleep won't come.

He tries to put a logical spin on everything that happened, works out various theories that would accommodate what he saw. The only one that suits is that he's losing it, and he's not ready to go there. Finally, he opens his eyes. Marley's still pecking away, her face concentrated by a serious expression. In her appearance and mien, she reminds him of girls he knew in LA in the eighties, many of them weekend punkers, holding down a steady job during the week, production assistants and set dressers and such, and then, on Friday night, they'd dress down, wear black lipstick and too much mascara, and go batshit crazy. But those girls were all fashion punks with a life plan and insurance and solid prospects, whereas Marley's a true edge-dweller with a punk ethos, living paycheck to paycheck, secure in herself, a bit of a dreamer, though her practical side shows itself from time to time—for a week or two she'll binge on schemes to resurrect her fiscal security; then, Pffft!, it all goes away and she's carefree and careless again.

These thoughts endanger Cliff's resolve to remain friends with her, and more dangerous yet is his contemplation of her physical presence. Frizzy blond hair framing a gamin's face; braless breasts, her nipples on full display through the thin fabric of her t-shirt; she's his type, all right. He understands that part of what's at play here is base, that whenever he's at a loss or anxious about something or just plain bored, he relies on women to sublimate the feeling.

Marley glances up, catching him staring. "Hey! You all right?"

"Yeah," he says. "Why?"

"You were looking weird is all." She closes the laptop. "You want anything?"

"No," he says, a reflex answer, but thinks about the things he wants. They're all momentary gratifications. Sex; surcease; to stop thinking about it. He suspects that the real curse of getting older is a certain wisdom, the tendency to reflect on your life and observe the haphazard path you've made, and then he decides that what he wants above all is to want something so badly that he stops second-guessing himself for a while. Just go after it and damn the consequences…though in reality, that's only another form of surcease.

"What do *you* want?" he asks.

She tips her head to one side, as if to see him more clearly. "I don't think I'm getting the whole picture here. Did something happen last night? You know, something more than what you told me? Because you're not acting like yourself."

"I'll tell you later." He shifts onto his side. "So what do you want? What would make you happy?"

She sets the laptop on the floor and comes over to the bed and makes a shooing gesture. "Scoot over. If this is going to be a deep conversation, I want to lie down."

He's slow to move, but she pushes onto the bed beside him and he's forced to accommodate her. She plumps the pillow, squirms about, and, once she's settled facing him, arms shielding her breasts, hands together by her cheek, she says, "I used to want to be a singer. I was in love with Tori Amos, and I was going to be like her. Different, but one of those chicks who plays piano and writes her own songs. But I didn't want it badly enough, so I just bummed around with music, gigged with a few bands and things like that. One of my boyfriends was a bartender. He taught me the trade, and I started working bar jobs. It was easy work, I met some nice guys, some not so nice. I was coasting, you know. Trying to figure it out. Now I think, I'm pretty sure, I want to be a vet. Not the kind who prescribes pills for sick cats and treats old ladies' poodles for gout. I'd like to work out in the country. Over in DuBarry, maybe, or down south in Broward. Cattle country. That would make me content, I think. So I'm saving up for veterinary college." She grins, fine squint lines deepening at the corners of her eyes. "Someday they'll be saying stuff like, "Reckon we better call ol' Doc Marley."

He's shamed, because this is all new information; he's known her for three years and never before asked about her life. He recalls her singing about the house and being struck by her strong, sweet voice, how she bent notes that started out flat into a strange countrified inflection. He doesn't know what to say.

"You look perplexed," she says. "You thought I was just an aging beach bunny, is that it?"

"That's not it."

"I suppose I am, technically, an aging beach bunny. But I'm making a graceful transition."

A silence, during which he hears cars pass. The beach is extraordinarily quiet, all the spring breakers sleeping in, waiting out the rain. He remembers a morning like this when he was eleven, he and some friends rode their bikes down past the strip of motels between Silver Beach and Main, hoping to see girls gone wild, and seeing instead spent condoms floating in the swimming pools like dead marine creatures, a lone girl crying on the sidewalk, crushed beer cans, the beach littered with party trash and burst jellyfish and crusts of dirty foam, all the residue of joyful debauch. It never changes. The gray light lends the furnishings, the walls, a frail density and a pointillist aspect—it seems the room is turning into the ghost of itself, becoming a worn, faded engraving.

"Why do you always act scared around me, Cliffie?" Marley asks. "Even when we were together, you acted scared. I know the age thing bothers you, but that's no reason to be scared."

"It's complicated," he says.

"And you don't want to talk about it, right? Guys really suck!"

"No, I'll talk about it if you want."

She looks at him expectantly, face partly concealed by dirty blond strings of hair.

"It's partly the age thing," he says. "I'm fifty-four and you're twenty-nine."

"Close," she says. "Thirty."

"All right. Thirty. Turning a year on the calendar doesn't change the fact it's a significant difference. But mostly it's this…blankness I feel inside myself. It's like I'm empty, and growing emptier. That's what I'm scared of."

"Well, I don't pretend to know much," Marley says. "I could be wrong, but sounds to me like you're lonely."

Could it be that simple? He's tempted to accept her explanation, but he's reluctant to accept what that may bring. Rain begins to fall more heavily, screening them away from the world with gray slanting lines.

"What do you see in me?" he asks. "I mean, what makes someone like you interested in a fifty-something used car salesman with a bad back. I don't get it."

"Wow. Once you start them up, some guys are worse than women. Out comes the rotten self-image and everything else." She glances up to the ceiling, as if gathering information written there. "I'll tell you, but don't interrupt, okay?"

"Okay."

"We're friends. We've been friends for going on four years, and I like to think we're good friends. I can count on you in an emergency, and you can count on me. True?"

He nods.

"You make my head quiet," she says. "Not last night, not when I'm in party mode. But most of the time, that's how I feel around you. You steady me. You treat me as an equal. With guys my age or close, I can tell what's foremost on their mind, and it's always a battle to win their respect. Like with Tucker. That may explain why I've got this thing for older men. They don't just see tits and a pussy, they see all of me. I'm speaking generally, of course. I get lots of horny old goats hitting on me, but they're desperate. You're not desperate. You don't have a need to get over on me."

"That might change," he says.

She puts a finger to his lips, shushing him. "Everything changes, everybody's kinky for something. Some guy shows up at my door with a muskrat, a coil of rope, and three pounds of lard, that's where I draw the line. But normal, everyday kinks…They're cool." She shrugs. "So it changes? So you're fifty-four with a bad back? So I'm kinky for older men? So what? And in case you're going to tell me you don't want to be a father figure, don't worry. When I'm around you, I'm always wet. Some times more than others, but it's pretty much constant. I don't think of you as my dad." She blows air through her pursed lips, as if wearied by this unburdening. "Fucking is just something I do with guys, Cliff. It doesn't require holy water and a papal dispensation. It's not that huge a deal."

"That's a lie," he says.

"Yeah," she says after a pause. "It's a fairly huge deal. All right. But what I'm trying to say is, if it doesn't work out, I'll cry and be depressed and hit things. My heart may even break. But it won't kill me. I heal up good."

The rain beats in against the window, spraying under the glass, drenching the ledge, spattering on the floor, yet Marley doesn't bother to close it. She sits up and, with a supple movement, shucks her t-shirt. The shape of a bikini top is etched upon her skin and in the half-light her high, smallish breasts, tipped by engorged nipples, are shockingly pale in contrast to her tan. It strikes Cliff as exotic, a solar tattoo, and he imagines designs of pale and dark all over her body, some so tiny they can only be detected by peering close, others needing a magnifying glass to read the erotic message that they, in sum, comprise. She lies down again, an arm across her tight, rounded stomach. Sheets of rain wash over the window, transforming it into a smeary lens of dull green and silvered gray, seeming to show a world still in process of becoming.

"So," Marley says. "You going in to work today?"

"Probably not," he says.

Chapter 7

Before going into work the following day, Cliff stops by the cottage. It's a sunny, breezy afternoon and all should be right with the world, but the stillness of the place unnerves him. He peels police tape off the doors, hurriedly packs a few changes of clothes and, as an afterthought, tosses his copy of *Sword of the Black Demon* into his bag. If things get uncomfortable at Marley's, he'll move to a motel, but he has determined that he's not going to spend another night in the cottage until the situation is resolved, until he can be assured that there'll be no reoccurrence of blue witches and flashing lights and two-hundred-foot tall swordsmen.

He pulls into Ridgewood Motors shortly before two and, from that point on, he's so busy that he scarcely has a chance to glance at the

Celeste. Jerry's in a foul mood because Stacey Gerone has run off and left him shorthanded.

"She's been screwing some rich old fart from Miami," Jerry says. "I guess she blew him so good, he finally popped the question. That bitch can suck dick like a two-dollar whore in a hurricane."

Dressed in his trademark madras suit and white loafers, Jerry cocks an eye at Cliff, doubtless hoping to be asked how he knows about Stacey's proclivities; he's brimming over with eagerness to divulge his conquest.

Jerry's pudgy, built along the lines of Papa Smurf, with a tanning-machine tan like brownish orange paint and a ridiculous toupee—he cultivates this clownish image to distract from his nasty disposition. Thanks to this and an endless supply of dirty jokes, ranging from the mildly pornographic to X-tra Blue, he's in demand as a speaker at Rotary Club and Chamber of Commerce dinners and has acquired a reputation for being crusty yet loveable. He acknowledges Cliff as a near-equal, someone who has the worldliness to understand him, someone in whom he can confide to an extent, and thus Cliff, knowing that Jerry will vent his temper on the other salesmen if he doesn't listen to him brag, is forced to endure a richly embroidered tale of Jerry's liaisons with Stacey, culminating with an act of sodomy described in such graphic detail, he's almost persuaded that it might have happened, although it's more likely that the verisimilitude is due to Jerry's belief that it happened, that through repetition his fantasy has become real.

This is the first Cliff has heard of the "rich old fart," but he's aware that Stacey played her cards close to the vest and there was much he did not know about her. He tries to nudge the conversation in that direction, hoping to learn more; but Jerry, made grumpy by his questions, orders him out onto the lot to sell some fucking cars.

A little after five o'clock, he's about to close with a young couple who've been sniffing around a two-year-old Bronco since the previous Friday, when Shalin Palaniappan strolls onto the lot. She walks up to Cliff, ignoring another salesman's attempt to intercept her, and says, "Hi."

Cliff excuses himself, steers Shalin away from the couple, and says, "I'm in the middle of something. Let me get somebody else to help you."

VACANCY

"I want you," Shalin says pertly.

"You're going to have to wait, then."

"I've waited this long. What's a few minutes more?"

With her baggy shorts and a pale yellow T-shirt, her shiny black eyes, her shiny black hair in a ponytail, her copper-and-roses complexion, she looks her age, fifteen or sixteen, a healthy, happy Malaysian teenager; but he senses something wrong about her, something also signaled by her enigmatic comment about waiting, an undercurrent that doesn't shine, that doesn't match her fresh exterior, like that spanking new Escalade with the bent frame they had in a few weeks before. He leaves her leaning against a Nissan 350-Z and goes back to the couple who, given the time to huddle up, have decided in his absence that they're not happy with the numbers and want more value on the toad they offered as a trade-in. Cliff feels Shalin's eyes applying a brand to the back of his neck and grows flustered. He grows even more so when he notices a young salesman approach her and begin chatting her up, bracing with one hand on the Nissan, leaning close, displaying something other than the genial manner that is form behavior for someone who pushes iron—then, abruptly, the salesman scurries off as if his tender bits have been scorched. Most teenage girls, in Cliff's experience, don't have the social skills to deal efficiently with the two-legged flies that come buzzing around, yet he allows that Shalin may be an exception. The couple becomes restive; now they're not sure about the Bronco. Cliff, aware that he's blowing it, passes them off to John Sacks, a decent closer, and goes over to Shalin.

"How can I help you?" he asks, and is startled by the harshness, the outright antipathy in his voice.

Shalin, looking up at him, shields her eyes against the westering sun, but says nothing.

"What are you looking to spend?" he asks.

"How much is this one?" She pats the Nissan's hood.

He names a figure and she shakes her head, a no.

"Do you have a car?" he asks. "We can be pretty generous on a trade-in."

"That's right. You always take it out in trade, don't you?"

Her snide tone is typical of teenagers, but her self-assurance is not, and her entire attitude, one of arrogance and bemusement, causes him to think that there's another purpose to her visit.

"I'm busy," he says. "If you're not looking for a car, I have other customers."

"Did you know I'm adopted? I am. But Bazit treats me like his very own daughter. He caters to my every whim." She reaches into a pocket, extracts a platinum Visa card and waggles it in his face. "Why don't we look around? If I see something I like, you can go into your song-and-dance."

He's tempted to blow her off, but he's curious about her. They walk along the aisles of gleaming cars, past salesmen talking with prospective buyers, pennons snapping in the breeze. She displays no interest in any of the cars, continuing to talk about herself, saying that she never knew her parents, she was raised by an aunt, but she's always thought of her as a mother, and when the aunt died—she was nine, then—Bazit stepped in. Not long afterward, they moved to America and bought the Celeste.

"There!" She stops and points at a silver Jag, an XK coupe. "I like that one. Can I take a test drive?"

"That's a sixty-thousand dollar car," says Cliff. "You want a test drive, I'll have to clear sixty thousand on your credit card."

"Do it."

He goes into the office and runs the card—it's approved. What, he asks himself, is a sixteen-year-old doing with that much credit? He knocks on Jerry's door and tells him that he has a teenage girl who wants to test-drive the SK.

"Fuck her," says Jerry without glancing up. "I've got a dealer who'll take it off our hands."

"Her card cleared."

"No shit? A rich little cunt, huh?" Jerry clasps his hands behind his head and rocks back in his swivel chair. "Naw. I don't want a kid driving that car."

"It's the girl from the Celeste."

"Shalin?" Jerry's expression goes through some extreme changes—shock, concern, bewilderment—that are then paved over by his customary. "What the hell. He throws a lot of business our way."

Cliff doubts that a man who rents motel rooms for twenty-nine bucks a night could be boosting Jerry's profits to any consequential degree, and he wonders what shook him up…if, indeed, he was shaken, if he wasn't having a flare-up of his heartburn.

Shalin, it turns out, knows her way around a stick shift and drives like a pro, whipping the SK around sharp corners, downshifting smoothly, purring along the little oak-lined back streets west of Ridgewood Avenue, and Cliff's anxiety ebbs. He points out various features of the car, none of which appear to impress Shalin. It's clear that she enjoys being behind the wheel and, when she asks if she can check out what the SK is like on the highway, he says, "Yeah, but keep it under sixty-five."

Soon they're speeding south on Highway 1 toward New Smyrna, passing through a salt marsh that puts Cliff in mind of an African place—meanders of blue water and wide stretches of grass bronzed by the late sun, broken here and there by mounded islands topped with palms; birds wheeling under a cloudless sky; a few human structures, dilapidated cabins, peeling billboards, but not enough to shatter the illusion that they're entering a vast preserve.

After a minute or two, Shalin says, "My mother and I…I mean, my aunt. We shared a unique connection. We resembled each other physically. Many people mistook us for mother and daughter. But the resemblance went deeper than that. We had a kind of telepathy. She told me stories about her life, and I saw images relating to the stories. When I described them to her, she'd say things like, 'Yes, that's it! That's it exactly!' or 'It sounds like the compound I stayed at on Lake Yogyarta.' I came to have the feeling that as she died—she was sick the whole time I was with her, in dreadful pain—she was transferring her substance to me. We were becoming the same person. And perhaps we were." She darts a glance toward Cliff. "Do you believe that's possible? That someone can possess another body, that they can express their being into another flesh? I do. I can remember being someone else, though I can't identify who that person was. My head's too full of my aunt's memories. It certainly would explain why I'm so mature. Everyone says that about me, that I'm mature for my age. Don't you agree?"

Scarily mature, Cliff says to himself. He doesn't like the direction of the conversation and tells her they'd better be heading back to the lot.

"Certainly. As soon as I see a turn-off."

She gooses the accelerator, and the SK surges forward, pushing Cliff back into the passenger seat. The digital readout on the speedometer hits eighty, eighty-five, then declines to sixty-five. She's putting on a little show, he thinks; reminding him who's in control.

"Aunt Isabel spoke frequently about the man who made her ill," Shalin goes on. "He was handsome and she loved him, of course. Otherwise she wouldn't have risked getting pregnant. He said he couldn't feel her as well when he wore a condom, and since this was at a time when protection wasn't considered important—nobody in Southeast Asia knew about AIDS—she allowed him to have his way."

A queasy coldness builds in Cliff's belly. "Isabel. Was she an actress?"

"You remember! That makes it so much easier. Isabel Yahya. You cracked jokes about her last name. You said you were getting your ya-yas out when you were with her. She didn't understand that, but I do."

She swings the SK in a sharp left onto a dirt road, a reckless maneuver; then she brakes, throws it into reverse, backs onto the highway, raising dust, and goes fishtailing toward Daytona.

"Take it easy! Okay?" Cliff grips the dashboard. "I didn't give her anything. She gave it to me. And it obviously wasn't AIDS, or I'd be dead."

"No, you're right. It wasn't AIDS, but you definitely gave it to her."

"The hell I did!"

"Before you became involved with Isabel, you slept with other women in Manila, didn't you?"

"Sure I did, but she's the one…"

"You were her first lover in more than a year!"

Shalin settles into cruising speed and Cliff, sobered by what she's told him, says, "Even if that's true…"

"It's true."

"...she could have seen a doctor."

"She did," says Shalin. "If you hadn't gotten her fired, perhaps she could have seen the doctor who attended you."

"What are you talking about? I didn't get her fired! She vanished off the set. I didn't know what had happened to her."

Shalin makes a dismissive noise. "As it was, Aunt Isabel went to a *bomoh*. A shaman. I can't blame you for that. She was a country girl and still put her trust in such men. But when he failed her, she wrote you letters, begging for help, for money to engage a western doctor. You never replied."

"I never got any letters."

"I don't believe you."

"She didn't have my address. How could she have written me?"

"She mailed them in care of your agent."

"That's like dropping them into a black hole. Mark...my agent. He's not the most together guy. He probably filed them somewhere and forgot to send them along."

They flash past a ramshackle fishing camp at the edge of the marsh, wooden cabins and a pier with a couple of small boats moored at its nether end. Their speed is creeping up and Cliff tells her to back it down.

"It's an astonishing coincidence that we bought the Celeste and you started working for Uncle Jerry," she says. "It almost seems some karmic agency is playing a part in all this."

Cliff doesn't know what troubles him more, the idea that the coincidence is not a coincidence, a thought suggested by her sly tone, or the implication that an intimate relationship exists between Jerry Muntz and the Palaniappans. Now that he thinks about it, he's seen Jerry, more than once, stop at the motel for a few minutes before heading home. He has no reason to assign the relationship a sinister character, yet Jerry wouldn't befriend people like the Palaniappans unless he had a compelling reason.

"All of what?" he asks.

"Aunt Isabel was a woman of power," says Shalin. "By nature, she was trusting and impractical, not at all suited for life in Manila or

Jakarta. She ended up in Jakarta, you know. In a section known as East Cipinang, a slum on the edge of a dump. We survived by scavenging. I'd take the things we found and sell them in the streets to tourists. We had enough to eat most days. Tourists bought from me not because they wanted the things we found, but because I was a very pretty little girl." Her lips thin, as if she's biting back anger. "Isabel could only work a few hours a day, and sometimes not that. Her insides were rotting. She received medicine from a clinic, but the disease had progressed too far for the doctors to do anything other than ease her pain. She'd lost her beauty. In the last years before she died, she looked like an old, shriveled hag."

"I'm sorry," Cliff says. "I wish I had known."

"Yes, you would have flown to her side, I'm sure. She often spoke of your generosity."

"Look, I didn't know. I can't be held responsible for something I didn't know was happening."

"Is that what it is to you? A matter of whether or not you can be held responsible? Are you afraid I'm going to sue you?"

"No, that's not..."

"Rest assured, I'm not going to sue you."

Her voice is so thick with menace, Cliff is momentarily alarmed. They're within the city limits now, driving in rush hour traffic past fruit stands and motels and souvenir shops, not far from the lot—he can't wait to get out of the car.

"Isabel, as I told you, was a woman of power," says Shalin. "In another time, another place, she would have been respected and revered. But ill, buried in the slums, power of the sort she possessed could do her no good."

"What the hell are you getting at?" he asks.

She flashes a sunny smile and goes on with her narrative. "Isabel loved you until the end. I know she hated you a little, too, but she maintained that you weren't evil, just profligate and vain. And slight. She said there wasn't much to you. You were terribly immature, but she had hopes you'd grow out of that, even though you were in your thirties when she knew you. She was basically a decent soul and power was something she used judiciously, only in cases where she could produce a good effect. It was among the last things she transferred to me." She sighs forlornly. "Taking control of me was the one selfish act she committed in her life. You can't blame her. The streets had left me damaged beyond repair and she was terrified of death. Of course these transfers are a bit like reincarnation, so it's not exactly Isabel who's alive. I mean, she is alive, but she's a different person now. There are things that are left behind during a transfer, and things added that belonged to the soul who once inhabited this body."

"You're out of your tree." He says this without much conviction. "All you're doing is screwing with me."

"Right on both counts."

She slows and eases into the turning lane across from the lot, waiting for a break in the traffic.

"Now," she says, "I use my power to get the things I want, to make my family secure. Sometimes I use it on a whim. You might say I use it profligately."

She edges forward, but brakes when she realizes she can't make the turn yet. A semi roars past, followed by a string of cars.

"One thing Isabel didn't transfer to me was her love for you," she says. "I imagine she wanted to keep that for herself, to warm her final moments. She was almost empty. All that was left was a shell, a few memories. Or maybe she didn't want me to love you. You know, in case I ever saw you again. Do you suppose that's it? She wanted me to hate you?"

"You can get by after that red pick-up," he says.

"I see it." She makes the turn, pulls into the lot and parks. "If that's so, if that's really what Isabel wanted, she got her wish," she says. "No child should have to endure East Cipinang. You have no idea of the things I was forced to do as a result of your nonchalance, your triviality. Your shallowness."

She looks as if she's about to spit on him, climbs out of the SK and then bends to the window, peering in at him. "This car won't do, I'm afraid," she says, blithely. "It corners horribly."

"What're you trying to pull?" he asks. "You were at my house the other night, weren't you?"

"If you say so."

"What the hell do you want from me?"

She straightens, as though preparing to leave, but then leans in the window again, her teeth bared and black eyes bugged. Except for the color of her skin, it's the face of the witch, vividly insane, without a single human quality, and Cliff recoils from it.

"If you want answers, watch Isabel's movie," she says, her face relaxing into that of a teenage girl. "I believe you have a copy."

Chapter 8

Cliff sits in his office for an hour, hour and a half, not thinking so much as brooding about Shalin's story. It's absurd, impossible, yet elements of it ring true, especially the part about him giving Isabel the STD. He digs deep, mining his memories, trying to recall how she was, how he felt about her, and remembers her as a simple girl, not simple in the sense of stupid, but open and unaffected, though it may be he's prompted by guilt to gild the lily. She didn't seem at all "a woman of power," but then he didn't take the time to know her, to look beneath the surface. His clearest memories relate to her amazing breasts, her dancer's legs and ass, and to what a great lay she was. He wishes he could remember a moment when he loved her, an instance in which he saw something special about her, but he was a superficial kind of guy in those days, and maybe still is.

Thoughts buzz him like mosquitoes, a cloud of tiny, shrill thoughts that swarms around his head, diving close just long enough to nettle his brain, questions about Shalin's story, more memories of Isabel (once a trickle, their flow has become a flood, but all relating to how she looked, smelled, felt, tasted), and disparaging thoughts, lots of them, remarking on, as Shalin put it, his triviality, his nonchalance, his shallowness. If he could go an entire day without his life being captioned by this dreary self-commentary...

VACANCY

The phone rings, and he picks it up, grateful for the interruption. His agent's mellow tenor brings all the infectious banality of SoCal to his ear. After an exchange of pleasantries, his agent says, "Listen, Cliff. I was in New York last week. I had this crazy idea and you know me, what the hell, I pitched it to a couple of publishers. I said, What if Cliff Coria wrote a book, a memoir, about his life in the movies. This guy's acted all over, I told them. Spain, Southeast Asia, Czechoslovakia. You name it. And he's smart. And he's seen celebrities in unguarded moments. He's kind of an insider-slash-outsider. He can give you a view from the fringes of Hollywood, and maybe that's the clearest view of all."

"I don't know, Mark."

"Don't you want to hear how they reacted?"

"Yeah."

"They were excited, Cliff. There could be serious money for you in this. And if the book does what I think it will, it'll generate significant heat out here."

The Celeste's Vacancy sign switches on in the twilight, seeming like a glowing blue accusation. Cliff lowers the Venetian blinds.

"I believe there'll be interest in you as a character actor," Mark goes on. "Not just cheesy parts. I think I'd be able to get you serious work. I know you can do this, Cliff. Remember those letters you used to send me? Like the one about Nicholson's ass hanging out of the car when he was banging that bit player? That was fucking hilarious! Come on! All I need is a few chapters and a rough outline."

Cliff assures his agent that he'll give it a try. He leaves a note for Jerry, saying he's going to take a few days off to deal with some personal problems, and then heads for Marley's place. Crossing the Main Street Bridge over the Halifax River, which bisects Daytona, he sees several old men fishing off the bridge, half in silhouette, motionless, with buckets at their feet, the corpses of blowfish and sting rays bloodily strewn along the walkway, and thinks that if he were ever to take up fishing, this is where he'd like to drop his line. The idea of joining those sentinel figures appeals to him, as does the thought of hauling up little monsters from the deep.

At the apartment Cliff pours a vodka from a bottle chilled in the freezer, turns on the TV, and pops *Sword of the Black Demon* into the DVD player. While the opening credits roll, he calls Marley and tells her he's coming up to the Surfside sometime between nine and ten. He fast-forwards through the movie until he finds the entrance of the witch queen and her chunky blue retinue; then he sits on the edge of the bed, sipping vodka, watching Isabel Yahya and the other women attending a ceremony in a torchlit cave made of acrylic fiber painted to look like rock—it involves the queen choosing a new fuck toy, a young Filipino youth with oiled muscles. She leads him to the royal chamber, where a bed with blue satin sheets awaits, screws his brains out and, while he's helpless, limp, and nearly unconscious from her amorous assault, she drains him of his soul, laughing as she coaxes it forth by means of a lascivious dance. The soul resembles a stream of pale smoke from which faces surface. Cliff assumes them to be the youth's memories. The smoke dwindles to a trickle and at long last, after much eye-rolling and twitching, the youth dies.

In another scene, Ricky Sintara, a striking young man with even larger muscles, also oiled, and Dak Windsor enter the cave, seeking to capture the queen and persuade her to divulge the whereabouts of the wizard who has loosed the black demon; but they are themselves captured by the royal guard. The queen drags Ricky off to suffer the same fate as the youth, but once in the sack, Ricky proves to be no ordinary man—his incomparable lovemaking renders the queen *hors de combat.* This is all shown tastefully—no actual penetration; only full frontal female nudity—and dredges up a chuckle from Cliff, because Ricky, a fine fellow and terrific drinking companion, would on occasion wear women's clothing when relaxing during the shoot and had a boyfriend who was prettier than the majority of the actresses.

Meanwhile, in another part of the cave, Dak is chained to the wall and Isabel is preparing to scourge him with an S&M dream of a whip whose lashes appear to be fashioned of live scorpions. He takes a few strokes, writhes in pain, calls out to God for assistance, using a specific phrase that causes Isabel to realize that he is the son of the doctor who saved her village from a cholera outbreak years before—she was a little girl at the time, but developed a crush on the teenage Dak that lasts to this day. Turned aside from the path of evil by the power of love, she frees Dak and they kiss, a miracle of osculation that changes her skin from blue back to a pleasing caramel, and together, along with Ricky, they flee the cave, carrying with them the comatose queen.

Lashed to a bed in Ricky's shack (the hero has hewed to his humble village origins), the queen strains mightily against her ropes, mimicking her earlier struggles in the act of love, breasts heaving, hips thrusting, tormented by Ricky's questions, and eventually she yields up her secrets. But that night, while Dak and Ricky are reconnoitering the wizard's lair, she calls out to Isabel, whom she still controls to an extent. By means of her occult powers and a cross-eyed, beetling stare, she coerces Isabel into untying her bonds. She then knocks her to the ground and stands over her, waggling her fingers and projecting dire energies from their tips, bursts of blue light that cause her former minion to shrivel, to grow desiccated and wrinkled, dying of old age in a matter of seconds.

Is that, Cliff asks himself, what Shalin wants him to believe may be in store for him? He recalls her talk about Isabel's premature aging, her comment regarding a karmic agency being involved in all of this—a sudden withering would be an apt punishment according to karmic law. But he refuses to believe Shalin capable of doling out such a punishment.

He goes to the refrigerator, pours another vodka, and watches the rest of the movie. The queen escapes through the surrounding jungle, but is killed by Ricky, who throws his magical dagger at her. It tumbles end over end, traveling hundreds of yards through the darkness, swerving around clumps of bamboo, tree trunks, bushes, and impales the fleeing queen through her malignant heart. Dak grieves for Isabel, but is bucked up by Ricky and rises to the moment with renewed zeal. With the help of a friendly shaman, they plot the attack: Dak will lead the simple villagers (there are always simple villagers in Filipino fantasy movies) in an assault on the wizard's palace, distracting the evil one so that Ricky can sneak inside and do him in.

The battle goes badly for Dak at first. The villagers are being hacked to pieces by the wizard's guard. All seems lost, but the ghost of Isabel appears, wreathed in swirling mist to disguise the fact the actress is no longer Isabel (a love scene between her ghost and Dak was intended for the night before the battle, but she vanished from the project and a rewrite was necessary), and she inspires him with a message of undying love and tells him of a secret tunnel into which they can lure the guard and fight them in a narrow confine, thus neutralizing their superior numbers. As this is happening, the Black Demon accosts Ricky outside the palace and all, again, seems lost. Not even he can defeat a giant. But the ancient gods, played by white-bearded men wearing silk robes and several busty Filipina babes in brocaded halters, intervene. They whisk Ricky and the Black Demon away to a cosmic platform surrounded by a profusion of stars and clouds of nebular gas (glowing, Cliff notices, rose and purple, green and white, like the lights he saw outside his cottage), shrink them to almost equal size (the demon still has a considerable advantage), and let them fight. Fending off blows with a magic bracelet given him by his dying father, a silvery circlet wrought from the stuff of a dying star, Ricky bests the demon and takes his sword—it is, by chance, the only weapon that can slay the wizard. He is returned to planet Earth where, after a torrid chase, the wizard changes into a huge serpent that Ricky chops into snake sushi.

In the final scene, also rewritten late in the game, a big celebration, Ricky wanders about the village, a girl on each arm, searching for his pal. Following an intuition, he divests himself of the ladies and enters the local temple, where he finds Dak on his knees, praying for the soul of Isabel at an altar surmounted by her portrait. He puts his hand on Dak's shoulder. The two men exchange sober glances. Then Ricky kneels beside him and adopts a prayerful attitude. Solemn music rises, changing to a bouncy disco theme as the screen darkens and the end credits roll.

Cliff thinks now that the last scene might have been intentionally ironic. He recalls that the director dogged Isabel throughout the shoot and seemed miffed when she got together with Cliff. He may have fired her because she wouldn't sleep with him and rewrote the scene to make a point. Not that this bears upon anything relevant to his current problem. He drains his vodka, idly gazing at the credits, puzzling over the film, wondering what Shalin wanted him to take from it. Maybe nothing. Maybe she just wanted him to endure the pain of watching it again. And then he spots something. A name. It flips past too quickly and he's not sure he saw it. He hits reverse on the remote, plays it forward, and there it is, the logical explanation he's been seeking, the answer to everything:

Special Effects: Bazit Palaniappan

He knew it! They've been trying to gaslight him the whole time. He remembers the F/X guy, a thin man in his fifties with graying hair who bore a passing resemblance to the owner of the Celeste. He must be Bazit the elder's son and dropped the Jr. after his father died. Why didn't he mention the connection? Surely he would have, unless he was too excited at seeing Dak Windsor. No, he would have mentioned it. Unless he had a reason to keep quiet about it...which he did. It occurs to Cliff that Bazit might be one of those soul transfers such as Shalin claimed to have undergone, but he's not buying that. With knowledge gained from his father, Bazit tricked up the dunes around Cliff's cottage and put on a show. Shalin must have assumed that he wouldn't watch the end credits.

Exhilarated, Cliff starts to pour another drink, then decides he'll have that drink with Marley. She gets off at ten—he'll take her out for a late supper, somewhere nicer than the Surfside, and they'll celebrate. She won't know what they're celebrating, but he's glad now that he didn't burden her with any of this. He trots down the stairs and out into the warm, windless night, into squeals and honks and machine gun fire from the arcades, happy shouts from the Ferris wheel, now lit up and spinning, and the lights on the miniature golf course glossing over its dilapidation, providing a suitable setting for the family groups clumped about the greens. The bright souvenir shops selling painted sand dollars and polished driftwood, funny hats and sawfish snouts, and the sand drifting up onto the asphalt from The World's Most Famous Be-atch (as an oft-seen t-shirt design proclaims), and the flashing neon signs above strip clubs and tourist bars along Main Street, the din of calliope music, stripper music, tavern music, and voices, voices, voices, the vocal exhaust of vacationland America, exclamations and giggles, drunken curses and yelps and unenlightened commentary—it's all familiar, overly familiar, tedious and unrelentingly ordinary, yet tonight its colors are sharper, its sounds more vivid, emblematic of the world of fresh possibility that Cliff is suddenly eager to engage.

Chapter 9

It's a good week for Cliff and Marley, a very good week. There is no recurrence of demons, no witches, no bumps in the night. Jerry is furious with him, naturally, and threatens to fire him, but he has no leverage—the job is merely a pastime for Cliff and he tells Jerry to go ahead, fire him, he'll find some other way to occupy his idle hours. He works on the book and is surprised how easily it flows. He hasn't settled on a title yet, but anecdotal material streams out of him and he's amazed by how funny it is—it didn't seem that funny at the time; and, though he's aware that he has a lot of cleaning up to do on the prose, he's startled by the sense of bittersweet poignancy that seems to rise from his words, even from the uproarious bits. It's as if in California, those years of struggle and fuck-ups, he realized that the dream he was shooting for was played-out, that the world of celebrity with its Bel Air mansions and stretch limos and personal chefs masked a terrible malformation that he hated, that he denied yet knew was there all along, that he didn't want badly enough because, basically, he never wanted it at all.

The relationship, too, flows. Cliff has his concerns, particularly about their ages, but he's more-or-less convinced himself that it's all right; he's neither conning Marley nor himself. He can hope for ten good years, fifteen at the outside, but that's a lifetime. After that, well, whatever comes will come. It's not that he feels young again. His back's still sore, he's beginning to recognize that he needs more than reading glasses, but he no longer feels as empty as he did and he thinks that Marley was spot-on in her diagnosis: he was lonely.

VACANCY

They make love, they go to the movies, they walk on the beach, and they talk about everything: about global warming, the NBA (Marley's a Magic fan; Cliff roots for the Lakers), about religion and ghosts and salsa, about dogs versus cats as potential pets, about fashion trends and why he never married, and veterinary school. Cliff offers to help with the tuition and, though reluctant at first, Marley says there's a well-regarded school in Orlando and she's been accepted, but doesn't know if she'll have enough saved to go for the fall term. Cliff has major problems with Orlando. There's no beach, no ocean breeze to break the summer heat, and he dreads being in such close proximity to the Mouse and the hordes of tourists who pollute the environment. Rednecks of every stamp, the blighted of the earth, so desperate in their search for fun that they make pilgrimages to Disneyworld and commingle with one another in a stew of ill-feeling that frequently results in knuckle-dragging fights between hairy, overweight men and face-offs between grim-lipped parents and their whiny kids. But he says, "Okay. Let's do it."

He's scared by what he's beginning to feel for her, and he's not yet prepared to turn loose of the pool ladder and swim out into the deep end; but his grip is slipping and he knows immersion is inevitable. At times, in certain lights, she seems no older than twenty. She's got the kind of looks that last and she'll still be beautiful when they cart him off to the rest home. That afflicts him. But then she'll say or do something, make a move in bed or offer a comment about his book or, like the other night at the movies, the first movie he's attended in years, reach over and touch his arm and smile, that causes him to recognize this is no girl, no beach bunny, but a mature woman who's committed her share of sins and errors in judgment, and is ready for a serious relationship, even if he is not. That liberates him from his constraints, encourages him to lose himself in contemplation of her, to see her with a lover's eye, to notice how, when she straddles him, she'll gather her hair behind her neck and gaze briefly at the wall, as if focusing herself before she lets him enter; how her lips purse and her eyebrows lift when she reads; how when she cooks, she'll stand on one foot for a minute at a time, arching her back to keep on balance; how when she combs out her hair after a shower, bending her head to one side, her neck and shoulder configure a line like the curve of a Spanish guitar. He wants to understand these phrasings of her body, to know things about her that she herself may not know.

The ninth morning after Cliff quit working for Jerry (he hasn't made it official yet, but in his mind he's done), he's lying in bed when Marley, fresh from a shower, wearing a bathrobe, tells him she's going to visit her mother in Deland; she'll be gone two or three days.

"I meant to tell you yesterday," she says. "But I guess I've been in denial. My mom's sort of demented. Not really, though sometimes I wonder. She never makes these visits easy."

"You want me to come along?"

"God, no! That would freak her out. Totally. Not because you're you. Any man would freak her out…any woman, for that matter. She'd hallucinate I'm having a lesbian affair, and then all I'd hear the whole time is stuff about the lie of the White Goddess and how we're in a time of social decline. It's going to be hard enough as it is." She hoists a small suitcase out from the back of the closet. "I want this visit to be as serene as possible, because the last day I'm there, I'm going to tell her about Orlando."

"It's not that big a move," he says. "You'll still be within an hour's drive."

"To her, it'll be an extinction event, believe me." She rummages through her underwear drawer. "One day you'll have to meet her, but you want to put that day off as long as you can. I love her, but she can be an all-pro pain in the butt."

Gloomily, he watches her pack for a minute and then says, "I'll miss you."

"I know! God, I'm going to miss you so much!" She turns from her packing and, with a mischievous expression, opens her robe and flashes him. "I've got time for a quickie."

"Come ahead."

She leaps onto the bed, throws a leg across his stomach, bringing her breasts close to his face; he tastes soap on her nipples. She rolls off him, onto her back, looking flushed.

"Better make that a long-ie," she says. "It's got to last for two days."

VACANCY

After she's gone, Cliff mopes about the apartment. He opens a box of Wheat Thins, eats a handful, has a second cup of coffee, paces. At length, he sits on the bed, back propped up by pillows, and, using Marley's laptop, starts working on the book. When he looks up again, he's surprised to find that four hours have passed. He has a late lunch at a Chinese restaurant on South Atlantic, then drives home and works some more. Around eight-thirty, Marley calls.

"This has to be brief," she says, and asks him about his day.

"Nothing much. Worked on the book. Ate lunch at Lim's. How about you?"

"The usual. Interrogation. Field exercises. Advanced interrogation."

"It can't be that bad."

"No, it's not...but I don't want to be here. That makes it worse."

"Are you coming back tomorrow?"

"I don't know yet. It depends on how much aftercare mom's going to need." A pause. "How's the book coming?"

"You can judge for yourself, but it feels pretty good. Today I wrote about this movie I did with Robert Mitchum and Kim..."

"Shit! I have to go. I'll call tomorrow if I can."

"Wait..."

"Love you," she says, and hangs up.

He pictures her standing in her mother's front yard, or in the bathroom, a little fretful because she didn't intend to say the L word, because it's the first time either of them have used it, and she's not sure he's ready to hear it, she's worried it might put too much pressure on him. But hearing the word gives him a pleasant buzz, a comforting sense of inclusion, and he wishes he could call her back.

He falls asleep watching a Magic game with the sound off; when he wakes, a preacher is on the tube, weeping and holding out his arms in supplication. He washes up but chooses not to shower, checks himself in the mirror, sees a heavy two-day growth of gray stubble, and chooses not to shave. He breakfasts on fresh pineapple, toast, and coffee, puts on a t-shirt, bathing suit, and flip-flops, and walks down to the beach. It's an overcast morning, low tide, the water placid and dark blue out beyond the bar. Sandpipers scurry along the tidal margin, digging for tiny soft-shelled crabs that have burrowed into the muck. People not much older than himself are power-walking, some hunting for shells. One sixty-something guy in a Speedo, his skin deeply tanned, is searching for change with a metal detector. During spring and summer, Cliff reflects, Daytona is a stage set, with a different cast moved in every few weeks. After the spring breakers, the bikers come for Bike Week. Then the NASCAR crowd flocks into town and everywhere you go, you hear them display their thrilling wit and wisdom, saying things like, "I warned Charlene not to let him touch it," and, "Damn, that Swiss steak looks right good. I believe I'll have me some of that." But the elderly are always present, always going their customary rounds.

Being part of the senior parade makes Cliff uncomfortable. In the midst of this liver-spotted plague, he fears contagion and he goes up onto the boardwalk. Most of the attractions are closed. The Ferris wheel shows its erector set complexity against a pewter sky; many of the lesser rides are covered in canvas; but one of the arcades is open, its corrugated doors rolled up, and Cliff wanders inside. Behind a counter, a short order cook is busy greasing the grill. Three eighth- or ninth-graders, two Afro-Americans and one white kid dressed hip-hop style, backward caps and baggy clothes, are dicking around with a shooter game. As he passes, they glance toward him, their faces set in a kind of hostile blankness. He can read the thought balloon above their heads, a single balloon with three comma-like stems depending from it: Old Fucking Bum. Cliff decides he likes playing an old fucking bum. He develops a limp, a drunk's weaving, unsteady walk. The kids whisper together and laugh.

At the rear of the arcade, past the row of Skee Ball machines, where they keep the older games, the arcade is quiet and dark and clammy, a sea cave with a low ceiling, its entrance appearing to be a long way off. Cliff scatters quarters atop one of the machines, Jungle Queen, its facing adorned with black panthers and lush vegetation and a voluptuous woman with black hair and red lips and silicon implants, her breasts perfectly conical. When he was a kid, he'd lift the machine and rest its front legs on his toes so the surface was level and the ball wouldn't drop, and he'd rack up the maximum number of free games and play all day. It didn't take much to entertain him, and he supposes it still doesn't.

He plays for nearly an hour, his muscle memory returning, skillfully using body English, working the flippers. He's on his way to setting a personal best, the machine issuing a series of loud pops, signifying games won, when someone comes up on his shoulder and begins watching. Ashford. Cliff keeps playing—he's having a great last ball and doesn't want to blow it. Finally the ball drops. He grins at Ashford and presses the button to start a new game.

Ashford says, "Having fun?"

"I can't lose," says Cliff.

Ashford looks to be wearing the same ensemble he wore during the interview, accented on this occasion by a fetching striped tie. The bags under his eyes are faintly purple. Cliff's surprised to see him, but not deeply surprised.

"Have you guys been watching my building?" he asks.

"You didn't answer the buzzer. I took a chance you'd be somewhere close by." Ashford nods toward the counter at the front of the arcade. "Let's get some coffee."

"I've got twelve free games!"

"Don't mess with me, Coria. I'm tired."

The two men take stools at the counter and Ashford sits without speaking, swigging his coffee, staring glumly at the menu on the wall, black plastic letters arranged on white backing, some of them cockeyed, some of the items misspelled ("cheseburgers," "mountin dew"), others cryptically described ("Fresh Fried Shrimp"). The counterman, a middle-aged doofus with a name badge that reads Kerman, pale and fleshy, his black hair trimmed high above his ears, freshens Ashford's coffee. Even the coffee smells like grease. The arcade has begun to fill, people filtering up from the beach.

"Are we just sharing a moment?" asks Cliff. "Or do you have something else in mind?"

For a few seconds, Ashford doesn't seem to have heard him; then he says, "Stacey Gerone."

"Yeah? What about her?"

"You seen her lately?"

"Not for a couple of weeks. Jerry said she ran off to Miami with some rich guy."

"I heard about that."

A shorthaired peroxide blond in a bikini, her black roots showing in such profusion, the look must be by design, hops up onto a stool nearby and asks for a large Pepsi. She has some age on her, late thirties, but does good things for the bikini. Ashford cuts his eyes toward her breasts; his gaze lingers.

"Ain't got no Pepsi," Kerman says in a sluggish, country drawl. "Just Coke."

"This morning around five-thirty, one of your neighbors found a suitcase full of Stacey Gerone's clothes in the dunes out front of your house." Ashford emits a small belch, covering his mouth. "Any idea how it got there?"

Alarmed, Cliff says, "I didn't put it there!"

"I didn't say you put it there. You're not that stupid."

"I haven't been to the house for three days. I just drove by to see if everything was all right."

The blond, after pondering the Pepsi problem, asks if she can have some fries.

"You want a large Coke with that?" asks Kerman.

Again the blond ponders. "Small diet Coke."

Kerman, apparently the genius of the arcade, switches on the piped-in music, and metal-ish rock overwhelms the noises of man and nature. Ashford, with a pained expression, tells him to turn it off.

"Got to have the music on after nine o'clock," says Kerman.

"Well, turn it fucking down!"

"You got no call to be using bad language." Kerman sulks, but lowers the volume; following Ashford's direction, he lowers it until the music is all but inaudible.

Ashford rubs his stomach, scowls, and then gets to his feet. "I have to hit the john. Don't go away."

As he walks off, the blond leans over the intervening stool and taps Cliff on the arm. "Do I know you? I believe I do."

Cliff mentions that he was once an actor, movies and commercials, and the blond says, "No, that's not it. At least, I don't think." She taps her chin and then snaps her fingers. "The Shark! You used to come in. You were seeing Janice for a while last year. I'm Mary Beth."

All the women at the Shark Lounge, waitresses and dancers alike, are working girls and, after hearing about how Janice has been doing, Cliff has an idea.

"Have you got time for a date this morning?" he asks.

That puts a hitch in Mary Beth's grin, but she says coolly, "Anything for you, sweetie."

"It's not for me, it's for my friend. He needs to get laid. He's a cop and the job's beating him up."

"You want me to ball a cop?"

"He'll welcome it, I swear. Make out you're a police groupie and you saw his gun or something. And don't let on I had anything to do with it."

"Whatever. It's two hundred for a shave and a haircut. You know, the basics."

"Shit! I don't have two hundred in cash."

"What about a credit card? I do Visa and Master."

She hauls up a voluminous purse from the floor beside her stool and digs out a manual imprinter.

"Hurry!" he says, looking toward the bathroom door as she imprints his card.

Once they've completed their transaction, he says, "I didn't mean to go all business on you. It was..."

"It's no thing. I do a lot of business with older guys this time of day. It beats night work. They're usually not freaks, so it's easy money."

"I know, but you were being friendly and I...."

"Oh, was I?" The blond shoulders her purse and smiles frostily. "You must have me confused for somebody else. I was working the room, Clifford."

"Cliff," he says in reflex.

"Okay. Cliff. I'm going to move to another stool so I can make eye contact with your buddy. But I'm down here most every morning, so if you need me for anything else, you just sing out."

Cliff doesn't know why he does this type of thing, plays pranks for no reason and without any point. He wonders if he had it in mind to compromise Ashford, to get something on him; but he doesn't believe it's about manipulating people. He figures it's like with the sea turtle—he's showing off, only for himself alone, his audience reduced to one. Another instance, he thinks, of his nonchalance.

Ashford returns and tells Kerman to bring him a glass of water. He swallows some pills, wipes his mouth, and says, "They should blow up that john. It's a fucking disaster area."

"I can help you with that."

"Huh?"

"I was in a demolition unit during Vietnam."

Ashford's eye snags on something—Mary Beth is sitting across from him, eating her French fries, giving each one a blowjob, licking off the salt and sucking them in. He tears himself away from this vision and says to Cliff, "We haven't been able to locate Miz Gerone, so officially you're a person of interest. If that blood on your house matches DNA the lab extracted from her hair brush, I'm going to have to bring you in."

Cliff offers emphatic denials of any involvement with her disappearance. "We fucked occasionally," he says, "but that was it. We didn't have much of an emotional connection."

"I know this is a frame. But the way you've handled everything, telling that story, lying about your girlfriend, it..."

"That wasn't a lie. I couldn't get back into my house because you were processing it. So I went over to Marley's after you released me, and things got deep. I swear to God that's the truth."

"Doesn't matter. It looks bad. You want to know something else that looks bad? I got a copy of one of your movies in the mail the other day. Jurassic Pork. Came in an envelope with no return address."

"Aw, Christ. I did that picture for the hell of it. I was curious to see what it was like."

"Somebody's trying to besmirch your character." Ashford chuckles. "They're doing a hell of a job, too, because you were definitely the shortest man in the movie."

"Yeah, yeah!"

"Prosecutors love to drop that sort of detail into a trial. Juries down here tend to think poorly of pornography. But the frame is so goddamn crude. The person doing the framing must have no comprehension of evidentiary procedure."

"So you believe me?"

"I wouldn't go that far, but I believe something's going on at the Celeste." Ashford has a sip of water, sneaks a peek at Mary Beth, who returns a wave, which he brusquely acknowledges. "You know of any way a used car can be given a new car smell?"

"Polyvinyl chloride," Cliff says. "The stuff they make dashboards out of. It comes in a liquid form, too. The manufacturers use it as a sealant. When a dealer has to take a car back on warranty, some have been known to slap on a coat of PVC and resell the car as new."

Ashford takes out his notebook. "What was that? The sealant?"

Cliff repeats the name. "The stuff's poison. Every time America has a whiff of a new car interior, they're catching a lungful of carcinogens."

Apparently unconcerned by this threat to the nation's health, Ashford says, "I might have found that Ford Escape. About five years ago, we were investigating a stolen car ring and we thought Muntz could be involved. We put a man into his service center in South Daytona. Nothing came of it, but I still had my suspicions. I went up there Tuesday and there was a red Ford Escape sitting out back under a tarp. I had one of our people take a look at it. It had that new car smell, but the engine number had been taken off with acid and the paint job wasn't the original. The car was originally gray, like the one you saw."

"If Jerry was chopping cars, they would have cut it up within an hour or two of bringing it into the shop," Cliff says. "It's been a month."

"He might have a special order for an Escape. It might be a present for one of Muntz's bimbos. Maybe he had a buyer and the guy has a cash flow problem. Who knows? Maybe it slipped his mind. Muntz is no Einstein."

Ashford's cough is plainly an attempt to disguise the fact that he's taking yet another look at Mary Beth. "He's got papers, but the name on them doesn't check out. He claims the guy came in off the street and said he won the car on a quiz show. I haven't got enough to charge him, but my gut tells me that was your Escape."

"So what's next?"

"I might check in to the Celeste tonight and see what's what. Vice has some expensive cars they use for undercover work. I can finagle one for the night, tell the guy on-duty at the yard I need it to impress some woman. That should get me into Room Eleven."

"You think that's a good idea?"

"I can't see what else to do. I don't have much time. If Gerone's DNA comes back a match to the blood on your house, you're going to become the sole target of the investigation."

"I thought you said you believed me!"

"I may buy your story. Some of it, anyway. But no one else does. The only reason you haven't been arrested is there's no evidence, no body. I'm on my own. The captain..." Ashford grimaces. "He's a results kind of guy. He'd love to make this case. It would look good on his resume. You're about as close to a Hollywood celebrity as we got around here, and a trial would get him exposure. It'd be huge on Court TV. He won't authorize me to do diddley until after the DNA comes back. If it's a match, you're in the shit."

"When's it due back?"

"Depends how far behind the lab's running. Maybe two-three days. Maybe tomorrow afternoon."

"Fuck!" Cliff tries to concentrate on the problem, but he's too agitated—he flashes on scenes from prison movies, the wavy smear of blood on his porch, the face of the witch. "You shouldn't do this alone."

Amused, Ashford says, "Yeah, it's going to be rough, what with demons and all."

"You don't know what happened to all those people."

"First of all, we don't know it's 'all those people.' We don't even know for sure about Gerone. Second..." He pushes back his coat to reveal his holstered weapon. "I'm armed, and I have thirty years on the job. I appreciate your motherly concern, but nothing's going to happen that I don't want to happen."

"Have you asked yourself why they only disappear people who rent Number Eleven?"

"Well," says Ashford after pretending to contemplate the question. "I guess because it has a magic stone buried underneath it."

"You don't have an answer, huh?"

"Maybe there's a hidden entrance," says Ashford, registering annoyance. "Or you just didn't see the people leave. Maybe they take them out in little pieces. I got way too many answers. I got them coming out of my ass. That's why I'm going up there, man. That's how you work a case."

Unhappy with this attitude, knowing he can't influence Ashford, Cliff says, "I don't understand why you're doing this for me."

"Jesus!" Ashford gives a derisive laugh. "You think I'm doing this for you? I don't give a flying fuck about you. I'm doing this because I enjoy it. I dig being a cop. I hate to see bad guys get away. And that's what's going to happen if you become the focus of the investigation. We might get Muntz and the What's-the-fuck's-their-names for auto theft, but if they're guilty of murder, I want to make sure they don't slide."

Cliff has new picture of Ashford as a rebel, a loner in the department who never advanced beyond the rank of sergeant because of his penchant for disobeying his superiors. He realizes this picture is no more complete than his original image of the man, but he thinks now that they're both part of Ashford's make-up. He wonders what pieces he's missing.

"Go on, get out of here," Ashford says, still irritated. "We're done. Go play your free games."

Cliff hesitates. "Give me your cell number."

"What the hell for?"

"If you're in there more than two hours, I'll call you."

Ashford glares at him, then extracts a card case from his jacket and flips a card onto the counter.

"Call me before you check in," says Cliff. "Right before. So I'll know when the two hours are up."

"Fine." Ashford signals Kerman, holds up his cup, and grins at Mary Beth. "See you later."

Chapter 10

As often happens when Cliff is under duress, he's inclined to put off thinking about crucial issues. He returns to Jungle Queen and finds that his place has been taken by a bald, sunburned, hairy-chested man in a bathing suit, a towel draped around his neck, who has frittered away all but two of his free games. Cliff watches for a bit, drawing a perturbed glance from the man, as if Cliff is the reason for his ineptitude.

He spends the rest of the morning pacing, puttering around the apartment, his mind crowded with thoughts about Stacey. They didn't care for each other that much, really. The relationship was based on physical attraction and sort of a mutual condescension—they both viewed the other as being frivolous and shallow. Nevertheless, the idea that she's been murdered makes him sick to his stomach. He switches on the TV, channel-surfs, and switches it off; he vacuums, washes dishes, and finally, at a quarter past one, needing to talk it out with someone, he calls Marley.

"I'm in the middle of something," she says. "I'll call you *tomorrow*."

From her emphasis on the word, he understands that she probably won't be home tonight, that she's trapped by her mother's impending breakdown.

He drives to the Regal Cineplex in Ormond Beach, where a movie's playing that he wants to see, but after half an hour he regrets his decision. It's not that the movie is bad—he can't tell one way or another—but sitting in the almost-empty theater forces him to recognize his own emptiness. It's still there; it hasn't gone away. He's reminded of the first month after he returned to Daytona, when he attended matinee after matinee. He missed being part of the industry, and watching movies had initially been a form of self-punishment, a means of humiliating himself for his failure now that the work wasn't coming anymore; but before long those hours in the dark, staring at yet not really seeing those bright, flickering celluloid lives, brought home the fact that he was missing some essential sliver of soul. He hadn't always missed it—he was certain that prior to Hollywood he'd been whole. Yet somehow, somewhere along the line, show biz had extracted that sliver and left him distant from people, an affable sociopath with no particular ax to grind and insufficient energy to grind it, even if he had one. He hoped Marley could bring him back to life, and he still hopes for that, but hope is becoming difficult to maintain.

He walks out into the empty lobby and stands at the center of movie displays and posters. Pitt and Clooney, Will Smith and Matthew McConaughey, posed heroically, absurdly noble and grim. He buys a bag of popcorn at the concession stand from a pretty blond teenager who, after he moves away, leans on the counter, gazing mournfully at the beach weather beyond the glass. Thinking that it was the violence of the film that started him bumming, he tries a domestic melodrama, then a bedroom farce, but they all switch on the Vacancy sign in his head. He drives back to Marley's apartment in the accumulating twilight, a stiff off-shore wind beginning to bend the palms, and waits for Ashford to call.

By the time the call comes at ten past nine, Cliff's a paranoid, over-caffeinated mess, but Ashford sounds uncustomarily ebullient.

"Black Dog, Black Dog! This is Dirty Harry Omega. We're going in! Pray for us!"

Cliff hears high-pitched laughter in the background. "Is someone with you? I thought you didn't have any back-up."

"I brought along the hoo..." He breaks off and asks his companion is it okay he refers to her as a hooker. Cliff can't make out the response, and then Ashford says, "I brought along the *beautiful, sexy* hooker you set me up with."

More laughter.

"Are you crazy?" Cliff squeezes the phone in frustration. "You can't..."

"He wants to know if I'm crazy," says Ashford.

An instant later, a woman's voice says, "Ash is *extremely* crazy. I can vouch for that."

"Mary Beth? Listen! I want you to have him pull over. Right now!"

"Everything's under control, Coria," says Ashford. "I'm on top if it."

"And behind it, too. And on the bottom." Mary Beth giggles.

"You can't take her in there!" says Cliff. "It's dangerous! Even if there's nothing…"

"Bye," says Ashford, and breaks the connection.

Stunned, Cliff calls him back, but either Ashford has switched off his phone or is not picking up.

There's the missing piece to the Ashford puzzle, the one that explains why he never rose higher than sergeant: He's a fuck-up, likely a drunk. He didn't sound drunk, but then he didn't sound sober, either. His friends on the force probably have had to cover for him more than once. He has to be drinking to pull something like this. Cliff tells himself that Ashford has survived this long, he must be able to handle his liquor; but that won't float. He should go over to the Celeste…but what if he fucks up Ashford by doing so? He puts his head in his hands, closes his eyes, and tries to think of something that will help; but all he manages to do is to wonder about Mary Beth. Recalling how she slipped into business mode this morning, he's certain Ashford is paying for her company. Six or seven hundred dollars, plus dinner and drinks—that would be the going rate for an all-nighter with an aging hooker. Ashford, he figures, must earn thirty-five or forty K a year. Spending a week's wage for sex would be doable for him, but he couldn't make a habit of it. But what if this is his farewell party and he's crashing out? Unwed, unloved by his peers, facing a solitary retirement—it's a possibility. Or what if he's on the take and this sort of behavior is commonplace with Ashford? Cliff has a paranoid vision of Jerry Muntz slipping Ashford a fat envelope. He rebukes himself for this entire line of speculation, realizing there's nothing to do except wait.

Thirty minutes ooze past. Wind shudders the panes, rain blurring the lights of the boardwalk, and he calls again. Ashford answers, "Yeah… what?"

He's slurring, his voice thick.

"Just checking on you," Cliff says.

"Don't fucking call me, okay? Call when it's been two hours...or I'll call."

"Are you in Number Eleven?"

"Yeah. Goodbye."

To ease the strain on his back, Cliff lies down on the bed and, perhaps as a result of too much adrenaline, mental fatigue, he passes out. On waking, he sits bolt upright and stares at the alarm clock. Almost midnight. If Ashford called, he didn't hear it, but he's so attuned to that damn ring...He fumbles for the phone and punches in Ashford's number. Voice mail. After a moment's bewilderment, panic wells up in him and he can't get air. Once his breathing is under control he tries the number again, and again is shunted to voicemail.

He talks out loud in an attempt to keep calm. "He's fucking me around," he says. "Motherfucker. He's twisting my brains like in high school. Or he forgot. He forgot, and now he and Mary Beth Hooker are passed out in bed at the Celeste."

Hearing how insane this monologue sounds, he shuts it down before he can speak the third possibility, the one he believes is true—that Ashford and Mary Beth are no more, dead and done for, presently being carted off to wherever the Palaniappans dispose of the bodies.

He flirts with the notion of calling the police, but what would be the point? If they're alive, all it would achieve is to attract more attention to him and that he doesn't need. If they're dead and he calls, he'll instantly become a suspect in multiple murders and they'd most likely pick him up. But he still has an out. He calls Marley. Voicemail. He leaves an urgent message for her to call him back. If he knew where her mother lived, the street address, he'd drive to Deland and pick her up, and they'd get the hell out of Dodge. Where they would go, that's a whole other question, but at least they'd be away from Shalin and Bazit. That's okay, that's all right. Tomorrow will be soon enough.

He tries Ashford a third time, to no avail, and lies down again. He doesn't think he can sleep, but he does, straight through to morning, a sleep that seems an eventless dream of a dark, airless confine in which insubstantial monsters are crawling, breeding, killing, speaking in a language indistinguishable from a heavy, fitful wind, coming close enough to touch.

Chapter 11

It's not unreasonable to think, Cliff tells himself, that Marley's still into it with her mother and that's why she hasn't called; but it's nine AM and he's growing edgy. He calls the police, asks to speak with Sgt. Ashford, and is put through to a detective named Levetto who says that Ashford's always late, he should be in soon, do you want to leave a message?

"No, thanks," says Cliff.

Screwing up his courage, he does something he should have done last night—call the motel.

"Celeste Motel," says Bazit. "How may I be of service?"

Cliff rasps up his voice to disguise it. "Number Eleven, please."

"Number Eleven is vacant, sir."

"I'm looking for some friends, the Ashfords. I could have sworn they were in Eleven."

A pause. "I'm afraid we have no one of that name with us. A Mister Larry Lawless and his wife occupied Number Eleven last night." Cliff thinks he detects a hint of amusement in Bazit's voice as he says, "They checked out quite early."

After trying Marley again, Cliff sits in his underwear, eating toast and jam, drinking coffee, avoiding thought by watching Fox News, when an idea strikes. He throws on shorts and a shirt, and heads for the arcade where he met Ashford the previous morning; he stakes out a stool at the counter, orders an orange juice from Kerman, and waits for Mary Beth to appear.

Last night's deluge has diminished to this morning's drizzle, but the wind is gusting hard. It's a nasty day. Churning surf ploughs the beach, massive, ugly slate-colored waves larded with white, like the liquidinous flesh of some monstrosity spilling onto shore, strands of umber seaweed lifting on its muddy humps. The bruised clouds bulge downward, dragging tendrils of rain over the land. A mere scatter of senior citizens are braving the weather; in the arcade, a handful of debased souls, none of them kids, are feeding coin slots with the regularity of casino habitués. If she's alive, the chances of Mary Beth putting in an appearance are poor, but Cliff sticks it out for more than an hour, scanning every approaching figure, prospecting the gray backdrop for a glint of whitish gold with black roots. His thoughts grab and stick like busted gears, grinding against each other, and the low music of the arcade, a muttering rap song, seems to be issuing from inside his head.

He reaches for his cell phone, thinking to try Marley, and realizes he has left it on the kitchen counter. He hurries back to the apartment and finds a message from Marley. "Hi, Cliffie," she says. "I'll be home soon. Mom's no longer threatening suicide. Of course, there could always be a relapse." A sigh. "I miss you. Hope you're missing me."

The message was left five minutes ago, so he calls her back, but gets her voicemail. It's twenty-three miles to Deland, a twenty-minute drive at Marley's usual rate of speed. At worst, he expects her to walk through the door in a couple of hours. But two o'clock comes and she's not yet back. He calls obsessively for the better part of an hour, punching in her number every few minutes. At three o'clock, he calls the police again and asks for Ashford. A different detective says, "I don't see him. You want to leave a message?"

"Is he in today?"

"I don't know," says the detective impatiently. "I just got here myself."

Cliff is astonished by how thoroughly the circumstance has neutralized him. He knows nothing for certain. There's no proof positive that Stacey is dead, no proof at all concerning the fates of Mary Beth and Ashford. There is some evidence that Jerry is involved in criminal activity, perhaps with the Palaniappans, but nothing you can hang your hat on. He has every expectation that Marley is safe, yet he's begun to worry. He can't raise the alarm, because no one will believe him and the police think he's a murderer. If truth be told, he's not sure he believes Shalin's story—events have gone a long way toward convincing him, but it's perfectly possible that she's playing mind games with him and that's all there is to it. When the DNA results come back, as they could any minute, at least according to Ashford, then there may be some proof, but if the DNA doesn't match Stacey's…*Nada.* Yet it's the very nebulousness of the situation that persuades him that his life has gone and is going horribly wrong, that he's perched atop a mountain of air and, once he recognizes that nothing is supporting him, his fall will be calamitous. He should do something, he tells himself. He should leave before the DNA comes back, pack a few things and put some miles between him and the Palaniappans whom—irrationally—he fears more than the police. He can call Marley from the road, though God knows what he'll say to her.

In the end, he takes a half-measure and drives to the cottage, deciding that he'll pack and wait there for Marley to call. The surf in Port Orange is as unlovely as that in Daytona, the sky as sullen. Wind flattens the dune grass, and the cottage looks vacant, derelict, sand drifted up onto the steps and porch. When he unlocks the inside door, a strong smell rushes out, a stale, sweet scent compounded of spoilage and deodorizers. Eau de Cliff. He tiptoes about nervously, peering into rooms, and, once assured that no one is lying in wait, he grabs a suitcase and begins tossing clothes into it. In a bottom drawer, underneath folded jeans, he finds his old army .45 and a box of shotgun shells. The shotgun has long since been sold, but the .45 might come in handy. He inspects the clip, making certain it's full, and puts it in the suitcase. Headlines run past on an imaginary crawl. Actor Slain In Deadly Shoot-out—details at eleven. He finishes packing, goes into the living room, and sits on the couch. A cloud seems to settle over him, a depressive fog. He can't hold a thought in his head. It's been years since he felt so unsound, as if the fluttering of a feather duster could disperse him.

The overcast turns into dusk, and for Cliff it's an eternal moment, a single, seamless drop of time in which he's embedded like an ancient insect, suspended throughout the millennia. He feels ancient; his bones are dry sticks, his skin papery and brittle. The phone rings. Not his cell, but his landline. He reacts to it sluggishly—he doubts Marley would call him at this number—but the phone rings and rings, a piercing note that reverberates through the house, disruptive and jarring. He picks up, listens, yet does not speak.

"Mister Coria? Hello?"

Cliff remains silent.

"This is Bazit Palaniappan, the owner of the Celeste Motel. How are you today?"

"What do you want?"

"I have someone here who wishes to speak with you."

Marley's voice comes on the line, saying, "Cliff? Is that you?"

"Marley?"

"I'm afraid she's too upset to talk further. I've arranged for her to have a lie-down in one of our bungalows."

"You fuck! You hurt her, I swear to God I'll kill you!"

Unperturbed, Bazit says, "Perhaps you could come and get her. Shall we say, within the next half-hour?"

"You bet your ass I'm coming! You'd better not hurt her!"

"Within the next half-hour, if you please. I can't tie up the room longer than that. And do come alone. She's very upset. I don't know what will happen if you should bring people with you. It might be too much for her."

His cloud of depression dissolved, Cliff slings the receiver across the room. He's furious, his thoughts flurry; he doesn't know where to turn, what to do, but gradually his fury matures into a cold, fatalistic resolve. He's fucked. The trap that the Palaniappans set has been sprung, but Marley...He removes the .45 from the suitcase, sticks it in his waist, under his shirt, and thinks, no, that won't be enough. They'll be watching for him, they'll expect a gun or a knife. His mind muddies. Then, abruptly, it clears and he remembers a trick he learned in blow-it-up school. He goes to the drawer in which he found the .45; he takes out two shotgun shells, hustles back to the living room, rummages through his desk and finds thumbtacks, strapping tape, and scotch tape. He makes a package of the shells, the scotch tape, a few thumbtacks, and a length of string; he drops his shorts and tapes the package under his balls. He's clumsy with the tape—his hands shake and it sticks to his fingers. The package is unstable. One wrong move and everything will spill onto the ground. He adds more tape. It's uncomfortable; it feels as if he shit his pants. He stands at the center of the room, and the room seems to shrink around him, to fit tightly to his skin like plastic wrap. He's hot and cold at the same time. A breath of wind could topple him, yet when he squeezes his hand into a fist, he knows how strong he is. "I love you," he says to the shadows, and the shadows tremble. "I love you."

Chapter 12

Cliff burns across the Port Orange Bridge. It's not yet full dark when he reaches the Celeste, but the Vacancy sign has been lit. Across the way, with its strings of lights bobbing in the wind and clusters of balloons and people milling everywhere, the used car lot might be a tourist attraction, a carnival without rides. He pulls up to the motel office and spots Bazit standing at the window, his arms folded. Bazit must see him, but he remains motionless, secure—Cliff thinks—with his hole card. He jumps out, heads for the door and, as he's about to open it, feels something hard prod his back.

"You stop there," says Au Yong, stepping back from him. She's training a small silver hangun on him and scowling fiercely. Cliff's right hand sneaks toward the .45, but Bazit emerges from the office and steers him into the shadows, where he pats him down. On discovering the .45, he makes a disapproving noise.

"I want to see Marley," Cliff says.

"You will see her," Bazit says. "In due course."

Au Young says something in Cantonese; Bazit responds in kind, then addresses Cliff in English. "My wife says for such a negligible man, you have a very powerful weapon."

"Fuck your wife," Cliff says. "I want to see Marley now."

Bazit continues patting him down, but does not check under his balls. "You will see her," he says. "And when you do, let me assure you, she will be unharmed. She is resting. Shalin is with her."

"You tell that bitch, if she…"

Bazit slaps him across the face. "I apologize, sir, for striking you. But you mustn't call my daughter a bitch or say anything abusive to my wife."

Again, he speaks to Au Yong in Cantonese—she looks at Cliff, spits on the grass, and goes into the office.

"This way, please." Bazit gestures with the .45, indicating that Cliff should precede him toward the rear of the motel, toward Bungalow Eleven. "Don't worry about your car. It will be taken care of."

As he moves along the overgrown path that winds back among palmettos, Number Eleven swelling in his vision, Cliff's throat goes dry and he feels a weakness in his knees, as might a condemned prisoner on first glimpsing the execution chamber. "Come on, man," he says. "Let me see Marley."

"I hope you will find your accommodations suitable," says Bazit. "At the Celeste, we encourage criticism. If you have any to offer, you'll find a card for that purpose on the night table. Please feel free to write down your thoughts."

At the entrance to Number Eleven, he unlocks the door and urges Cliff inside. "There's a light switch on the wall to your left. Is there anything else I can do before I bid you goodnight?"

Cliff opens the door and steps in. Of the hundred questions he needs answered, only one occurs to him. "Was it your father who did the special effects for *Sword of the Black Demon*?"

"No, sir. It was not." Bazit smiles and closes the door.

Cliff switches on the overhead and discovers that the lights of Bungalow Eleven are blue. It doesn't look as bad as he imagined. No dried blood, no spikes on the walls. No bone fragments or ceilings that open to reveal enormous teeth. He tries the door. Locked from without—it appears to be reinforced. He fends off panic and goes straight to work, dropping his shorts and unpeeling the tape that holds the package. The entrance to the room is a narrow alcove, perfect for his purposes. He tapes a shotgun shell to the back of the door, the ignition button facing out. Then he tapes a thumbtack to the wall slightly less than head-high, the point sticking through the tape, aligning it so that the door will strike it when opened. He has to use the string to sight the job, but he's confident that he's managed it. The bathroom door slides back into the wall, so it's no good to him. He searches for a hidden entrance. Discovering none, he tapes the second shell to the front door, a foot-and-a-half lower than the first, and lines it up with a second thumbtack.

An easy chair occupies one corner of the room. He drags it around, angles it so that it faces the door, and sits down. Booby-trapping the door has taken it out of him. He thinks that the adrenaline rush wearing off is partly to blame for his fatigue, but he's surprised how calm he feels. He's afraid—he can almost touch his fear, it's so palpable—but overlying it, suppressing it, is a veneer of tranquility that's equally palpable. He supposes that this is what some men feel in combat, a calmness that permits them to function at a high level.

The blue light, which annoyed him at first, has come to be soothing, so much so that he finds himself getting sleepy, and he thinks that the Vacancy sign may have had a similar effect when he stared at it from the used car lot. He wants to stay alert and he looks around the room, hoping to see something that will divert him. The windows are covered by sheets of hard plastic dyed to resemble shades. Except for them, everything in Number Eleven is blue. The toilet, the rugs, the bed table coated in blue paint. The sheets on the bed are blue satin, like the witch queen's sheets in the movie. That bothers him, but not sufficiently to worry about it. He tries to estimate how long he's been here. Maybe thirty, forty minutes... The sheets seem to ripple with the reflected light, gleams flowing along them as if they're gently rippling, and he passes the time by watching them course the length of the bed.

He thinks this could be it, the sum of the Palaniappans' vengeance—they've finished with their games, and in the morning they'll reunite him and Marley. They appear to know everything about him, where he is at any given moment...all that. Perhaps they know he's basically decent and that he didn't intend to injure Isabel. That thought planes into others about Isabel, and those in turn plane into memories of the movie they made together. He can't recall its name, but it's right on the tip of his tongue. Devil Something. Something Sword. She flirted brazenly with him on the set, but there was an untutored quality to her brazenness, as if she didn't have much experience with men and knew no other way to achieve her ends. He recalls seeing her off the set, in a Manila hotel, room service on white linen, high windows that opened onto a balcony, how she danced so erotically he thought his cock would explode, but once he was inside her, that part of him calmed down and he could go all night. It's a wonder he didn't notice she loved him, because all these years later he sees it with absolute clarity. She would lie beside him, stroking his chest, gazing into his eyes, waiting for him to reciprocate. He thought she was trying to impress him with her devotion, to trap a rich American for her husband, and, while that might have been true, he failed to recognize the deeper truth that underscored her actions. It's the same with Marley, and he understands that, at least in the beginning, he treated her with equal deference, dealing with her as one might a sexy puppy that was eager to bounce and play. It was convenient to feel that way, because it absolved him of responsibility for her feelings.

Other memories obtain from that initial one, and he becomes lost, living in a dream of Isabel, and when a point of blue light begins to expand in midair, right in front of him, he thinks it's part of the movie he's replaying, part of the dream, and watches from a dreamlike distance as it expands further, unfolds and grows plump in all the right places, evolving into the spitting image of Isabel as she was in *The Black Devil's Sword* or whatever, blue skin, black nipples, lithe and curvy, her secret hair barbered into exotic shapes, and she's dancing for him, only this dance is different from the one she used to do, more aggressive, almost angry, though he knows Isabel didn't have an angry bone in her body... it's as though she has no bones at all, her movements are so sinuous and supple, bending backwards to trail her hair along the floor, then straightening with a weaving motion, hips and breasts swaying, a sheen of sweat upon her body as she flings her fingers out at him, like the queen...in the movie...when she danced...

Cliff feels pain, not an awful pain, but pain like he's never felt before, as if an organ of which he has been unaware, a special organ tucked away beneath the tightly packed fruits of heart, liver, spleen, kidneys, and intestines, insulated by their flesh, has been opened and is spilling its substance. It's not a stabbing pain, neither an ache nor a twinge, not the raw pain that comes from an open wound or a burning such as eventuates from an ulcer; but though comparably mild, not yet severe enough to combat his arousal, it's the worst pain he has known. A sick, emptying feeling is the closest he can come to articulating it, but not even that says it. He understands now that this is no movie and that something vital is leaking out, being drawn from his body in surges, in trickles and sudden gushes, conjured forth by blue fingers that tease, tempt, and coax. He tries to relieve the pain by twisting in the chair, by screaming, but he's denied the consolation of movement—he cannot convulse or writhe or kick, and when he attempts to scream, a scratchy whisper is all he can muster. It's not that he's being restrained, but rather it seems that as the level of that vital essence lowers, he's become immobilized, his will shriveled to the point that he no longer desires to move, he no longer cares to do anything other than to suffer in silence, to stare helplessly at the beautiful blue witch with full breasts and half-moon hips, sweat glistening on her thighs and belly, who is both the emblem and purveyor of his pain.

His vision clouds, his eyes are failing or perhaps they are occluded by a pale exhaust, a cloud-like shadow of the thing draining from him, for he glimpses furtive shapes and vague lusters within the cloud; but they are unimportant—the one wish he sustains, the one issue left upon which he can opine, is that she be done with him, and he knows that she is nearly done. His being flickers like a shape on a silent screen, luminous and frail. But then she dwindles, she folds in upon herself, shrinking to a point of blue light, and is gone. Her absence restores to him an inch of will, an ounce of sensitivity, yet he's not grateful. Why has she left him capable of feeling only a numb horror and his own hollowness? He wants to call her back, but has no voice. In frustration, he strains against his unreal bonds, causing his head to wobble and fall, and sits staring at his feet. Sluggish, simple thoughts hang like drool from the mouth of whatever dead process formed them, the final products of his mental life.

After a while, an eon, a second, he realizes that the pain has diminished, his vitality is returning, and manages to lift his head when he hears a click and sees the door being cautiously opened. A woman with frizzy blond hair peeks in. He knows her—not her name, but he knows her and has the urge to warn her against something.

"Cliff!" she says, relief in her voice, and starts toward him, bursting through the door.

Two explosions, two blasts of fire, splinter the wood and fling her against the wall, painting it with a shrapnel of blood, hair, scraps of flesh and bone. She flops onto the floor, an almost unrecognizable wreckage, face torn away, waist all but severed, blood pooling wide as a table around her. But Cliff recognizes her. He remembers her name, and he begins to remember who she was and why she was here and what happened to her. He remembers nights and days, he remembers laughter, the taste of her mouth, and he wants to turn from this grisly sight, from the burnt eye and the gristly tendons and the thick reddish black syrup they're steeping in. He wants to yell until his throat is raw, until blood sprays from his mouth; he wants to shake his head back and forth like a madman until his neck breaks; he wants very badly to die.

From outside comes the sound of voices, questioning voices, muted voices, and then a scream. Cliff understands now how this will end. The police, a murder trial, and a confinement followed by an execution. As Marley recedes from life, from the world, he is re-entering it, reclaiming his senses, his memories, and he struggles against this restoration, trying with all his might to die, trying to avoid an emptiness greater than death, but with every passing moment he increases, he grows steadier and more complete in his understanding. He understands that the law of karma has been fully applied. He understands the careless iniquity of humankind and the path that has led him to this terrible blue room. With understanding comes further increase, further renewal, yet nonetheless he continues to try and vomit out the remnant scrapings of his soul before Shalin returns to gloat, before one more drop of torment can be exacted, before his memories become so poignant they can pierce the deadest heart. He yearns for oblivion, and then thinks that death may not offer it, that in death he may find worse than Shalin, a life of exquisite torment. That in mind, he forces himself to look again at Marley's disfigured face, hoping to discover in that mask of ruptured sinews and blackened tissue, with here and there a patch of skull, and, where her neck was, amidst the gore, the blue tip of an artery dangling like a blossom from a flap of scorched skin....hoping to discover an out, a means of egress, a crevice into which he can scurry and hide from the light of his own unpitying judgment. He forces himself to drink in the sight of her death; he forces himself and forces himself, denying the instinct to turn away; he forces himself to note every insult to her flesh, every fray and tatter, every internal vileness; he forces himself past the borders of revulsion, past the fear-and-trembling into deserts of thought, the wastes where the oldest monsters howl in the absence; he forces himself to persevere, to continue searching for a key to this doorless prison until thick strands of saliva braid his lips and his hands have ceased to shake and cracked saints mutter prayers for the damned and blood rises in clouds of light from the floor, and in a pocket of electric quiet he begins to hear the voice of her accusatory thoughts, to respond to them, defending himself by arguing that it was she who originally forced herself on him, and how could he have anticipated any of this, how can she blame him? You should have known, she tells him, you should have fucking known that someone like you, a jerk with a trivial intelligence and the morals of a cabbage and a blithe disregard for everything but his own pleasure, must have broken some hearts and stepped on some backs. You should have known. Yeah, he says, but all that's changed. I've changed. With a last glimmer of self-perception, he realizes this slippage is the start of slide that will never end, the opening into a hell less certain than the one that waits upon the other side of life. He feels an unquiet exultation, a giddy merriment that makes him dizzy and, if not happy, then content in part, knowing that when they come for him, the official mourners, the takers under, the guardians of the public safety, those who command the cold violence of the law, they'll find him looking into death's bad eye, into the ruined face of love, into the nothing-lasts-forever, smiling bleakly, blankly...

Vacantly.

DOG-EARED PAPERBACK OF MY LIFE

My name, Thomas Cradle, is not the most common of names, yet when I chanced upon a book written by another Thomas Cradle while looking up my work on Amazon (a pastime to which I, like many authors, am frequently given), I thought little of it, and my overriding reaction was one of concern that this new and unknown Cradle might prove the superior of the known. I became even more concerned when I learned that the book, *The Tea Forest*, was a contemporary fantasy, this being the genre into which my own books were slotted. Published in 2002, it was ranked 1,478,040 in Amazon sales, a fact that eased my fears somewhat. According to the reader reviews (nine of them in sum, all five stars), the book was a cult item, partly due to its quality and partly because the author had disappeared in Cambodia not long after its publication. I found it odd that I hadn't heard of Cradle and his novel before; out of curiosity, I ordered a used copy and put the incident from mind.

The book arrived ten days later, while I was proofing my new novel, working on a screenplay based on my third novel, for which I was being paid a small fortune, and negotiating to buy a home in the Florida Keys, a property to which some of the screenplay money would be applied. The package lay on my desk unopened for several weeks, buried under papers. By the time I got around to opening it, I had forgotten what it was I ordered. My copy of *The Tea Forest* turned out to be a dog-eared trade paperback, the pages crimped and highlighted in yellow marker throughout, rife with marginalia. On the cover, framed by green borders, was a murky oil painting depicting a misted swamp with an almost indistinguishable male figure slogging through waist-deep water. I looked on the spine. The publisher was Random House, also my publisher. That made it doubly odd that I hadn't heard of the book. What the hell, I asked myself, were they doing publishing two Thomas Cradles in the same genre? And why hadn't my editor or agent made me aware of this second Cradle?

I turned the book over and glanced at the tiny author photo, which showed a bearded, unkempt man glaring with apparent contempt at the camera. I skimmed the blurbs, the usual glowing overstatement, and read the bio:

> "Thomas Cradle was born in Carboro, North Carolina in 1968. He attended the University of Virginia for two years before dropping out and has traveled widely in Asia, working as a teacher of English and martial arts. He currently lives in Phnom Penh. *The Tea Forest* is his first novel."

A crawly sensation moved down my neck and spread to my shoulders. Not only did Cradle and I share a name, we had been born in the same town in the same year and had attended the same university (though I had graduated). I'd also trained in Muay Thai and Shotokan karate during high school—if not for a herniated disc, I might have pursued these interests. I had a closer look at the author photo. Lose the beard, shorten the hair, drop twenty-five pounds and six years, and he might have been my twin. The contemptuous glare alone should have made the likeness apparent.

Someone, I told myself, was playing a practical joke, someone who knew me well enough to predict my reactions. When I opened the book, something would pop out or a bad smell would be released...or perhaps it would be a good-natured joke. Kim, my girlfriend, had the wherewithal to doctor an old photograph and dummy up a fake book, but I would not have thought she possessed the requisite whimsy. I dipped into the first chapter, expecting the punchline would be revealed in the text; but after five chapters I recognized that the book could not be the instrument of a prank, and my feeling of unease returned.

The novel documented a trip down the Mekong River taken by four chance acquaintances, beginning in Stung Treng on the Cambodian-Lao border, where the four had purchased a used fishing boat, to Dong Thap Province in the extreme south of Vietnam. It was an unfinished journey fraught with misadventure and illness, infused with a noirish atmosphere of low-level criminality, and culminated with a meditation on suicide that may well have foreshadowed the author's fate.

Judging by the wealth and authenticity of the background detail and by the precisely nuanced record of the first-person narrator's emotional and mental life, the novel was thinly disguised autobiography; and the configuration of the narrator's thoughts and perceptions seemed familiar, as did the style in which the novel was written: It was my style. Not the style in which I currently wrote, but the style I had demonstrated at the start of my career, prior to being told by an editor that long, elliptical sentences and dense prose would be an impediment to sales (she counseled the use of "short sentences, less navel-gazing, more plot," advice I took to heart). Cradle Two's novel was no mere pastiche; it was that old style perfected, carried off with greater expertise than I had ever displayed. It was as if he had become the writer I had chosen not to be.

I went to Amazon again, intending to have another look at the webpage devoted to *The Tea Forest* and perhaps find the author's contact information; but I could not locate the page, and there was no evidence anywhere on the Internet of a second Thomas Cradle or his novel. I tried dozens of searches, all to no avail. I emailed the seller, Overdog Books, asking for any information they might have on the author; they denied having sold me the book. I sent them a scan of the packing slip, along with a note that accused them of being in collusion with one of my enemies, most likely another writer who, envious of my success, was mocking me. They did not respond. I riffled through the pages of the novel, half-expecting it to dematerialize along with the proof of its existence. I had often made the comment that if ever I were presented with incontrovertible evidence of the fantastic, I would quit writing and become a priest. Though I was not yet prepared to don the cassock, the book in my hands seemed evidence of the kind I had demanded.

The narrative of *The Tea Forest* was episodic, heavy on the descriptive passages, many of them violent or explicitly sexual; and these episodes were strung together on a flimsy plotline that essentially consisted of a series of revelations, all leading the narrator (TC by name, thereby firmly establishing that Cradle Two had not overstrained his imagination during this portion of the creative process) to conclude that our universe and those adjoining it were interpenetrating. He likened this circumstance to countless strips of wet rice paper hung side by side in a circle and blown together by breezes that issued from every quarter of the compass, allowing even strips on opposite points of the circle to stick to each other for a moment and, in some instances, for much longer; thus, he concluded, we commonly spent portions of each day in places far stranger than we were aware (although the universes appeared virtually identical). This, he declared, explained why people in rural circumstances experienced paranormal events more often than urban dwellers: They were likely to notice unusual events, whereas city folk might mistake a ghost for a new form of advertising, or attribute the sighting of an enormous shadow in the Hudson River to chemicals in the air, or pay no attention to the fact that household objects were disappearing around them. It also might explain, I realized, why I was no longer able to unearth any record of the novel.

I had the book copied and bound and FedExed the copy to my agent. The cover letter explained how I had obtained it and asked him to find out whatever he could. He called two mornings later to congratulate me on a stroke of marketing genius, saying that *The Tea Forest* could be another Blair Witch and that this hoax concerning a second Thomas Cradle was a brilliant way of preparing the market for the debut of my "new" style. When I told him it wasn't a hoax, as far as I knew, he said not to worry, he'd never tell, and declared that if Random House wouldn't go for the book, he'd take me over to Knopf. At this juncture, I began to acknowledge that the universe might be as Cradle Two described, and, since there would be no one around to charge me with plagiarism, I saw no reason not to profit from the book; but I told him to hold off on doing anything, that I needed to think it through and, before all else, I might be traveling to Cambodia and Vietnam.

The idea for the trip was little more than a whim, inspired by my envy of Cradle Two and the lush deviance of his life, as evidenced by *The Tea Forest*; but over the ensuing two months, as I reread sections of the novel, committing many of them to memory, the richness of the prose infected me with Cradle Two's obsessiveness (which, after all, was a cousin to my own), and I came to speculate that if I retraced his steps (even if they were steps taken in another universe), I might derive some vital benefit. There was a mystery here that wanted unraveling, and there was no one more qualified than I to investigate it. While I hadn't entirely accepted his rice paper model of the universe, I believed that if his analogy held water, I might be able to perceive its operations more clearly through the simple lens of a river culture. However, one portion of the novel gave me reason for concern. The narrator, TC, had learned during the course of his journey that in one alternate universe he was a secretive figure of immense power, evil in nature, and that his innumerable analogs were, to some degree or another, men of debased character. The final section of the book suggested that he had undergone a radical transformation, and that idea was supported by a transformation in the prose. Under other circumstances, I would have perceived this to be a typical genre resolution, but Cradle Two's sentences uncoiled like vipers waking under the reader's eye, spitting out a black stream of venom from which the next serpent would slither, dark and supple, sleekly malformed, governed by an insidious sonority that got into my head and stained my dreams and my work for days thereafter. Eventually I convinced myself that Cradle Two's gift alone was responsible for this dubious magic and that it had been done for dramatic effect and was in no way a reflection of reality.

The book, the actual object, became an article of my obsession. I liked touching it. The slickness of the cover; the tacky spot on the back where a clerk or prior owner had spilled something sticky or parked a wad of chewing gum; the neat yet uninspired marginalia; the handwritten inscription, "To Tracy," and the anonymity of the dedication, "For you"; the faintly yellowed paper; the tear on page 19. All its mundane imperfections seemed proofs of its otherworldliness, that another world existed beyond the enclosure of my own, and I began carrying the book with me wherever I went, treating it as though it were a lover, fondling it, riffling its pages, fingering it while I drove, thinking about it to the point of distraction, until the idea of the trip evolved from a whim into a project I seriously considered, and then into something more. Though I was ordinarily a cynical type, dismissive of any opinion arguing the thesis that life was anything other than a cruel and random process, my affair with the book persuaded me that destiny had taken a hand in my life, and I would be a fool not to heed it (I think every cynic's brassbound principles can be as easily overthrown). And so, tentatively to begin with, yet with growing enthusiasm, I started to make plans. As a writer, I delighted in planning, in charting the course of a story, in assembling the elements of a fiction into a schematic, and I plotted the trip as though it were a novel that hewed to (but was not limited by) the picaresque flow of Cradle Two's voyage along the Mekong. There would be a woman, of course—perhaps two or three women—and here a dash of adventure, here a time for rest and reflection, here the opportunity for misadventure, here a chance for love, and here a chance for disappointment. I laid in detail with the care of a master craftsman attempting a delicate mosaic, leaving only one portion undone: the ending. That would be produced by the alchemy of the writing or, in this instance, the traveling.

I intended to hew closely in spirit to the debauched tenor of Cradle Two/TC's journey, and I hoped that by setting up similar conditions, I might have illuminations similar to his; but I saw no purpose in duplicating its every detail—I expected my journey to be a conflation of his experience. The lion's share of his troubles on the trip had stemmed from his choice of boats, so rather than buying a leaky fishing craft with an unreliable engine for cheap, I arranged to have a houseboat built in Stung Treng. The cost was negligible, four thousand dollars, half up front, for a shallow-draft boat capable of sleeping four with a fully equipped galley and a new engine. Once I completed the trip, I intended to donate it to charity, a Christian act that, given the boat's value in U.S. dollars, would allow me to take a tax write-off of several times that amount. I informed Kim that I'd be going away for six to eight weeks, roughing it (she considered any activity that occurred partially outdoors to be roughing it) on the Mekong, far from five-star hotels and haute cuisine and that she was welcome to hook up with me in Saigon, where suitable amenities were available. However, I cautioned her that I would be attempting to recreate the mood described in *The Tea Forest*, and this meant I would be seeing other women. Perhaps, I suggested, she should seize the opportunity to spread her wings.

Kim, a tall, striking brunette, had an excellent mind, a background in microbiology, and a scientist's dispassionate view of human interactions. We had discussed marriage and discussed rather more the possibility of having children, but until we reached that pass, she was comfortable with maintaining an open relationship. She told me to be careful, a reference both to safe sex and to the problems I'd had in compartmentalizing my emotional life, and gave me her blessing. I then contacted my agent and instructed him to sell *The Tea Forest* while I was gone. These formalities out of the way, I had little left to do except lose some weight for the trip and cultivate a beard—I thought this would help get me into character—and wait for the end of the fall monsoon.

—

I flew to Bangkok and there took passage on the Ubon Ratchatani Express toward the Lao border, berthed in an old-fashioned sleeping car with curtained fold-down beds on both sides of the aisle. I spent a goodly portion of the evening in the bar car, which reeked of garlic and chilis and frying basil, drinking bad Thai beer, trying to acclimate myself to the heat that poured through the lowered windows. From Ubon, I traveled by bus to Stung Treng, a dismal town of about twenty-five thousand at the confluence of the Mekong, the Sesan, and the Sekong Rivers. It was a transit point for backpackers, a steady trickle of them, the majority remaining in town no more than a couple of hours, the length of time it took for the next river taxi to arrive. I had thought to pick up a companion in one of the larger Cambodian towns downriver, but as I would be trapped in Stung Treng for three days while the boat was being fitted and provisioned, I posted signs at the border, in the open-air market, and around town, advertising a cruise aboard the *Undine* (the name of my houseboat) in exchange for personal services. Women only. See the bartender at the Sekong Hotel.

I was heading back to the hotel, passing through the market when a mural painted on a noodle stall caught my eye. Abstract in form, a yellowish white mass of cells or chambers, spreading over the front and both sides of the stall—though crudely rendered, I had the idea that it was the depiction of microscopic life, one of those multicelled monstrosities that you become overly familiar with in Biology 101. It was such an oddity (most of the stalls were unadorned, a handful decorated with religious iconography), I stopped to look and immediately drew a gathering of young men, curious to see what had made me curious and taking the opportunity to offer themselves as guides, procurers, and so forth. The stallkeeper, an elderly Laotian man, grew annoyed with these loiterers, but I gave him a handful of Cambodian riels, enough to purchase noodles for my new pals, and asked (through the agency of an interpreter—one of the men spoke English) what the mural represented.

"He don't know," said the interpreter. "He say it make peaceful to look at. It make him think of Nirvana. You know Nirvana?"

"Just their first couple of albums," I said. "Ask him who painted it."

This question stimulated a brief exchange, and the interpreter reported that the artist had been an American. Big like me. More hair. A bad man. I asked him to inquire in what way the man had been bad, but the stallkeeper would only say (or the interpreter could only manage to interpret) that the man was "very bad." I had only skimmed the last half of *The Tea Forest*, but I seemed to recall a mention of a creature like that depicted by the mural, and I suspected that the mural and the bad man who had created it might be evidence supporting Cradle Two's theories.

That afternoon I staked out a table in the Sekong's bar and was amazed by how many women volunteered for my inspection. Two balked at the sexual aspects of the position, and others were merely curious; but eleven were serious applicants, willing and, in some cases, eager to trade their favors for a boat ride and whatever experiences it might afford them. I rejected all but four out of hand for being too young or insufficiently attractive. The first day's interviews yielded one maybe, a thirty-four-year-old Swedish schoolteacher who was making her way around the world and had been traveling for almost five years; but she seemed to be looking for a place to rest, and rest was the last thing on my mind.

The bar was a pleasant enough space—walls of split, lacquered bamboo decorated with travel posters, Cambodian pop flowing from hidden speakers, and a river view through screen windows. A standing floor fan buzzed and whirred in one corner, yet it was so humid that the chair stuck to my back, and the smells drifting up from the water grew less enticing as the hours wore on. Late on the second day, I was almost ready to give up, when a slender, long-legged woman with dyed black hair (self-barbered, apparently, into a ragged pageboy cut), camo parachute pants, and an oft-laundered Olivia Tremor Control T-shirt approached the bar. She unshouldered her backpack and spoke to the bartender. I signaled to him that she passed muster. He pointed me out, and she came toward my table but pulled up short a couple of feet away.

"Oh, gosh!" she said. "You're Thomas Cradle, aren't you?"

Flattered at being recognized, I said that I was.

"This is fantastic!" She came forward again, dragging the backpack. "I shall have to tell my old boyfriend. He's a devoted fan of yours, and he'll be terribly impressed. Of course, that would make it necessary to speak with him again, wouldn't it?"

She was more interesting-looking than pretty, yet pretty enough, with lively topaz eyes and one of those superprecise British accents that linger over each and every syllable, delicately tonguing the consonants, as if giving the language a blowjob.

"It's hellish outside," she said. "I must have a cold drink. Would you care for something?"

Her face, which I'd initially thought too young, mistaking her for a gangly teenager, had a waiflike quality; a white scar over one eyebrow and small indentations along her jaw, perhaps resulting from adolescent acne, added a decade to my estimate.

"I'll take a Green Star, thanks," I said. "No ice."

"Gin for me. Tons of ice." Her mouth, bracketed when she smiled by finely etched lines, was extraordinarily wide and expressive, appearing to have an extra hinge that enabled her crooked grin. "I'll just fetch them, shall I?"

She brought the drinks, had a sip, closed her eyes, and sighed. Then she extended a hand, shook mine, and said, "I'm Lucy McQuillen, and I loved your last book. At least I think it's your last." She frowned. "Didn't I hear that you'd stopped writing...or were giving it up or something? Not that your presence in Cambodia would refute that in any way."

"I have got a new novel coming out next spring," I said.

"Well, if it's as good as the last, you'll have my ten quid."

"The critics will probably say it's exactly the same as the last."

We teetered on the brink of an awkward silence, and then she said, "Shall I tell you about myself? Would that be helpful?"

"That's why I'm here."

"Okay. I'm thirty-one...thirty-two next month, actually. I've lived in London all my life. I graduated from the Chelsea School of Design and worked at a firm in the city for a while. Five years ago I started my own firm, specializing in urban landscape design. We were doing spectacularly well for a new business..."

A foursome of prosperous-looking Cambodian men entered the bar, laughing and talking; they acknowledged us, inclining their heads and pressing their hands together in a prayerful gesture, a gesture that Lucy returned, and they took seats at a table against the back wall.

"To put it succinctly," Lucy went on, "I'm a victim of multiculturalism. My East Indian accountant stole from me, quite a large sum, and fled to India. I couldn't recover. It was an absolute disaster. I'm afraid I was a mess for some time thereafter. I had a little money left in personal accounts, and I started out for India, planning some pitiful revenge. I'm not certain what I had in mind. Some sort of Kaliesque scenario, I suppose. Gobbets of blood. His wife screaming in horror. Of course, I didn't go through with it. I bypassed India completely, and I've been bumming around Southeast Asia for a couple of years. My money's running low, and, to be frank, this voyage would extend my trip and give me the time and leisure to write a new business plan."

"You must be good at what you do," I said. "To be so successful at such a young age."

"I've won awards," she said, grinning broadly.

"I would have thought, then, you could have found investors to bail you out."

"As I said, I was a mess. Certifiably a mess. Once they noticed, investors wouldn't touch me. I've calmed down a great deal since, and I'm ready to have at it again."

She fit into the "too eager" category, yet I found her appealing. The Cambodian men burst into applause, celebrating something one of them had done or said. The light was fading on the river, the far bank darkened by cloud shadow. I asked Lucy if she understood the requirements of the position.

"Your sign was somewhat vague," she said. "I may be misreading it, but I assume 'companion' is another word for girlfriend?"

"That's right."

"May I ask a question?"

"Go for it."

"Surely a man of your accomplishment must have a number of admirers. You're not bad looking, and you obviously have money. I don't understand why you would be in the market."

"It's in the nature of an experiment," I said. "I can assure you that you won't be harmed or humiliated in any way."

"A literary experiment?"

"You might say."

"You know, I didn't intend to seek the position," she said. "I was just...intrigued. But I must admit, having Thomas Cradle on my resumé would do wonders for my self-esteem." She had a deep drink of her gin-and-tonic. "If the position is offered, I do have two conditions. One you've already spoken to—I'm not into pain. Short of sea urchins and safety pins, I'm your girl. I believe you can expect me, given a modicum of compatibility, to perform my duties with relish."

"And the second condition?"

"Instead of leaping into the fire, as it were, I'd prefer we took some time to become comfortable with one another. Give it a day or two. Will that be a problem?"

"Not at all."

One of the Cambodian men bought us fresh drinks. He spoke no English, but Lucy chatted him up in his own tongue and then explained that his friend had received a promotion, and he would like us to join them in a toast. We complied, and, after bows and prayerful gestures all around, I asked if she had studied Cambodian.

"I pick up languages quickly. One of my many gifts." She gave another lopsided smile. "I do have some bad habits I should mention. I tend to run on about things. Talk too much. Just tell me to stuff it. People have been telling me that since I was a child. And I'm a vegetarian, though I have been known to eat fish. I'm picky about what I consume."

"My cook's big on veggies," I said. "Too much so for my tastes."

"You have a cook?"

"A Vietnamese kid. Deng. He's crew and cook. The pilot's an old guy in his sixties. Lan. He speaks decent American, but he doesn't talk to me much…not so far, anyway."

"La-de-da!" said Lucy. "Next you'll be telling me you have your own private ocean."

A breeze stirred the placid surface of the river, but it had no effect on the humidity in the restaurant.

"There's one thing more," Lucy said. "I'm afraid it may erase whatever good opinion you've formed of me, but I can't compromise. I smoke two pipes of opium a day. One at noon, and one before sleeping. Sometimes more, if the quality's not good." She paused and, a glum note in her voice, said, "The quality is usually good in these parts."

"You have an adequate supply on hand?"

She seemed surprised by this response, unaware that her confession had put her into the lead for the job. "I've enough for the week, I think."

"Is opium the actual reason you want to extend your trip?" I asked.

"It's part of it. I won't lie to you. I recognize I'll have to quit before I return to London. But it's not the main reason."

Another backpacker, a short woman with frizzy blond hair, entered and, after peering about, approached the bartender. I signaled him to send her away. Lucy pretended not to notice.

"Would you like to see the boat?" I asked.

An alarmed look crossed her face, and I thought that this must be a major step for her, that despite her worldliness she was not accustomed to giving her trust so freely. But then she smiled and nodded vigorously.

"Yes, please," she said.

—

The sun was beginning to set as I rowed out to the *Undine*, moored some thirty yards from shore. A high bank of solid-looking bluish gray cloud rose from the eastern horizon, its leading edge ruffled and fluted like that of an immense seashell, a godly mollusk dominating the sky; fragments of dirty pink cloud drifted beneath, resembling frayed morsels of flesh that might have been torn from the creature that once inhabited the shell, floating in an aqua medium. The river had turned slate colored, and the houseboat, with its cabin of varnished, unpainted boards and the devilish eyes painted on the bow to keep spirits at bay, looked surreal from a distance, like a new home uprooted and set adrift on a native barge, its perfect, watery reflection an impressionist trick. Lan sat cross-legged in the bow. So unchanging was his expression, his wizened features appeared carved from tawny wood, his gray thatch of hair lifting in the breeze. Deng, a cheerful, handsome teenager clad in a pair of shorts, scrambled to assist us and lashed the dinghy to the rail. He exchanged a few words in Vietnamese with Lucy and then asked if we were hungry.

The same breeze that had not had the slightest effect at the bar here drove off the mosquitoes and refreshed the air. We sat in the stern, watching the sunset spread pinks and mauves and reds across the enormous sky, staining hierarchies of cumulus that passed to the south. The lights of Stung Treng, white and yellow, beaded the dusky shore. I heard strains of music, the revving of an engine. Deng brought plates of fish and a kind of ratatouille, and we ate and talked about the French in Southeast Asia, about America's benighted president ("A grocer's clerk run amok," Lucy said of him), about writing and idiot urban planners and Borneo, where she had recently been. She had an edge to her personality, this perhaps due to working with wealthy and eccentric clients, rock stars and actors and such; yet there was a softness underlying that edge, a genteel quality I responded to, possibly because it reminded me of Kim…though this quality in Lucy seemed less a product of repression.

Deng took our plates, and Lucy asked if I had anyone back in the States, a wife or girlfriend. I told her about Kim and said she might meet me in Saigon.

"I suppose that's where I would leave you," she said. "Assuming you deem me suitable." Her mouth thinned. "I probably shouldn't put this out there, because whenever I show enthusiasm, you become reticent. But this is so wonderful." Lucy's gesture embraced the world as seen from the deck of the *Undine*. "In order to get rid of me, you may have to throw me overboard." She sat forward in the deck chair. "What are you thinking about?"

I saw no reason to delay—the prospect of spending another day at the Sekong was not an engaging one. "Welcome aboard," I said.

"Oh, gosh!" She pushed up from the chair and gave me a peck on the lips. "That's marvelous. Thanks so much."

We went inside, and I showed her the shower, the galley, and the king-size bed; then I left her to wash up and stood looking out over the river, listening to the loopy cries of lizards, alerted now and again by the plop of a fish. Night had swallowed all but the lights on the shore, and I could no longer make out Lan in the bow. Deng sat on the roof, legs dangling, reading a comic by lantern light. I felt on the brink of something ineluctable and strange, and I suspected it had to do more with Lucy than with the voyage. Kim's caution notwithstanding, I anticipated losing a piece of my soul to this forthright, tomboyish, opium woman. When I went back down, I found her on the bed, her legs stretched out, toweling her hair, wearing only a pair of panties. It looked as if two-thirds of her length were in her legs. Bikini lines demarked her small, pale breasts. A brass box of some antiquity rested on the sheets beside her.

She came out from beneath the towel and caught me staring. "I know," she said. "I'm revoltingly thin. I look better when I've put on five or six pounds, but I can't keep weight on when I'm traveling."

"You know that's bullshit," I said. "You look great. Beautiful."

"I'm scarcely beautiful, but I do have good legs. At least so I've been told." She stared at her legs, pursed her lips as if reappraising them; then she said, "I came all the way from Vientiane today, and I'm exhausted. So if you don't mind, I'll indulge my filthy habit earlier than usual this evening." She patted the box. "It's awfully bright in here. Can something be done?"

I joined her on the bed, switched on a reading lamp, and cut the overheads.

"Much better," she said.

She opened the box, removed a long pipe of wood and brass, and unwrapped yellowish paper from a pressed cake of black opium.

"I'll be completely useless once I've smoked," she said. "However, you may touch me if you like. I enjoy being touched when I'm high."

I asked if she would be aware of what was going on. "Mmm-hmm. I may act as though I'm not, but I know."

"Where do you like to be touched?"

"Wherever you wish. My breasts, my ass." She glanced up from her preparations. "My pussy. Go lightly there, if you will. Too much stimulation confuses things in here." She tapped her temple.

She pinched off a fragment of opium and began rolling it into a pellet, frowning in concentration; her hands and wrists were fully illuminated, but the rest of her body was sheathed in dimness; she might have been a trim young witch up to no good purpose, drenched in the shadow cast by her spell, preparing a special poison that required a measure of light for efficacy. She plumped the pillows, making a nest, and lay on her side.

"Kiss, please," she said.

Her lips parted and her tongue flirted with mine. She settled into the pillows and lit the pipe, her cheeks hollowing as she sucked in smoke. She relit the pipe three times, and after the last time, she could barely hold it. After watching her drowse a minute, I stripped off my clothes and lay facing her, caressing her hip, tasting the chewy plug of a nipple. Her eyes were slitted, and I couldn't tell if she was focusing on me, yet when my erection prodded her thigh, she made an approving noise. I slipped a hand under her panties, rested the heel of it on her pubic bone, thatched with dark hair, and let the weight of one finger come down onto her labia. The intimacy of the touch seemed to distress her, so I reluctantly withdrew the finger, but I continued to touch her intimately. Holding her that way became torture.

"Lucy?" I whispered.

She didn't appear to be at home. Her breathing was shallow; a faint sheen of sweat polished her brow. I had no choice but to relieve the torment as best I could.

I hadn't thought that I could take such pleasure from fondling a nearly comatose woman. The thought that she was submitting to me had been exciting. I had walled off such practices from my sexual life, yet I now found myself imagining variations on the act, and I believed that Lucy would be a willing partner to my fantasies. The woman I'd met in the bar had, over the course of a few hours, been transformed into a practicing submissive. I had known other women to exhibit a manner markedly different from that they later presented, women who, upon feeling secure in the situation, had changed as abruptly as Lucy. But Cradle Two's rice-paper model was in my head, people shunting back and forth between universes without realizing it, and I thought if I could see those women now, I would view their sudden transformation in a new light, and I speculated that this Lucy might not be the same who had climbed into the dinghy with me. One way or another, I had presumed her to be a normal, bright woman who had survived a shattering blow, but it was evident that she had picked up a kink or two along the road to recovery.

In the morning I woke to a drowned gray light, the cabin windows spotted with rain. Lucy was sitting up in bed, inspecting her stomach.

"I'm all sticky," she said, and gave me a sly smile. "You were wicked, weren't you?"

"Don't you remember?"

She gave the matter some study, screwing up her face, as might a child, into a mask of exaggerated perplexity. "It's a little hazy. I definitely remember you touching me." She scooted down beneath the sheets, snuggling close. "It made for a decent icebreaker, don't you think? There'll be less reason for nerves when we make love."

"Now you mention it, I doubt there'll be any." I clasped my hands behind my neck. "Last night was surprising to me."

"A sophisticate like you? I wouldn't have believed it possible to surprise you."

I caught her by the hair and pulled her head away from my chest, irritated by the remark. Judging by her calm face, she didn't mind the rough treatment, and I tightened my grip.

"I wasn't mocking you," she said. "I'm your admirer. Honest. Cross my heart and spit on the pope."

I released her, astonished by the behavior she had brought out in me. She flung a leg across my waist, rubbing against me, letting me feel the heated damp of her.

"Would you care to see another of my tricks?" she asked.

"What do you have?"

"Oh, I've got scads." She folded her arms on my chest, rested her chin upon them, and gazed at me soberly. "You'd be surprised, I mean really, really...*really* surprised, how wicked I can be."

—

Travel has always served to inspire me, as it has many writers, as it apparently did my alter ego; yet the farther we proceeded down the Mekong, the more I came to realize that there was a blighted sameness to the world and its various cultures. Strip away their trappings and you found that every tribe was moved by the same passions, and this was true not only in the present but also, I suspected, in ages past. Erase from your mind the images of the kings and exotic courtesans and maniacal monks that people the legends of Southeast Asia, and look to a patch of ground away from the temples and palaces of Angkor Wat—there you will find the average planetary citizen, a child eating the Khmer equivalent of a Happy Meal and longing for the invention of television.

The landscape, too, bored me. Like every river, the Mekong was a mighty water dragon, its scales shifting in hue from blue to green to brown, sometimes overflowing its banks, and along the shore were floating markets, assemblies of weathered gray shanties resting upon leaky bottoms that were not much different from shacks on the Mississippi or huts along the Nile or the disastrous slums of Quito spilling into the Guayas, fouling it with their wastes...and so I did not delight, as travelers will, in the scenting of an unfamiliar odor, because I suspected it to be the register of spoilage, and I derived no great pleasure from the dull green uniformity sliding past or in the sentinel presence of coconut palms, their fronds drooping against a yellow morning sky, or the toil of farmers (though one morning, when we passed a village where people were washing their cows in the river, I felt a twinge of interest, remarking on the possible linkage between this practice and the Saturday morning ritual of washing one's car in a suburban driveway). Neither did I have the urge to scribble excitedly in my journal about the quaint old fart who sold Lucy a bauble in a floating market and told a story in pidgin English about demons and witches, oh my! Nor did I, as might an ecotourist in his blog for true believers, fly my aquatic mammal flag at half-mast and rant about the plight of the Irrawaddy dolphins (yet another dying species) that surfaced from muddy pools near the town of Kratie. And I did not exult, like some daft birder, in the soaring river terns and kingfishers that dive-bombed the waters farther south. I was solely interested in Lucy, and my interest in her was limited.

Within a week we had developed an extensive sexual vocabulary, and though it stopped short of sea urchins and safety pins, we were depraved in our invention—that was how I might have characterized it before embarking upon the relationship, though I came to hold a more liberated view. Depravity always incorporates obsession, but our obsession had a scholarly air. We were less possessed lovers than anthropologists studying one another's culture, and because we made no emotional commitment, our passion manifested as a scientific voyeurism that allowed us to explore the scope of actual perversity with greater freedom than would have been the case if our hearts were at risk. We approached each other with coolness and calculation. "Do you like this?" one of us would ask, and if the answer was no, we would move on without injured feelings to a new pleasurable possibility. Apart from badinage, we talked rarely, and when not physically involved, we went away from each other, she to craft her business plan, sketching and writing lists, and I to sit in the stern and indulge in a bout of self-loathing and meditate on passages from *The Tea Forest* that reflected upon my situation. Five days on the Mekong had worked a change in me that I could not comprehend except in terms of Cradle Two's novel. Indeed, I lost much of the urge to comprehend it, satisfied to brood and fuck my way south. I felt something festering inside me, some old bitterness metastasizing, sprouting black claws that dug into my vitals, encouraging me to lash out; yet I had no suitable target. I yelled at Deng on occasion, at Lan less frequently (I had grown to appreciate his indifference to me); but these were petty irritations that didn't qualify for a full release, and so I lashed out against myself.

Of my many failings, the most galling was that I had wasted my gifts on genre fiction. I could have achieved much more, I believed, had I not gone for the easy money but, like Cradle Two, had been faithful to my muse. Typically, I didn't count myself to blame but assigned blame to the editors and agents who had counseled me, to the marketers and bean counters who had delimited me, and to the people with whom I had surrounded myself—wives and girlfriends, my fans, my friends. They had dragged me down to their level, seduced me into becoming a populist. I saw them in my mind's eye overflowing the chambers of my life, the many rooms of my mansion, all the rooms in fantasy and science fiction, all the crowded, half-imaginary party rooms clotted with people who didn't know how to party, who failed miserably at it and frowned at those few who could and did, and yearned with their whole hearts to lose control, yet lacked the necessary passionate disposition; all the corridors of convention hotels packed with damaged, overstuffed women, their breasts cantilevered and contoured into shelf-like projections upon which you could rest your beer glass, women who chirped about Wicca, the Tarot, and the Goddess and took the part of concubine or altar-slut in their online role-playing games; all the semi beautiful, equally damaged, semi-professional women who believed they themselves were goddesses and concealed dangerous vibrators powered by rats' brains in their purses and believed that heaven could be ascended to from the tenth floor of the Hyatt Regency in Boston, yet rejected permanent residence there as being unrealistic; all the mad, portly men with their bald heads and beards and their eyeballs in their trouser pockets, whose wives caught cancer from living with them; all the dull hustlers who blogged ceaselessly and had MacGyvered a career out of two ounces of talent, a jackknife, and a predilection for wearing funny hats, and humped the legs of their idols, who blogged ceaselessly and wore the latest fashion in emperor's new clothes and talked about Art as if he were a personal friend they had met through networking, networking, networking, building a fan base one reader at a time; all the lesser fantasists with their fantasies of one day becoming a famous corpse like Andre Breton and whose latest publications came to us courtesy of Squalling Hammertoe Woo Hoo Press and who squeezed out pretentious drivel from the jerk-off rags wadded into their skulls that one or two Internet critics had declared works of genius, remarking on their verisimilitude, saying how much they smelled like stale ejaculate, so raw and potent, the stuff of life itself; all the ultrasuccessful commercial novelists (I numbered myself among them) whose arrogance cast shadows more substantial than anything they had written and could afford, literally, to treat people like dirt; all the great men and women of the field (certain of them, anyway), the lifetime achievers who, in effect, pursed their lips as if about to say "Percy" or "piquant" when in public, fostering the impression that they squeezed their asscheeks together extra hard to produce work of such unsurpassed grandiloquence...Many of these people were my friends and, as a group, when judged against the entirety of the human mob, were no pettier, no more disagreeable or daft or reprehensible. We all have such thoughts;

we find solace in diminishing those close to us, though usually not with so much relish. And while I kept on vilifying them, spewing my venom, I recognized they were not to blame for my deficiencies and that I was the worst of them all. I had all their faults, their neuroses, their foibles, and then some—I knew myself to be a borderline personality with sociopathic tendencies, subject to emotional and moral disconnects, yet lacking the conviction of a true sociopath. The longer I contemplated the notion, the more persuaded I was to embrace the opinion espoused in *The Tea Forest* that Thomas Cradles everywhere were men of debased character. The peculiar thing was, I no longer took this judgment for an insult.

Our fifth day on the river, Lucy scored a fresh supply of opium from a floating market, and that night, a dead-still night, hot and humid as the inside of an animal's throat, once she had prepared a pipe, she held it out to me and said, "I believe the time is right."

"No, thanks," I said.

She continued to offer the pipe, her clever face ordered by a bemused expression, like a mother forcing her infant son to try a new food, one she knows he will enjoy.

"I've smoked pot," I said. "But I don't know about this."

"I promise you, you'll have a grand old time. And it'll help with the heat."

I took the pipe. "What do I do?"

"When I light the pipe, draw gently on it. You mustn't inhale deeply, just enough to guide the smoke."

It was as she said. Once guided, the smoke seemed to find its own way, plating my throat and lungs with coolness and enforcing a dizzy, drifty feeling. I lost track of what Lucy was doing, but I think she, too, smoked. We lay facing one another, and I became fascinated by the skin on her lower abdomen, pale and, due to shaving, more coarsely grained than the rest. My limbs were heavy, but I managed to extend a forefinger and touch her. The contact was so profound, I had to close my eyes in order to absorb the sensations of warmth and softness and muscularity. With effort, because I had little strength and not much volition, I succeeded in slitting my eyes, focusing on an inch of skin higher up, a tanned, curving place. My focus narrowed until I appeared to be looking at a minute fraction of her whole, a single tanned atom, and then I penetrated that atom and was immersed in a dream, something to do with a lady swimming in a pool floored by a huge white lotus, its petals lifted by gentle currents, and an anthropomorphic beast with the head of a mastiff who ate cockroaches, pinching off their heads, draining them of a minim of syrupy fluid that he chased with diamonds, grabbing a handful from a bowl at his elbow and crunching them like peanuts, a fabulous adventure that was interrupted, cut off as if the channel had been switched, and replaced by the image of a night sky into which I was ascending.

The lights in the sky appeared scattered at first but grew brighter and increasingly unified, proving to be the visible effulgence of a single creature. It was golden-white in color and many chambered, reminding me of those spectacular, luminous phantoms that range the Mindanao Trench, frail complexities surviving at depths that would crush a man in an instant; yet it was so vast, I could not have described its shape, only that it was huge and golden-white and many chambered. Its movements were slow and oceanic, a segment of the creature lifting, as though upon a tide, and then an adjacent segment lifting as the first fell, creating a rippling effect that spread across its length and breadth. All around me, black splinters were rising toward the thing, sinister forms marked by a crookedness, like hooked thorns. Dark patches formed on its surface, composed of thousands of these splinters, and it began to shrink, its chambers collapsing one into the other like the folds of an accordion being compressed. Unnerved, I tried to slow my ascent, and as I twisted and turned, flinging myself about, I glimpsed what lay behind me: a black, depthless void picked out by a single, irregular gray shape, roughly circular and, from my perspective, about the size of a throw rug. The gray thing made me nervous. I looked away, but that did nothing to ease my anxiety, and for the duration of my dream—hours, it seemed—I continued my ascent, desperate to stop, my mind clenched with fear. When I woke near first light, my heart hammered and I was covered in sweat. I recalled the mural in Stung Treng, noting the crude resemblance it bore to the glowing creature, but a more pressing matter was foremost in my thoughts.

I put my hand on Lucy's throat and shook her. She felt the pressure of my grip. Her eyes fluttered open, widened; then she said, "Is this to be something new?"

"What did you give me last night?" I asked. "It wasn't opium."

"Yes, it was!"

"I've never seen a record of anything like what I experienced."

"Not everything is written down, Tom." She moved my hand from her throat. "You're so very excitable. Tell me about it."

I summarized my evening and she said, "You may have had some sort of reaction. I doubt it will reoccur."

"I'm not smoking that shit again."

"Of course you won't." She sat up. "But to more pressing business. I may get my period today—I'm feeling crampy. So, if you want to get one in before the curse is upon me, this morning would be the time."

—

Lan had his work cut out for him. North of Kampong Cham, the Mekong was more than a mile wide, but massive dry-season sandbars rendered the river almost impassable. Often there was a single navigable channel and that had to be located, so we went more slowly than usual, with Deng going on ahead of the *Undine* in the dinghy, taking soundings. To break the monotony, we camped one night on an island where we found driftwood caught in the limbs of trees fifteen and twenty feet high, pointing up the dramatic difference in water level between the rainy season and the dry. We erected a tentlike structure of mosquito netting and lounged beneath it, drinking gin and watching a strangely monochromatic sunset bronze the western sky, resolving into a pageantry of yellows and browns. Deng cooked over an open fire on the beach, preparing a curry. As darkness closed down around us, there was an explosion of moths, nearly hiding him from view (we glimpsed him squatting by the fire, a shamanic figure occulted by flurrying wings), and when he brought the curry to us, what was supposed to be a vegetarian dish had been thickened by uncountable numbers of moths. Lucy had a nibble and declared it to be: "Not bad. They give it kind of a meaty flavor." I had been incredibly careful about food since arriving in Asia, wanting to spare myself the misery of stomach problems, but I was hungry and stuffed myself.

The following morning I was stricken with severe diarrhea. I blamed the moths and Deng. He kept out of my way for the next two days. On the third day, while resting in the stern, I caught sight of him on the island helping Lucy fly a kite, and then, later that afternoon, I saw him sneaking into our cabin. Thinking he might be stealing, hoping for it, in fact (I was feeling better and wanted an excuse to exercise my temper), I went inside. Lucy was sitting on the bed, leaning toward Deng, whose back was to me. He appeared to be fumbling with his shorts. I shouted, and after tossing me a terrified glance over his shoulder, he bolted for the door.

"What the fuck's going on?" I asked.

"For God's sake," Lucy said. "Don't act so wronged."

I was taken aback by her mild reaction—I had expected a denial.

"I took pity on him," she said. "There's no reason for you to be upset."

"You felt bad, so you were going to blow him?"

She frowned. "If you must know, I was going to manipulate him."

"A hand job? Oh, well. If I'd known that's all it was...Shit. My mom used to give the paperboy hand jobs. Dad would look on and beam."

She gave me a defiant look.

"Are you serious?" I asked. "You don't see you did anything wrong?"

We held a staring contest, and then she said, "Can you imagine being sixteen, trapped on a boat with people who're having sex as much as we do? He was pathetic, really."

"So he came to you and asked for a hand job? And you said, 'Oh, Deng, soulful child of the Third World...'"

"He asked for considerably more than that. I told him it was all I could manage." She crossed her legs and gazed out at the river. "Since we've been going at it, I've had an almost ecumenical attitude toward sex. It's not as though we're in love, yet that's the feeling I get when I'm in love. It makes me wonder if I've ever been in love."

"Ecumenical? You mean like you want to spread it around?"

"That's one way of putting it," she said frostily.

"I don't want you to feel that way. I'm territorial in the extreme."

"Yes, I'm beginning to grasp that." She stretched out on the bed, placed her hand on a paperback that lay open beside her. "It won't happen again."

I sat next to her on the edge of the bed. "Is that all you have to say?"

"Do you want an apology? I apologize. I should have known it would distress you." She waited for me to respond and then said, "Should I leave? I'd rather not, but it's your boat. If you're determined to view what I've done as a betrayal..."

"No, I'm just confused."

"About what?"

"About your attitude...and mine. I don't understand why I'm not angrier."

"Look," she said. "Do you really believe I'm seeking another sexual outlet? That I'm not getting enough? Nymphomaniacs don't get this much."

"Yeah, okay," I said, still dubious.

"So, are we going to move past this?"

If she was lying, she deserved a pass on the basis of poise alone. I grudgingly said, "It might take me a while."

"How long would you reckon 'a while' to be? Long enough for you to feel horny again?"

To get her off the subject, I asked what she was reading.

She showed me the cover of *The Tea Forest* and said, "I'd forgotten how brilliant this was."

It took me a second or two to process her remark. "You've read *The Tea Forest*? Before this trip, I mean?"

"Didn't I tell you?"

"You said you'd read one of my books, but you never said which."

"This was the only one I could find. The clerk in the bookstore mentioned that you'd gone off writing…or something to that effect. I guess he wasn't aware of your recent work."

I told her I was feeling queasy and, taking the satellite phone, went into the stern and called my agent. I asked if he had turned over every stone in hunting for a book called *The Tea Forest* by Thomas Cradle. He was concerned for my well-being and asked if I wasn't carrying this a little too far; he told me that they had begun publicizing the hoax, and hundreds of fans (including librarians, collectors, and so forth) had written in to my website claiming to have done exhaustive searches, none yielding a result. That left me with the proposition, however preposterous, that Lucy was not of this universe…not this particular Lucy, at any rate. I had no idea when the current incarnation had come aboard or when she might disembark, and then I realized something that, if I hadn't been flattered by her recognition of me at the Sekong Hotel, might have alerted me to her origin much earlier. I had grown a beard and let my hair grow long, drastically altering my appearance. It was Cradle Two whom she had recognized, probably from his author photograph, and this helped establish that she, the Lucy of the Sekong Hotel, had shifted over from an adjoining universe. Or perhaps I had been the one who shifted. According to Cradle Two, so many people and things were constantly shifting back and forth, that such distinctions scarcely mattered.

Picking through this snarl of possibility, I thought that Lucy and I might have shifted many times during the previous two weeks and that the Lucy of the Sekong might not be the Lucy of this moment—*The Tea Forest* must exist in more than one universe—and it occurred to me that the novel presented a means of crudely defining the situation. Every hour or so for the remainder of the day, I asked Lucy a question pertaining to *The Tea Forest*. She answered each to my satisfaction, which proved nothing; but the next morning, while she trimmed her toenails in the stern, I asked if she found the ending anticlimactic, and she said crossly, "Are you mad? You know I haven't had time to read it."

"The ending?" I asked. "You haven't read the ending?"

"I haven't even begun the book! Must I repeat that information every half-hour?"

Two hours later I asked her a variation on the question, and she replied that the ending had been her favorite part of the novel and followed this by saying that it would have been out of character for TC to complete the journey. He was a coward, and his cowardice was its own resolution. To end the book any other way would have been dramatically false and artistically dishonest. I (Cradle Two) was a modernist author, she said, prowling at the edges of the genre, and had I taken TC into the tea forest, I would have had to lapse into full-blown fantasy, something she doubted I could write well. She went on to dismiss much of postmodernism as having "an overengineered archness" and, except for a few exemplary authors, being a refuge for those writers whose "disregard for traditional narrative (was) an attempt to disguise either their laziness or their inability to master it." She concluded with a none-too-brief lecture on cleverness as a literary eidolon, a quality "too frequently given the stamp of genius during this postmillennial slump."

After listening to her ramble on for the better part of an hour, I was disinclined to ask further questions, and truthfully there was no need—I had proved to my satisfaction that Cradle Two's model of the universe was accurate in some degree, and I wanted Wicked Lucy back, not this pretentious windbag. I went outside and paced the length of the *Undine*, sending Deng scuttering away, and tried to make sense out of what was going on, overwhelmed by feelings of helplessness brought on by my new understanding of the human condition, a condition to which I had paid lip service, yet now was forced to accept as an article of faith. "The river was change," Cradle Two (and perhaps Cradles 3, 4, 5, ad infinitum) had written. "It flowed through the less mutable landscape, carrying change like a plague, defoliating places that once were green, greening places that once were barren, mutating the awareness of the people who dwelled along it, infecting them with a horrid inconstancy, doing so with such subtlety that few remembered those places as having ever been different." It had been my intention to shoot straight down the Mekong to the delta and spend most of the six weeks there; but now, recalling this passage,

I felt a vibration in my flesh and panicked, fearing that the vibration, my fixation on the delta, and, indeed, every thought in my head, might reflect the inconstancy cited by Cradle Two. I had begun to feel a pull, a sense of being summoned to the delta that alarmed me; I sloughed this off as being the product of an overwrought imagination, but nonetheless it troubled me. For these reasons, I decided to break the trip, as Cradle Two's narrator had done, hoping to find stability away from the river, a spot where change occurred less frequently, and stop for a week, or perhaps longer, in what once had been the capitol of evil on earth, Phnom Penh.

—

In the future I expect there to be systems that will allow a boy on a bicycle, balancing a block of ice on his handlebars, to pedal directly from Phnom Penh into the heart of Manhattan, where thousands will applaud and toss coins, which will stick to his skin, covering him like the scales of a pangolin, and he will bring with him wet heat and palm shadow and a sudden, fleeting touch of coolness in the air, and there will follow the smells of moto exhaust, of a street stall selling rice porridge sweetened with cinnamon and soup whose chief ingredient is cow entrails, the dry odor of skulls at Tuol Sieng prison, marijuana smoke, all the essences of place and moment, every potential answer to the Cambodian riddle fractionated and laid out for our inspection. Until then, it will be necessary to travel, to not drink the water, to snap poorly composed pictures, to be hustled by small brown men, to get sick and rent unsatisfactory hotel rooms. I yearned for that future. I wanted to live in the illusion that persuades us that true-life experience can be obtained on the Internet. Barring that, I wanted to find lodgings as anti-Cambodian as possible, one of the big American-style hotels, an edifice that I felt would be resistant to the processes of change. Wicked Lucy, however, insisted we take a room at the Hotel Radar 99, where she had stayed on a previous visit.

The hotel was situated in an old quarter of the city, well away from modernity of the kind I favored, and no element of the place seemed to have the least relation to the concepts of either radar or ninety-nine. The building was three stories of decrepit stone that had been worn to an indefinite salmon hue—it might originally have been orange or pink (impossible to say which)—and had green French doors that opened onto precarious balconies with ironwork railings. Faded, sagging awnings skirted that section of the block, overhanging restaurants and shops of various kinds; and parked along the curb at every hour of day or night were between ten and twenty motos, the owners of which, according to Lucy, provided the guests, mostly expats, with drugs, women, and whatever else they might want in the way of perversity. You entered through a narrow door (the glass portion painted over with indigo) and came into a dark green-as-a-twilit-jungle foyer, throttled with ferns and fleshy-leaved plants. There was never anyone behind the reception desk. You were compelled to shout, and then maybe Mama-san (the elderly Japanese woman who owned the place) would respond, or maybe not. Beyond lay a tiny courtyard where two clipped parrots squabbled on their perch. Our room was on the second floor, facing back toward the entrance, the metal number 4 turned sideways on the door. Apart from lizards clinging to the wall, its decor was purely utilitarian: a handful of wooden chairs; a writing desk that may once have had value as an antique; three double beds about which mosquito netting could be lowered, all producing ghastly groans and squeaks whenever we sat on them and playing a cacophonous avant-garde freakout each time we made love. The bathroom was also an antique, with a claw-footed bathtub, a chain-pull toilet, and venerable tile floors. Stains memorializing lizard and insect death bespotted the cream-colored walls and high ceilings. Everything smelled of cleaning agents, a good sign in those latitudes.

I spent five days rooted to the room, trying to deny and resist change, infrequently stepping out onto the balcony to survey the street or going into the corridor overlooking the courtyard to observe the tranquil life of the hotel. I could detect no change in my surroundings—proof of nothing, but I grew calmer nonetheless. A German couple was staying in the room on our left, two Italian girls on our right. Farther along: Room 2 was home to a pair of twenty-somethings: a thin, long-haired man with a pinched, bony face and a Canadian flag embroidered on his jeans and a gorgeous gray-eyed blonde with full breasts and steatopygian buttocks. She was the palest person I had met in Cambodia, her skin whiter than the bathroom tiles (covered, as they were, by a grayish film). I never saw her leave the room, not completely. She would open the door and, without letting loose of it, as if it were all that kept her from drifting away, offer a frail, zoned, "Hi," then hover for a while, looking as though she were going to make some further comment, before fluttering her fingers and vanishing inside. Once at noon, when the sunlight brightened the courtyard floor, casting a lace of shadow from a jacaranda tree onto the stone floor, she performed this ritual emergence half-nude, dressed in a tank top, her pubic hair a shade darker than that on her head, yet firmly within the blonde spectrum. It became evident that she was distressed about her boyfriend—he was overdue, probably off buying drugs (heroin or opium, I guessed), and she hoped these appearances at the door would hurry him along.

After five days Lucy tired of indulging me, of bringing me food, and coaxed me outside. I began taking walks around the immediate neighborhood, but I had no desire to explore farther afield. I had been to Phnom Penh twenty years before, and I had snapped pictures of the temples of Angkor Wat, skulls, the Killing Fields, crypts overgrown by the enormous roots of trees, and I had slept with expat girls and taxi girls, and I had partied heartily in this terrible place where death was a tourist attraction, getting kicked out of bars for fighting and out of one of the grand old colonial hotels along the river for public drunkenness. I needed no further experience of the country and was content to inhabit a few square blocks, reconciling myself to the idea that things had always changed around me, and how were you to distinguish between normal change and a change promulgated by a transition from one universe to the other? Did such a thing as normal change even exist? People, for example, were so predictable in their unpredictability. Amazing, how they could do a one-eighty on you at the drop of a hat, how their moods varied from moment to moment. Perhaps this was all due to physics, to universes like strips of rice paper blown by a breeze and touching each other, exchanging people and insects and corners of rooms for almost identical replicas; perhaps without this universal interaction people would be ultrareliable and their behavior would not defy analysis, and every relationship would be a model of logic and consistency, and peace could be negotiated, and problems, great and small alike, could be easily solved or would never have existed. Perhaps the breeze that blew the strips of rice paper together was the single consequential problem, and that problem was insoluble. I understood that what had panicked me was a fundamental condition of existence, one that a mistaken apprehension of consensus reality had caused me to overlook. I further understood that I could adapt to my recently altered perception of this condition and found consolation in the idea that I could train myself to be as blind as anyone.

Around the corner from the hotel was a restaurant that sold fruit shakes. A young girl tended it. She stood behind a table that supported a glass display case in which there were finger bananas, papayas and several fruits I could not identify, bottled milk and various sweeteners in plastic tubs. She spent much of her day cleaning up after a puppy that wandered among a forest of table legs, sniffing for food, pausing now and again to piss and shit—thus the fecal odor that undercut the sugary smell of the place. In the darkened interior were blue wooden chairs and tables draped in checkered plastic cloths and poster ads featuring Cambodian pop stars stapled to the walls. On the fourth day after I started going out, Lucy and I were having fruit shakes when the blonde girl from the hotel wandered in, clutching a large straw bag of the sort used for shopping. She sat against the back wall, staring out at the street, where a couple of moto cowboys were attempting wheelies, the *brraaap* of their engines overriding the restaurant's radio. Lucy waved to her, but the blonde gave no reaction. Her skin was faintly luminous, like ghost skin, and her expression vacant.

"I'm going to see what's wrong," Lucy said.

"Nothing's wrong," I said. "She wants a shake."

Lucy pitied me with a stare. "I'll be back shortly."

She joined the blonde at her table, and they spoke together in muted voices. With their heads together, one light and one dark, they posed a yin-yang juxtaposition, and as I sipped my shake, I thought about having them both, a fleeting thought that had no more weight than would the notion of taking a shot at Cate Blanchett. One of the moto cowboys pulled up facing the restaurant and shouted—he wore what looked to be a fishing hat with a turned-up brim, the word LOVE spelled out in beads on the crown, and he appeared to aim his shout at the blonde. She paid him no mind, busy conferring with Lucy. He shrugged, spoke to someone on the sidewalk I couldn't see, and rode off. The puppy bumped into my foot. I nudged him aside and concentrated on sucking a piece of papaya through my straw. When I looked up, Lucy had taken the blonde by an elbow and was steering her toward our table.

"This is Riel," Lucy said. "Riel, this is Thomas."

Her eyes lowered, the blonde whispered, "Hi."

"That's an interesting name," I said. "It's spelled the same as the currency?"

The question perplexed her, and I said, "Cambodian money. The riel? Is it spelled the same?"

"I guess." At Lucy's prompting, she took a seat. "It's French. Like Louis Riel."

"Who?" I asked.

"A famous Canadian. The Father of Manitoba."

"I didn't know Manitoba had a father," said Lucy pertly.

"Tell me about him," I said.

"People say he was a madman," Riel said. "He prayed obsessively. They hanged him for treason."

"And yet he fathered Manitoba." Lucy grinned.

"Mitch says they must have named the money over here for him, too," Riel said.

The counter girl, who had ignored her to this point, came over and asked if she wanted something.

"Make her a banana shake," Lucy said, surprising me that she would know what Riel wanted.

I asked Riel if she was from Manitoba, and she said, "Yes. Winnipeg." Then she asked Lucy if she could have custard apple instead of banana.

I inquired as to who Mitch was, and Lucy said, "The ass who was with her. He ran off with their money. I told her she should stay with us until she figures out what to do."

This snatch of conversation summed Riel up—she saw her beauty as a type of currency and was, perhaps, mad—and summed up our relationship with her as well. It seemed Lucy had found someone more submissive than she herself was. She sent messages with her eyes saying that she wanted this to happen.

"Yeah, sure," I said.

Riel greedily drank her shake, eschewing a straw. She was, if you overlooked her drug abuse, a sublime creature possessed by a serene absence.

Once she finished her shake, Lucy went off with her, saying that they were going to "get something" for Riel. I went back to the hotel and read and stared out the window. The sky was almost cloudless, a few puffs drifting high, but then it flickered, the entire blue expanse appearing to wink out, like a television image undergoing a momentary loss of power, and a large cloud roughly resembling a canoe appeared in the lower sky; the roofline above which it floated also seemed different, though I couldn't have told you how. But the canoe-shaped cloud...I was certain it had not been there seconds before. I expected another flicker, and when none came, I was relieved; and yet I felt again that summoning toward the south. A longing pervaded me, a desire to be on the move, and that longing intensified, faded, intensified...It was as if, having risen to the bait of *The Tea Forest*, something was tugging gently on the line, trying to set the hook deep before reeling me in.

After an hour the women returned and went into the bathroom, where they remained for twenty-five minutes. When they emerged, Riel was topless and wobbly. A trickle of blood ran down her arm—it might have been a scarlet accessory designed to contrast with her milky skin. With an arm about her waist, Lucy helped her to lie on the bed next to ours, cleaned away the blood, and wrangled off her jeans. Riel fell into a light sleep. Lucy started to disrobe.

"What was all that in the bathroom?" I asked, putting down my book.

"She had trouble getting a vein." Lucy skinned out of her panties. "I assisted."

"And now?"

She put a finger to her lips and stretched out beside Riel and began to caress her. This male fantasy held no particular appeal for me in the abstract, yet now I was captivated by Lucy's tenderness and thoroughness. She left no area of Riel's skin unexplored, licking and rubbing against her with the delicacy of a cat. The bed played an oriental music of squeaks and *sproings* when she went down on her, a lengthy symphony with prolonged, hushed spaces between the notes, reflecting discrete movements of Lucy's fingers and tongue. They achieved a simultaneous climax, Lucy digging between her own legs with her left hand, letting forth a gasp, and Riel, becoming active at the end, crying out while holding Lucy's head in place.

Lucy wiped her mouth dry on the sheet. She crossed to the bed upon which I lay and took my hand, saying she wanted to watch me make love to Riel. I needed no urging, but her eagerness made me self-conscious and briefly reinstituted a morality that viewed the world through prim spectacles and characterized such behavior as degenerate and vile. I said something to the effect that I didn't know or I wasn't sure, a delaying action; but Lucy pressed a condom into my hand.

"Hurry," she said. "While she's still wet."

—

I liked how Riel, a sleepy heroin girl, would coast in sex, gliding, billowing, alone on her white ocean when I was joined to her. That first time, though, when she gazed up at me with Chinese eyes, those gray irises and shrunken pupils gazing out from a beautiful porcelain mask, old eyes weary of something, perhaps of everything, she seemed the embodiment of a Zen wisdom—by sinking to the bottom of the world, surrendering herself to its flood, she had gained infinite knowledge through the rejection of knowledge. I turned her onto her stomach in order to avoid her eyes, wishing to remain ignorant of whatever she might know about me in her Buddha ignorance, and soon roused a clanking, violent music from the bed.

Riel was all about appetite. When she ate, she ate wholeheartedly, and when she drank, she drank single-mindedly, and when she was inspired to talk, she talked a blue streak, and when she fucked, although stoned, never as active as Lucy, she gave it her all. I asked her if heroin didn't muffle the sexual drive, and she said, "Yes…but once you get started, it's kind of cool." She and Lucy and I deployed our bodies in every possible permutation, and over the span of several days, I learned there was a qualitative difference between their addictions, one that defined their drugs of choice. Compared to Lucy's elaborate ritual with the pipe, Riel's affair with the needle had a decidedly American character (stick it in and get off). This distinction carried over into their attitudes toward sex, and I was led to generalize that whereas opium women might prefer to grill thin slices of your heart, skewering each with a toothpick, devouring it over a period of years, heroin girls will, if given the chance, swallow it in three quick bites. Riel became increasingly needy—needy for food, alcohol, drugs, and orgasms. I could empathize with her boyfriend. Had we been alone together, I would have dumped her myself. Beauty is not sufficient compensation for a demanding nature. But with Lucy to share the load, her demands were acceptable.

I discovered that a threesome required more drama to sustain it than did a twosome, and at first we manufactured drama. Games became the order of the day. Often Lucy and Riel would get high, leaving me to orchestrate these exercises. I enjoyed having two women, limp as dolls, whom I could exploit however I chose. When that became boring, I let Lucy take the lead. One afternoon she insisted I read a passage from *The Tea Forest* before having sex with Riel. The passage involved Cradle Two's narrator speaking to a German girl he had picked up in a Phnom Penh bar during the break in his trip. He had just finished helping her fix and was dictating the terms of their relationship. In speaking the lines, I felt an absolute conviction, as if my voice and Cradle Two's had merged:

" 'If you have to puke again,' I said, 'go outside, okay?'

"The girl tried to focus, but she gave it up; her head lolled, and an arm slipped off the sofa, her fingers trailing in the vomit.

" 'I'm not your pimp,' I told her. 'I'm not going to be your pimp. What I'm going to do is use you to attract a certain class of man. You want to fuck for money, okay, I'll pay you. Don't let the men I set you up with pay you. You'll probably have to do two or three tricks. For now, though, I'll be the only one fucking you. I need to make sure you can do the things they like. I'll keep you in dope and give you a place to live. I'll regulate your drugs...that way you won't get too big a habit. You have to learn to manage your habit. You can't do that, you're on your own.' "

Prior to this, I had, of course, recognized the resonance between the addition of Riel to our union and Cradle Two's novel—indeed, I had done little other than recognize such resonances since beginning the trip. More to the point, reading the passage brought home to me how much of the veneer of the civilized man had worn off. I was a long walk from becoming an unregenerate criminal like the narrator of *The Tea Forest*, and perhaps I would never achieve that level of criminality; but I was headed down the path he had trod. At one point I considered calling Kim and making a stab at redemption, hoping that her rational voice would reorient me; but Lucy and Riel stared at me with dull opiated expectancy from a nipple-to-nipple embrace, and I decided that the call could wait.

We started going out at night into the neon-braided streets of central Phnom Penh, putting on one-act plays in the thick, hothouse air, treating that city of a million souls as if its mad traffic and buzzing motos, its brutal history and doleful present, were merely a backdrop for our entertainments. We, or rather Lucy and Riel, sought out fortune-tellers, those who lined the riverbank by day, when the parks were thronged with tai chi practitioners and tourists and badminton players, and by night, when the poor gathered with their children to squat along the embankment eating boiled eggs and fried beetles, and the prosperous fortune-tellers with fancy booths at Wat Phnom, their altars adorned with strings of Christmas tree lights, candles, incense, and bowls of fruit, and cluttered with porcelain sages, Ramayana monkeys, Buddhas with holographic halos sheltering beneath gilt parasols...A more generous writer might have inferred that this profusion of seers and charlatans was but a veneer masking the rich spiritual life of the populace, always in communion with the city of ghosts that interpenetrated with and cast a pall over the city of blood and stone; and yet it meant nothing to me, or, to be accurate, it might someday provide the background detail for a story, and if a host of sad phantoms had materialized before me, creatures with bleak, negative eyes and bodies of lacy ectoplasm, I would have taken due notice and then done my best to ignore them, being consumed by other mysteries. We shooed away beautiful lady-boys and Cambodian kids with dyed Mohawks who were trying to prove something by bumming cigarettes from Americans, and we discouraged the taxi girls who came at platoon strength from alley mouths and bars, girls in their teens and maybe younger, chirping slogans from the hookers' English phrase book and then retreating in sullen disarray, chiding one another in singsong Khmer for being too aggressive or not aggressive enough. We disregarded the entreaties of ragged amputees and blind men with bowls, and we ate hallucinatory food from stalls, bugs and guts and whatnot, and inspected vendors' wares—the arms dealers were of especial interest to me. They commonly operated on street corners (some nights, in certain quarters, there seemed to be one on almost every corner) and offered a wide selection of handguns and ammo, the odd assault weapon—hardly surprising in a country where you could, I'd been told, blow away a cow with a rocket launcher for a fee of two hundred dollars, less if you were prepared to haggle. I saw in them the future of my own country, where death was celebrated with equal enthusiasm, although candy-coated by Technicolor and video games and television news. When the coating finally wore off, as it threatened to do, there we would all be, in Cambodia.

As we strolled along Street 51 one night, after a late supper at a grand old colonial hotel on the riverfront near Wat Phnom hill, we happened upon a blue wall bearing the painted silhouette of a girl flying a kite, a Beardsley-like illustration; beside it were the words HEART OF DARKNESS BAR. In addition, there was a painting on the door very much like the mural on the market stall in Stung Treng. I wanted to check the place out, intrigued by the mural, by the name of the bar and the juxtaposed irony of the sign, but Lucy said it was dangerous, that the Coconut Gang hung out there, and someone had recently been murdered on the premises.

"What's a Coconut Gang?" I asked.

"Rich assholes. Khmer punks and their bodyguards. Please! Let's go somewhere else."

"All I want is to have a quick look."

"This is no place to play tourist."

"I'm not playing at anything. I'm a writer. I can use shit like this."

"Yes, I imagine being shot could prove an invaluable resource. Silly me."

"Nothing like that's going to happen."

"Do you have the slightest idea of where you are? Haven't you noticed this is a hostile environment? They don't care if you're a bloody writer. They don't discriminate to that degree. To them, you're simply an idiot American poking his nose in where it's not wanted."

A smattering of Cambodians had paused in their promenade to kibbitz, amused by our argument. Feeling exposed, I said, "All right. Fine... whatever. Let's just go, okay?"

Lucy looked around. "Where's Riel?"

We found her in the entryway of the club, staring at a stuffed green adder in a bottle and being stared at by two security men. Mounted on walls throughout the main room were dozens of bottles, some containing snakes, other objects less readily identifiable, and bizarre floral arrangements, someone's flawed conception of the Japanese form. Riel evaded Lucy's attempt to corral her and went deeper into the club, which was also a misconception, an Asian version of a western bar with a big dance floor and booths but with the details, the accents, all wrong. The dance floor was packed with Cambodian men and taxi girls and young expats working out to "Smells Like Teen Spirit." As we proceeded through the club, every couple of feet we crossed into a zone dominated by a new perfume or cologne.

We located a niche in the crowd at the bar, and when the harried bartender deigned to notice us, we ordered drinks. The clamor and the loud music oppressed me, and the young Khmer men in body-hugging silk shirts and gold watches and Italian shoes who eyed Riel made me uneasy. I wasn't disturbed by the possibility of her straying—my attitude toward her was devoid of possessiveness—but I presumed she might be a source of trouble; though the place did not seem dangerous, just another drunken revel in post-millennial Southeast Asia, expressing the relief Asians felt on having survived the worst life had to offer, or so they believed…or so I thought they believed. I realize now that it was the same party, more or less, that has been going on for as long as there have been party people.

One drink, I estimated, would be the limit of my tolerance for the Heart of Darkness; but a college-age American kid pushing through the press, Dan Something, muscular and patchily bearded, a frat type on holiday, was brought up short by the sight of Riel. He struck up a shouted conversation with her, bought her a second drink, and invited us to join him and his friends in one of the many private rooms that opened off the main space; there we could talk more comfortably. Riel turned him down, but Marilyn Manson's "Tainted Love" started to play, a song that made me want to break things, particularly Marilyn Manson, and I accepted.

Inside the private room (black walls; furnished with a grouping of easy chairs and a sofa; centered by a coffee table upon which lay a pack of cigarettes, cigarette papers, and a heap of marijuana), Dan introduced us to Sean, a hulking, three-hundred pound, shaven-headed version of himself, his lap occupied by a teenage taxi girl in T-shirt and knock-off designer jeans, tiny as a pet monkey by comparison, and Mike, also accessorized by a taxi girl, a lean, saturnine guy with evil-Elvis sideburns, multiple facial piercings, and tats, the most prominent being a full sleeve on his right arm, a gaudy jungle scene that was home to tigers, temples, and fantastic lizards. Dan, Riel, Lucy, and I squeezed onto the sofa; I was all but pushed out of the conversation, and had to lean forward to see what was happening at the opposite end, where Dan had isolated Riel, sitting between her and Lucy. Air conditioning iced the room, and the din of the dance floor was reduced to a thumping rumor.

Dan and Sean (Sean was a little man's name—in a perfect world, he would have been named Lothar) had recently arrived from Thailand and spoke rapturously of Khao San Road, the backpacker street in Bangkok. This identified them, if they had not already been so identified, as a familiar species of idiot. Khao San was a strip of guesthouses, internet cafés, bars, tattoo joints, travel agents, etc., where each night, indulging in the distillation of the backpacker experience, hundreds of drunken expats assembled to gobble deep fried scorpions and buy sarongs and wooden bracelets at the stalls lining the street, and—their faces growing solemn—to swap stories about the spiritual insights they had received while whizzing past some temple or another in a VIP bus. They had hooked up with Mike, a college bud, in Phnom Penh. He had been in-country for less than three weeks yet talked about Cambodia with the jaded air of a long-term resident. I guessed him to be the brains of the outfit.

Dan held forth at some length about his hour-and-a-half tour of the Killing Fields, explaining to the ever-so-blitzed Riel (she had added three drinks and the better part of two joints to her chemical constituency) how it had been majorly depressing, yet life affirming and life changing. The Cambodian people were awesome, and his respect for them was so heartfelt, I mean like totally, that he managed to work up a tear, a trick that foretold a future in show biz and may have achieved the desired response among the inebriated breeding stock back in Champaign-Urbana, where he attended school, inducing them to roll over and spread, overborne by the sensitive depths of his soul; but it zipped right past Riel. Listening to him gave me a feeling of superiority, and I could have kept on listening for quite some time; but Lucy was unhappy, pinched between me and Dan, and I thought it appropriate to drop a roach into the conversational soup.

Leaning forward, I asked, "Why don't you have a taxi girl like your pals here?"

Dimly, Dan seemed to perceive this as a threat to his ambitions toward Riel. A notch appeared in his brow, and he squinted at me meanly. Then inspiration struck, perhaps an illumination akin to his moral awakening at the Killing Fields. He acquired an expression of noble forbearance and said, "I don't do whores."

Sean loosed a doltish chuckle; the faces of the taxi girls went blank.

"Seriously," Dan said, addressing first me, then Riel. "I revere women too much to want to just use their bodies."

"Shit, man," Mike said, and he burst out laughing. This set everyone to laughing, with the exception of Riel. Our laughter drowned out Dan's earnest protests, and once it had subsided, Mike confided to us that Dan's girl had fled the room. "She was one psycho bitch," he said. "One second she's grabbing his junk, the next she's talking a fucking mile a minute, pointing at shit."

"What was she pointing to?" Lucy asked.

"Fuck if I know. I was too wasted, and she was talking Cambodian, anyway."

Lucy inquired of the taxi girls in Khmer and, following a back-and-forth, gave her report. "She said the room was different."

"Huh?" said Sean.

"That's what they told me."

"I like being used," Riel said out of the blue.

This alerted even Dan, who had been sulking.

"It makes me feel, you know..." Riel spaced on the thought.

"How *does* it make you feel?" asked Mike.

Riel deliberated and said at last, "When Tom comes inside me, it's like I'm being venerated." She turned her calm face to me. "I wish you'd come in me without a rubber, so when I walk around I could feel it running down my thigh. It'd be like a reminder of what you felt. Of what I felt." She looked to Lucy. "You know what I mean? Isn't it that way for you?"

Lucy's head twitched—it might have been a nod—and she compressed her lips. The college boys stared at me in wonderment. They had,

I thought, taken me for a relative or some kind of neutered loser. The taxi girls were transfixed, hanging on Riel's every word.

"It's because I'm beautiful, I feel that way, I think. Mitch always told me I was beautiful. Lately he wasn't being honest, but he believed it once upon a time. Now, with you guys..." She smiled at Lucy and me. "I'm this exotic country you've traveled to. Like Cambodia. I'm a lot like Cambodia. The land of beautiful women." She waved at the taxi girls. "You're absolutely perfect. You are. You've got these perfect titties. So firm, I don't have to touch them to know."

Sean's girl blushed; he gaped at Riel.

"Mine are too soft." She glanced at her breasts. "Don't you think?"

Lucy and I answered at the same time, her saying, "No," and me saying, "They're fine."

This, the implication that the three of us were in a relationship, provoked Mike to say delightedly, "Fuck!"

"Could I have another drink?" asked Riel, and, turning to Dan: "Maybe you could bring me a drink?"

He hesitated, but Mike said, "Yeah, get us all one, man," and he went off with our drink order; the door opening allowed a gust of music inside.

Lucy started to speak, but Riel cut in line and said to me, "Mitch wanted to sell me to other men, but I wouldn't let him. I wonder if that's why he left."

"Beats me," I said.

"You wouldn't sell me, would you, Tom?"

I had a pretty fair buzz going, but nevertheless I noted that this was another disturbing resonance between my life and *The Tea Forest.* "There's no need," I said. "I'm rich."

With a finger, Riel broke the circle of moisture her glass had made on the table. "I don't guess it matters. Someone's always using you."

"Oh, for heaven's sake! I am fed up with your dreary pronouncements!" Lucy put the back of one hand against her brow, a move suitable to an actress in a silent film, and imitated Riel's fey voice: "It's all so morbidly banal!" She dropped the impersonation and said angrily, "If you reduced your drug intake, you might have a sunnier outlook."

Unruffled, Riel said, "You're not where I am yet. You'll have to increase your drug intake to catch up."

Sean and Mike glanced at each other. I could almost see a word balloon with two downward spikes above their heads, saying in thought italics: *This is way cool!* The taxi girls lost interest and idly fondled their new best friends; but their interest was restored when Riel asked Mike if he planned to have sex with his girl there in the room.

"If you'll have sex with Tom and Lucy," he said.

"No," I said.

"Why not, man? We're all friends."

"Little orgy action. Yeah," said Sean, and had a toke off a joint that his taxi girl held to his lips.

"You haven't even introduced us to your dates," I said to Mike. "That's not very friendly."

"Hey, fuck yourself, dude," said Sean, suddenly gone surly, no doubt due to some critical level of THC having been surpassed.

Mike said, "Oh-oh! You don't want to be getting Sean upset. My man's third team All American. He's a beast."

Sean glared at him. "Fuck you, too."

"Really?" I leaned back and crossed my legs. "What position do you play? No, let me guess. You're an *offensive* lineman, right?"

Lucy put a cautioning hand on my knee.

"Nose guard," said Sean, unmindful of the emphasis I'd placed on the word *offensive*.

Riel started singing, a breathy, wordless tune that drew everyone's notice, and then broke it off to say, "Your friend's been gone a long time."

"It's nuts out there," said Mike. "He's probably still trying to get served."

"Or hooking up with another whore." Sean extended a hand to Mike, who slapped him five but did so listlessly, as though out of obligation.

The door flew inward, and a diminutive Cambodian, one of the gold watch/silk shirt crowd, with a high polish to his hair and an inconsequential mustache, burst into the room, along with the pumping beat of a Madonna song. He shouted at the taxi girls. Behind him was an older man whose eyes ranged the room. Lucy caught at my hand. The taxi girls, too, shouted; their shrill voices mixed incoherently with that of the younger man. Sean dumped his taxi girl onto the floor and stood, his face a beefy caricature of disdain. The older man produced an automatic pistol from behind his back, aimed it at Sean, and spoke to him sharply in Khmer.

"Get down!" Lucy said. "He's telling you to get on your knees!"

Looking dumfounded, Sean obeyed. The taxi girl scrambled up, confronting the young man. They both began to yell, and then he punched her flush in the face, knocking her to the floor. Sean said something, I wasn't sure what. The older man butt-ended him, and he slumped across the taxi girl's legs. She sat against the wall, dazed and bleeding from the mouth. The other taxi girl was still shouting, but the shouts seemed remote, as did the sight of Mike frozen in his chair. The shock I had felt when the incident began had evolved into the kind of fright that grips you when your car spins out of control on an icy road; everything slowed to a crawl. Lucy sheltering against my arm, Riel gazing with mild interest at the gun, Sean moaning and clutching his head—all that was in focus, remarkably clear, yet it was like a child's puzzle with a very few pieces that I couldn't solve. I had the knowledge that whatever was going to happen would happen, and I would die in that little icy black room with Madonna woodling about love and a hooting, arm-waving, hip-shaking crowd attempting to cover up the unappetizing facts of their existence with celebration.

The young man (he couldn't have been more than eighteen or nineteen) strode to the center of the room. I was half-hidden behind Lucy, pressed back into the cushions, and until then I don't think he had been able to see me unimpeded. He did not look my way at first—he plainly wanted to strut, to bask in his dominance; but when his eyes fell on me, his prideful expression dissolved. He put his hands together, fingers and palms touching as if in prayer, and inclined his head and jabbered in Khmer.

Bewildered, Lucy said, "He's apologizing to you. He's begging you not to tell his father and asking your forgiveness."

I gawked at her.

"Say something," she said sotto voce. "Act in control."

It had been years since I smoked, but I needed a cigarette to marshal my wits. I reached for the pack on the table and lit one. "How can I forgive him when this animal is holding a gun on us? Ask him that."

Lucy spoke to the young man, and he snapped at the bodyguard, who lowered the gun and withdrew. The young man then reassumed his prayerful posture.

"Tell him he can go," I said. "If he leaves immediately, I won't tell his father."

She relayed the message, and the young man backed toward the door, bowing all the while.

"Wait!" I said, and Lucy echoed me in Khmer.

The young man stopped, holding his pose. I let him stew in his own juices, and his hands began to tremble—his fright increased my spirits more than was natural.

"Tell him to take care of our bill before he goes," I said. "And have them turn the music down."

"Jesus fuck!" Mike said once he had gone. "I thought we were dead! What the fuck just happened?"

Sean struggled up into a sitting position. His taxi girl tried to minister to him, but he brushed her away.

"Shit!" said Mike, and then repeated the word.

The other taxi girl kneeled beside her friend and mopped blood from her mouth and chin.

Lucy, regaining her poise, said to me, "He must have mistaken you for someone else."

"Who the fuck are you, guy?" Mike asked. "Some kind of fucking…?" His imagination failed him and he said again, "Shit!"

"Tom's a hero," said Riel, smiling goofily.

"Apparently so." Lucy picked up her drink and saluted me with an ironic toast. "A hero to villains, at any rate. Could there be something you haven't told us?"

With a groan, Sean heaved up from the floor and flopped into the chair—he was one unhappy nose guard. "That guy like to bust my fucking skull."

"Have a drink," said Mike.

The volume of the music was cut in half. I asked Riel to close the door, and, reaching out languidly, she pushed it shut, putting an end to Madonna. I butted my cigarette, yet it had tasted good, and I lit another. The smoke was hitting me like opium fumes, making my head swim. "Maybe we should go."

"Oh, do you think so?" asked Lucy nastily. "We might as well stay now. What more could happen?"

"I'd like to have my drink," said Riel. "Where's…you know, your friend?"

"Dan," said Mike. "Yeah, where the fuck is he?"

The taxi girls went to hover beside their men. Lucy's eyes pried at me, trying to see whatever it was she had overlooked in me. She knew something wasn't kosher. I was on my third cigarette when Dan reentered, carrying a tray of drinks.

"You missed out, man," said Mike. "Tom saved our fucking ass."

He delivered an exaggerated play by play of the assault and my "heroics," and Sean, pressing an iced drink to his head, provided color commentary. "That was one cold dude, man" and "I didn't know what the fuck he was talking about" were exemplary of his contribution. In response to this last, I asked Lucy what had been the young Khmer's problem.

"He accused Nary…" She indicated Sean's girl. "Of giving the third girl—the one who left—drugs."

"Why? Because she freaked out about the room?"

Lucy spoke to the girls and then said, "The girl has a fondness for Ecstasy. Dith, the young guy, had forbidden her to use any more. They have a relationship, though I can't quite gather what it is, and he believed that these two slipped her some in a drink. They claim she just started behaving oddly. She said a mirror vanished off the wall."

"Crazy bitch," said Dan.

"Let's go." I stood, followed in short order by Lucy. "You coming, Riel?"

She held up a forefinger, addressed herself to her drink, and chugged it in two swallows.

Dan put on a woebegone look. "Hey, come on! You guys don't have to go."

But Riel was already at the door. She paused to flutter a ditsy wave. "'Bye, Danny," she said.

—

The *Undine* was moored at the port facility on the Tonle Sap, a short distance from where it joined the Mekong and close by a huge multistory barge, its paint weathered to the grayish white of old bone. In years past this had housed a dance hall, a brothel by any other name, and now the top floor was home to the offices of the Cambodian Sex Workers Union and other such organizations. Womyn's Agenda For Change, the sign above one door spelled out in English. The following morning, sitting in the stern of the *Undine*, I watched streams of taxi girls trundling along the balconies, passing in and out of rooms where their sisters had once slaved, busy being empowered, fighting the good fight against the corporate giants that sought to use them as guinea pigs to test experimental AIDS vaccines. I supposed their sisterhood boosted morale and saved lives, and I knew it was dangerous work. Lucy compared them to the Wobblies back in the 1920s and said many girls had been murdered for their efforts. Yet to my eyes they might as well have been streams of ants plucking a few last shreds of tissue off a carcass—they had no conception of the forces mounted against them, no clue how absurd and redundant a name was Womyn's Agenda For Change.

Since my arrival in Phnom Penh, the changes (flickerings in the sky, subtle alterations in urban geography, etc.) had grown more frequent or, due to an increased sensitivity on my part, more observable. The episode with the taxi girl and the vanishing mirror was the first evidence I'd had that anyone else noticed them, though the evidence was impugned by the possible use of drugs. If the changes were observable by others, if this were other than a localized effect, and if it occurred in a place less disorderly than Phnom Penh, it would be the lead story on the news. I expected that when I reached Dong Thap the changes might be even more drastic. The prospect unnerved me, yet it held a potent allure. Like the narrator of *The Tea Forest,* I was being drawn to complete the journey and I wanted to complete it. The previous night's incident had convinced me that I was undergoing a transformation like the one documented by Cradle Two in the novel. I had taken undue pleasure in the exercise of control over the young Khmer in the Heart of Darkness, and I wondered if the person for whom he had mistaken me could have been the alpha-Cradle, that secretive, powerful figure, the Platonic ideal of Cradles everywhere. The notion that I was evolving into such a ruthless and decisive figure was exhilarating. I had never possessed either quality in great measure, and the proportions of the man, the fear he inspired, were impressive. Yet I was being pulled in another direction as well, and that was why I had returned to the *Undine* and sat in the stern, the satellite phone in my lap, ignoring the faint, sweetish reek of sewage, gazing at the barge and at eddies in the brown water.

When I called Kim, she answered on the third ring and told me this wasn't a good time. I asked if she had company. She was noncommittal, a sure sign that one of my colleagues, or one of hers, was lying in bed beside her. I said it was important, and she said, "Hang on."

I pictured her slipping into a robe, soothing the ruffled sensibilities of her lover, and carrying the phone into the living room. When she spoke again, her tone was exasperated.

"You don't call for three weeks, and now you just have to speak to me?" she said. "I got so worried I called Andy [my agent], and of course you'd called him. This is so typical of you."

I apologized.

"Are you in trouble?" she asked. "Do you want to run off to Bali with some teenage nymph and jeopardize everything we've built together?"

"It's not that."

"Because if that's the case, I'm sick and tired of having to coax you back. I'm ready to give you my blessing."

"It's not that! Okay? I want you to do me a favor. Andy was going to make copies of *The Tea Forest.* Did he send one to me?"

"I don't know. You have a package from him. I put it with the rest of your mail."

"That's probably it. Could you take a look?"

While she checked, my eyes returned to the barge. A number of women were kneeling on the foredeck, painting signs for a protest, and others had gathered in the bow, listening to a speaker who was talking into a hand-held megaphone, doing a bit of consciousness-raising. Now and then her high-pitched voice blatted out and there was a squeal of feedback.

"It's here," Kim said. "Do you want me to express it?"

"I want you to read it."

"Thomas, I don't have the time."

"Please. Read it...as soon as possible. I can't talk to you about what's happening until you've read it."

There was a silence, and then she said, "Andy told me you were developing some worrisome obsessions about the book."

"You know I'm a..."

"Just a second."

A man said something in the background; after that I heard nothing. When Kim came back on, she said with anger in her voice, "You have my undivided attention."

"Sorry."

"It's not important. You were saying?"

I'd lost the thread, and it took me a second to pick it up.

"I'm not the kind of guy who's likely to lose it," I said. "You know that."

"Are you doing a lot of drugs?"

"Did Andy say he thought I was?"

"Not in so many words, but...yeah."

"Well, I'm not. There are some strange correspondences, very strange, between the book and what's going on here. I need another point of view."

"All right. I'll read it Wednesday night. I can't until then. Tomorrow's a nightmare."

A drop of sweat trickled into my eye, and I wiped it away. Not even eight-thirty, and the temperature was already into the nineties. I felt a sudden upsurge of emotion and realized how much I missed Kim. Though I had tried to throw my heart in a new direction, though Lucy was an interesting woman and, without doubt, more sexually adventurous than Kim, I was ready for some home cooking, and I asked Kim if she was planning to meet me in Saigon.

"If you still want me to," she said.

We discussed when she would come, at which hotel she should stay, and spent some time repairing the rift in the relationship. I was so consoled by the familiarity of her voice, so excited by the predictable promise it conveyed, I suggested that we could marry in Saigon, a suggestion she did not reject out of hand, saying we should table the matter until she arrived. I thought we both had concluded that these adventures, these dalliances no longer served a purpose—they had become interruptions in our lives, and it was time we moved on. Yet when I hung up, it was as though I had cut myself off from her. I felt a total lack of connection and regretted having mentioned marriage. I went into the bow and asked Lan if we could head south in the morning. He sat facing the river and its farther shore, his legs dangling over the side of the houseboat, wearing a grease-stained pink T-shirt and shorts; he pushed a shock of gray hair from his eyes and peered up at me like an old turtle, blinking, craning his stiff neck.

"Anytime," he said. "Need provisions."

"Send Deng into town."

He chuckled, showing his gapped yellow teeth. "Deng."

"What's so funny?" I asked.

"Gone. You scare him. He tells me you are a bad man. He says a bad man is unlucky for people around him."

I thought Deng's leaving probably had more to do with Lucy than with his perception of my character. "You don't believe that, do you?"

"Maybe," said Lan.

"Then why haven't you deserted?"

"No reason." He fixed his eyes on a barge loaded with crates chugging upstream, crapping an oil slick and black fumes. "Need provisions," he said.

—

That afternoon, under an overcast sky, we visited a market on the outskirts of the city, a place where the pavement ended and green countryside could be seen off along the main road; the streets widened to form an open area—a square, if you will—of tapioca-colored dirt amid dilapidated buildings, none more than two stories tall. Infirm-looking, vertically compromised stalls of weathered wood were clumped alongside the buildings, pitched at eccentric angles. If you squinted and let your eyes slide out of focus, they resembled old, hobbling, gray-skirted women, some leaning together, who had paused for breath during a constitutional and never stirred again. The majority of the stalls were the offices of fortune-tellers, and this was the reason for our visit: Lucy's favorite fortune-teller could be found there. Why she picked him out of all the fortune-tellers in Phnom Penh, I hadn't a clue. He offered no complicated graphs and charts to demark your fate, as did many. His method was to rub dirt into her palm to make the lines stand out and mutter abstractions about her future until she was satisfied. Perhaps appearance played a part in her choice. Iron-gray hair fell in tangles over his chest and shoulders, and tattoos, faded to intricate blue scratchings, wrote an illegible legend on his arms, chest, neck, and forehead. He had a wispy goatee, wore a wraparound that covered his loins, and could usually be found smoking a cigar-sized spliff, which may have accounted for his benign gaze. His colleagues, most neatly dressed in western-style clothing, free of tattoos and spliffs, gave him a wide berth.

While Lucy consulted her wizard and Riel dawdled at a stall that sold cheap jewelry, I walked through thin crowds along one of the market streets leading off the square and, after a bout of token haggling, bought a U.S. army-issue Colt .45 and six clips of ammo from an arms dealer. Though old, the weapon appeared to be in good working order. The dealer encouraged me to test fire it, but I was afraid that I might be reported—I had no conception of the legalities attendant upon buying a gun. I tucked the pistol into my waist, beneath my shirt, and hustled back toward the square. A block along from the arms dealer, I stopped dead in my tracks. Standing in the doorway of a building on the corner was a bearded man dressed identically to me—shorts, sandals, a black T-shirt—and with an identical (as far as I could determine from a distance of forty feet) face and build. I imagined that we wore the identical stunned expression. We locked gazes for a moment, and as I hurried toward him, he ducked into the interior of the building. I raced after him, through the door and into the midst of twenty or thirty people slurping noodles at wooden tables, nearly knocking over a waitress who carried a load of dirty dishes. Her irritation gave way to confusion. She glanced toward the kitchen, then at me, and that told me all I needed to know. I ran through the kitchen and out onto the street behind the restaurant. There was scant pedestrian traffic—some kids kicking around a soccer ball, two women talking, a man looking under the hood of a beat-up yellow Toyota—and no sign of my double. I walked along in the direction of the square, peering into doorways, my excitement draining. What could we have said to each other, anyway? We could have compared notes on Cradleness, on what it meant to be a Cradle, for all the good that would do. Possibly I could have learned something new about the delta, but nothing, I thought, that would have greatly illuminated its central mystery. It had been a strange thing to see myself, yet now, at a remove from the moment, I questioned whether he had actually been my double. A bearded man in shorts and a black T-shirt at a distance of forty feet who had fled when approached by a stranger on the run: I told myself he might have been anyone.

In my absence, the center of the square had been taken over by an elephant. It was kneeling, a heap of fresh dung close by its hindquarters, and Riel stood at its side, like a princess beside a weathered castle wall, talking to a boy in shorts, twelve or thirteen, mounted behind the animal's neck. A farmer's son, I thought, who had ridden the family tractor into town to show it off. I found a stall adjacent to Lucy's wizard that sold coffee sweetened with condensed milk and sat on a rickety folding chair and watched Riel trying to entice the boy into giving her a ride (he kept wagging his finger no, and scowling), while the elephant flexed its trunk and blinked away flies, presenting an image of stuporous discontent.

The crowds were thinner in the square than they had been on the side streets, so Riel was the object of much attention, especially from the male stallkeepers. I sipped my coffee and thought about the gun pushing against my pelvic bone, imagining it had been snatched from the hand of a dead officer during the Vietnam conflict and wondering how many lives it had snuffed out. It had been an impulse buy, although the impulse was informed by a lifelong fear of and fascination with guns and was given a quasi-rational basis by the idea that I might need it once we reached the delta. It was a steel phallus, a social ill, all those things that left-wing politics said it was; yet its cold touch warmed me and added weight to my purpose, enabling the fantasy that my mission there was important.

Lucy finished her consultation and joined me for coffee. "It's going to rain," she said.

The clouds had gone from a nickel color to dark gray brushed with charcoal; the muggy heat and the smell of the elephant's dung had thickened. I laid an envelope on the table by Lucy's hand.

"What's this?" she asked, fingering it.

"Severance pay," I said.

She met my eyes steadily, and I thought she would object or demand an explanation; but she only looked away, her face neutral.

"So what did he tell you, your guy? What's in your stars?" I asked, breaking a silence.

"Obviously not a trip south," she said. "Oh, well. Like they say, all good things..."

"I hope it's been good."

She appeared to rebound. "It's been an adventure...and good." She grinned. "No complaints on this end."

"It's about time you went home and kick-started that career, don't you think?"

"Advice? And from someone who should know better?" she said merrily. "I shall have to reevaluate my impression of you."

"Just a thought."

The stallkeeper switched on a radio and tuned into a station playing reggae—Peter Tosh and elephants, the essence of globalization. Lucy inspected the contents of the envelope. "This is a lot of money," she said. "It's too much, really."

"I was hoping you'd see to Riel."

She nudged the envelope over to my side of the table. "I don't want to be responsible."

"I thought you fancied her."

"The lesbian thing…it's my exhibitionist side coming out. It works for me when the right guy is around. Otherwise…" She wrinkled her nose.

"Look, I'm not expecting you to spend much time on this. Give it a week or so, and try to pass her off to someone decent. That shouldn't be much of a problem. Maybe you can trick her onto a plane back to Winnipeg. If she stays here, she's bound to run into someone who'll fuck her up worse than she already is."

"All right. I'll do my best for her, but…I'll do my best."

I took her hand, letting my fingers mix with hers. "I'm going to be in London next spring. I'll give you a call, see how you're doing."

"I'm likely to be busy," she said after a pause. "But, yes. Do call, please."

We held hands for ten or fifteen seconds, reestablishing the limits of our limited affection, and then Lucy said, "Oh, my gosh. Look what she's doing now."

Riel had stepped around to the front of the elephant, facing it, and was dancing, a slow, eloquent, seductive temple-girl dance, arms raised above her head, hips swaying, as if trying to charm the beast. The elephant appeared unaffected, but everyone in the square had stopped what they were doing to watch. A livid stroke of lightning fractured the eastern sky, its witchy shape holding against the sullen moil of clouds, and was followed by a peal of thunder that rolled across green fields into the city. As it passed, the sky flickered, the clouds shifted in their conformation; but such phenomena had grown so commonplace, I would not have noticed except that it added a mysterious accent to the scene.

"Do you think she's in any danger?" Lucy asked.

"From the elephant? Probably not," I said. "The boy seems calm."

"We should fetch her, anyway. It's time we went back." She tucked the envelope into her bag, yet made no move to stand. "Whatever comes, I think we've helped her."

"We provided a place where she didn't have to worry about survival. But I don't think we can claim to have helped."

"What should we have done? Put her in a clinic? She wouldn't last a day. We're not her parents…and it's not as if she cares a fig about us. She'd be off in a flash if something better happened along."

"Maybe something better will come along. That's why I gave you the money."

Lucy acknowledged this gloomily.

"She may care about us more than you think," I said. "Her attachment to the world is flimsy, but we became her world for a few weeks. Flimsy or not, she formed an attachment."

"Isolate one moment, if you can, when she demonstrated genuine affection."

"That little speech she gave at the Heart of Darkness. I…"

"I knew you'd bring that up."

"I realize it was done for shock value. But it was inspired by a kernel of affection."

Lucy's fortune-teller scurried out from his stall and made a playful run at Riel—his shoulders were hunched and arms dangling, as though he were pretending to be a monkey tempted by a piece of fruit yet afraid to touch it. She continued to dance, and he wove a path about her, feinting, lunging at her, and scooting away; whenever he came near, he scattered some sort of powder at her feet. The scene held a curious potency, like a picture on a card, the representation of an archetype in a Cambodian Tarot, an image that seemed easily interpretable at first glance, but then, in the way of many Asian scenes, came to seem an impenetrable riddle: the wizard scuttling forward and retreating and the mystery void girl, the blonde sacrifice, lost in abandon, in holy, slow dementia, dancing before the massive, dim-witted, iconic beast. Lucy mentioned again that we should be going. Another peal of thunder, an erratic rumbling, hinted at something souring in the darkened belly of the sky. Vendors hastened to cover their merchandise, unrolling cloths and makeshift awnings. A sprinkle of rain fell, yet still we sat there.

—

"Snake country. That is what my daddy called Vietnam whenever he'd had a few, referring not only to his service in the delta, but to the country at large. He'd reach a garrulous stage in his drunk and deliver himself of some bloody, doleful tale, staring into his glass as if relating his wartime experiences to gnats that had drowned in a half-inch of Jim Beam. I think these stories were intended as self-justification, explaining in advance why he was probably going to kick the crap out of me later on, capping off his evening with a spot of exercise; but I heard them not as apology or warnings about the world's savagery—they had for me the windy lilt of pirate stories, and I loved to hear him lying his ass off, boasting of his prowess with a fifty-millimeter machine gun, blowing away gooks from the stern of a swift boat, dealing death while his comrades were shot to pieces around him...and, oh, watching them die had ripped the heart from his chest—the survivor's guilt he felt, the nightly visitations from torn, shattered corpses. Yet he couldn't help that he had been made of sterner stuff than they, and, when you got right down to it, he had relished his days in Vietnam. He had been called, he said, and not by love of country. If he had it to do over, he wouldn't so much as step on a bug for a country that hadn't done squat for him. No, he was convinced that he had been summoned to an unguessable purpose that he could never put a name to, that had nothing to do with war. That was the sole element of his narrative that rang true, the part about being summoned, and this was likely due to the fact that I could relate to such a summons. He hated the Vietnamese, but he was a natural-born hater, and I doubt now that he ever went to Vietnam. He showed me no mementos or photos of him and his buddies, and the stories lacked detail, though as the years wore on, he added detail (whether his memory improved or he was polishing a fictional history, his stories caused me to become fixated on guns and violence, and this led me to do a crime that earned me a nickel in the prison camp at Butner). His war record was the only thing he took pride in, yet it may all have been a drunken fantasy. 'The goddamn gooks make wine out of snake's blood,' he muttered once before passing out, and the conjuration of that image, red-like-pomegranate wine that beaded on the lip of a glass in a yellow-claw hand, the drops congealing thick as liquefied Jell-O, sliding down the throat in clots, slimy and narcotic—that said it all for me about snake country.

"Unlike my daddy, who came with guns blazing and the ace of death in his eye, I had the shits when I entered Vietnam, and several degrees of fever. I lay in the bottom of the boat, trying to hold in my guts, and avoided looking at the sky, which was playing its usual tricks, only with greater frequency—to look at it intensified my fever. We had some trouble at the border post. The Vietnamese run a tighter ship than does Cambodia, and since we didn't have enough money for a respectable bribe, the officials threatened to confiscate our boat; but then Jordan helped them get an overloaded pick-up unstuck from a muddy ditch, and after that they were all smiles and stamped our passports and waved us through into a portion of the Mekong renowned for its whirlpools. We were cautioned that much larger craft than ours had been sucked under, but we negotiated this treacherous stretch without incident and, below the town of Chau Doc, entered an area known as the Nine Dragons, where the river split into nine major channels, and there were as well minor channels, islands, and a maze of man-made canals spider-webbing an enormous area. At a riverside gas station, we received directions to the Kinh Dong Tien, the canal that would carry us toward the tea forest.

"The boating life on the canals was more lively than we had yet encountered, even in the vicinity of Phnom Penh, and was so dense that signs on the riverbank directed traffic, warning when not to pass on the left and such. There were mobile floating rice mills, boats loaded with construction supplies, with coconuts, plumbing fixtures, furniture, watermelons, and so forth, and the banks were crowded with shacks, and beyond them were fields reeking of DDT. People stared openmouthed at us and laughed at our wretched condition—covered with insect bites and sores, putting along in that wreck of a boat, the rudder held on with adhesive tape, the engine sputtering. Some of them, moved by charitable impulse, offered assistance, and others offered produce and drinking water, but I was in no mood to accept their charity. My fever had worsened, and the spiritual darkness that afflicted me had deepened to the point that I saw everything through a lens of distaste and loathing. Every smile seemed mocking, every friendly gesture masked an inimical intent, and I wanted nothing to do with this infestation of small brown people who swarmed over the delta, polluting it with their pesticides, with their shitting, squalling babies, and their brute insignificance. 'You don't go hunting termites with a rifle,' Daddy once told me. 'You poison their fucking nest.' Recalling that comment, I thought maybe he had gone to Vietnam after all..."

—

Not long after the events described in this passage, Cradle Two's narrator (and, I would guess, Cradle Two himself) grew too ill to go on, or, as the narrator implies, he used illness as an excuse for quitting because his fear of what lay ahead came to outweigh the pull he felt to complete the journey. After being treated at a local clinic, he recuperated in Phnom Penh and there wrote the ending to the book, claiming to be in mental communion with a multiplicity of Thomas Cradles, several of whom managed to enter the tea forest; yet even if you accepted this to be true, it was not a true resolution—he lost contact with the various Cradles once they passed beyond the edge of the forest, and so he contrived an ending based on clues and extrapolation.

I had been wise not to emulate Cradle Two's journey to the letter, I realized. As I've mentioned, the lifestyle he was forced to adopt due to lack of funds left him prone to disease and injury, whereas I, traveling in comfort aboard the *Undine*, had maintained my health. I had no doubt that I would see journey's end; but now that I was on the final leg, I debated whether or not I wanted to see it. The spiritual darkness remarked on by Cradle Two's narrator had descended upon me in full, though it might be more accurate to say that my social veneer had been worn away by the passage along the river and my dark nature revealed. I understood my essential character to be cold and grasping, violent and cowardly, courageous enough should my welfare demand it, yet terrified of everything, and I was, for the most part, comfortable with that recognition. (All men possessed these qualities, although I—and, I assumed, my fellow Cradles—must have them in spades.) When Kim called, presumably to report on her reading of *The Tea Forest,* I refused to answer. She rang and rang, calling every half hour; I switched off the satellite phone, not wishing to be distracted from steeping in my own poisonous spirit, basking amid thoughts that uncoiled lazily, turgidly, like serpents waking from a long sleep...like Cradle Two's ornate sentences. Yet as my bleakness grew, so did my fear. I wanted to retreat from the delta, to return to my old secure life. The fear was due in large measure to what I saw whenever I set foot out of the cabin. As we drew near Phu Tho, the hamlet that served as the jumping-off place for the tea forest, the changes that twitched and reconfigured the clouds, that caused mirrors to vanish from walls and rooftops to assume new outlines, became constant, and I felt myself to be the only solid thing in the landscape. It was like watching time-lapse photography. A village glided past, and I saw tin roofs rippling with change, acquiring rust, brightening with strips of new tin, dimpling with dents that would the next second be smoothed out, and a group of people coming from their houses to stare and wave would shift in number and alignment, vanishing and reappearing, wearing shabbier or more splendid clothes, and the sky would darken with running clouds, lighten and clear, the clouds then reoccurring, assuming different shapes, and the green of the fields would vary from a pale yellow-green to a deep viridian, and every shade in between; and Lan at his post in the prow, he would change, too, his skull narrowing and elongating, stubble sprouting from his chin, one leg withering, a cane materializing by his hand—yet before long he was hale once again. I sequestered myself in the cabin, doing my best to ignore disappearing pots and suddenly manifesting piles of dirty clothing. I had nothing to guide me through this leg of the journey—I had gone farther along the path than Cradle Two, and his novel made no mention of this phenomenon. On half a dozen occasions, I was on the verge of ordering Lan to turn the boat and make for Phnom Penh, but I persevered, though my heart fluttered in my chest, itself registering (or so I feared) the process of change as we slipped back and forth between universes, approaching an unearthly nexus. And then, less than five miles from Phu Tho, either the changes ceased or they became unobservable. We had reached a place where all things flowed into one, the calm at the heart of the storm.

Phu Tho itself was unremarkable, a collection of small concrete-block houses, painted in pastel shades, gathered about a landing and a ranger station (a mosquito-infested tin hut) where you gained admission to the national park beyond, a wetlands that contained the tea forest. But the canal and its embankment in the vicinity of Phu Tho was a graveyard of boats: motor launches, rafts, dinghies, sailboats of every size, barges. Thousands had been dragged onto land and an uncountable number of others scuttled—in order to clear a channel, I conjectured, though that reason no longer applied, for the channel had been blocked with submerged and partially submerged craft, and our progress was halted more than a mile from the hamlet. To reach it, I would have to pick my way on foot across the drowned hulks of a myriad boats.

We arrived at our stopping point in early morning, when drifts of whitish fog lay over all, ghosting the forest of prows and masts emerging from the water and the wreckage of crushed and capsized hulls spilling over the shore as if a tsunami had driven them to ruin. The majority (like the *Undine*) were adorned with painted eyes to drive away evil spirits, and these could be seen peering at us through the gauzy cover, seeming to blink as the fog thickened and thinned—it was an eerie and disconcerting sight, its effect amplified by the funereal silence that held sway, accented by the slop of the tide against the houseboat, an unsavory sound that reminded me in its erratic rhythm of an injured cur licking a wound. The people we had talked to along the canals would surely have told us of this obstruction, and it followed, then, that Phu Tho, this Phu Tho, must be a singular place designed to mark journey's end for every Thomas Cradle (excepting those who failed to complete their journeys), and that in other Phu Thos, life went on as always, the canal busy with its usual traffic, and that I was, despite Lan's presence, for all intents and purposes, alone.

I packed a rucksack with a change of clothes, protein bars, water, the gun, binoculars, a coiled length of rope, a first-aid kit, an English-Vietnamese pocket dictionary, repellent, and my dog-eared copy of Cradle Two's novel, thinking that his ruminations about the tea forest might be of value. Lan was waiting on deck, dour as ever; before I could instruct him, he said, "I stay here three days. Then I go. Bring police." Phu Tho spooked him, though you couldn't have determined this from his expression. I felt oddly sentimental about leaving him behind, and as I began my trek to shore, negotiating a path of slippery, tilted decks and slick hulls, tightroping along submerged railings, I speculated about his past and why he had stuck it out with me. I decided that it must have to do with habits cultivated during the Vietnam conflict—he may have been an army scout or ARVN and thus had developed a love-hate relationship with Americans. Before long, however, the exigencies of the crossing demanded my full attention. Twice I had to retrace my steps and seek a new route, and once, when I was up to my neck in water, I nudged something soft, and a bloated, eyeless face emerged from the murk and bobbed to the surface. I kicked the body away in revulsion, but I had the impression that the face had belonged to a man of about my size and weight. This was more than a graveyard for boats. I imagined that many more Cradles might be asleep in that deep.

A third of the way to shore, I stopped to rest atop the roof of a sunken launch. The sun was high, showing intermittently between leaden clouds; the fog had burned off, and though the heat was intense, I was grateful for it. I felt a chill that could not be explained by my immersion in water. The stillness and the silence, the corpse I had disturbed, the regatta of dead ships, looking more ruinous absent its ghostly dress and stretching, I saw now, for miles along the canal, a veritable boat holocaust: It was such a surreal scene, its scope so tremendous, I quailed before it; yet as always something drove me on. I was around fifty, sixty yards from shore, taking another rest, when music kicked in from one of the houses. It carried faintly across the water, but I could make out Little

Richard telling Miss Molly it was all right to ball. The song finished, and after an interval, Sly Stone's "Everyday People" began to play. That sunny jingle served to heighten Phu Tho's desolate air. I wiped sweat from my eyes and scanned the houses, trying to find the source of the music. No people, no dogs or pigs or chickens. Banana fronds lifted in a breeze, but no movement otherwise. I took a look through my binoculars. On the façade of a pale green house was a mural like the one I'd seen in Stung Treng, and again in Phnom Penh, depicting a yellowish, many-chambered form. The next song was Neal Diamond's "Girl, You'll Be a Woman Soon." Whoever was selecting the music had begun to piss me off.

The boats close in to the hamlet were relatively undamaged, still afloat, and this made the going easier. I scrambled ashore to the tune of "Low Rider" and rested on an overturned dinghy, the moisture steaming out of my clothing. I took the gun from my pack, tucked it into my waist, and headed for the pale green house, walking across a patch of mucky ground bristling with weeds and, apart from butterflies and some unseen buzzing insects, devoid of life. The vibe I received from Phu Tho was not so much one of abandonment (though it clearly had been abandoned), but of its impermanence, of the tautness to which its colors and shape were stretched over an inscrutable frame. It was as if at any moment my foot would punch through the rice paper illusion of earth into the void below; yet I had a firm confidence that this would not happen, that its frailty, its temporality, was something I simply hadn't noticed before but that had always been there to notice—frailty was an essential condition of life—and that I noticed it now spoke to the fact that I had come to a place less distant (in some incomprehensible way) from the source of the feeling. This was a complex and improbable understanding to have reached in the space of a hundred-foot walk, with music blasting and all the while worrying about what was inside the house and whether it had been wise to swim in water as foul as that in the vicinity of the hamlet; yet reach it I did, for all the benefit it bestowed.

The song faded, and the *put-put* of a generator surfaced from the funk, the singer advising his listeners to take a little trip, take a little trip with him, and an enormous man stepped from the door. He was well over three hundred pounds (closer to four, I reckoned), and stood a full head taller than I, clad in shorts and sandals and a collarless, sweat-stained shirt sewn of flour sacking. His arms and legs were speckled with inflamed insect bites, and his complexion was a sunburned pink, burst capillaries reddening his cheeks and nose; but for these variances, his bearded face, couched in an amused expression, was the porcine equivalent of my own.

"You're late to the party, cuz," he said in a voice rougher than mine, a smoker's voice with a country twang.

I was slow to respond, daunted by him.

"Better come on in," he said. "Looks like you could use a sit-down."

The floors of the house were of packed dirt carpeted with straw mats, and the mats were filthy with fruit rinds, empty bottles, crumbs, magazines (porn and celebrity rags), and all manner of paper trash. Centerfolds were taped to the walls. A bare, queen-sized mattress took up one end of the room; at the opposite end was a mildewed easy chair without legs and two card tables with folding chairs arranged beside them; a small TV-DVD player sat on one of the tables, DVDs scattered around it, and there was also a record player of the sort high school girls used to own in the sixties to play 45s. Sitting by the record player, holding a stack of 45s in her lap, was a slim, worn-looking Vietnamese woman of about thirty wearing a print smock. The man introduced her as Bian, but he didn't bother to introduce himself. He wedged himself into the easy chair—it was a tight fit—and sighed expansively. The sigh seemed to enrich the sickening organic staleness that prevailed in the house, and I pictured the individual molecules of the scent as having the man's pinkish coloration and blobby shape.

"Want a beer?" He spoke to Bian in Vietnamese. "She'll bring us a couple."

She went into the back room, a thin silver chain attached to her ankle slithering behind her, anchored to a stone half-buried in the floor. The man saw me staring at it and said, rather unnecessarily, "I didn't keep her on a leash, the bitch would be gone."

"No doubt," I said.

Bian brought the beers and stationed herself once again by the record player—taped to the wall above her head, like a dream she was having, an airbrushed redhead with pendulous breasts gazed at a porn star's erection delightedly and with a trace of wild surmise, as if it were just the bestest thing ever.

My initial take on the fat man, that he might be the powerful Ur-Cradle, had waned. He was a gargantuan redneck idiot, and my astonishment at his presence, at having this sorry proof of what I had previously only supposed, was neutralized by his enslavement of Bian and his repellent physical condition. On the face of things, he was a step or three farther along the path to the true Cradle than I was, a distillation of the Cradle essence. I didn't trust him, and I let my beer sit untasted. Yet at the same time I had a sympathetic reaction to him, as if I understood the deficits that had contributed to his character.

I asked where he had gotten the beer, and he said, "Some of the boys hijacked supply barges to get here. Hell, with what's on them barges, a man could survive for years. I been here must be four, five months and I hardly put a dent in it."

"By 'the boys,' you mean men like us? Thomas Cradles?"

"Yeah." He groped for something on the floor beside his chair, found it—a rag—and mopped sweat from his face. "Not all of them look like us. I guess their daddies slept with somebody different. But they all got the same name, least the ones I talked to did. Most push on through without stopping, they're so damn eager to get into the tea forest."

"Apparently you weren't that eager."

"Look at me." He indicated his massive belly. "A man my size, I'm lucky I made it this far, what with the heat and all. I was about half dead when I got here. Took me a while to recover, and by the time I did, the urge wasn't on me no more. That was strange, you know, 'cause I was flat-out desperate to get here. But hey, maybe the animal can't use fat junkies. Anyhow, I figured me and Bian would squat a while and make a home for the boys. You know, give them a place to rest up, drink a few beers...get laid." He shifted about in his chair, raising a dust. "Speaking of which, twenty bucks'll buy you a ride on Bian. She might not look it, but she got a whole lot of move in that skinny ass."

Bian cast a forlorn glance my way.

"I'll pass," I said. "What can you tell me about the tea forest?"

"Probably nothing you don't know. Some boys been coming back through lately, ones that didn't make it all the way to wherever. They're saying the animal don't need us no more. Whatever use it had for us, it's about over with...Least that's the feeling they got."

"The animal?"

"Man, you don't know much, do you? The animal. The creature-feature. It's painted on the wall outside. You telling me you never seen it before?"

I told him what I had seen, the murals, the creature in my opium dream, and that I had sworn off drugs for fear of seeing it again.

"Well, there's your problem, dude," he said, and gave a sodden laugh. "I mean, shit! How you expect to pierce the veil of Maya, you don't use drugs? You sure you're a Cradle? 'Cause from what I can make out, most of us stayed stoned the whole damn trip."

It was in my mind to tell him that if he was any example, most of us were serious fuck-ups; but instead I asked what he thought was going on.

"'Pears we all see it a little different," he said. "This one ol' boy, he told me he figured what we saw wasn't exactly what was happening. It was like a symbol or a...I don't know. Something."

"A metaphor?"

He didn't appear familiar with the word, but he said, "Yeah...like that. Everyone I've talked to pretty much agrees the animal needs us to protect it from something." His brow furrowed. "Those splinters you saw when you were high? I reckon they're like these stick figures I saw. Every time I did up, I'd see them standing around parts of the animal, guarding it like. Fucking weird, man. Scared the shit out of me. But I kept on seeing them 'cause I couldn't do without ol' Aunt Hazel."

The reference eluded me.

"Heroin," he said. "I had a monster habit. First week after I kicked, it was like I caught the superflu." He had a swallow of beer, wiped his mouth with the back of his hand. "Now the next question you're going to ask is, How come it chose us? Everybody's got a theory. Some I've heard are fucking insane, but they all boil down to basically the same thing. Something about us Cradle boys is pure badass."

His prideful grin told me that he was satisfied with this explanation and would be unlikely to have anything more intelligent to say on the subject. "You said some of them came back? Are they still here?"

He shook his head. "They couldn't get shut of this place fast enough. If you're after another opinion...way I hear it, some boys are still wandering around the fringe of the forest. They didn't feel the urge strong enough, I guess. Or they were too weak and gave out. You could talk to them. The ones that come back used park boats, so getting to the forest ain't nothing."

Bian said something in Vietnamese, and the man said, "She wants to know if you're going to fuck her."

"I don't think so," I said.

He relayed this information to Bian, who appeared relieved. "You can always change your mind. Bian don't care. She's a regular scout... ain't you, darling?" He reached out and chucked her under the chin. "You don't know what you're missing. She's got a real educated pussy." He settled back in the chair and gave me a canny look. "I bet you're a writer."

Surprised, I said, "Yeah," and asked how he knew.

"I didn't *know*. Us Cradles tend to be literary types more often than not. And seems like the boys who ain't interested in Bian are mostly writers...though there's been a couple like to wore her out. But what I was getting at, seeing how you're a writer, maybe you can make sense of their scribbles. I got a whole bunch of their notebooks."

"You have their journals?"

"Journals...notebooks. Whatever. I got a bunch. The boys that stop in, they figure they're going to need food and water more than anything else. They buy provisions and leave their stuff for me to hold. If you want to check it out, it's in the back room there."

It took him two tries to lever himself out of the chair. Going with a rolling, stiff-ankled walk, he preceded me into the room and pointed out the possessions of other Cradles scattered willy-nilly among crates of canned goods and stacks of bottled water and beer: discarded packs, clothing, notebooks, and the usual personal items. Copies of *The Tea Forest* could be seen poking out from this mess, as ubiquitous as Lonely Planet guides in a backpacker hotel. I squatted and began leafing through one of the notebooks. The handwriting was an approximation of my own, and the words...The notebooks were a potential gold mine, I realized. If this one were typical of the rest, I could crib dozens of stories from them, possibly a couple of novels. It struck me anew how odd all this was, to be seeking clues to a mystery by poring over journals that you yourself had written...or if not quite you, then those so close to you in flesh and spirit, they were more than brothers. Intending to make a comment along these lines, I half-turned to the fat man and caught a blow on the head that drove splinters of light into my eyes and sent me pitching forward on my stomach into a pile of clothing. If I lost consciousness, it was for a second or two, no more. Woozy, my face planted in a smelly T-shirt, I felt him patting down my pockets, pulling out my wallet, and heard his labored wheezing. My right hand was pinned beneath me, but I was able to slide my fingers down until I could grip the Colt and, when he flipped me onto my back, I aimed the gun at the blur of his torso—my vision had gone out of whack—and pulled the trigger. Nothing happened. My finger was outside the trigger guard. He grabbed the barrel, tugging and jerking at the Colt, grunting with effort, dragging me about, while I hung on doggedly, trying to fit my finger into the guard.

Everything moved slowly, as if I were trapped beneath the surface of a dream. I recall thinking what a dumb son of a bitch he was not to knock my arm aside and use his weight against me; and I had other thoughts as well, groggy, fearful thoughts, a dull wash of regrets and recriminations. And I realized I should have known from the disorderly state of the various Cradles' possessions that the fat man was not holding them in safekeeping, that he had simply emptied their packs on the floor while going through them, and the men whose lives they represented were probably adrift in the canal...and then my finger slipped inside the guard. There was a blast of noise and heat and light, a searing pain in my hand, and two screams, one of them mine.

My eyes squeezed shut, clutching my wrist; it was all I could do at first to manage the pain. I knew the Colt had exploded, and my sole concern was the extent of my injuries. Though it bled profusely, the wound seemed minor—the explosion had sliced a chunk out of the webbing of skin between my forefinger and thumb. My ears rang, but I soon became aware of a breathy, flutelike sound and glanced at the fat man. He lay sprawled among his victims' dirty laundry, head and shoulders propped against a crate, staring at me or, more likely, at nothing, for his eyes did not track me when I came to a knee; he continued to stare at the same point in space, whimpering softly, his pinkish complexion undercut by a pasty tone. He, too, was clutching his wrist. His hand was a ruin, the fingers missing, except for a shred of the thumb. With its scorched stumps and flaps of skin, it resembled a strange tuber excavated from the red soil of his belly. His lower abdomen was a porridge of blood and flesh, glistening and shuddering with his shallow breaths—it appeared that swollen round mass was preparing to expel an even greater abomination from a dark red cavity in which were nested coils of intestine. I'd never seen anyone's guts before, and though it was a horrid sight, the writer in me took time to record detail. Then his sphincter let go, and revulsion overwhelmed me.

I staggered to my feet and spotted Bian frozen in the doorway, watching the fat man die with a look of consternation, as if she had no idea how to handle this new development. Dizzy, my head throbbing, I stepped over the fat man's legs. I could do nothing for him; even had there been something, I wouldn't have done it. Bian had retaken her chair in the front room and was fingering her 45s, the image of distraction. I sat opposite her, removed the first-aid kit from my pack, and cleaned my wound with alcohol. A thought occurred to me. I pulled out my English-Vietnamese dictionary and found the word for key.

"*Danh tu?*" I said, pointing to her chain. I went through several variant pronunciations before she grasped my meaning. She said something in Vietnamese and mimed plucking something from a hip pocket.

"Okay, I get." She made a keep-cool gesture. "I get."

I bandaged my hand, and as I secured the bandage with tape, the fat man, emerging from the safe harbor of shock, began pleading for God's help, babbling curses, lapsing now and again into a fuming noise. Bian selected a record, fitted it onto the spindle, and his outcries were buried beneath the strings and faux-pomp of "MacArthur Park." The music started my head to pounding, but it was preferable to hearing the fat man groan.

The sky had opened up, and rain was falling, a steady downpour that would last a while. I saw no reason to hang around. I repacked my rucksack and nodded to Bian, who responded in kind and gazed out the door, tapping a finger in time to the beat. As I walked down a weedy slope toward the park ranger's shack, I could find in myself no hint of the profound emotion that was supposed to come with taking a life, with having violated this most sacrosanct and oft-breached of taboos, and I pondered the question of whether I would feel the same if I had killed a non-Cradle. I'd had a bond of sorts with the fat man, yet I had a minimal reaction to his death, as if the life I'd taken were mine by rights, thus negligible...though he might not be dead. Another song, "Nights In White Satin," began to play, presumably to drown out his cries; yet I thought Bian might be unmindful of his condition and was simply luxuriating in the lush, syrupy music that she had taken refuge in during her months of enslavement. I marveled at the calmness she displayed upon exchanging captivity for freedom. Perhaps it was an Asian thing, a less narcotized appreciation of what Riel had known: Someone was always using you, and thus freedom and captivity were colors we applied to the basic human condition. Perhaps what was a cliché in our culture bespoke a poignant truth in hers.

—

Writers tend to romanticize the sordid. They like to depict a junkie's world, say, as edgy, a scraped-to-the-bone existence that permits the soul of an artist to feel life in his marrow and allows him to peer into the abyss. Many of them believe, as did Rimbaud, or at least tout the belief, that derangement of the senses can lead one to experience the sublime; but for every Rimbaud there are countless millions whose senses have been deranged to purely loutish ends, and I am inclined to wonder if *le poete maudit* achieved what he did in spite of drugs and debauchery, not because of them. Whatever the case, I was convinced, thanks in part to the example set by my gargantuan pod brother, that the sordid was merely sordid. I might be disagreeable and sarcastic, but my efforts to bring forth my inner Cradle had been pretty feeble: kinky sex and a smattering of mean-spirited thoughts. Those were minor flaws compared to murder and enslavement. If the trait for which the "animal" needed us had anything to do with our innate repulsiveness, that might explain why I felt its call less profoundly than the others.

It was midafternoon when I set out for the tea forest in a motor launch left by (if the fat man were to be believed) one or another returning Cradle, with the rain falling hard, drenching my clothes, and the sky as dark as dusk. Rain pattered on the launch, hissed in the reeds, and had driven to roost the birds that—so my guidebook attested—normally stalked the wetlands. I followed a meandering watercourse through marshes toward a dark jumbled line in the distance. My head was bothering me. I felt cloudy, vague, gripped by a morose detachment, and assumed I had suffered a mild concussion. Images of Kim, of Lucy and Riel (most of them erotic in nature), were swapped about in my head, as were concerns about the new novel, about my health, about what would happen now that the end of the journey was at hand, and a belated worry that Bian would report me for killing her captor. However, as I drew near the forest, a feeling of glory swept over me. I was on the brink of doing something noble and essential and demanding self-sacrifice. The feeling seemed to come from outside myself, as if—like mist—it surrounded the forest in drifts through which I was passing, emerging now and again, returning to my confused state.

At the verge of the forest, I cut the motor and glided in, catching hold of a trunk to stop myself. The melaleuca tea trees (there must have been thousands, their lovely fan-shaped crowns thick with leaves, extending as far as the eye could see) were between twenty and thirty feet high, and I estimated the depth of the water to be about four feet, lapping gently at the trunks. They cast an ashen shade and formed a canopy that shielded me from the worst of the rain. A smell of decomposition fouled the air—I wrapped a T-shirt about the lower half of my face to reduce the stench. Peering through the gloom, I spotted other boats, all empty, and bodies floating here and there, bulking up from the dark gray water, their shirts ballooned taut with gasses. The trees segmented my view, offering avenues of sight that were in every direction more or less the same, as if I were trapped in some sort of prison maze.

I restarted the motor and had gone approximately two hundred yards into the forest when I noticed a thinning of the trees ahead and a paling of the light that might signal a clearing; but I could not discern its extent or anything else about it. The bodies that islanded the water near the boundary of the forest were absent here, and this gave me pause. I cut the engine again and surveyed the area, I could discern no particular menace, yet I had an apprehension of menace and reacted to every sound, jerking my head this way and that. Unable to shake the feeling, I decided a retreat was in order. I swung the boat around and was about to restart the engine, when I spotted a gaunt, bearded man sitting in the crotch of a tree.

At first I wasn't sure the figure was not a deformity of the wood, for his hair and clothing were as gray as the bark of the tree, and his skin, too, held a grayish cast; but then he lifted his hand in a feeble salute. He was lashed in place by an intricately knotted system of rags that allowed him a limited range of motion. His features were those of a Cradle, yet whereas the Cradles I had met with previously were of the same approximate age as me, he appeared older, though this might have been the result of ill usage. "How's it going?" he asked. His voice, too, was feeble, a scratchy croak. I asked why he had lashed himself to the tree.

"If I were you I'd do the same," he said. "Unless you're just going to turn around and leave."

I let the boat come to rest against the trunk of a tree close to his.

"Seems a waste," he said. "Coming all this way and then not sticking around for the show."

"What show?"

He made an elaborate gesture, like a magician introducing a trick. "I don't believe I could do it justice. It's something you have to see for yourself." He worked at something caught in his teeth. "I think this'll be my last night. I need to get back to Phnom Penh."

Nonplussed, I asked why he hadn't gone farther into the forest.

"I'm not a big believer in an afterlife."

"So you're saying the ones who continue on past this point, they die?"

"Questions of life and death are always open to interpretation. But yeah…that's what I'm saying. There's two or three hundred of us left in the forest. Some cross over every day. They're half-crazy from being here, from eating bugs and diseased birds. Stuff that makes your insides itch. They finally snap." He glanced toward the clearing. "It's due to start up again. You'd better find something to tie yourself up with. What I did was strip clothes off the corpses."

"I've got something."

I secured the launch to the trunk. The crotch of the melaleuca was no more than a foot above water level and, once I had made myself as comfortable as possible, I removed the coil of rope from my pack. The man advised me to fashion knots that would be difficult to untie and, when I asked why, he replied that I might be tempted to untie them. His affable manner seemed sincere, but we were no more than fifteen feet apart, and my visit with the fat man had made me wary. I kept the knots loose. Once settled, I asked the man how long he had been in the forest.

"This'll be my fifth night," he said. "I was going to stay longer, but I'm almost out of food, and my underwear's starting to mildew. I want to leave while I'm still strong enough to top off that fat fuck in Phu Tho."

"I wouldn't worry about him."

"Oh, yeah?"

"I dealt with him," I said, wanting to give the impression of being a dangerous man.

"He tried something with you?"

"I didn't give him the opportunity."

I asked if he lived in Phnom Penh, and as the light faded, he told me he operated a small business that offered tours catering to adventure travelers interested in experiencing Cambodia off the beaten path. He went into detail about the business, and although his delivery was smooth, it seemed a rehearsed speech, a story manufactured to cover a more sinister function. I let on that I was also a businessman but left the nature of the business unclear. Our conversation stalled out—it was as if we knew that we had few surprises for the other.

The rain stopped at dusk, and mosquitoes came out in force. I hoped that my faith in malaria medication was not misplaced. With darkness, a salting of stars showed through the canopy, yet their light was insufficient to reveal my neighbor in his tree. I could tell he was still there by the sound of his curses and mosquito-killing slaps. I grew sleepy and had to struggle to keep awake; then, after a couple of hours, I began to cramp, and that woke me up. I asked how much longer we had to wait.

"Don't know," the man said. "I thought it would be coming earlier, but maybe it won't be coming at all. Maybe it's done with us."

Irritated, I said, "Why the hell won't you tell me what's going on?"

"I don't know what's going on. I've got some ideas, but they're pretty damn crazy. You seem stable, a lot more so than most of the pitiful bastards left out here. What I was hoping was for you to give me your take on things and see if it lines up with mine. I don't want to predispose you to thinking about it one way of the other. Okay?"

"The fat guy, he said he thought that whatever it is—the animal, he called it. He thought the animal wanted our help because the Cradles were badasses."

"Could be. Though I wouldn't say badass. Just plain bad. Rotten." I heard him shifting about. "Wait and see, all right? It shouldn't be much longer."

I spent the next hour or thereabouts hydrating and rubbing cramps out of my legs. One night of this, I told myself, was all I was going to take. The cramps abated, and I began to feel better. However, my mind still wasn't right. I alternated between alertness and periods during which my thoughts wandered away from the forest, wishing I had never left home, wishing Kim was there to steady me with her cool rationality, wishing that we could make a real family and have babies, wondering if I would see her again, not because I felt imperiled and believed I might not survive the tea forest but because of my commitment-phobic character and faithless heart. It was in the midst of this reverie that the man in the tree beside me said, "Here it comes."

I could see no sign of "it," only darkness and dim stars, and asked in which direction he was looking and what he saw.

"Don't you feel that?" he asked.

"Feel what?"

The next moment I experienced a drowsy, stoned sensation, as if I had taken a Valium and knocked back a drink or two. The sensation did not intensify but rather seemed to serve as a platform for a feeling of groggy awe. I saw nothing awe-inspiring in my immediate surrounding, but I noticed that the darkness was not so deep as before (I could just make out my neighbor in his tree), and then I realized that this increased luminosity, which I had assumed was due to a thinning of mist overhead, was being generated from every quarter, even from under the water—a faint golden-white radiance was visible beneath the surface. The light continued to brighten at a rapid rate. In the direction of the clearing, the trees stood out sharply against a curdled mass of incandescence and cast shadows across the water. I began to have some inner ear discomfort, as if the air pressure were undergoing rapid changes, but nothing could have greatly diminished my concentration on the matter at hand. It appeared the forest was a bubble of reality encysted in light—light streamed from above, from below, from all the compass points—and, as its magnitude increased, we were about to be engulfed by our confining medium, by the fierce light that burned in the clearing, a weak point in the walls of the bubble that threatened to collapse. Filamentous shapes that might have been many-jointed limbs materialized there and then faded from view; bulkier forms also emerged, vanishing before I could fully grasp their outlines or guess at their function…and then, on my left, I heard a splashing and spotted someone slogging through the chest-deep water, moving toward the clearing at an angle that would bring him to within twenty or twenty-five feet of my tree, reminding me of the man portrayed on the cover of *The Tea Forest.* As the figure came abreast of the tree, I saw it was not a man but a woman wearing a rag of a shirt that did little to hide her breasts and with hair hanging in wet strings across features that, although decidedly feminine, bore the distinct Cradle stamp. She passed without catching sight of me.

What prompted me to attempt her rescue, I can't say. Perhaps a fragment of valorous principle surfaced from the recesses of my brain and sparked sufficiently to disrupt my increasingly beatific mood. More likely, it was the desire to learn what it would be like to (essentially) fuck myself—would I prove to be a screamer or make little moans? Or perhaps it was the beatific mood itself that provided motivation, for it seemed to embody the concept of sacrifice, of giving oneself over to a higher purpose. I undid the knots that bound me to the tree and jumped down and went splashing after her. She heard me and wheeled about, and we stared at one another. The light had grown so intense that she was nearly cast in silhouette. Dirt was smeared across her brow and cheeks and neck. She had a wild, termagant look.

"I won't hurt you," I said, hoping to gentle her. "I promise. Okay?"

Her expression softened.

"Okay?" I came a step forward. "I want to help. You understand?"

She brought her right hand up from beneath the water and lunged toward me, slashing at my throat with a knife. She had me cold, though I saw it at the last second and tried to duck...but she must have slipped. She fell sideways, and I toppled backward. The next I knew, we were both floundering in the water. I locked onto her right wrist, and we grappled, managing to stand. Turned toward the source of that uncanny light, she hissed at me. Droplets of water beaded her hair and skin. They glowed like weird, translucent gems, making her face seem barbarous and feral. Her naked breasts, asway in the struggle, were emblems of savagery. She kneed me and clawed and, whenever our heads came together, she snapped at my cheek, my lip; but I gained the advantage and drew back my fist to finish her...and slipped. I went under, completely submerged, and swallowed a mouthful of that stew of filth and decomposition. When I bobbed back up, I found her standing above me, poised to deliver a killing stroke. And then there was a flat detonation, *blam*, like a door slamming in an empty room. Blood sprayed from her elbow, and she was spun to the side. She staggered and screamed and clutched her arm, staring up into the tree to which the gaunt man was secured—he was aiming a snub-nosed pistol. Cradling her arm, the woman began to plough her way toward the clearing, hurrying now, glancing back every so often. I clung to a trunk and watched her go. The man made some comment, but my ears were still blocked by the changes in air pressure, and I was too disoriented to care what he said.

The forest brightened further, and the light around me gained the unearthly luster favored by artists of the late Italian Renaissance that you sometimes get when the afternoon sun breaks through storm clouds, and the break widens and holds, and it appears that everything in the landscape has become a radiant source and is releasing a rich, spectral energy. Close by what I presumed to be the edge of the clearing, the trees—both their crowns and trunks—had gone transparent, as if they were being irradiated, shifted out of existence. As the woman approached these trees, a tiny dark figure incised against the body of light, she suddenly attenuated and came apart, dissolving into a particulate mass that flew toward the center of the light. I could see her for the longest time, dwindling and dwindling, and this caused me to realize that I had no idea of the perspective involved. I had known it was vast, but now I recognized it to be cosmically vast. I was gazing into the depths of a creature that might well envelop galaxies and minnows, black holes, Chomolungma, earth and air and absence, all things, in the same way it enveloped the tea forest, seeming to have created it out of its substance, nurturing it as an oyster does a pearl. And this led me to a supposition that would explain the purpose of my journey: Like pearls, the Cradles were necessary to its health...and it may have been that the whole of mankind was necessary to cure it of or protect it from a variety of disorders; but for this particular disorder, only Cradles would serve.

I did not reach this conclusion at once but over the course of an interminable night, watching other deracinated Cradles—twenty or more—cross the drowned forest to meet their fate, repeating the transition that the woman had made. The druggy reverence I had earlier felt reinstituted itself, though not as strongly as before, and I felt a compulsion to join them, to sacrifice my life in hopes of some undefined reward, a notion allied with that now-familiar sense of glorious promise. I believe my fight with the woman, however, had put me out of that head enough so that I was able to resist—or else, having nearly run out of Cradles, the thing, the animal, God, the All, whatever you wished to call it, needed survivors to breed and replenish its medicine cabinet (giving the Biblical instruction "Be fruitful and multiply" a new spin) and thus had dialed back the urgency of its summons.

Toward dawn, the light dimmed, and I was able to see deeper into the thing. I noticed what might have been cellular walls within it and more of the ephemeral, limb like structures that I had previously observed. At one point I saw what appeared to be a grayish cloud fluttering above a dark object—it looked as if one of the lesser internal structures had been coated with something, for nowhere else did I see a hint of darkness, and there was an unevenness of coloration that suggested erosion or careless application. The fluttering of the cloud had something of an animal character—agitated, frustrated—that brought to mind the approach-avoidance behavior of a mouse to a trap baited with cheese, sensing danger yet lusting after the morsel. I recalled my opiated vision aboard the *Undine*, the gray patch that had been chasing after the luminous void-dweller, and I thought the coating must be the blood and bones of countless Cradles reduced to a shield that protected it from the depredations of the cloud. Soon it passed from view, seeming to circulate away, as though the creature were shifting or an internal tide were carrying it off.

A deep blue sky pricked with stars showed among the leaves overhead, the last of the light faded, and I continued to squat neck-deep in the water, staring after it, trying to find some accommodation between what I thought I had known of the world and what I had seen. While I was not a religious man, I was dismayed to have learned that the religious impulse was nothing more than a twitch of evolutionary biology. I could place no other interpretation on the event that I had witnessed. The parallels to the peak Christian experience were inescapable. I was dazed and frightened, more so than I had been in the presence of the creature. My fear had been suppressed by the concomitant feelings of awe and glory, and though I knew it had not truly gone anywhere, that it still enclosed all I saw and would ever see, now that it was no longer visible, I feared it would return…and yet I was plagued by another feeling, less potent but no less palpable. I felt bereft by its absence and longed to see it again. These emotions gradually ebbed, and I became eager to put that oppressive place behind me. I splashed over to the tree where I had tied up the boat and began fumbling with the line.

"Hey, brother," said the man in the tree adjacent to mine. "Take me with you."

Anxiety floored the superficial nonchalance of his tone. He still held the pistol, though not aiming it at me. I told him to find his own boat—there were plenty around.

"I don't have the will to leave," he said. "And if I don't leave, that thing's going to get me." He offered me the pistol. "You have to help me. I won't try anything." He laughed weakly. "The shape I'm in, it wouldn't matter if I did."

I knew he had been playing me, that his every word and action had been designed toward this end; but he *had* saved my life. I took the gun and told him to bind his hands as tightly as he could manage. When this was done, I helped him down from the tree and into the boat. He was frail, his skin loose on his bones, and I guessed that he had lied to me, that he had been in the forest far longer than five nights. I checked his bonds, settled him into the bow, and climbed in. The man seemed greatly relieved. He pressed his fists to his forehead, as if fighting back tears. When he had recovered, he asked what I thought about things now that I had seen the show. I summarized my reactions and he nodded.

"You didn't carry out the metaphor as far as I did," he said. "But yeah, that pretty much says it."

I asked him to explain what he meant by carrying out the metaphor.

"If you accept that our bad character is what makes us useful to it... or at least is symptomatic of the quality that makes us useful. Our psychic reek or something." He broke off, apparently searching for the right words. "You saw that gray, swarming thing? How it seemed reluctant to come near the part that was treated? Coated, as you said."

"Yeah. So?"

"Well, given that we were the element holding off the gray thing, and that our one outstanding characteristic is our essential crumminess, my idea is that the animal used us for repellent."

I stared at him.

"You know," he said. "Like mosquito repellent. Shark repellent."

"I got it."

"It's just a theory." He obviously assumed that I disagreed with him and became a bit defensive. "I realize it trivializes us even more than how you figured it."

I unscrewed the gas cap and peered inside the tank—we had enough fuel for the return trip.

The man chuckled and said, "It's kind of funny when you think about it, you know."

—

All journeys end in disappointment if for no other reason than that they end. Life disappoints us. Love fails to last. This has always been so, but the disappointment I felt at the end of my journey may relate more to a condition of our age of video games and event movies. To have come all this way and found only God—there should have been pirates, explosions, cities in ruins, armies slinking from the field of battle, not merely this doleful scene with a handful of Cradles and a glowing bug.

A better writer than I, the author of *The Tea Forest*, once said, "After you understand everything, all that's left to do is to forget it." I doubted my understanding was complete, but I saw his point. I could return home and lash myself to a tree and never leave again; I could make babies with Kim and subsume my comprehension of the world, the universe, in the trivial bustle of life. Perhaps I would be successful in this, but I knew I'd have to work at it, and I worried that the images I retained from my night in the forest would fatally weaken my resolution.

During the ride back, the man became boastful. I empathized with this—it gave you a heady feeling to have abandoned God, to have left Him in His Holy Swamp, trolling for Cradles, and though you knew this wasn't actually the case, that He was still big in your life, you had to go with that feeling in order to maintain some dignity. When we reached Phnom Penh, the man said, I'd be treated like a king. Anything I wanted, be it women, drugs, or money, he'd see I got more than my share, a never-ending bout of decadent pleasures. Could he be, I wondered, the Ur-Cradle, the evil genius at the center of an Asiatic empire, the crime lord before whom lesser crime lords quailed? It was possible. Evil required no real genius, only power, a lack of conscience, and an acquisitive nature such as I had seen at work in the tea forest. Men were, indeed, made in Its Image...at least writers and criminals were. Whatever, I planned to put the man ashore at the nearest inhabited village and then head for Saigon and, hopefully, Kim.

Another passage from *The Tea Forest* occurred to me:

> "...He had tried to make an architectural statement of his life after the tea forest, to isolate a geometric volume of air within a confine whose firm foundations and soaring walls and sculptural conceits reflected an internal ideal, a refinement of function, a purity of intent. Though partially successful in this, though he had buried his memories of the forest beneath the process of his art, he became aware that the task was impossible. One journey begat another. Even if you were to remain in a single place, the mind traveled. His resolves would fray, and, eventually, everything he had accomplished and accumulated—the swan of leaded crystal keeping watch from the windowsill, the books, the Indonesian shadow puppets that haunted his study, the women, his friends, the framed Tibetan paintings, the madras curtains that gaudily colored the bedroom light, his

habit of taking morning tea and reading the Post at Damrey's stall in the Russian Market, the very idea of having possessions and being possessed—these things would ultimately become meaningless, and he would escape the prison he had fashioned of them into the larger yet no less confining prison of his nature, and he would begin to wonder, What now? When would the monster next appear and for what purpose? How could he, who had been granted the opportunity to understand so much, know so little?"

It was a dreary prospect that Cradle Two painted, one I chose to deny. Unlike him, I had performed a redemptive act by saving the man—that signaled hope for improvement, surely—and I believed that, with Kim's help, I could shape a world that would contain more than my ego and ambition. I would learn to make do with life's pleasures no matter how illegitimate they were. And if I thought too much about the forest, why then I could write about it. *The Tea Forest* need not be a stand-alone book. A sequel might be in order, one that further explored the nature of the animal; perhaps a trilogy, a spiritual odyssey with a well-defined and exalting ending. I smelled awards, large advances. Small things, yet they delighted me.

The sun was up and the air steamy, baking the weeds and the little houses, when we came to Phu Tho. A putrid stench proceeded from the pale green house where the fat Cradle had died, and the innumerable ruined and stranded boats looked almost festive in the morning light, like the remnants of a regatta at which too good a time had been had by all. We had reached the banks of the canal when I remembered something. I told the man to wait, that I had left certain of my possessions in the fat man's house. He sank to the grass, grateful to have a rest. I walked back to the house and peeked in the door. Bian had fled and taken her records. I tied my T-shirt about my nose and mouth to cut the smell and steeled myself. It promised to be a disgusting business, retrieving the notebooks of my dead brothers, but I had my career to think of.

HALLOWEEN TOWN

This is the story of Clyde Ormoloo and the willow wan, but it's also the story of Halloween, the spindly, skinny town that lies along the bottom of the Shilkonic Gorge, a meandering crack in the earth so narrow that on a clear day the sky appears to those hundreds of feet below as a crooked seam of blue mineral running through dark stone. Spanning the gorge is a forest with a canopy so dense that a grown man, if he steps carefully, can walk across it; thus many who live in Halloween must travel for more than a mile along the river (the Mossbach) that divides their town should they wish to see daylight. The precipitous granite walls are concave, forming a great vaulted roof overhead, and this concavity becomes exaggerated near the apex of the gorge, where the serpentine roots of oak and hawthorn and elm burst through thin shelves of rock, braiding their undersides like enormous varicose veins.

Though a young boy can toss a stone from one bank to the other, the Mossbach is held to be quite a broad river by the citizenry, and this is scarcely surprising, considering their narrow perspective. Space is at a premium and the houses of the town, lacking all foundation, must be bolted to the walls of the gorge. Their rooms, rarely more than ten feet deep, are stacked one atop another, like the uneven, teetering columns of blocks erected by a toddler, and are ascended to by means of external ladders or rickety stairs or platforms raised by pulleys (a situation that has proved a boon to fitness). A small house may reach a height of forty feet, and larger ones, double stacks topped off by ornamental peaked roofs, often tower more than eighty feet above the Mossbach. When families grow close, rooms may be added that connect two or more houses; thereby creating a pattern of square shapes across the granite redolent of an enormous crossword puzzle; when feuds occur, these connecting rooms may be demolished. Public venues like O'Malloy's Inn and the Downlow have expanded by carving out rooms from the rock, but for much of its length, with its purplish days and quirky architecture and night mists, Halloween seems a habitation suited for a society of intelligent pigeons...though on occasion a purely human note is sounded. Sandy shingles notch the granite shore and piers of age-blackened wood extend out over the water, illumined by gas lamps or a single dangling bulb, assisting the passage of the flat-bottomed skiffs that constitute the river's sole traffic. Frequently you will see a moon-pale girl (or a dark-skinned girl with a peculiar pallor) sitting at the end of such a pier beneath a fan of radiance, watching elusive, luminous silver fish appearing and disappearing beneath the surface with the intermittency of fireflies, waiting for her lover to come poling his skiff out of the sempiternal gloom.

—

At forty-one, Clyde Ormoloo had the lean, muscular body of a construction worker (which, in fact, he had been) and the bleak disposition of a French philosopher plagued by doubts concerning the substantive worth of existence (which, in essence, he had become). His seamed face, surmounted by a scalp upon which was raised a crop of black stubble, was surpassingly ugly, yet ugly in such a way that appealed to women who prize men for their brutishness and use them as a setting to show off the diamond of their beauty. These women did not stay for long, put off by Clyde's unrelenting and perhaps unnatural scrutiny. Three years previously, while working a construction site in Beaver Falls, Pennsylvania (his home and the birthplace of Joe Namath, the former NFL quarterback), he had been struck a glancing blow to the head by a rivet dropped from the floor above and, as a result, he had begun to see too deeply into people. The injury was not a broken spine (he was in the hospital one night for observation), yet it paralyzed Clyde. Whereas before the accident he had been a beer guzzler, an ass-grabber, a blue-collar *bon vivant*, now when he looked into a woman's eyes (or a man's, for that matter), he saw a terrible incoherence, flashes of greed, lust, and fear exploding into a shrapnel of thought that somehow succeeded in contriving a human likeness. His friends seemed unfamiliar—he understood that he had not known them, merely recognized the shapes of their madness. He asked questions that made them uncomfortable and made comments that they failed to grasp and took for insults. Increasingly, women told their friends they didn't know him anymore and turned away when he drew near. Men rejected him less subtly and formed new friendships with those whose madnesses complemented their own.

"Sooner or later," said one of his doctors, "almost everyone arrives at the conclusion that people are chaotic skinbags driven by the basest of motives. You'll adjust."

None of the doctors could explain Clyde's sudden increase in intelligence and they were bemused by his contention that this increase was a byproduct of improved vision. In Clyde's view, his new capacity to analyze and break down the images conveyed by light lay at the root of his problem—the rivet had struck his skull above the site of the visual cortex, had it not? At the movies, in rock clubs, in any poorly lit circumstance, he felt almost normal, though most movies—themselves creations of light—seemed designed to inspire Pavlovian responses in idiots, and thus Clyde began attending the local arthouse, hiding his face beneath a golf cap so as not to be recognized.

"Try sunglasses," suggested a specialist.

Sunglasses helped, but Clyde felt like a pretentious ass wearing them day in, day out during the gray inclemency of a Beaver Falls winter. He considered moving to Florida, but knew this would be no more than a stopgap. The sole passion he clung to from his old, happy life (never mind that it had been an illusion) was his love of football, and for a while he thought football might save him. He spent hours each night watching ESPN Classic and the NFL Network. Football was the perfect metaphor, he thought, for contemporary man's frustration with the limitations of the social order, and therein rested its appeal. Whenever the officials (who in the main were professional men, lawyers, accountants, insurance executives, and the like, apt instruments of repression) threw their yellow flags and blew their silver whistles, preventing a three-hundred-pound mesomorph from ripping out a young quarterback's throat, they were in effect reminding the millions tuning in that they could expect no more than a partial fulfillment of their desires... and yet they did this with the rabid participation of the masses, who dressed in appropriate colors, rooting for the home team or the visitors, but acknowledging by the sameness of their dress that there was only one side, the side that sold them jerseys and caps. Thus football had evolved into a training tool of the corporate oligarchy, posing a dreary object lesson that conditioned proles to accept their cancer-ridden, consumerist fates enthusiastically. Having thought these things, the game lost much of its appeal for Clyde. And so, plagued by light, alone in a world where solitude is frowned upon, if not perceived as the symptom of a deviant pathology, he petitioned the town of Halloween to grant him citizenship.

—

The population of Halloween fluctuates between three thousand and thirty-eight hundred, and is sustained at those levels by the Town Council. At the time Clyde put in his application, the population hovered around thirty-two hundred, so breaching the upper limit would not be a problem. To his surprise, the decision to reject or approve him would not be rendered by the council in full session, but by a committee of three men named Brad, Carmine, and Spooz, and the meeting was held at the Sub-Café, an establishment that had been excavated out of the granite, a neon sign was bracketed to the rock above the entrance, indigo letters flashing on and off, producing eerie reflections in the water, and the interior looked a little like Brownie's back in Beaver Falls, with digital beer signs and some meager Christmas decorations and piped-in music (the Pogues were playing when he entered), TVs mounted here and there, maple paneling and subdued lighting, photographs of former patrons on the walls, tables, a horseshoe-shaped bar and waitresses wearing indigo Sub-Café T-shirts. A comforting mutter arose from the crowd at the bar, and two of the committee were seated at a back table.

Carmine and Spooz, it turned out, were cousins who did not share a family resemblance. Spooz was a genial, round-cheeked man in his mid-thirties, already going bald, and Carmine was five or six years younger, lean and sallow, with a vulpine face, given to toothpick-chewing and lip-curling. Brad, who had to be called away from a group gathered around a punchboard, was a black guy with baby dreads, a real beanpole, maybe six-six or six-seven. He brought a beer over for Clyde and gave him a grin as he pulled a chair up to the table. They drank and talked small and Clyde, gesturing at the TVs, asked if they had cable.

"Shit, no," said Carmine, and Spooz said, "The cable and the satellite company are having a turf war, so nobody can get either one."

"Cable wouldn't work down here, anyway," said Carmine. "Satellite, neither."

"How come?" Clyde asked.

"We got a service that burns stuff for us," Spooz said. "They send DVDs down the next day."

"Ormoloo," said Brad. "That's French, isn't it? Doesn't it have something to do with gilding?"

"Beats me." Clyde drained his glass and signaled the waitress to bring another round. "My dad was this big old guy who founded a hippie commune out in Oregon. He changed his name legally to Elephant Ormoloo. When my mom married him, she changed hers to Tijuana Ormoloo. When she divorced him, she changed it back to Marian Bleier. She told me I could choose between Bleier and Ormoloo. I was ten years old and pissed at her for leaving my dad, even though he'd been screwing around on her, so I chose Ormoloo. Anyway..." Clyde resettled in his chair. "I don't think my dad even realized it sounded French. He used to buy these Hindu posters from a head shop. You know, the ones with blue goddesses and guys with elephant heads and all that. He loved those damn posters. I think he was trying for a Hindu effect with the name."

After a silence during which the PA system began piping in the Pretenders, Carmine shifted his toothpick from one side of his mouth to the other with his tongue and said, "Too much information, guy."

Irritated, Clyde said, "I thought you wanted to know shit about me."

"Take it easy, man," said Brad, and Spooz, with an apologetic look, said, "We want to get to know you, okay? But we got a lot of ground to cover here."

Clyde hadn't noticed any particular rush on the part of the committee, but kept his mouth shut.

Spooz unfolded a wrinkled sheet of paper and spread it on the table. To make it stay flat, he put empties on it top and bottom. The paper was Clyde's application.

"So, Cliff," Spooz said. "Seems like you've got a very excellent reason for wanting to move here."

"That's Clyde, not Cliff," said Clyde.

Spooz peered at the paper. "Oh…right."

The waitress delivered their beers and plunked herself down in the chair next to Clyde. She was a big sexy girl, a strawberry blonde with a big butt, big thighs, big everything, kind of an R. Crumb woman, albeit with a less ferocious smile.

"You going to sit in, Joanie?" Brad asked.

"Might as well." She winked at Clyde. "I ain't making no money."

"I thought you guys were going to decide," said Clyde, feeling that things were becoming a bit arbitrary. "Can just anybody get in on this?"

"That's how democracy works," said Carmine. "They do it different where you come from?"

"Maybe he doesn't like girls." Joanie did a movie star-quality pout.

"I like girls fine. I…It's…" Clyde drew a breath and let it run out. "This is important to me, and I don't think you're taking it seriously. You don't know my name, you're not asking questions. My application looks like it's been in the wastebasket. I'm getting the idea this is all a big joke to you people."

"You want me to fuck off, I will," Joanie said.

"I don't want anybody to fuck off. Okay? All I want is for this to be a real interview."

Carmine gave him the fisheye. "You don't think this is a real interview?"

"We're in a freaking bar, for Christ's sakes. Not the town hall."

"So what're you saying? The interview's not real unless it's in a building with a dome?" Carmine spat on the floor, and Joanie punched him in the arm and said, "You going to clean that up?"

"This is the town hall," Carmine said.

"Uh-huh. Sure it is," said Clyde.

Brad tapped him on the arm in order to break up the stare-down he was having with Carmine. "It's the truth, dude. Anywhere the committee meets, it's the town hall."

Carmine popped a knuckle. "I suppose where you come from, they do that different, too."

"Yeah, matter of fact." Clyde fixed him with a death stare. "One thing, they don't let sour little fucks decide anything important."

"All right, all right," Spooz said. "Let's everybody calm down. The man wants some questions. Anyone have a question?"

Carmine said meanly, "I got nothing," and Brad appeared to be mulling it over.

"What sort of work you do?" Joanie asked.

Clyde started to point out that the question had been answered on his application; but he was grateful for this much semblance of order and said, "Construction. I'm qualified to operate most types of heavy machinery. I do carpentry, masonry, roofing. I've done some wiring, but just basic stuff. Pretty much you name it." He glanced at Carmine and added, "Too much information?"

Carmine held out a hand palm down and waggled it, as if to say that Clyde was right on the edge of overcommunicating.

Brad said, "I don't believe we've got any construction going, but he could start out down at the Dots."

Spooz agreed and Clyde was about to ask what were the Dots, when Joanie cut in and asked if he had a girlfriend.

"How about we keep it serious?" said Spooz.

"I am serious!" she said.

"Naw," said Clyde. "No girlfriend. But I'm accepting applications."

Joanie took a pretend-swat at him with a menu.

Brad followed with a question about his expertise in furniture building, and then Spooz and Joanie had questions about his long-term goals (indefinite), his police record (nothing heavy-duty since he was kid), and his health concerns (none as far as he knew). They had other questions, too, which Clyde answered honestly. He began to relax, to think that he was making an overall good impression—Brad and Joanie were in his corner for sure, and though Spooz was Carmine's cousin, Clyde had the idea that they weren't close, so he figured as long as he didn't blow it, he was in.

The atmosphere grew convivial, they had a few more beers, and at last Spooz said to his colleagues, "Well, I guess we know enough, huh?"

Joanie and Brad concurred, and Clyde asked if they wanted him to go away so they could talk things over. Not necessary, they told him, and then Carmine said, "Here's a question for you. How do you feel about the Cowboys?"

At a loss, Clyde said, "You talking about the Dallas Cowboys?"

Carmine nodded, and Clyde, assuming that this didn't require a legitimate answer, said, "Screw 'em. I'm a Steelers fan."

Brad, who had been resting his elbows on the table, sat back in his chair. Joanie was frozen for a second and then busied herself in bussing the table. Spooz lowered his eyes as if deeply saddened. Carmine smiled thinly and inspected his fingernails.

"Are you fucking kidding me?" Clyde said. "That was a serious question?"

Brad asked what time it was, and Spooz checked his watch and said it was six-thirty.

"Hey," said Clyde. "You need me to be a Cowboys fan, I'll be a Cowboys fan. I don't give a good goddamn about football, really."

That seemed to horrify them.

"What do you want from me? You want I should paint myself silver and blue every Sunday? Come on!"

"Monday," said Brad. "We don't get the games until Monday."

Spooz's stern expression dissolved into a grin. "I can't keep this up. Congratulations, man."

Baffled for the moment, Clyde said, "What are you talking?"

"You've been jumped in. This was like your initiation. The council accepted you last week."

"You'll be on probationary status for six months," Joanie said. "But it's more-or-less a done deal."

Brad and Spooz both shook his hand, and Joanie gave him a hug and a kiss with a little extra on it, and people came over from the bar to congratulate him. Clyde kept saying happily, "I can't believe you guys were just busting my chops. You fuckers had me going there!"

Carmine, who apparently had taken a real dislike to him, waited until the crowd around Clyde had dissipated to offer a limp handshake. "Don't get giddy," he said, putting his mouth close beside Clyde's cheek. "Things might not work out for you here."

—

Walnuts are Halloween's chief export, its only source of income (apart from the occasional tourist and the post office, which does a bang-up business once a year, stamping cards and letters) and are prized by connoisseurs in the upper world for their rich, fruity flavor, a flavor derived from steeping in the ponds south of town known as the Dots—three of them, round as periods, they create an elision interrupting the erratic black sentence of the Mossbach. Recently there have been complaints that the walnuts are no longer up to standard. The mulberries and plants that, dissolved into a residue, suffuse the walnuts, imbuing them with their distinct taste, no longer fall from the sky crack in profusion; and neither do the walnuts fall so thickly as they once did, plop-plop-plopping into the water like a sort of wooden hail. Nowadays the townspeople are not above importing mulberries and certain weeds and even walnuts, and dumping them into the ponds, a practice decried by connoisseurs; yet they continue to pay the exorbitant prices.

Each morning Clyde would pole his skiff (something more difficult to do than it would appear) from the north end of town, where he had found temporary living quarters, to the Dots. He recalled how it had been going to work in Beaver Falls, steering his pickup past strip malls with gray snow banked out front, his seat littered with half-crushed cans and fast food garbage, pieces of bun, greasy paper, a fragment of tomato, a dead French fry, the heater cooking it all into a rotten smell, while the idiot voices of drive-time America yammered and puffy-faced, sullen, half-asleep drivers drank bitter coffee, listening to Howard Stern and Mancow Muller, trying to remember the gross bits with which to amuse their friends…and he contrasted that with the uncanny peace of going to work now, gliding downstream beneath the still-darkened seam of sky, the only sound that of his pole lifting and planting, inhaling the cool, damp smell of the river mixed with fleeting odors of fish death and breakfasts cooking and limeflowers (a species with velvety greenish-white blooms peculiar to Halloween, sprouting from the dirt and birdlime that accumulated on the ledges), and occasionally another skiff coming toward him, the boatman saluting, and his thoughts glided, too, never stressed or scattered, just taking in the sights, past the simple, linear houses spread out across the rock walls like anagrams and scrambles, the blurred letters of the neon signs flickering softly in the mist, the lights at the end of spidery docks glowing witchily, haloed by glittering white particles, and once he reached the Dots, shallow circles of crystalline water illuminated in such a way as to reveal their walnut-covered bottoms (yet not enough light to trouble him), he would put on waders and grab a long rake and turn the walnuts so as to ensure they received the benefits of immersion on all sides equally.

Between fifty and sixty men and women joined him on the morning shift and he became friendly with several, and friends with one: Dell Weimer, a blond, overweight transplant from Lake Parsippany, New Jersey, where he had managed a convenience store. Dell had recently finished a short stretch in the Tubes, the geological formation that served as Halloween's main punitive device, and would say nothing about it other than that it was "…some evil shit." He was forthcoming, however, about the rest of the town in which he had lived for six years.

One morning Dell straightened from his labors and, as he was wont to do, clutched his back and began grousing about the job. "Fuck a bunch of walnuts," he said on this occasion. "Here we are breaking our butts for nothing!"

Clyde asked him to explain, because he had been led to believe the town depended on the walnuts, and Dell said, "Ever hear of Pet Nylund?"

"Sounds familiar."

"You know. The rock star guy."

"Yeah…yeah! My ex used to like his stuff. Real morbid crap."

"He's born and raised in Halloween."

"You're kidding?"

"Yeah, he lives here when he's not in L.A. I'll show you his place. He bought up all the land around the gorge—he must own a fucking million acres. He invested heavy in energy and bioengineering stocks about thirty years ago and the stock went through the roof."

"Bioengineering. Tinkering with genes and all that?"

"Right. He had his own company come down in here…Mutagenics, I think their name was. They were doing experiments south of the Dots, flushing shit into the river. Don't eat nothing come out of that river, son, 'less you want to grow gills." Dell paused to work out a kink. "Like I was saying, they flushed their chemicals so they washed away underground. The Mossbach goes subta—…you know."

"Subterranean."

"Yeah, right. God only knows what's growing down there. The Mutagenics people couldn't leave fast enough, so you know some bad shit happened. But even though the water here's okay, the fishies got that poison in 'em and there is some weird-looking stuff in that river. Anyhow, Pet's worth billions, so he endows the town. Now the town's a billionaire, too. Nobody's got to work, except for Nylund struck a deal with the council. In return for the endowment, people have to live like always until after he dies. He doesn't want to watch the place change and he knows the money's bound to change it. After he's gone, he don't give a damn about what happens, but for now we got to bust our behinds." Dell winced and rubbed his back again. "If he shows his face around here, I might do us all a favor and off the son-of-a-bitch."

That night in the Sub-Café, Clyde asked Joanie, with whom he was having a thing, if the Pet Nylund story was true.

"Who told you? Dell, I bet," she said. "That lazy bastard's going to wind up back in the Tubes."

She told the bartender that she was going on break and hustled Clyde out onto the pier that fronted the bar. The mist was thick and, although he heard people laughing out on the water, he couldn't see past the end of the pier. Eight or nine skiffs were tied up to the pilings; the current made them appear to nudge against each other with ungainly eagerness, like pigs at a trough.

"You're not supposed to know any of that stuff until you're off probation," Joanie said.

"Why not?"

"Because knowing about it might make you unmotivated."

"There's no reason to think it'll make me less unmotivated five months from now."

Joanie cast about to see if anyone was within earshot. "It's all about the benefits, see. They kick in once you're a citizen. Retirement, full medical...and I mean full. They'll even pay for a tummy tuck, anything you want. Nylund thinks if the probationers knew, they wouldn't get into the spirit of the town. They'd just be faking it."

The water slurped against the pilings, as if a big something had given them a lick.

"Dell mentioned this company, Mutagenics."

"You don't want to be talking about that," said Joanie, affecting a sober expression. "And don't you even think about going south of the Dots. We got this one idiot who goes south a lot, but one day she's going to turn up missing. Happens eventually to everybody who pokes their nose down there."

"So what's up with that?"

"If I could tell you, I'd probably be missing. I don't go there. Ever. But don't talk about it, okay? With Dell or anyone…except with me. I don't want you getting in trouble. With me…" She threw a stiff punch to the point of his shoulder. "You're already in trouble."

"Ow! Jesus!" He grabbed her and pulled her against him. He squeezed and her breath came out in a trebly *oof.* Her eyes half-closed and she ground her hips against him. The mists swirled and thickened, sealing them off from the Sub-Café, until only a vague purplish flickering remained of the sign.

"Ouch," Joanie said.

—

Ms. Helene Kmiec, the widow of Stan Kmiec, former head of the town council, was at thirty-six a relatively young woman to have endured such a tragedy, and this perhaps explained her emotional resilience. Since her husband's death eight months ago in a boating accident south of the Dots, she had taken a succession of lovers and started a new business involving the use of a webcam and bondage gear (this according to Dell, who further stated that Ms. Kmiec, a petite blonde with, in his words, "trophy-sized balloons," could give him a spanking any old time she wanted). She also took in boarders. The remainder of her time was devoted to the care and feeding of the town's sole surviving cat, a Turkish angora named Prince Shalimar who had survived for five and a half years, considerably longer, it was believed, than any other cat in Halloween's shadowy history.

"Something around here likes cats a *leetle* too much," she said to Clyde on the occasion of their first meeting. "People claim to have seen it, but this is all they've come up with."

She handed Clyde a photocopied poster with an artist's rendering of a raggedy Rorschach inkblot looming over a cat and underneath it the words:

REWARD!!!

For information leading to the capture of

Halloween's Cat Killer

Beneath that was Ms. Kmiec's contact information.

"It's not much to go on," Clyde said, and tried to hand back the poster. Ms. Kmiec told him to hang onto it—she had plenty more.

"The damn thing's fast," she said. "Fast and sneaky. Hard to get a handle on its particulars. At least that gives you a general idea of its size." She studied the picture. "It's nailed damn near every cat in town for the past forty years, but it's not getting Princey."

"You think it's the same one's been doing it all that time?"

"Doesn't matter," she said. "It comes around here, I got something for it. One or many, old or young, that sucker's going down."

"Why don't you get a dog?"

"Dogs get taken by things in the river. Cats have the good sense to stay clear of the water."

They were sitting together on a sofa in her cramped, fourth-floor living room, a ten-by-eight-foot space with a door that connected to a corridor leading to the house next door. Its cadmium yellow walls were dense with framed photographs, many of them shots of Ms. Kmiec in various states of undress, and the largest depicting her arm-in-arm with the late Mr. Kmiec, a pudgy, white-haired gent whose frown lines and frozen smile implied that such an expression did not come easily to his face. In this photograph she wore an ankle-length skirt, a cardigan, and a prim, gone-to-Jesus expression, leaving the impression that she had stepped away from the sexual arena before her time, an error since corrected. The skirt and the cardigan had been replaced that day with a gold dressing gown loosely belted over a skimpy black latex costume.

"There's one thing we should get straight before you move in," she said. "For the record, I did not kill my husband. You may hear talk that I did..."

"I'm not big on gossip," Clyde said, avoiding looking at her for fear he might see the truth of her statement—the light in the room was brighter than he would have liked.

"...but I didn't. Stan was a chore and we didn't always get along. There's times now I still resent him, but he was a good guy at heart. He was always helping me with my projects. Matter of fact, he was helping me out the day he died. We were down south looking for the cat killer and something snaked over the side of the skiff and took him under. Wasn't a thing I could have done. People say if I'd loved Stan, I would have gone in after him. Maybe there's some truth to that. I did love him, but Stan was twenty-six years older than me. Maybe I didn't love him enough."

She inched forward on the sofa, reached out her hand and touched Mr. Kmiec's image on the wall opposite. She seemed to be having a moment and Clyde waited until she had leaned back to ask what she had meant by "something snaked over the side."

"South of the Dots there's a lot of strange flora and fauna," she said. "We don't know half what's there. Don't you be going down that way until you get acclimated." She patted his knee. "We wouldn't want to lose you."

A masculine wail of distress floated up from below and Ms. Kmiec jumped to her feet. "Oh, damn! I forgot about him! Here I am chattering away and...I don't know what I'm thinking!" She fingered out a key from the pocket of her robe and passed it to Clyde. "I have to take care of something. Can you show yourself up? It's the eighth floor."

Clyde said, "Sure," and scrunched in his knees so she could get past.

"Now I put you right above the Prince's room," she said as she stood in the open door, a section of the gorge's granite wall visible behind her. "I know you're bound to have company, and I don't care about that. But I made certain the bed in that room is extra stable, because the Prince hates sharp noises. So if the headboard comes loose and starts banging, or whatever, do your best to fix it temporarily and I'll get someone in to do repairs ASAP. All right?"

She shrugged out of her robe and tossed it onto the arm of the sofa and started down the ladder, seeding Clyde's brain with an afterimage of pale, shapely legs and swelling breasts restrained by narrow, shiny strips of rubber. A second later her head popped back into view.

"If you want, look in on the Prince. He loves new people." Her brow furrowed, as if trying to recall some further instruction; then she brightened and said, "Welcome to Kasa Kmiec!"

—

The eighth floor was a room with a half-bath added on. Within a ten-by-twelve space, it contained a captain's bed with shelves in the bottom, a wicker chair, bookshelves and a TV niche built into the walls, a stove and sink, and small refrigerator. It was as cunningly crafted as a ship's cabin, with every inch of space utilized. Initially Clyde felt he might break something whenever he moved, but he adapted to his new quarters and soon, when lying on the bed, he began to have a sense of spaciousness.

He enjoyed sitting in the wicker chair after work with the lamp dialed low, vegetating until his energy returned, and then he would turn the light on full. He had discovered that he liked being smart when alone, liked the solitary richness of his mind, and he would sketch plans for the house he intended to build after he got off probation; he would read and speculate on subjects of which he had been unaware prior to the accident (Indian influences on Byzantine architecture, the effects of globalization upon Lhasa and environs, et al.); but always his thoughts returned to the town where he had sought refuge, whose origins no one appeared to know or question, whose very existence seemed as mysterious as the nation of Myanmar or the migratory impulses of sea turtles. He had supposed—unrealistically, perhaps—that the people of Halloween would have a clearer perspective on life than did the people in Beaver Falls; but they had similar gaps in their worldview and ignored these gaps as if they were insignificant, as if by not including them in the picture, everything made sense, everything was fine. He had hoped the town would be a solution, but now he suspected it was simply another sort of problem, more exotic and perhaps more complex, one that he would have to leave the light on a great deal in order to resolve if he hoped to get to the bottom of it.

When he heard the winch complain, the chain slithering through the pulley, signs that Joanie was on her way up in the elevator that operated above the fifth floor, he would dim the lamp so he would be unable to perceive the telltales that betrayed the base workings of her mind and the fabrication of her personality. She understood why he did this—at least he had explained his troubles—but it played into her appreciation of herself as an entry-level girlfriend, and she often asked if she wasn't pretty enough for him, if that was why he lowered the lights. He told her that she was more than pretty enough, but she grew increasingly morose and would say she knew they were a short-term thing and that he would someday soon find someone who made him happy, as would she, and it was better this way—this way, when the inevitable happened they would stay friends because they had been honest with each other and hadn't gotten all deluded, and until then, well, they'd have some fun, wouldn't they? Even in the half-dark, he realized it was a self-fulfilling prophecy, that her low self-esteem foredoomed the relationship. Understanding this about her, having so much apperception of the human ritual, dismayed him and he would try to boost her spirits by telling her stories about his life topside (the citizens of Halloween referred to other parts of America as "topside" or "the republic") or by mocking Mrs. Kmiec's cat.

Beside the bed was a trapdoor that had once permitted egress to the floor below, but now was blocked by a sheet of two-inch plexiglass—a plastic cube had been constructed within the old wooden room for the protection of its sole inhabitant, a fluffy white blob with a face and feet. When Clyde first opened the trapdoor, Prince Shalimar had freaked out, climbing the walls, throwing himself at the inner door; now, grown accustomed to Clyde and Joanie peering at him, he never glanced in their direction. The place was a cat paradise filled with mazes upon which to climb, scratching posts, dangling toys, and catnip mice. Infrequently the Prince would swat at one or another of the toys; now and then he would chew on a catnip mouse; but a vast majority of his time was spent sleeping in a pillowed basket close to his litter box.

"It's not even a cat anymore," Joanie said one evening as they looked down on the Prince, snoozing on his pillow. "It's like some kind of mutant."

"Ms. Kmiec gives him enemas," said Clyde.

"You're kidding!"

"Swear to God. I looked down there one time and she had a plastic tube up his butt."

"Did she see you?"

"Yeah. She waved and went on with her business."

"Wasn't the cat pissed?"

"She was wearing work gloves and holding him down, but by the time I looked, he seemed to have quit struggling and was just lying there."

Joanie shook her head in wonderment. "Helene is very, very weird."

"Do you know her?"

"Not so much. She used to come in the bar with Stan. She's always been weird. My big sister was the same year in school as with her—she says Helene was already into the dominatrix stuff when she was a kid. She quit doing it for Stan."

"Maybe she didn't quit. Maybe Stan was her only client for a while."

"Maybe."

Joanie leaned against him and Clyde draped an arm over her shoulder; the edge of his hand nudged her breast. They watched as the Prince gave a mighty fishlike heave and managed to flop onto his back.

"He doesn't even have the energy to miaow anymore," Clyde said. "He makes this sound instead. 'Mrap, mrap.' It's like half a miaow. A shorthand miaow."

Joanie caught his hand and placed it full on her breast. "Something happens to Helene, the poor bastard won't stand a fighting chance. Nobody else is going to do for him the way she does. He'll be like a bonbon for that fucking thing."

They made loud, sweaty love with no regard for Prince's sensibilities, banging the headboard against the wall, and afterward, with Joanie snoring gently beside him, Clyde was unable to rid himself of the image and lay thinking that they were all bonbons, soft white things in their flimsy protective shells, helplessly awaiting the emergence of some black maw or circumstance.

—

Seven weeks after his arrival in Halloween, Clyde was working with a group of twenty or twenty-five in the central Dot, when he heard from

Mary Alonso, a sinewy, brown-skinned gay woman in her early thirties, that Dell had been banished.

"'Banished'?" he said, and laughed. "You can't banish people, not since the Middle Ages."

"Tell that to Dell." Mary leaned against the rocky wall, a pose that stretched her T-shirt across her diminutive breasts, making them look like lumps of muscle. "They sent him up to the republic and he can't come back. He'd been to the Tubes nine times. The tenth time and you're gone."

"Is that some kind of rule? Nobody told me."

"When you're through probation you get a book with the town laws. There aren't many of them. Don't kill anybody, don't rape anybody, don't screw up constantly. I guess they got Dell on the don't screw up constantly."

"What the hell? Don't you have people believe in the Constitution down here?"

"The Constitution's not what it used to be," Mary said. "Guess you didn't notice."

"Well, how's about Helene Kmiec?"

"Huh?"

"Helene Kmiec. Chances are she killed her husband. The way Joanie tells it, they didn't hardly investigate."

"I wouldn't know about that." Mary started raking again.

"Is Dell still around? Are they holding him somewhere?"

"Once they decide you're gone, you're gone. Only reason I know about it, I was at home and Tom Mihalic come around saying I had to work Dell's shift."

Distraught, Clyde threw aside his rake and went splashing away from the ranks of toiling men and women, stomping down hard, trying to crush as many walnuts as he could. He didn't slow his pace until he had gone halfway along the narrow channel between the second and third Dot, and then only because he noticed the light had paled.

Unlike the other two Dots, the third and largest (some ninety feet in diameter) lay at the bottom of a hole that appeared to have been punched through from the surface—probably an old sinkhole—and was open to the weather. At present it was raining straight down, raining hard (a fact that wasn't apparent back in the second Dot, where the walls of the Shilkonic all but sealed them off from the sky), and the pond was empty of laborers. The effect was of a pillar of rain resembling one of those transporter beams used in science fiction movies, except this was much bigger, a ninety-foot-wide column of excited gray particles preparing to zap a giant up from the bowels of an ashen planet, making a seething sound as it did, and amplifying the omnipresent damp smell of the gorge. Staring at it, Clyde's anger planed away into despondency. He and Dell hadn't been that close. They had gone out drinking three or four times, and he'd visited Dell's place to watch DVDs, and they hung out during their lunch breaks, and that was it. But their relationship had the imprimatur of friendship. Dell's breezy, profane irreverence reminded him of his friends back in Beaver Falls. People gossiped about each other a lot in Halloween, yet he recognized that they shied away from certain people and subjects: Pet Nylund and why there was no cable TV and what had happened to Helene Kmiec's husband, to name three. Dell had talked freely about these and other taboos, though most of his talk was BS (perhaps that explained why he'd been banished), and while Clyde had been reluctant to respond in kind, due to his probationary status, neither had he discouraged Dell. A fly's worth of guilt traipsed across his brain and he brushed it aside, telling himself that Dell was his own man and he, Clyde, wasn't about to make this into a soap opera of recriminations and what-ifs.

By the time he reached the pond, the rain had stopped. Under ordinary circumstances, he kept clear of the third Dot (Spooz, as a representative of the council, had written a note excusing him from work there because of his sensitivity to light), yet Clyde felt he needed every jot of intellect in order to deal with his emotions and he moved out into the pond, glancing anxiously at the turbulent sky and the gaping crack of the gorge across the way—less than two months in town and he had already become an agoraphobe. To his left, a section of the granite wall evolved into a ledge. He boosted himself onto it and sat with his legs dangling. Twenty feet farther to the left lay a beach of sand and dirt and rubble, where grew several low bushes surrounding a stunted willow, the sole tree in all of Halloween. Clyde considered the complicated patterns of the bare twigs, thinking this was something the supporters of intelligent design, mistaking (as they frequently did) mere intricacy for skillful engineering, might point to in order to demonstrate the infinite forethought that had gone into God's universal blueprint. Hell, he could do a better job himself, given the right tools. For starters, he'd outfit everyone with male and female genitalia so they wouldn't be constantly trying to fuck one another over, and once they had experienced the joys of childbirth, they would likely stop trying to fuck *themselves* over, recognizing that survival was overrated, and would abandon procreation to the lesser orders and become a species of bonbon who placidly waited for extinction, recognizing this to be the summit of human aspiration. That question settled, he turned his attention to the matter at hand. He had been wrong in trying to banish Dell from mind, basically duplicating the action of the town. Not that he cared to hold onto guilt or any other emotion where Dell was concerned, but he needed to think about why he had been banished and how this might apply to him. He began to whistle—Clyde was an accomplished whistler and had gotten in the habit of accompanying himself while thinking. Whistling orchestrated his thoughts into a calm and orderly pattern, preferable to their usual agitated run. The sinkhole responded with a hint of reverb, adding a mellifluous quality to his tone, distracting him, and it was then he spotted a woman with pale skin and shoulder-length auburn hair peering at him through the willow twigs.

"Jesus!" said Clyde, for she had given him a start.

The twigs sectioned her face like the separations of a jigsaw puzzle, causing her to appear, as she turned her head, like a stained glass image come to life. She stepped out of cover, hopped up onto the far end of the ledge, scowled and said, "Get out of my way."

She was slender and tall, and had on a white sundress that, being a little damp, clung to her body. She wore kneepads and elbow pads, and on her feet were a pair of brown sports shoes.

"Aren't you cold?" Clyde asked.

She pulled a pair of thin gloves from the pocket of her skirt and put them on. In a town where pale women predominated, her pallor was abnormal, like chalk. Her mouth was so wide, its corners seemed to carry out the lines of her slanted cheekbones, and was perfectly molded, the lips neither too full nor too thin, lending her an air of confidence and serenity; her eyes, too, were wide, teardrop-shaped, almost azure in color. She let the scowl lapse into a mask of hostile diffidence, but her face was an open book to Clyde. Her confidence was not based on her beauty (in truth, he didn't perceive her as beautiful, merely attractive—she was too skinny for his tastes), but spoke to the fact that she had little regard for beauty...and not much regard for anything or anyone, if he read her right. She told him once again to move it so she could pass, and Clyde, irritated by her peremptory manner, pointed at the water and said, "Go around."

"I don't want to get wet," she said.

"Yeah, I just bet you don't. That would be icky."

She affected a delighted expression and laughed: two notes, sharply struck, from the treble end of a keyboard. "You're being clever, aren't you? Now let me by."

Clyde was tempted to make her squeeze past, and perhaps he would have done so once upon a time, but he was fascinated by the way her face changed with the movement of eyes and mouth, with every shift in attitude, one moment having an Asian cast, the next seeming entirely Caucasian, and the next expressing an alien quality...and this grounded the charge of his anger. Wondering how old she was (he would not have been surprised to learn she was forty or twenty-five), he eased off the ledge and into the water.

As she walked past him on long, muscular legs, he tried to make nice, saying, "My name's Clyde."

"How appropriate," she said.

When she reached the end of the ledge, she grabbed a miniscule projection of stone, placed the toe of one shoe in an equally imperceptible notch, and then went spidering across the granite face, making the traverse with such speed and precision, it was as if she were wearing sucker pads on her fingers and toes. Within seconds she had disappeared into the channel that led back to the second Dot.

"Whoa!" said Clyde.

HALLOWEEN TOWN

—

He told no one about having seen the woman. He did not tell Joanie because he knew she would leap to the conclusion that his interest was more than casual (which it wasn't, or so he believed) and be upset; he did not tell Mary Alonso, who had taken Dell's place as a source of gossip and information, and with whom he went out for drinks on occasion, usually along with Mary's partner, Roberta, a fey, freckly, dark-haired girl, because he didn't want to learn that the pale woman was a shrew or unstable—he preferred to let her remain a mystery (since we rarely feel compelled to mythologize the humdrum or the ordinary, his interest was likely more than casual). He began coming in early to work and staying late, using the time to practice his whistling in the reverb chamber of the third Dot, hoping to catch sight of her again. He worked on octave jumps, trills and ornamental phrasings, and developed a fresh repertoire of standards and novelty tunes. After a month he became sufficiently confident to essay a few numbers of his own composition ("fantasies," he called them), foremost among them a ballad that he entitled "Melissa"—he thought the woman looked like a Melissa.

Whistling, for Clyde, was its own satisfaction, but when Mary Alonso told him about the talent contest held at the Downlow every year and urged him to enter, he thought, What the hell? He devoted himself to perfecting "Melissa," adding a frill or two, reworking the somber middle passage, trimming the coda so the song fit within the contest's fourminute limit, and one afternoon in March, with the contest less than a month away, while he sat practicing on the ledge, with a circle of wintry blue sky overhead and shadow filling the sinkhole, all except for a slice of golden light at the brim, the woman, dressed in jeans and a burgundy sweater, came poling a skiff from the south, emerging from the darkness of the gorge with lanterns hung all over the prow and sides and stem. Something about her posture announced her even before he made out her face. She beached the skiff near the willow and climbed onto the ledge and took a seat about three feet away. Her flat azurine stare seemed as hostile as before, but Clyde saw curiosity in her face. Neither of them spoke for a couple of ticks and then she said, "That's a cool tune, man."

"It's something I'm working on," he said.

"You made it up?"

"Yeah."

"Very cool. What's it called?"

"'Melissa.'"

"Is she your girl…your wife?"

"I don't know why I called it that. The only Melissa I ever knew was back in grade school."

"It sounds classical. You ever hear the opera, *Pelléas et Mélisande*, by Debussy?"

"I don't think so."

She appeared to have run out of questions.

"What's it about, the opera?" asked Clyde.

"I don't remember much. This sad chick's married to this prince, but she's in love with his brother. She cries a lot. It's kind of a bummer. Your thing reminded me of it."

She kicked her heels against the rock and gazed out across the pond. Clyde realized that at this distance he should be reading her more clearly—he should have seen past the level of body language into her chaotic core, where need and desire steamed upward and began to solidify into shards of thought; yet he could find no trace of her fundamental incoherence…or else, unlike the rest of mankind, she was fundamentally coherent, her personality rising in a smooth, uninterrupted flow from its springs, a true and accurate extension of her soul.

"Not the notes," she said. "The feeling."

"Huh?" said Clyde.

"Your song. It reminded me of the opera. Not the melody or anything, but the feeling." She said this with a trace of exasperation and then asked, "Why're you staring at me?"

He was inclined to tell her that she had a smudge on her cheek (which she, in fact, did) or that she looked familiar; but she gazed at him with such intensity, he half-suspected that his inability to see into her basements signaled a commensurate ability on her part to see into his—afraid of being caught in a lie, then, he told her about his accident and its aftermath and explained how she appeared to be something of an anomaly, at least as regarded his hypothesis concerning light, intellect, and the chaotic underpinnings of human personality.

"Must be I'm in your blind spot," she said. "Because I feel pretty chaotic...at least most of the time."

That he might have a blind spot disturbed him more than the thought that she might be a freak of nature.

"Light-based intelligence," she said musingly. "What about Milton? He wrote great shit after he went blind."

"I haven't found a theory yet that explains everything or everyone. I suppose he's an exception, like you."

He thought she might be losing interest in the conversation and asked if she commonly hung out in the third Dot.

"Only during the season," she said in a fake upper-crust accent. Letting up on the sarcasm, she added, "I pass through when I go exploring down south. And when I need to be by myself, I'll stake out a spot next to the willow."

"So if I see you beside the willow, I should beat it?"

"Not necessarily," she said, and grinned. "You could whistle and see what develops. I've always had a thing for musicians." With an easy motion, she pushed up to her feet. "I've got to get back. See you around, maybe."

Clyde restrained himself from asking her to stay. "Hey, what's your name?"

"Annalisa."

She moved off and Clyde, watching the roll of her hips, knowing it was the wrong thing to do yet unable to suppress the urge, let out an appreciative whistle, an ornate variation on the wolf whistle that he had devised for just such occasions and often used to excellent effect, the intricacy of his embellishment compensating for the cornball tactic. Annalisa rolled her eyes, but he noticed a little extra sway in her walk as she went toward the skiff. He thought "Annalisa" was a much better title than "Melissa," and he decided then and there to break up with Joanie.

—

Usually Joanie was eager to go to his place, but that night, perhaps sensing trouble, she resisted being alone with him and they went for a drink at the Downlow, a labyrinthine nightclub excavated from the rock. Bass-heavy ambient music rumbled from hidden speakers. The rooms were lit by plastic boulders that shifted from dull orange to violet to blue-green, and served as tables; these were enclosed by groupings of sofas and easy chairs. There were decorative touches throughout—potted ferns; a diminutive statue that might have been Mayan or Olmec; a poster of Pet Nylund with his hair flying, face obscured, twisting the strings of his guitar—but not enough of them to create a specific statement. The overall effect was of a tiki bar in Bedrock whose interior decorator had been fired halfway through the job.

They chose an empty side room with an aquarium built into the walls, populated by fish with strange whiskery antennae and others without eyes. Clyde recognized none of them and asked Joanie what kind they were. She replied, "Who do you think I am? A fish scientist?" She looked sullen in the orange light, angry in the violet, depressed in the blue-green.

A waitress brought their drinks and, since Joanie's mood showed no sign of improving, Clyde got straight to the point. He had worked out what he felt was a tactful approach, but he had barely begun when Joanie broke in and asked, "Who is she?"

Defensively, Clyde said, "You think I've been unfaithful?"

She scooted an inch or two farther away. "Don't bullshit me. Men don't jump unless they got some place to land."

"I met this woman, all right?" said Clyde. "But we haven't done anything yet."

"Who is she?"

"If you weren't so goddamn negative about our relationship. If you didn't always…"

"Oh, it's my fault?" She made a noise like the Prince did when he sneezed. "I guess I should have known from experience. I been dumped on more times than your toilet seat, so it must be me..."

"See, that's what I'm talking about! You're always putting yourself down."

"It must be me and not the dickwads I go out with."

"Maybe all I need is a break," said Clyde. "A little space."

Joanie injected an artificial brightness into her voice. "What a good idea! I'll give you space while you cozy up to what's-her-buttass and I'll just hang loose in case things don't work out."

"Goddamn it, Joanie! You know that's not what I mean."

"Tell me who she is."

Reluctantly, Clyde said, "I only met her a couple of times. Her name's Annalisa."

For a second Joanie was expressionless; then she spewed laughter. "Oh, man! You hooked up with the willow wan?"

"I haven't hooked up with anybody!"

She put her head down and shook her head back and forth; her hair glowed orange as it swept the top of the boulder.

"What'd you call her...the willow what?"

Joanie's voice was nearly inaudible above a lugubrious bass line. "Wan. The willow *wan*. It's what everybody calls her."

"I don't get it."

"Because she's pale as birdshit and always acts crazy and hangs out by the willow tree and she does all kinds of crazy things."

"What's she do that's crazy?"

"I don't know! Lots of things."

"There must be something specific if everyone thinks she's crazy."

"She's all the time going down south of the Dots. You have to be crazy to go there." A look of entreaty crowded other emotions from her face, yet Clyde still saw anger and hurt. "She's gaming you, man. You don't want to mess with her. She games all the guys. She's Pet Nylund's ex-wife, for God's sake! She still lives with him."

"What do you mean?"

"Am I speaking Spanish? She fucking lives with him. In his house."

Some evidence of the disappointment he felt must have surfaced in his expression, for upon registering it she snatched her purse and jumped up from the sofa. He caught her wrist and said, "Joanie…"

She broke free and stood with her chin trembling. "Stay out of the Sub for a while, okay?"

A tear spilled from the corner of her eye and she rubbed it frantically, as if trying to kill a stinging insect; then she said something he didn't catch and ran from the room.

Clyde had the impulse to offer consolation, but the weight of what she had said about Annalisa kept him seated. Though they had established the frailest of connections, nothing really, he felt betrayed, hurt, angry, everything Joanie had appeared to feel—the idea floated into his mind that she might want him to suffer and had lied about Annalisa. But if it were a lie, it would be easy to disprove and thus it was probably true. He downed his drink in two swallows and went into the main room, a semicircular space with twenty or thirty of the boulder tables and a bar with a marble countertop and a stage, currently unoccupied, against the rear wall. Joanie was doing shots at the bar, bracketed by two men who had their hands all over her; when she saw him she gave her hair an assertive flip and pretended to be deeply interested in what one man (a big sloppy dude with long hair and a beard, Barry Something) was saying. He scanned the tables, hoping to spot a friendly face among the people sitting there. Finding none, he walked out onto the pier, sat on a piling under the entrance lights and listened to the gurgling of the Mossbach. Off along the bend, on the elbow of the curve, Pet Nylund's house staggered up the cliff face, three side-by-side, crookedy towers, their uppermost rooms cloaked in darkness. Lights were on in several of the lower rooms. Clyde toyed with the notion of going over and busting through the door and venting his frustrations in a brawl. It was a bonehead play he would once have made without thinking, and that he now stopped to consider the consequences and hadn't simply acted out his passions with animal immediacy, never mind it was the rational thing to do…it dismayed him. Carmine, he told himself, might have been right in his estimation: maybe Halloween wasn't going to work out for him.

Laughter from the doorway and Joanie emerged from the Downlow arm-in-arm with the two men she'd been flirting with at the bar. The bearded man caught Clyde staring and asked what he was looking at. Clyde ignored him and said, "Don't do this to yourself, Joanie."

She hardened her smile and Barry Something put a hand on Clyde's chest and suggested he back the fuck off. The touch kindled a cold fury in Clyde that spread throughout his body, as if he'd been dunked in liquid nitrogen. He saw everything with abnormal clarity: the positions of the men, Joanie's embittered face, the empty doorway, the green neon letters bolted to the rock. He spread his hands as though to say, no harm, no foul, and planted his right foot and drove his fist into Barry's eye. Barry reeled away, went to his knees, grabbing his face. Joanie started yelling; the other man sidled nervously toward the entrance. Barry moaned. "Aw, fuck! Fuck!" he said. An egg-shaped lump was already rising from his orbital ridge. Clyde grabbed Joanie's arm and steered her toward his skiff. She fought him at first, but then started to cry. Some onlookers stepped out of the bar, drinks in hand, to learn what the fuss was about. Not a one of them moved to help Barry, who was rolling around, holding his eye. Talking and laughing, they watched Clyde pole the skiff into the center of the river. "Chickenshit bastard!" someone shouted. From a distance, the tableau in front of the bar appeared to freeze, as if its batteries had died. Joanie sat in the stern, her knees drawn up, gazing at the water. Her tears dried. Once or twice she seemed on the verge of speaking. He thought he should say something, but he had nothing to offer, still too adrenalized, too full of anger at Barry, at himself, too caught up in the dismal glory of the fight, confused as to whether it had validated his hopes for Halloween or had been an attempt to validate them. When they reached her pier, Joanie scrambled up onto it without a word and raced into her tiny, two-room house and slammed the door.

—

Working alongside him the following morning, Mary Alonso, who had gotten a buzzcut and a dye job, leaving a half-inch of blond stubble that he thought singularly unattractive, filled Clyde in on Annalisa.

"She shares the house with Pet, but she's not *with* him, you know," she said. "She keeps to her half, he keeps to his. Joanie was being a bitch, telling you that without telling you the rest. Not that I blame her."

"For real? She's not sleeping with him?"

"She did once after the divorce, but it was sort of a reflex."

Clyde flipped a rotten walnut up with his rake, caught it in midair and shied it at the wall, provoking a stare from another worker, whom the walnut had whizzed past. "How'd you hear that?"

"Before me and Roberta got together, Annalisa had a girl crush on Roberta. She thought she might be gay, but…" Mary strained to break up a clump of walnuts that had become trapped in underwater grass. "Turned out she wasn't. Not even a little." She scowled at Clyde. "Don't look so damn relieved!"

Clyde held up a hand as though in apology. "So Roberta told you about her?"

"Yeah. They stayed friends and she talks to Roberta sometimes. But don't get too happy. Her head's fucked up from being with Pet all those years. She tells Roberta she's going to leave, but she never does. There's some kind of bizarre dependency still happening between her and Pet."

Clyde went back to work with a renewed vigor, thinking that he might be the man to dissolve that bond. The weather was crisp and clear, and the sky crack showed a cold blue zigzag like a strip of frozen lightning that the ragged line of laborers beneath appeared to emulate. A seam of reflected light from the water jittered on the rock walls.

"I'm worried about you, man," said Mary. "I love you, and I don't want to see you get all bent out of shape behind this thing."

"You love me!" Clyde gave a doltish laugh.

Mary's face cinched with anger. "Right. Mister Macho. You think all love is is the shit that makes you feel dizzy. Everything else is garbage. Well, fuck you!" She threw down her rake and went chest to chest with him. "Yeah, I love you! Roberta loves you! It's amazing we do, you're such an ass-clown!"

Startled by this reaction, Clyde put a hand on her shoulder. "I didn't mean to piss you off."

She knocked his hand away, looking like she was itching to throw a punch.

"I wasn't thinking," Clyde said. "I was..."

"For someone claims to have a problem with smarts, you do a lot of not-thinking." She picked up her rake and took a swipe at the walnuts.

The other workers, who had paused to watch, turned away and engaged in hushed conversations.

"You're so caught up in your own crap, you can't see anything else," said Mary, who had toned down from fighting mad to grumpy.

"We've established I'm a dick, all right?" Clyde said. "Now what're you trying to tell me?"

"Annalisa's not Pet's wife, and she's not his girlfriend, but she's his business because she lets herself be his business. Until that changes she's poison for other guys. That's the number one rule around here, even though they didn't write it down: Don't fuck with Pet Nylund's business."

"Or what? You go to the Tubes?"

"Keep being a dick. You'll find out."

Mary raked walnuts with a vengeance, as if she wanted to rip out the bottom of the Dot. Clyde rested both hands on the end of his rake and, as he gazed at the other workers, some intent on their jobs, some goofing off, some pretending to be busy, and then glanced up at the gorge enclosing them like the two halves of a gigantic bivalve, its lips almost closed, admitting a ragged seam of sky, at the gray walls stained with lichen and feathered with struggling ferns, he had an overpowering sense of both the unfamiliar and the commonplace, and realized with a degree of sadness what he should have understood long before: Halloween wasn't, as he had hoped, an oasis with magical qualities isolated from the rest of the country; it was the flabby heart of dead-end America, a drear, crummy back alley between faceless cliff tenements where the big ones ate the little ones and not every dog had his day.

—

For almost a week he took to sitting each night beneath the dangling seventy-five watt bulb at the end of Ms. Kmiec's pier, hoping to catch Annalisa returning in her skiff from down south. He was a fool, he knew that—he had no reason to believe she felt anything for him, and the wonder was that he felt so much for her; yet he was unable to resist the notion (though he wouldn't have admitted it, because saying the words would have forced him to confront their foolishness) that they had connected on an important level. To provide himself with an excuse for sitting there hour after hour, he borrowed one of Stan Kmiec's old fishing rods and made a desultory cast whenever he sighted an approaching skiff. Briefly, he became interested in trying to land one of the silvery bioluminescent fish that flocked the dark water, but they proved too canny and the only thing he snagged was what he thought to be some sort of water snake, a skinny writhing shadow that snapped and did a twisting dance in midair, and succeeded in flinging out the hook…and yet he heard no splash, as if it had flown off into the night.

The sixth night, unseasonably warm and misty (it had been like that all week and the bugs and bats were out in force), he spotted a skiff coming from the south with no light hung from its bow and knew it had to be Annalisa. She paused when she noticed him, letting the skiff glide. He whistled the opening bars of "Annalisa." She turned the skiff, brought it alongside the pier, and said brightly, "What's up?"

"Fishing." He indicated the rod. "Thinking."

She smiled. "Ooh. That must be hard work. Maybe I shouldn't interfere."

She had on jeans and a turtleneck and an old saggy gray cardigan; her hands were chapped and smudged with dirt, and her reddish brown hair (redder, he thought, than the last time he had seen her) was tied back with a black ribbon.

"The damage is done," he said. "Come sit a while."

She looped a line over a piling and he gave her a hand up. She settled beside him, her hip nudging his. She let out a sigh and looked across the water to the houses on the far side, a game board of bright and dark squares, their walls barely discernible and their piers lent definition by diffuse pyramids of wan light and whirling moths at their extremities. She smelled of shampoo and freshly turned earth, as if she had been gardening.

"I see Milly's working late," she said.

"Milly?"

"Milly Sussman. Don't you even know your neighbors?"

"Guess not."

"You need to get out more. How long have you been here? Three, four months? I should think you would have noticed Milly. Statuesque. Black hair. An extremely impressive woman."

"Maybe…yeah."

With her hair back, her face seemed more Asian than before; her prominent cheekbones and narrow jaw formed a nearly trapezoidal frame for her exotic features, making them appear stylized like those of a beautiful anime cyborg. From all her tics and eye movements and the working of her mouth, he read a mixture of desire and fear. Something left a trail of bubbles out on the river. Three glowing silver fish hovered in the water beneath her Doc Martens. She peered at them and asked, "You catch anything?"

"Yep. I hooked me a nice-looking one."

"You're being clever again. I can tell." She kicked her heels idly against the side of the pier. "We missed out, not living in the age of courtly speech. I could say, like, uh, 'Hooked, sir? Thy hook is not set deep enough!' And you could…"

He placed a hand on the back of her neck and drew her gently to him and kissed her. She pulled away and, with a nervous laugh, said, "Better watch it. You'll get girl cooties." The second time he kissed her, she displayed no reluctance, no resistance whatsoever. Her tongue darted out so quickly, it might have been an animal trapped in the cave of her mouth, desperate to escape, if only to another cave. He caught her waist, pulling her closer, and slipped his hand under the turtleneck, up along her ribcage to her breast, rolling the nipple with his thumb. Their teeth clicked together, they clawed at one another and sought fresh angles of attack, striving to penetrate and to admit the other more deeply. The kiss was brutish, clumsy, an expression of red-brained lust, and Annalisa surfaced from it like a diver with bursting lungs, exclaiming, "Oh god!"

After a few beats they kissed again, and were more measured in their explorations, yet no less lustful. Clyde was about to suggest they move things to his bedroom, but Annalisa spoke first.

"I can't do this now." She tugged the turtleneck down over her breasts. "I'm sorry. Really, really sorry. But I have to go."

"Go where?"

"Home. I don't want to, but..."

Despite himself, resentment crept into his voice. "Home to Pet."

Annalisa cut her eyes toward him and finished straightening her clothes. "It's complicated."

"You going to explain it to me?"

"Yes, but I can't now." She rebuttoned the top button of her jeans.

"When am I going to see you?"

"I'm not sure."

"I don't understand," he said. "You wanted me to kiss you."

"I did. Very much." She reached behind her head and retied her hair ribbon. "Since we're being candid, I want to make your eyes roll back. But it's dangerous. *This* was dangerous. I shouldn't have let it happen."

"How's it dangerous?"

"You could die."

She said this so flatly, he had to laugh. He wasn't sure whether she was telling the truth or attempting to scare him off. He stared at her, perhaps sadly, because she reacted to his expression by saying, "For God's sake! It was only a kiss." He continued to stare and she said, "Okay, the losing-consciousness part, that was new." She climbed into the skiff, undid the line, and held onto the piling. "I'm incredibly motivated to be with you. You probably sensed that."

He nodded happily.

"There's a safe way we can be together," she went on. "But you have to give me time to work it out. Weeks, if necessary. Maybe a month. Can you do that? If not, tell me now, because Pet is insane. It's not that he's suspicious or jealous. He is batshit crazy and he hurts people."

"I can do it."

A flapping of wings overhead, followed by a long quavering cry that sounded like a man running out of breath while blowing trebly notes on a harmonica.

"If it takes a little longer even," Annalisa said, "promise you'll trust me."

"Promise."

"You won't do anything stupid!"

"I'll be cool."

"Shake on it."

She gave his hand a vigorous shake and trailed her fingers across his as she disengaged.

"All right. See you soon," she said, and made a rueful face. "I'm sorry."

It was slightly unreal watching her glide away into the dark and, after she had vanished, he felt morose and insubstantial, like a ghost who had suddenly been made aware of all the sensory richness of which he was deprived. The enclosure of the gorge, though invisible, oppressed him. Dampness cored his bones. It was impossible to hold onto promises in all that emptiness. Whatever it was that made bubbles out in the river was still making them, trawling back and forth in front of the pier, closing the distance with each pass, lifting the water with each turn, causing swells. Clyde walked away from the pier, chased by the whisper of the water, the gleeps and tweetlings of frogs and other night creatures, and wearily climbed the ladder to his apartment.

—

They saw one another more frequently than he'd expected over the days that followed, running into each other in the bars, on the river, sometimes contriving to touch, and one afternoon, when Mrs. Kmiec sent him to Dowling's (Halloween's eccentric version of a supermarket and its most extensive building, four interconnected tiers of eight stories each) to pick up kitty litter, Annalisa accosted him in Pet Supplies, eighth floor, fourth tier, and drew him out through a door behind the shelves into a narrow space between the rear wall and the cliff face, and there she hiked up her skirt and they made violent, bone-rattling love balanced on girders above eighty feet of nothing, braced against rock that had been ornately tagged by generations of teenagers who had used the spot before them, swirls of orange, silver, blue, red, and fat letters outlined in black, most of them cursing the authority of man or god, whatever agency had ruled their particular moment, all their hormonal rebellion confined to this not-so-secret hideaway. Annalisa was sweet and shifty, cunning with her hips, yet she nipped his neck, marking his throat, and left a long scratch on his rib cage, and spoke in tongues, in gasps and throaty noises. It seemed less an act of abandon for her than one of desperation. Afterward he asked if this is what she'd had in mind when she mentioned a safe way of being together. "I couldn't wait," she said, staring at him with tremulous anxiety, as if the wrong word would break her, shatter the almost Asian simplicity of her face. He felt this to be the case, that she had put herself in physical and mental jeopardy by taking this step, and he realized that her strength and apparent independence was a carefully constructed shield that had prevented him from seeing what lay behind it—he still could not make out the roots of her trouble, but he sensed something restive, dammed up, a powerful force straining for release.

The week before the talent contest they held auditions at the Downlow. The stage was lit with a spot that pointed up the tawdryness of the glittery silver Saturns and comets on the dark blue painted backdrop; but there were amps and a good PA and professional quality mikes, everything a performer might need. Waiting to go on, through what seemed an interminable sequence of stand-up comics with no sense of timing, accordion players, twirlers, off-key vocalists, tap dancers, rappers, and a man who could put a foot behind his ear while standing and repeat everything you said backward (Clyde's favorite), he had several drinks to ease his nerves and oil his instrument…perhaps one too many, for when his turn came, following a sax player who noodled a decent rendition of "My Favorite Things," he announced that he would be performing an original composition entitled, "'Annali...uh, Melissa.'" A guy in the back asked him to repeat the title and he said, "Sorry. I'm a little nervous. That's 'Melissa Anne.'"

Pet Nylund was supposed to be in the audience and, as he adjusted the mike, adding a bit touch of reverb, Clyde searched for him (though he couldn't recall his face and wasn't certain what he would be like after so many years away from the limelight), but the spot blinded him. He warmed up with a scale, which drew catcalls, but after he had performed, he received scattered applause, which was better than most had done. Afterward he was given a packet containing an entry number and forms, and told he was in. His main competition was the sax player, a black chick named Yolanda who sang a wicked version of "Chain of Fools," and a young guy who did a one-man-band comedy act that was borderline obscene and a real crowd-pleaser. The singer and the young guy were one-two, he figured, but he stood a good chance for third place money, three hundred bucks and a Pet Nylund box set, enough to buy Annalisa something nice. He'd give the box set to Mary for Roberta, who was a fan.

He had another drink at the bar, looked around again for Annalisa and Pet, and talked to Spooz for a bit. Spooz complimented him on his whistling and said he should hang out—Brad would be along soon. Brad had a job topside that kept him running and was hardly ever around, and Clyde would have liked to stay and talk sports with him; but lately he preferred being alone with his thoughts of Annalisa to the company of others, so he begged off.

The lights were on in Ms. Kmiec's living room and, as he ascended the ladder, taking pains not to slip, because drunken ladder mishaps were a common occurrence in Halloween (only the week before Tim Sleight, whom Clyde knew from the Dots, had gotten a load on and plunged two floors, narrowly missing a granite outcropping and splashing in the river), Ms. Kmiec's door flew open and, framed in a spill of yellow glare, she leaned out and said merrily, "Clyde Ormoloo! Come have a drink!"

Her hair was pinned up loosely, riding atop her head like the remains of some blond confection, a soufflé that had fallen, a wedding cake that had been dropped. She had on a black lace peignor and a pair of matching panties; her unconfined breasts bobbled as she swayed in the doorway. She or someone had made bullseyes of her nipples with concentric circles of green ink. He assumed she was trashed and warned her to be careful.

"Clyde Ormoloo-loo!" She pouted. "You get in here right now! There's someone wants to see you!" She sang this last sentence and leaned farther out and beckoned to Clyde.

He scaled the remaining rungs, pushed past her and closed the door to prevent her from doing a half-gainer into the Mossbach.

The yellow room was as always, but for three notable exceptions: Prince was curled up on the sofa, his head tucked into his stomach, and the large framed photograph of Stan and Helene had been defaced by the realistic cartoon (also in green ink) of a stubby erect penis sticking out from the center of Mr. Kmiec's forehead. An aromatherapy candle that had gone out sprouted from a blue glass dish on the coffee table—the packaging, which lay on the floor, said it was Tyrrhenian Musk, a product of Italy, but it smelled like charred Old Spice to Clyde. He had the idea that he was interrupting one of Helene's private sessions.

"See!" Helene said. She leaned into Clyde. "Princey's here!"

With some effort she lifted Prince, cradling him like a baby, and pressed him into Clyde's chest, as if expecting him to hold the animal. Prince yielded an annoyed, "Mrap," and struggled weakly. Clyde saw that the door leading to the adjoining house stood partway open.

"Is someone here?" he asked.

Helene buried her face in Prince's tummy and made growly noises, offending the cat still more.

A big tanned woman with strong features, muscular arms and legs, several inches taller than Clyde, black hair tumbled about her broad shoulders, entered from the corridor, bottle in hand. Her face reminded him of the image of an empress embossed on a Persian coin that his dad once showed him, too formidable to be beautiful, yet beautifully serene and leonine beneath her ringleted mane. She wore a red Lycra sports bra and shorts that did their best to control an exuberant bust and mighty rear end. His first thought was that she must be a transsexual, but there was no sign of an Adam's apple and her hands were slender and finely boned—three rings, none a wedding band, adorned them, including a significant diamond nested among opals.

"Hello," she said in a humid contralto. "I'm Milly. And you must be Clyde. Would you care for some apple brandy? It's sooo good!"

"Yeah...okay." Clyde perched on the couch beside Helene, who was still making much over the cat. Recalling Annalisa's description, he said, "You're Milly Sussman?"

"The same."

Moving with a stately grace, Milly took a seat in an easy chair and poured a dollop of brandy each into three diminutive glasses shape like goblets.

"I thought you owned the house across the way," Clyde said.

"I own two houses." She held up two fingers for emphasis. "One's basically an office. Helene?"

"Yes, please!" She scooted to the edge of the couch. Prince writhed free, fell with a thud to the floor, and waddled off to find a quieter spot.

"New friends," Milly said, lifting her glass.

Helene chugged the brandy; Clyde had a sip.

"It is good," he said, setting down his glass. "I notice you have a tan. That's unusual around here."

Milly examined her arms. "I'm just back from three glorious weeks in Thailand. Well, not *just* back, but I was there recently. A little island not far from Kosumui. You should have seen me then. I was nearly absolutely black. But now..." She heaved a dramatic sigh. "I'm entombed in Halloween once again."

Helene went over to the portrait of her late husband and studied it with her head cocked.

"You must like it here," Clyde said. "I mean, two houses."

"It has its charms." Milly crossed her legs. "Lately, however, I find it limiting. And you?"

Helene hunted for something on the end table beside the easy chair, was impeded in her search by the folds of her peignor and shrugged out of it. She located what she had been looking for—a Magic Marker—and stood sucking on the tip, apparently contemplating an addition to her work. Though for seven, eight seconds out of ten on the average, Clyde's thoughts turned to Annalisa, the sight of Helene almost naked was difficult to ignore.

Milly repeated her question: "And you?" Her smile seemed to acknowledge Clyde's distraction.

"I liked it better when I first arrived," he said. "I guess maybe I'm finding it limiting, too."

With a knee resting on the arm of Milly's chair, Helene drew on the portrait.

Milly ran a hand along her thigh, as if to smooth out an imaginary wrinkle in the skin-tight Lycra. "Perhaps there's a way we can help one another exceed those limits."

Choosing his words with care, Clyde said, "We're probably talking about different sorts of limits."

"Ah." Her face impassive, she sipped her brandy.

They endured a prickly silence; then Clyde asked, "So what do you do...for a living?"

"I have a foundation that funds cottage industries in the Third World. I was a lawyer; I suppose I still am. But the law..." She made a disaffected noise.

"We could use some cottage industries here. This raking walnuts thing gets pretty old."

"Actually I was speaking to Pet about that very thing before I left for Thailand. Of course we don't need them, but diversity might infuse the people with a better attitude. Raking walnuts, packaging walnuts, shipping walnuts, all this ridiculous drudgery... It reinforces the notion that he owns them. But he insists on running the town his way. Pet's an unpleasant little man. He's one of the reasons I'm thinking about leaving."

"Never met the guy."

"I did some legal work for him during the nineties. I liked him then, but he's changed a great deal since he stopped performing."

"There!" Helene backed off a few paces to assess her work. Atop Stan Kmiec's head she had created the line drawing of a parrot that, its head turned sideways, was threatening to bite the stubby appendage protruding from his brow.

"Very nice," said Milly. "Clyde and I were talking about Pet, dear. Anything you'd care to contribute?"

"Pet's an even bigger prick than Stan," she said absently, and cast about the room. "I think Prince went over to your place."

She headed off along the connecting corridor, weaving from wall to wall.

"Well," said Clyde, sliding to the edge of the sofa. "I've got work in the morning. Walnuts to rake."

"A question before you go," Milly said. "I realize that men—many of them—find me too Amazonian for their tastes. Is that why you turned me down?"

Clyde was startled by her frankness.

She smiled. "Be truthful, now!"

"It's more a case of my head not being in the right place," he said.

She put her glass on the coffee table, leaning close to him as she did. He became aware of the smallness of the room, and the heated scent of her body, and had a paranoid flash, recalling movies featuring women of her dimension and fitness level who served villains, generally of Eastern European origin, as paid assassins; yet he picked up nothing from her other than a gloomy passivity.

"I've got stuff on my mind," he said. "Life stuff, you know."

Milly sank back into the cushions, again crossing her legs. "Helene told me you were unattached."

A scream ripped along the corridor between the houses, followed by an explosive crash of glass breaking. Clyde and Milly sprang to their feet at nearly the same moment and, due to the cramped quarters, her head struck him on the point of the chin, knocking him back onto the sofa and sending white lights shooting into his eyes, while she went down heavily between the easy chair and the end table. She managed to unwedge herself and struggled up into a crouch, when Helene rushed in and bowled her over again. Helene yanked at a drawer in the end table, pulling it completely out and spilling a large pistol, a .357, onto the floor.

"Son-of-a-bitch got Prince!" she said tearfully.

She cocked the gun and scampered across the coffee table between Milly and Clyde; she flipped a row of wall switches and threw open the door. Exterior lights bathed the granite cliff and the neighboring houses in an infernal white radiance, illuminating every crevice and projection. From the sofa, Clyde had a glimpse of something unusual. Traversing the cliff ten yards above them was a greenish black creature—at that distance it resembled an enormous cabbage that had been left out in the rain and rotted, losing all but an approximation of its spherical form, its leaves shredded and hanging off the central structure like the decaying rags of a homeless person. It moved rapidly, albeit in a series of fits and starts, growing taller, skinnier, pausing, then shrinking and becoming cabbage-like again, its body flowing between those poles, as if its means of perambulation involved muscular contractions and expulsions of air similar to those utilized by an octopus. Still groggy, Clyde sat up, hoping for a clearer look, but Helene blocked the doorway. She braced against the doorframe, adopting a shooter's stance, and squeezed off three rounds that boomed across the gorge and shattered the air inside the yellow room. Clyde stumbled up off the sofa just as she said, "Damn it!" and began fumbling with the gun. She tugged on the trigger, holding the weapon at such an angle that, if it hadn't been jammed, it would have blown off her foot.

"Wait!" he said, going toward her.

A petulant expression replaced one of stupefied determination. She transferred the gun to her left hand and, playing keep away, thrust it out over the gorge, a clumsy movement that caused her to overbalance. She flailed her arms, clutched at the air, shrieked in terror and toppled out the doorway. Clyde made a dive for her and snagged an ankle, stopping her fall, but momentum swung her against the side of the house—she smacked into the wall headfirst and went limp. The edge of the doorway cut into the back of Clyde's arms. He eased forward, so his arms were clear, his torso and head extended over the gorge, and firmed up his grip, paying no mind to Milly's hysterical advice. The dark river and the diminished pier and the strip of yellow-white sand beside it looked like really keen accessories to a toy model of the town. He closed his eyes to forestall dizziness. Other voices were heard. A man poked his head out the window of the house next door and told him not to let go. Someone else called from below, telling him to swing Helene out over the river and let her drop into the water, as if a forty-foot plunge were nothing to fear. Women's voices shrilled; thick, sleep-dulled male voices rumbled and children squeaked. It seemed the gunshots had waked half the population of Halloween and they each and every one were offering stupid suggestions.

"Milly! Get behind me," he said. "Grab my ankles."

She did as told and immediately began yanking him into the room.

"No, stop…stop!" he said. "Don't pull until I tell you. Okay?"

Inch by inch, Clyde worked his grip higher on Helene's leg. Sweat broke on his forehead. Helene was not a heavy woman, but he couldn't get his back into the lift and a hundred-ten, hundred-twenty pounds of dead weight took a toll on his arms. Her head kept banging against the house and he decided this was a good thing—if she woke and went to thrashing about, he might lose her. The lights gave him a headache and the small crowd that had gathered on the shingle below distracted him. Once he had secured a hold on Helene's knee, he told Milly to pull him about six inches back. She tugged on his ankles and Clyde twisted onto his side, a movement that swung Helene's free leg toward him. Holding her by the knee with one arm, he trapped the other leg and locked both hands behind her thighs. He told Milly to pull him six inches farther, and when she did, he heaved on Helene, shifting her up along his body to a point where he had a grip on her hips and buttocks, and a faceful of lace panties.

"Okay," he said to Milly. "Bring us in."

Once they were inside the room, Milly dragged Helene off him. The cheer that arose from the gorge was fainter than he might have expected, as if a sizable portion of those watching had been rooting against them. Blood smeared Helene's mouth and chin, most coming from her nose—Clyde thought it might be broken. While Milly ministered to her, he had a seat on the sofa and pounded the rest of his brandy. He poured another glass and knocked down the lion's share of that. The muscles in his shoulders burned. Helene came back to the world crying and carrying on about Stan, how ashamed she was for defacing his picture. She didn't remember a thing about the accident or Prince, but planted a bloody kiss on Clyde's mouth in gratitude after Milly brought her up to speed. Milly decided to take Helene over to her place, where she could better care for her, and said she'd be back to check on him as soon she made Helene comfortable.

Clyde closed his eyes and thought about the cat-killer (it wasn't the first inexplicable thing he'd seen here, but it certainly staked claim to being the headline on Weird News), and about Prince *mrapping* around Cat Heaven, and about Annalisa, what lay ahead for them and how it would be…and then he was being shaken awake by Steve Germany, a squat, shaven-headed man, all his features crowded together toward the center of his face, a walnut raker who worked nights as a bouncer at the Downlow, and another bouncer, Dan or Dave, he couldn't recall, sat next to him, and Spooz studied him from the easy chair, his double-chinned mug pale as an onion, and said, "Man, did you screw up," and there was a fourth guy, a scrawny, shriveled-up, narrow-shouldered geezer with a prunish face (except for a young man's sneering mouth) and his gray hair in a pony tail, wearing a midnight blue velvet jacket over a T-shirt bearing the design of a Chinese character on the chest and black jeans belted with a buckle in the shape of a P flocked round by silver birds (it looked as if he'd borrowed his grandson's clothes) and this enfeebled gangster of love, this Lilliputian Monster of Rock (Clyde knew he was Pet Nylund), produced a pocket tape recorder, clicked the play button, and Clyde heard his own voice say, "'Annali…Melissa,'" pause, crackle, and then, "Sorry. I'm a little nervous. That's 'Melissa Anne.'"

"Do you know who I am?" Pet asked in a sandpapery wheeze, and Clyde, realizing that he was in deep shit, understanding that it didn't much matter how he responded, answered, "George Michaels's dad?"

Pet bared his teeth in a yellow smile. "Tube his ass!"

—

The tubes were situated at the opposite end of town from the Dots, occupying the summit of a sixty-foot-high granite mound and hidden by a high concrete block wall overgrown by lichen—it looked like an old WWII gun emplacement guarding the entrance to Halloween. That evening, however, it radiated evil energies visible to Clyde as pulsating streams of gray vapor and had the gargantuan aspect of an ancient citadel, a habitat fit for wizards and eldritch beasts. After the one-sided struggle to subdue him, someone had given Clyde an injection. Nothing calmative. His heart raced, his nerves twitched, and his thoughts flared like fireworks, illuminating one or another heretofore hidden corner of his brain before being dissipated by a new pyrotechnic display of insights and colors. Tattered glowing white wings without bodies, the relics of revenant birds and angels, swerved near and then vanished into the purple gloom; troll faces materialized from the coarse rock and spoke booming words, like the magic words in a children's book, and the black water acquired a skin of serpent scales. If he had not been trussed like a mummy, thin ropes pinning his arms to his sides and lashing his legs together, he could have gotten behind the hallucinations, and he would have offered a vociferous complaint if he hadn't also been gagged. As it was, he rolled about, rocking the skiff, until Spooz kicked him in the liver.

Making jokes at his expense, they lugged him up from the river and through a door and laid him down on a concrete slab lit by arc lamps, a penitentiary setting that had the industrial look and soul-shriveling feel and dry negative smell of an execution ground. A single star shone in the sky crack, its name unknown, so he called it Azrael, then Disney, then Fremont Phil or Capricorn Sue, depending on its sex. He lifted his head and saw six, no, seven perfectly round openings in the concrete, one of them covered with a piece of sheet iron, a winch mounted above each, and he flashed on the idea that perfectly round holes were a motif in Halloween, there were the Dots and the Tubes and...well, there were a couple of examples, anyway, and he imagined that some gigantic, perfectly round, acid-exuding worm or humongous beetle with diamond-hard mandibles had bored the holes, and pictured gaping mouths waiting at the bottom to be fed. A voice among other voices, Brad's voice, distracted him, and he tried to find him, craning his neck, rolling his eyes, a friend come to intercede, and Brad kneeled beside him, his stubby dreadlocks looking like a tarantula hat, and hooked a chain to one of the ropes strapping his chest and said, "Sorry, man. Nothing personal." He measured the width of Clyde's shoulders with a tape and said, "Number Five'll do," and Clyde made eye contact with him and saw only a core impersonality—the man derived pleasure from being impersonal, from just doing his job and following orders, the glad-handing, Dallas Cowboy-loving torturer of Halloween town, and he couldn't fathom why he had failed to see this before and supposed that the blackness of Brad's skin absorbed the light and thus prevented him from…no, no, no, don't go there, he chuckled inwardly at the nuttiness of worrying about being politically correct, like a prisoner of the Inquisition fretting over his eczema, and then he was picked up and suspended over Number Five, and felt the chain grow taut, Brad steadying him as he was lowered, saying with relish, the last voice Clyde heard, "If you twist around too much, man, you'll rub off the chain and we'll have to fish you out with hooks," and Clyde, at eye-level with Brad's feet, envisioned hooks tearing off chunks of flesh grown too soft and rotten to impale, an image he carried down into the dark, the dank, claustrophobia-inducing dark of a pit that fit around him more tightly than a coffin, down, down, down, scraping the walls (the tube was canted at a slight angle), scarcely enough room to tip back his head and see the coin of lesser darkness above being devalued, dwindling and dwindling until it was the size of a half dollar, a quarter, a dime…and that was when he fell, bumping and battering his way to the bottom. A shred of instinct came into play and he bent his knees as much as possible to absorb the blow, landing with most of his weight on the left foot, the resultant pain so bad it seemed to fill his entire body until he forced it back, compressed it into a throbbing ache beneath his knee, shifting onto his right foot to alleviate it further, and yet the pain was still very bad, burning like a cancer in the bone, and something slithered, rattled, clinked down the tube and lashed him across the face, chipping a tooth, and he tasted blood (they had dropped the chain, or else it had torn loose from the winch) and he panicked and tried to spit out the gag and scream for what must have have been a couple of minutes before he recognized the chain attached to his chest remained taut and they had flung down a second chain. Playing a trick. Having their little joke. Anger helped him deal with the pain, but he was incapable of sustaining it. Time grew sluggish, the seconds oozed past, each one a complex droplet of fear, agony, hope, fatalism, despair. He began to see and hear things that he hoped were unreal. Fish with fangs and cicatrice grins swam at him through the walls. The stone was a living depth of stone, breathing in and out, each contraction bruising his ribs, compressing his lungs. He couldn't think, poisoned by shock and trauma, and he wished they would finish him, drench him with scalding water or drown him in oil…it didn't matter. Ragged, grating voices doubled by echoes told him things about himself that he thought only he knew, things he hadn't known, and things he wanted to deny. He said her name as though it were a charm against them, Annalisa, and kept on saying it until it became as meaningless as rosary devotions. The voices persisted and told him lies about her. *That whey-faced bitch gamed you, man. Every night she goes home to that yellow smile and those gnarly bones. You know what they do? Think about it. What was she? His groupie? And she still lives with him? Come on! You think that's going to change? Look where you are. She gave up a little tongue, a little tit, and threw you a quickie…now she's laughing at you while Pet's hitting that big white butt of hers over and over and…*

The voices became garbled, too many to hear, an inchoate stew of vowels and consonants that eventually faded, leaving only a single voice, that of a young man saying, "Holy Mary, Mother of God, pray for us now and at the hour of our death, amen," speaking so rapidly, the words ran together, and then, "…blessed be the fruit of thy womb, Jesus, Holy Mary…" repeating this fragment, this same broken prayer, again and again. It annoyed him that the guy didn't know the words and he tried to beam them at him (it sounded like he was right next door), and the guy must have received the transmission, because he began to say it correctly, Hail Mary, full of grace, the Lord is with theeblessedartthouamong…

etcetera. Clyde got caught up in the rhythm of the prayer, in the sheer velocity of it. He seemed to be skittering across the prayer's surface as if it were a globe and he was a spider seeking to maintain his place by scuttling along the equator, but the globe spun too quickly and, dizzy from the spin, he lost traction and was blown off into the abyss, pinwheeling down into a noiseless, bottomless dark where there was a complete absence of pain and even spiders feared to tread.

—

A transformative thought visited Clyde, dropping down from the aether where it customarily dallied, occasionally occupying the minds of cosmic beings, the type of thought with which, if he could have mastered it, he might have comprehended the process of the world as though it were a problem in simple arithmetic, or effect the path of astronomical objects, or divine the future by the mere contemplation of a grape. Of course he was incapable of mastering it—it was too vast, too important, surrounding him the way a balloon might surround an ant. He inhaled its heady atmosphere, trying to absorb all the intelligence he could, but retained only fragments that translated into useless homily, some garbage about fitting a purpose to his life and finding (or was it founding?) a kingdom, and one item more specific, no less fragmentary, the phrase, "...below the fifty-seventh parallel." Yet he took these things to heart. He passed through the skin of the thought, clung to its outer surface until it wafted away, leaving him woozily awake and marginally aware of his surroundings, his leg aching (but the pain greatly diminished), watching a boatman—an indistinct black figure—thrust with his pole, making a faint splash and sending the skiff skimming beneath a dim sprinkle of white stars, dull and unwinking as bread crumbs on a dark blue cloth. He lay in the prow, with someone breathing regularly beside him (he was too exhausted to turn his head and determine who), and flirted with the notion that the ancient Greeks had been accurate concerning their speculations on the afterlife, and old What's-his-face, Charon, had come to ferry them across the River Styx into the mouths of Hell. Though this was patently untrue (he smelled rotten walnuts and suspected they were crossing the third Dot), he had no doubt that the imagery was apt, that one of Pet's boys had been ordered to take them south and dump the bodies. He struggled to kindle a spark of rebellion, to resist this fate, but fatigue and whatever narcotic had been given him for the pain muffled his fire. He just wanted to sleep. Before passing out, the last question he asked (of whomever it is we ask these questions) was, he wondered if this was what had happened to Dell…

They were crossing an underground lake, a stretch of water whose dimensions were impossible to judge—the walls and ceiling were lost in darkness, though lamps had been hung off the sides and both ends of the skiff, making them look, Clyde supposed, like one of those strange electric creatures that inhabited ocean trenches. Light from a lantern in the stern sprayed around the mysterious figure of the boatman, somewhat less mysterious now that he could see baggy jeans and a green down jacket patched with duct tape, a hood hiding the face. His leg throbbed and there was a considerable swelling beneath the knee (his trousers had been cut away). He eased onto his side and came face-to-face with a young brown-skinned man wearing a sleeveless T-shirt and clutching a blanket about his shoulders, gathered at the throat, a pose that made him appear boyish; yet his arms were thick and well muscled, those of a man. A gash on his cheekbone leaked a pink mixture of blood and serum. As if registering the weight of Clyde's scrutiny, his eyes fluttered open, murmured something, and closed them again.

"That's David Batista," said Annalisa. "Pet's editor. He was in the tube next to you."

She pushed back the cowl and shook out her hair; she had puffy half-circles under her eyes. Clyde wanted to ask a basic question, but his tongue stuck to his palette.

"Are you okay?" she asked.

He wetted his lips and swallowed. "Leg hurts."

"Yeah, Roberta says it's fractured."

"Roberta?"

"Mary Alonso's Roberta. I'll give you another pill."

At her feet, he noticed a tarpaulin covering someone wearing jeans and a pair of gray boots.

"And that," she said in a deliberate manner. "That is Pet."

Energy appeared to run out from her, rendering her a stony figure whose pallid animating principle stemmed from some un-alive source, as if the name pronounced had the power to transform warmth into cold, joy into hatred, every vital thing into its deathly opposite, and she stood motionless, frozen to her pole, with sunken cheek and haunted eye, a steerswoman dread and implacable, more so than Charon. Then, stepping back from the place where memory or emotion had borne her, she thrust with the pole, propelling the skiff into a channel with pitted walls like those of an old castle. Clyde felt a cold blush of anxiety that, although triggered by her reaction, seemed a general anxiety springing from every element of their situation.

Annalisa fed him a white tablet not much larger than a pinhead, warned him to keep his hands clear of the water, saying, "There's things in there will take it off," and returned to her position in the stern. Batista woke and slid over to allow Clyde more room; then he sat up and Clyde asked him what was going on.

"All I know is these four women pulled us out and tubed Brad," Batista said. "Milly Sussman…you know her? Big, good-looking woman! She seemed to be the one running the show. She had the gun, anyway. She said she wanted us put somewhere safe until things got settled, so Annalisa's taking us south. I don't know what they've got in mind for Pet."

Annalisa was off in her own world, not listening to the conversation.

"If half the stuff in his memoirs is true," Batista went on, "they can drop him in the Tubes and leave him for all I care."

Clyde recognized Batista's voice as that of the guy who had said his Hail Marys wrong, if that were possible; he thought about inquiring whether or not he, Batista, had heard his advice, but decided it would be too much of a complication. "That's what you were doing?" he asked. "Helping him write his memoirs?"

Batista nodded. "Routing out a sewer would have been cleaner work. I told him I was quitting, so he tubed me." He shot Clyde an appraising look. "Did they give you drugs? This guy I know said they had drugs that made it worse."

"They gave me something nasty," Clyde said.

The white tablet kicked in. He felt warm, muddled, distant from pain. He luxuriated in the sense of bodily perfection that attended even the movement of a finger and admired the swelling on his shinbone for the subtlety of its coloration. A cloying vegetable scent infused the air and this, too, pleased him, though he was not able to identify it. The most apt comparative he could find (only this odor was far more acidic) was the incense his mom had ordered from a catalogue during her charismatic Catholic phase, Genuine Biblical Times Incense from Jerusalem, smell what our Lord and Savior smelled, and she had hated the stuff, said she couldn't get the stink out of her new sofa, so Clyde had appropriated the incense and used it to mask the smell of pot.

They emerged from the channel into another section of the gorge, skimming along beneath a gray-blue sky, a broad expanse in relation to Halloween's sky crack. The cliffs here were perpendicular to the river and higher than the cliffs in town. Some ninety or a hundred feet wide, the Mossbach had here acquired a murky greenish tint, meandering between steep, sloping banks from which sprouted dense tangles of strange vegetation: blackish green grass sprinkled with starfish-shaped white blossoms and stubby, many-branched trees that resembled a hybrid of bonsai and gorgonians, the majority of these were also blackish green, yet some of the fans were tinged with indigo. Dark globular bushes, each with thousands of tiny leaves, quivered as they drifted past, and vines, some thick as hawsers, others fine as wires, looped in and out like exposed veins feeding the micro-environment. The place had the dire atmospherics of a wicked fairy tale, a secret grotto poisoned by the presence of an evil spirit, and the early morning light held a pall that seemed a byproduct of the pungent odor (Clyde thought he recognized the base smell as cat shit, but doubted that could be right). Fat insects with wings like fractured blades of zircon wobbled drunkenly from shrub to shrub, giving the impression that the work they did was making them ill.

They rounded a bend and Clyde, glancing over his shoulder, was presented with a vista that to his eyes, grown accustomed to confined spaces, was a virtual Grand Canyon of confinements. Here the shore widened and the cliffs made him think of illustrations in children's dinosaur books, having a Paleolithic jaggedness, their summits tattered with mist. Bracketed to the rock was a Halloween house of black metal (two columns of six stories). The walls had a dull chitin-like finish that lent the rooms (quite a bit larger than usual) the aspect of twelve rectangular beetles crawling up the cliff in tight formation. Fifteen feet below the first floor of the house, directly beneath it, tucked flush against the rock and fronted by a pebbly shingle that continued on to fringe the shoreline farther south, stood a flat-roofed, one-story building painted bluish green, a shade too bright to be called viridian. Clyde soon realized that paint was not responsible for the color—the structure was furred with lichen, the odd patch of raw concrete showing through. In one such spot the stenciled black letters MU AGE beneath a portion of a skull-and-crossbones added an indefinite yet ominous caption to the scene. Mutagenics, Clyde said to himself, remembering his conversation with Dell. The window screens were rusted but intact; the door was cracked open. To the left of the building lay a plot of fenced-in, furrowed dirt. Ordinary ferns sprouted from the rock above it, fluttering in the breeze as if signaling for help, hoping to be rescued from the encroachment of more alien growth. One thing distinguished the place above all else, verifying Clyde's suspicions concerning the odor: cats of every breed and description sunned themselves on the building's roof, peeped from thickets, crept along the margin of the water, perched primly in rocky niches and gazed scornfully down on those below. The shingle, their sandbox, was littered with turds. He took them to be feral descendants of the survivors of the cat-killer, yet they reacted with neither aggression nor fear and merely turned an incurious eye toward the intruders. There were hundreds of them, yet they made precious little noise, a scattering of miaows where one might have expected an incessant caterwauling. Some rubbed against Batista's ankles as he half-carried Clyde to the lee of the building and helped him sit with his back to the wall.

The derelict building; the house of black metal; the strangely silent cats; the unusual vegetation; the sluggish jade river winding between towering cliffs—these things caused Clyde to envision that they were characters in a great unwritten fantasy novel by Joseph Conrad, the ruins of civilization subsumed by elements of an emergent one ruled by the sentient offspring of our former housepets and, in this semi-subterranean backwater, the narrator and a handful of his friends were attempting to stave off the inevitable eternal night of their species by swapping anecdotes about mankind's downfall, individual tales of apocalyptic folly that, taken in sum, constituted a mosaic of defeat and sounded the death knell of the human spirit. He pictured a venerable storyteller, his gray-bearded jaw clenched round a pipe stem, rotted teeth tilted like old gravestones in the tobacco-stained earth of his gums, puffing vigorously to keep his coal alive and exhaling a cloud of pale smoke that engulfed his listeners as he spoke and seemed by this noxious inclusion to draw their circle closer… Clyde laughed soddenly, amused by his ornate bullshit.

From the skiff, an outcry.

At the water's edge Annalisa stood over Pet, who was on his knees, his hands bound. He still had on his dark blue velvet jacket. She whacked him across the shoulders with her pole and he laboriously got to his feet. Clyde felt divorced from the situation and tracked the progress of a gray tabby as it sneaked near one of the globular bushes, made a sinuous, twisting leap, snatched a bug from midair and fell to tearing it apart. Another cat jumped down from the roof, eyed them with middling hostility, and sauntered off. Batista pressed his shoulder against the door of the Mutagenics building and forced it open—the swollen wood made a *skreeking* noise. After a minute he hunkered down beside Clyde, who asked what he had found inside.

"A bunch of nothing," said Batista. "Couple of lab tables and a file cabinet. A door…probably leads up into the house."

Urged on by Annalisa, Pet came stumbling up from the shingle. Clyde thought of an old Italian vampire movie in which the main vampire had been exhumed from his crypt, a skeleton, but after a starlet's blood had been drizzled on his fangs, he gradually reacquired sinew and flesh and skin—Pet appeared to be stuck partway through that process. Annalisa inserted the pole between his ankles, tripped him, and he went sprawling.

"Crazy bitch!" He wiped sand from his mouth with his coat sleeve. "Think this'll get you anything?"

"Don't worry about me," Annalisa said. "You're the one with the problem."

"I got no problem," said Pet with a smirk. "Brad and the guys'll be coming around the bend any minute, and you'll be on your haunches, begging for a bone."

"Watch your mouth!" Clyde had been aiming for belligerence, but the words were so slurred, they came out, "Wushamou."

"You don't know her, pal. She'd go down on a sick monkey if she thought she'd gain an edge." Pet chuckled. "Remember the tour with Oasis, honey? Man, you guys should have seen her. I told her..."

Batista had been juggling some pebbles in his palm—he shied one at Pet, striking him in the chest.

"It won't be Brad coming," Annalisa said. "It'll be Milly."

"Milly?" Pet snorted. "That's crap! She wouldn't be involved in something this stupid."

No one said anything.

Pet looked at them each in turn. "What are you people fucking trying to pull?"

Annalisa sat next to Clyde and asked how he was doing. "What's in those pills you gave me?"

"Morphine sulfate."

Clyde grunted. "I must be doing okay, then."

Pet shifted, trying to get comfortable. "This is all about him? This mutt?"

"Why not?" said Annalisa. "It doesn't have to be, but sure, let's make it about him."

She rested her head on Clyde's shoulder. The contact warmed him—he hadn't noticed that he was cold—and left him feeling dozy. For a minute or ten, the only sounds were the rush of the river and the cats.

"I'm hungry," said Batista.

"Me, too." Pet propped himself on an elbow. "What say we scrag a few cats and roast 'em? We can have a picnic. Got any mint jelly? I hear roast cat's great with mint jelly."

Annalisa leaned forward, trembling and tense. "You hungry?" Uneasiness surfaced in Pet's face.

"I said, are you hungry?"

That drained-of-life quality she had displayed earlier was back. Clyde had a hunch that she intended to kill Pet and caught at her arm; but she was already moving toward Pet. She strode past him, however, and fumbled with the garden gate; she flung it open, causing consternation among the cats trailing after her, and dug with her hands in the dirt, uprooting two big onions dangling from their stalks.

She brought them to Pet, pushed them at him. "Eat these."

"Fuck you!" He turned away.

"Don't be afraid," she said in a wound-tight voice. "They won't poison you any more than you've already been poisoned."

An inch of apprehension crept into his defiant expression.

"That's right," she said. "For over a year I've been bringing you treats from my garden. If you weren't afraid of doctors, a checkup might have revealed cancer. You must be riddled with it by now."

Pet tried to shrug it off, but he was plainly rattled.

"Of course you're such a toxic little freak," she went on, "could be you just absorb the shit. Maybe it's actually making you healthier."

She paused, as if giving this possibility its due consideration, and then swung the onions, striking Pet in the face, knocking him onto his back. She straddled him and hit him again and again, her hair flying into her eyes. Each blow thudded on bone. He tried to buck her off, but in a matter of seconds his body went limp. She kept on hitting him, taking two-handed swings, gasping with every one, like the gasps she uttered when she made love. The cats nearest her shrank from the violence, wheeling about and scampering off. Clyde yelled for her to stop and, in no particular hurry, Batista went over, threw his arms around her and pulled her away. She resisted, but he was too strong—he lifted her and whirled her about. The onions flew from her hand, bouncing and rolling to Clyde's feet. They were mushed and lopsided, dirt and speckles of blood clinging to their pale surfaces.

"Let me go," she said dully.

He released her and she gave him a little shove as she stepped away. She walked down to the river and pushed back her hair and stood gazing upstream. Flecks of onionskin were stuck to the blood on Pet's face. His eyes were shut and the breath shuddered out of him. Clyde couldn't tell if he was conscious. Batista hovered betwixt and between as if unable to decide with whom to align himself. One of the cats started lapping at the blood on the onions, ignoring Clyde's halfhearted attempts to shoo it away.

He called out to Annalisa—she backhanded a wave, a gesture of rejection he chose to interpret as her needing a moment. He felt the morphine taking him as his adrenaline rush faded and he did his best to keep his mind focused. He wanted to comfort her, yet he doubted that she could be comforted or that comfort was the appropriate medicine. He could relate to her outburst of rage against a man who had misused her. Everyone was mad that way, but mad enough to be a poisoner? To delight in secret over another's slow demise? That required a refined madness, a spiritual abscess that might prove to be untreatable. He drew in a shaky breath and was cold again. The landscape no longer seemed so epic and exotic, humanized and made paltry by her violent excess. Just a bunch of filthy cats, an abandoned building and some cliffs.

Batista came over and sat down. After a minute or two, so did Annalisa. Clyde draped an arm about her. She relaxed beneath the weight and cozied into him and he let go of his questions, persuaded by the animal consolation of her body. The cats, filling in the open spaces they had vacated, seemed emblems of normalcy, sniffing and shitting, batting at bugs, much in the way the world goes on following the hush created by an explosion, with people scurrying about, engines starting, all the noise and talk and bustle paving over a cratered silence, all the clocks once again ticking in unison.

HALLOWEEN TOWN

—

The sun was not yet in view, but a golden tide had scrubbed the shadows from the top of the western cliff wall and, as the light brightened, some of the place's eerie luster was restored. About a half-hour after the beating, Pet sat up. He shot a bitter glance toward Annalisa and lowered his head. His left eye was swollen shut, his forehead bruised. Blood from his nose reddened his lips and chin, and he breathed through his mouth. No one spoke to him. He cast about, as though searching for something to occupy himself; then he lay back down and turned onto his side, facing away from them. Soon afterward the cats retreated, withdrawing swiftly into the underbrush to the south, a cat stampede that left nary a one in sight.

"Where are they going?" Batista asked.

Annalisa disengaged from Clyde, wearily lifting his arm away. She said something that sounded like "lurruloo," and peered south along the shore. Clyde heard a yowling, a cacophony of small, abrasive voices, and saw a greenish black something slide out of the brush and onto the shingle: the cat killer surrounded by a tide of cats. Whenever it shrank, spreading out into its rotted-cabbage mode, cats leapt onto its "skirts," clinging to them as it grew tall and spindly.

"Help me get him up!" Annalisa said to Batista.

Together they hustled Clyde into the building, a wide single room of unpainted concrete, dappled with lichen and reeking of mildew, empty but for lab tables and a filing cabinet, the floors littered with glass and other debris. A recessed black metal door set in the rear wall. They started to lower him to the floor, but he insisted upon remaining upright, propped against one of the tables. Pet scrambled inside as Batista shut the door. Out the window, Clyde saw the creature, utilizing its peculiar means of locomotion, slip along the shingle and come to a halt beside the skiff. Stretched to its full height, seven feet or thereabouts, it reminded him of a bedraggled Christmas tree that had been left out for the garbage and lost its pyramidal form, become lopsided and limp; instead of a plastic star, it was topped off by a glabrous, football-shaped, seemingly featureless head, dark olive in color. A few cats still clung to it, nibbling the fringes of its skin. The ground in its wake was strewn with half-conscious cats—some rolled onto their backs in a show of delight—and others could be seen wobbling off into the brush. The creature's body rippled, its loose flaps of skin creating a shimmying effect, and it produced a loud ululation, "Lurruloo," that had the throatiness and wooden tonality of a bassoon, deflating as the last note died—close at hand, now it looked less like a melted cabbage than an ugly green-and-black throw rug with a funny lump at the center. A bloated white cat that bore a striking resemblance to Prince waddled out from behind it and collapsed on its side.

"All this thing's doing is getting cats fucked up," Clyde said, peering around Batista, who was hogging the window. "It's not killing them."

"They love cats," Pet said. "The cats keep 'em groomed and the lurruloo turn 'em into cat junkies. It's people they kill."

"Because you and those idiot friends of yours were hunting them." Annalisa spat out the words.

"Uh-huh, sure. They were carrying peace signs and singing 'Kumbaya' before we came along. What do you think happened to the Mutagenics people?"

"Yeah, what did happen to them?" Batista asked. "Your memoirs are a little blurry on the subject."

"There's more than one of these things?" asked Clyde.

"Pet stranded them here," Annalisa told Batista. "They tried escaping through the caves. No one's sure what happened."

"The caves?" said Clyde.

"What was I supposed to do? Let 'em tell the world about their exciting new species?" Angry, Pet took a step toward her. "It would have been the end of Halloween, man. Soldiers and scientists all over the place."

Annalisa banged her fist against the filing cabinet. "If you hadn't poisoned their environment, you would never have known they were there. They would have never been motivated to visit the surface."

"Fuck a bunch of Greenpeace bullshit!" Pet affected a feminine voice: "You realize they're not animals, don't you? They steal cats and destroy TV cables. Surely you can see they're intelligent? They deserve our protection."

Pet was reacting, Clyde observed, as if the beating had never occurred, either because he felt equal to Annalisa now that she was onion-less, or because argument was simply a pattern they had developed. For that matter, she was reacting more-or-less the same. It made him wonder if beatings might also be one of their patterns.

"They don't like it here!" she said. "Why do you think they only send one up at a time?"

"If they only send one," said Clyde, "how can you tell there's more than one?"

Pet sniffed. "I don't fucking care why. But if they keep coming, I'll give 'em more than chemicals to worry about."

"I doubt that," Annalisa said. "When Milly gets here we're going to have a discussion about them...and you."

"I'm still betting on Brad."

"We tubed Brad. By now some of the others are probably down there with him, and Milly has the rest of your thugs doing doggie tricks. You shouldn't have gotten so tight with your lawyer. She knows all the right buttons to push."

"Hey!" Clyde yelled. "Does somebody want to answer my questions?"

Annalisa looked at him dumfounded, as if she had only just noticed his presence.

"What you said those about things sending one up at a time?" Batista turned from the window. "There's three outside now."

Pet and Annalisa crowded him out the way.

"I see one out front." Annalisa.

"There's one...behind the fence." Pet.

"Where's the third?"

The light from the window was suddenly blotted out. Pet and Annalisa backed away, and Clyde found himself looking into a maw of glistening, grayish meat that overspread the window screen. The lurruloo made a squelching noise—its flesh convulsed and it sprayed a thick, clear liquid onto the mesh, which began to yield a thin white smoke.

"Jesus Christ! That's acid!" Batista said. "Can it squeeze through there?"

"It's not real strong," said Annalisa. "It'll take at least ten, fifteen minutes to eat through the mesh."

With a sprightly air, Pet produced a prodigious key ring bearing a couple of dozen keys and shook them so they jangled. "Don't sweat it, man. I got this covered."

He crossed the room to the black door, fiddled with the keys, and unlocked it. Clyde continued to be fascinated by the lurruloo. Its insides were as ugly as a raw mussel, pulsing and thickly coated with juice. An outer fringe of its skin was visible at the bottom of the window—it was lined with yellowish hooks of bone not much bigger than human teeth that bit into the concrete.

Beyond the door a cramped spiral stair had been carved out of the rock. Though Batista helped him, ascending the stair started Clyde's leg throbbing again. Annalisa offered another pill, but he turned her down, wanting to keep his head clear. Opening off the stairs was a space twice the size of a normal room in Halloween, furnished with a pool table, a red-and-inky blue Arabian carpet, and a teak sofa and chairs upholstered in a lustrous red fabric splotched with mildew. The black metal walls were figured by a rack half-full of cues, an erotic bas relief and two louvered windows that striped the room with light, items that completed a modernistic take on American Bordello. Clyde lowered himself carefully onto the sofa, Pet sprawled in a chair, and Batista hung by the door. Annalisa climbed the interior stair, which corkscrewed up through the ceiling at one end of the room, returning after a brief absence carrying a pair of lace panties. She dropped them in Pet's lap and sat beside Clyde.

"I thought you quit using this place," she said.

Pet smiled—there were still traces of blood on his teeth. He tossed the panties onto the floor.

"You're such a shithead," she said.

"What do you care?"

"I *don't* care...but it pisses me off, you lying to me."

"It wasn't me, okay. It must have been one of the guys."

"You promised me nobody..."

"What is it with you two?" Clyde pushed himself up against the sofa cushion and looked at Annalisa. "You just tried to kill him. Hell, you've been trying to kill him for a year! And now you're upset because he's lying?"

"I told you, it's complicated," she said weakly.

"Naw, this isn't complicated. This is deeply twisted!" Clyde inched away from her in order to get some separation. "We're in trouble here, and you two are carrying on like it's *Days of Our Lives*."

Annalisa's eyes filled. "We're not in trouble. The lurruloo can't climb metal."

"Great! Good to know. But that doesn't answer my question. I..."

"How's this for an answer, tough guy?" Pet kicked the bottom of Clyde's left foot.

His eyes shut against the pain, Clyde heard a noise as of metal under stress and seemed to feel the room shift. Annalisa screamed and fell against him. Pet squawked and there was a thudding noise, followed by Batista cursing. When he opened his eyes, he saw the room was at a severe tilt. Batista lay on the floor, rubbing his head. Pet still sat in his chair, gripping both arms, a confused, wizened monkey in a blue velvet jacket. Boosting herself up, Annalisa walked downslope to the nearest window and peered through the vents.

"God," she said. "There must be fifty of them outside."

Batista joined her at the window. "I thought you said the acid wasn't strong. It must be eating through the brackets."

"They had to have done most of the damage beforehand." She glanced at Pet. "Not intelligent, huh?"

The room sagged downward again.

"We've got to get higher." Pet headed for the stairs.

"Not a smart idea," said Batista. "If they weakened these brackets, they might have done the ones higher up, too. You want to fall from forty feet? Sixty feet?"

"Annalisa!" Wincing, Clyde stood, balancing on one foot and the sofa arm, in too much discomfort to worry about clearheadedness. "I need a pill."

"Let's go back down." Pet's voice held a note of panic.

"You're not opening that door," said Batista, blocking his way. "They're bound to be in the lab by now...and on the stairs. Give me the keys."

Clyde let the pill Annalisa handed him begin to dissolve under his tongue.

Batista motioned to Annalisa. "Help me turn the sofa over. Pet...get under a chair or something."

Ignoring Pet's dissent, Batista and Annalisa got the sofa turned and they crowded beneath it, Clyde first, Annalisa in the middle, facing him, and then Batista, the cushions muffling their bodies. Clyde put a fist through the cloth back of the sofa and grabbed onto a wooden support strut. He could hear Pet muttering and then it was quiet, except for the three of them breathing. He'd had no time to be afraid and now it was so unreal... He thought people on an airplane in trouble might feel this way, that somehow it was going to blow over, that nothing was really wrong, that the hand of God would intervene or the pilot would discover a miraculous solution, all in the moment before the plane began its final plunge and hope was transformed into terror. Annalisa buried her face in his shoulder and whispered, "I love you." If she had spoken earlier he would have questioned the words, he would have asked how could she love him and be involved with a sickness like Pet Nylund? How could she be distracted from love by a petty hatred, even the greatest hatred being a petty indulgence when compared to love? Things being what they were, however, he repeated the words inaudibly into her hair and, as if saying made it so, he felt love expand in him like an explosion taking the place of his heart, an overwhelming burst of tenderness and desire and regret that dissolved his doubts and recriminations, a sentimental rush that united with the rush of the morphine and eroded his sensibilities until he was only aware of her warmth and the pressure of her breasts and the fragrance of her hair...A shriek of metal, the room jolted downward once more and then came free of its brackets entirely and fell, slamming edge-on into the roof of the Mutagenics lab. It rolled off the roof, smashed into the ground sideways, rolled again. They managed to maintain the integrity of their shelter somewhat through the first crash, but when the room began to roll, the sofa levitated, leaving them clutching the cushions, and Clyde went airborne during the second crash and lost consciousness. The next he knew, Batista was shouting, pulling him from beneath a chair and some heavy brown fabric that he thought might be the carpet backing. He was disoriented, his vision not right. Sunlight spilled into the room, which was tilted, the furniture jumbled against what once had been a wall, half-submerged in water. Annalisa kneeled in the water, fluttering her hands above Pet, who lay partly beneath some bulky object. Her hands were red and her down jacket was smeared with redness as well. Clyde blacked out again and was shaken awake by Batista, who jammed a pool cue into his hand and yelled once again. He glanced up at the sun, the cliffs, and recognized that he was outside. Befuddled, he gazed at the pool cue. Batista, bleeding from a cut on his scalp, asked if he could deal with it. Clyde wasn't clear on the precise nature of "it," but thought it best to go along with the program. His vision still wasn't right, but he gripped the cue purposefully and nodded.

"I'll go get her," Batista said, and moved off down the slope, disappearing through a gash in the black metal surface the size and approximate shape of a child's wading pool.

Clyde realized he was sitting about a third of the way up the side wall of the room, and realized further that the room was in the river, sticking out of the sun-dazzled green water like a giant domino with no dots. What did they call blank dominoes? He couldn't remember. His head ached, the glare hurt his eyes, and his leg was badly swollen—he could feel a fevered pulse in it, separate from the beat of his heart. He started to drift, but a scream from below, from within the room, brought him back. Annalisa. He reacted toward the gash, but movement was not a viable option. Even morphine couldn't mask the pain that a slight change of position caused. He tightened his grip on the cue and, when Annalisa screamed again, he tuned it out.

Cats seethed along the shore in front of the Mutagenics lab; their faint cries came to him. They appeared interested in something on the opposite side of the Mossbach, but Clyde could see nothing that would attract such concentrated interest, just granite and ferns, swarming gnats and… His chest went cold with shock. Twenty, twenty-five feet above was an overhanging ledge and a dozen or so lurruloo were inching along it, some of their hooks latching onto the cliff wall, some onto the ledge, unable to secure a firm hold on either. The extreme end of the ledge was positioned over the uppermost portion of the half-sunken room and, should this be their intent, would allow them to drop onto the metal surface one or two at a time. Gritting his teeth, Clyde turned in order to face those that dropped. More lurruloo were plastered to the cliff above the ledge, looking at that angle like an audience of greenish black sombreros with misshapen crowns and exceptionally wide, not-quite-symmetrical brims. Thirty or forty of them. *Goofy-looking buggers, but deadly*, said an inner voice with a British Colonial accent. *Saw one take old MacTavish back in '98. 'Orrible, it was!* He made a concerted effort to straighten out, focusing on the end of the ledge, and became entranced by the patterns of the moss growing beneath it.

A tinkly piano melody began playing in his mind, something his grandmother had entertained him with when he was a kid, and it was playing still when the first lurruloo slipped off the ledge, spreading its fleshy skirts (for balance?) and landed thirty feet upslope with a wet, sloppy thump. Its hooks scrabbled for purchase on the metal as it slid, doing a three-quarter turn in the process, trying to push itself upright, yet incapable of controlling its approach. Holding the cue like a baseball bat, he timed his swing perfectly, cracking the back of its bulbous head, served up to him like a whiffle ball on a post three feet high. He heard a crunch and caught a whiff of foulness before it spilled into the water. His feeling of satisfaction was short-lived—two more dropped from the ledge, but collided in midair, knocking one into the river. The other landed on its side, injuring itself. As it slid past, its skirts flared at the edges, exposing dozens of yellowish hooks, perhaps a muscular reflex in response to trauma, and one tore a chunk from Clyde's right thigh. Not serious, but it pissed him off.

"Batista!" he shouted, and a warbling, hooting response came from overhead, as if the lurruloo were cheering…or they might be debating alternative strategies, discussing the finer points of inter-species relations.

Two more skidded toward him, one in advance of the other. Clyde balanced on a knee, his bad leg stuck out to the side like a rudder, and bashed the lead lurruloo in the head, then punched at the other with the tip of the cue—to his surprise, it penetrated the lurruloo's skull to a depth of five or six inches. Before its body slipped from the cue, its bulk dragged him off balance, causing him to put all his weight on his bad leg. Dizzy, with opaque blotches dancing in his vision, he slumped onto the sun-heated metal. His leg was on fire, but he felt disconnected from it, as if it were a phantom pain. Human voices sounded nearby. He braced up on his elbows. Batista was boosting himself up through the gash and Annalisa sat beside it—she shook her head in vehement denial and talked to her outspread, reddened hands. Clyde couldn't unscramble the words. Batista rushed up the slope, pool cue at the ready, and, reminded of duty, Clyde fumbled for his cue, grabbed the tip, sticky with a dark fluid, and made ready to join the fray. But Batista was doing fine on his own, laying waste to the lurruloo as they landed, before they could marshal a semblance of poise, knocking the pulpy bodies, dead and alive, into the river. In his sleeveless T-shirt and shorts, Batista the Barbarian. Clyde chortled at the image—a string of drool eeled between his lips.

The lurruloo on the ledge broke off their attack and began a withdrawal, flowing up the cliff face, while those above offered commiseration (this according to Clyde's characterization of their lugubrious tones). Wise move, he said to himself. Better to retreat, to live and multiply and create the legend of the demon Batista, his Blue-Tipped Stick of Doom. Annalisa stared at him emptily and then, making an indefinite noise, she crawled up beside him. He caressed her cheek and she leaned into the touch. Her mouth opened, but she didn't speak. He cradled her head, puzzled by her silence. They weren't out of the woods yet, but they had survived this much and he thought she should be happier. *He* should be happier, excited by the victory, however trivial. But her silence, her vacant manner, impelled him to confront questions he couldn't cope with at present. Their future, for one. She seemed nearly lifeless, not like previously, her energies channeled into some dread purpose, but more as though a light had guttered out inside her, reducing her to this inert figure.

"Oh, wow," said Batista.

Hundreds of lurruloo had joined those on the cliff wall and they were wheeling as one, united in a great circular movement as though in flight from a predator, like a herd of wildebeest or a school of fish; but instead of fleeing, they continued to circle, creating a pattern that grew increasingly intricate—a great spiral that divided into two interlocking spirals, and this, too, divided, becoming a dozen patterns that fed into one another, each having a variant rhythm, yet they were rhythms in harmony with one another, the whole thing evolving and changing, a greenish black inconstancy that drew the eye to follow its shifting currents. It was a beautiful, mesmerizing thing and Clyde derived from it a sense of peace, of intellect sublimated to the principles of dance. He understood that the lurruloo were talking, attempting to communicate their desires, and the longer he watched them flow across the cliff face, the more convinced he became of their good intentions, their intrinsic gentleness. He imagined the pattern to be an apology, an invitation to negotiate, a statement of their relative innocence… Shots rang out, sporadic at first, a spatter of pops, then a virtual fusillade. The pattern broke apart, the lurruloo scattering high and low into the south, twenty or thirty of their dead sinking into the Mossbach, the leakage from their riddled corpses darkening the green water. Clyde had been so immersed in contemplation, he felt wrenched out of his element and not a little distressed—he believed he had been on the cusp of a more refined comprehension, and he looked to see who had committed this act of mayhem. Two skiffs had rounded the bend in the river and were making for the wreckage of the metal room. Three men with rifles stood in the first and Clyde's heart sank on recognizing Spooz among them; but his spirits lifted when he spotted a tanned figure clad in sweat pants and a bulky sweater in the second skiff: Milly. They pulled alongside and made their lines fast to what remained of a bracket. Batista, appearing hesitant, as if he, too, had been shocked by the slaughter, helped Milly out of the skiff and gave her the digest version of what had happened, concluding with Pet's death, the battle, and its unusual resolution.

"The last bunch who were exposed to that hypnotic thing—I think it was about seven years age—only one survived. You're lucky we came along when we did." Milly cocked an eye toward Annalisa. "How's she doing?"

Batista made a negative noise. "She's not communicating too well."

Milly nodded sadly. "I always thought she'd be what killed Pet."

Batista's eyes dropped to her breasts. "She gave it the old college try."

The river bumped the skiffs against the side of the room, causing a faint gonging; clouds passed across the sun, partially obscuring it; with the dimming of the light, as if to disprove his theories, Clyde felt suddenly sharper of mind.

Milly rubbed Batista's shoulder, letting her fingers dawdle. "Why don't you ride back with me? It'll give us a chance to talk about your situation."

She summoned Spooz and the other men. They hopped onto the half-submerged room and two of them peeled Annalisa away from Clyde. She went without a word, without a backward look, and that made another kind of pain in his chest, the kind morphine couldn't touch. Milly squatted beside him, Spooz at her shoulder, and asked how he was.

"Real good," he said. "For someone who doesn't know what the hell's going on. When were you people going to tell me about the lurruloo?"

"I'm sure Annalisa wanted to tell you. It's supposed to be on a need-to-know basis."

"It's obvious Helene didn't need to know."

Milly shrugged, but said nothing.

"Seems irresponsible to me," Clyde said. "Maybe even criminal."

"Things in Halloween are going to run differently, now."

"And you're going to be running them?"

"For a while."

He jerked his head at Spooz. "Is he part of the new order?"

"If he toes the line."

"What about Brad?"

"Brad's not part of anything anymore."

In her serene face he read a long history of cunning and ruthlessness—it was like looking off the end of a pier in Halloween and seeing all the grotesque life swarming beneath the surface.

"The king is dead, long live the queen," said Clyde. "Is that it? I'm getting the idea this whole thing fit right in with your plans. I mean, it couldn't have worked out any better, huh?"

"I'm not going to have trouble with you, am I?" she asked mildly.

"Me? No way. Soon as I'm able, me and Annalisa are putting this place in the rear view."

Milly mulled this over. "That might be a good idea."

With a sincere expression, Spooz extended a hand, as if to help him up. "Square business, guy. I was just doing my job. No hard feelings?"

"Get your damn hand out of my face," Clyde said. "I can manage my own self."

—

"Just below the fifty-seventh parallel..." included a lot of frozen territory: parts of Russia, Latvia, Lithuania, Bellarus, Sweden, Denmark, Canada, and Alaska. Ridiculous, to hang onto a fragment, a hallucinated phrase, a misfiring of neurons, out of all that had occurred, but he couldn't shake the idea that it was important. Clyde had yet not founded, or found, a kingdom, but he had fitted a new purpose to his life, and it was for that reason he had parked his pickup in front of the neighborhood Buy-Rite on a cold December Saturday morning in Wilkes-Barre, Pennsylvania, waiting for the pharmacy to open so he could refill Annalisa's migraine prescription. The migraines turned her into a zombie. She would lie in bed for a day, sometimes two days at a time, unable to eat, too weak to sit up, capable of speaking no more than a couple of words. Between the migraines and the anti-psychotics, they'd had maybe three good weeks out of the six months since they left Halloween. Those weeks had been pretty splendid, though, providing him hope that a new Annalisa was being born. Her psychologist was optimistic, but Clyde doubted she would ever again be the woman he originally met, and perhaps that woman had never truly existed. The knots that Pet Nylund tied in her had come unraveled with his death and they seemed to have been what was holding her together. Life in their apartment was so oppressive, so deadly quiet and gloomy, he had taken a job driving heavy equipment just to have a place to go. The guys on site thought him aloof and strange, but chalked that up to the fact that his wife was sick, and they defended him to their friends by saying, "The man is going through some shit, okay?"

His breath fogged the windshield and, tired of wiping it clear, he climbed down from the truck and leaned against the cold fender. The sun was muted to a tinny white glare by a mackerel sky, delicate altocumulus clouds laid out against a sapphire backdrop. A stiff wind blew along the trafficless street, chasing paper trash in the gutters, flattening a red, white, and blue relic of the recent presidential election against the Buy-Rite's door for a fraction of a second, too quickly for him to determine which candidate it trumpeted. Not that it much mattered. The glass storefronts gave back perfect reflections of the glass storefronts on the opposite, sunnier side of the street. Quiznos. Ace Hardware. Toys 'R' Us was having a pre-Christmas sale. The post-apocalyptic vacancy of the place was spoiled by a black panel van that turned the corner and cruised slowly along and then pulled into the space next to Clyde's pickup. An orange jack-o-lantern with a particularly jolly grin was spray-painted on the side of the van—it formed the O in dripping-blood horror movie lettering that spelled out HALLOWEEN. The window slid down to reveal Carmine's sallow, vulpine face. He didn't speak, so Clyde said, "What a shocker. Milly sent you to check up on us, did she?"

Carmine climbed out and came around the front of the van. "I had some business in town. She wanted me to look you up. See if you need more money and like that."

"As long as the checks from the estate keep coming, we're cool," said Clyde. "How'd you find me?"

"I went over to your place. This woman told me you'd be here."

"Annalisa's nurse."

"Whatever." Carmine examined the bottom of his shoe. "How's she making it…Annalisa?"

"It's slow, but she'll be fine." Clyde waved at the van. "This is new, huh?"

Carmine looked askance at the jack-o-lantern. "Milly's trying to encourage tourism. She's putting on a Halloween festival and all kinds of shit."

"You think that's wise? All you need is for a couple of tourists to get picked off by the lurruloo."

"They aren't a problem anymore."

"What do you mean?"

"They're not a problem. Milly handled it."

"What are you talking? She wiped them out?"

"That's not your business."

Despite having less than fond memories of the lurruloo, Clyde found the notion that they had been exterminated more than horrifying, but was unable to think of an alternative way by which Milly could have handled it.

"Jesus, it's fucking cold!" Carmine jammed his hands into his pockets and shuffled his feet. "So what's life like in the republic?"

"Less benefits, little bit more freedom. It's a trade-off."

"Doesn't sound like so good a deal to me."

"That's your opinion, is it?"

Carmine gave a dry laugh. "I got to book. Any messages you want sent back?"

"How's Roberta and Mary Alonso?"

"They're in dyke heaven, I guess. They were married a few weeks back."

"No shit?"

"Milly made a law saying gay marriage is legal. Now she expects all the fruits to flock to Halloween." Carmine spat off to the side. "Got to hand it to her. She knows how to get stuff done."

"She makes the trains run on time."

Puzzled by the reference, Carmine squinted at him, then walked around to the driver's side of the van.

"Did Helene Kmiec kill her husband?" Clyde asked.

"How the fuck should I know?" Carmine started the engine.

"I'm serious, man. It's bugging me. It's the only question I have about Halloween I don't know the answer to."

"That's the only one you got?" Carmine backed out of the parking space and yelled, "Man, did you even know where you were living?"

Clyde watched until the black speck of the van merged with the blackness of the street, wishing he'd asked after Joanie. He reached for a cigarette, the reflex of an old smoker, and said, "Fuck it." He walked along the block to a newsstand that was opening up and bought a pack of Camel Wides. Out on the sidewalk, he lit one and exhaled a plume of smoke and frozen breath. Maybe Milly had blown up the entrance to the lurruloo's caves, sealing them in—maybe that was all she had done. What, he asked himself, would the penalty be for the genocide of a new intelligent species? Most likely nobody would give a damn, just like him. They had their own problems and couldn't be bothered. He thought about the 57th parallel and what might lie below it, and he thought about Annalisa's sharp tongue and wily good humor, subsumed beneath a haze of drugs. He thought about a local bar, once a funeral home, that now was painted white inside, every inch and object, with plants in the enormous urns and round marble tables, usually filled with seniors—it troubled him that she liked to drink there.

"Hey, buddy!" The newsstand owner, an elderly man with a potbelly and unruly wisps of gray hair lying across his mottled scalp like scraps of cloud over a wasteland—he beckoned to Clyde from the doorway and said, "You can smoke inside if you want." When Clyde hesitated, he said "You're going to freeze your ass. What're you doing out there?"

Clyde told him, and the old man said, "She's always late opening on Saturday. Come on in."

With Clyde at his heels, the owner walked stiff-legged back inside, took a seat on a stool behind the counter, picked up a lit stogie from an ashtray and puffed on it until the coal glowed redly.

"Screw those bastards in the legislature telling us we can't smoke in our own place," said the owner. "Right?"

"Right."

There must have been a thousand magazines on the shelves: drab economic journals; bright pornos sealed in plastic; hockey, boxing, football, wrestling, MMA, the entire spectrum of violent sport; women's magazines with big, flashy graphics; *People, Time, Rolling Stone*; magazines for cat fanciers and antique collectors and pot smokers, for deer hunters and gun freaks and freaks of every persuasion; magazines about stamps and model trains, Japanese films and architecture, country cooking and travel in exotic lands; magazines in German, Italian, French. Clyde had patronized dozens of newsstands in his day, but never before had he been struck by the richness of such places, by the sheer profligacy of the written word.

"They tell you a man's home is his castle, but you know how that goes," said the owner, winking broadly at Clyde. "The little woman takes control and pretty soon you can't sit in your favorite chair unless it's covered in a goddamn plastic sheet. But a man's place of business now, that's his kingdom. That's how come I named this place like I did."

"What's that?" Clyde asked.

The owner seemed offended that he didn't know. "Kingdom News. People come in sometimes thinking I'm a Christian store, and I tell 'em to check out the name. Herschel Rothstein, Proprietor. I ain't no Christian. The point I'm making, shouldn't nobody tell a man he can't smoke in his damn kingdom."

Clyde wondered if the owner and his newsstand might not have been summoned from the Uncreate, perhaps by the same entity that had visited him after his ordeal in the Tubes, so as to pose an object lesson. He had been considering kingdoms in grandiose terms, a place requiring a castle, at least a symbolic one, and great holdings; yet now he recognized that a kingdom could be a small, rich thing, an enterprise of substance somewhere below the 57th parallel. A newsstand, a bar, a fishing camp—someplace quiet and pristine where Annalisa would heal and thrive.

A young woman dressed in cold weather yuppie gear came in to buy a paper and wrinkled her nose at the smell of the old man's cigar. He flirted outrageously with her and sent her away smiling, and they sat there, the owner on his stool, Clyde on a stack of *Times-Leaders*, laughing and smoking and talking about the bastards in the state legislature and the bigger bastards down in Washington, recalling days of grace and purity that never were, forgetting the wide world that lay beyond the door, happily cursing the twenty-first century and the republic in its decline, secure for the moment in the heart of their kingdom.

ROSE STREET ATTRACTORS

Those who knew Jeffrey Richmond, if anyone could be truly said to have known him, viewed him as an acquaintance merely, the sort of person one tolerates because he belongs to a certain circle, yet avoids due to his unpleasant character or dubious connections. He was a slight black-haired chap in his middle thirties, beardless and brown-eyed, sharp-featured and plain of dress, possessed of a subdued public manner, and whenever he chanced to visit the Inventors' Club, his fellows hid themselves behind the pages of a newspaper or pretended to be engrossed in a conversation concerning a cricket match or a minor political issue, or else they bluntly ignored him. On most such visits he would sit in one of the club's deep leather chairs and drink a glass or two of port and then take his leave, both entrance and exit unmarked by the least notice; but infrequently he would attach himself to a group of men engaged in a discussion concerning some aspect of science or mechanics, and even more infrequently he would interject a comment that another member might acknowledge in a distant tone, saying, "Ah, Richmond," before turning away. Whereupon the group would close ranks against him and he would drift back to his chair. He had endured that state of affairs for the past three years, ever since joining the club, and when I inquired as to the reasons underlying this consistent display of contempt, I was told that Richmond, holder of a dozen patents relating to a diverse range of industries, from textile to armaments, and thus wealthy, had chosen to live in the pernicious slum of St. Nichol and was thought to have family in the district—even if untrue it was apparent to the discerning eye, so my informant claimed, that his exposure to the evils endemic to the place had thoroughly corrupted him.

My own status at the club was hardly secure—although I came from a prominent Welsh family with business connections in London, I was but a probationary member and twenty-six years old (all the full members were at the least five years my senior), and otherwise suspect because, despite holding a medical patent, I was an alienist, a discipline not yet accorded the banner of respectability. I had joined the club in order to gain access to the upper classes through its membership, which counted a smattering of dukes and lords among their number, hoping that when one or another of their relations suffered an affliction for which medical science had no obvious remedy, they might call upon me. Indeed, I had already experienced a degree of success, having assisted in the treatment of Sir Thomas Winstone's nephew, whose opium addiction was rooted in a childhood trauma. It was my hope that by attending the ills of parasites like Winstone's nephew, I might garner sufficient wealth to establish clinics that would provide treatment of the mentally afflicted among the lower classes superior to that they received in hospitals such as Bedlam and Broadmoor. And so, while I felt something of an ideological kinship with Richmond, for the sake of my goals I became complicit in shunning him, addressing him with a reserve that verged on rudeness. I would have never done more than tip my hat and nod to the man had he not forced himself upon me.

One foggy autumn evening, a fog so thick that the streetlamps were transformed into inexplicable glowing presences like those said to hover intermittently above the northern marshes, I was returning home from the club, keeping a hand on the clammy bricks to guide me through especially dense eddies, when I heard boot heels behind me. I paid them scant attention until, on rounding a corner onto a poorly lit lane, their pace quickened and, fearing a footpad, I darted ahead and secreted myself in the doorway of an apothecary shop, holding my shooting stick at the ready. Seconds later a man wearing a greatcoat emerged from the billowing fog and passed my hiding place. He stopped several yards farther along and peered about. I recognized Richmond, but did not show myself, hoping he would continue on his way. However, he turned back and, realizing that I would almost certainly be seen, I stepped forth from the doorway and said, "Are you following me, sir?"

He did not seem in the least taken aback by my sudden appearance, but rather smiled and said in a high-pitched, nasal voice, like that of an Irish tenor with a cold, "There you are, Prothero. I thought you had eluded me."

"So you admit it—you were following me. May I ask why?"

"I hoped it might prove less of an embarrassment if I pressed my business with you away from the confines of the club."

This shamed me, since I was a snob by association and not by nature; yet I maintained a cool manner. "I'm unaware of any business between us."

"That remains to be seen. I require the services of an alienist for a day or two. If you come with me to Saint Nichol, I will double your usual fee."

My interest was piqued, but I had concerns. "Tonight? At this hour?"

"If you fear for your safety, let me assure you that at no hour of day or night is Saint Nichol markedly less perilous." A smile touched the corners of his mouth and I had the idea that it was a mocking smile. "While I cannot guarantee with absolute certainty that you will survive the experience," he went on, "I swear that you will be as safe in my company in Saint Nichol as you would be on any other street in London."

I hesitated and, apparently attributing my hesitancy to greed, Richmond said, "Name your price, then. I will gladly pay it."

"Money is not at issue," I told him. "Mental ailments—and I presume this is why you have sought me out, to treat such an ailment—are not easily corrected. I am no carpenter who can repair your steps or patch a hole in your roof in a few hours."

"I do not expect you to effect a cure, simply to give me your counsel."

"On what subject? Is there a patient you wish me to observe?"

"Two. Myself and one other."

I started to speak, but he said, "You have questions for me. That I understand. And I intend to answer them. But my answers, insufficient as they are, will be far more revealing in light of what I have to show you."

Without waiting to learn whether or not I would accept his invitation (I fully intended to accept, seduced by the air of mystery attaching to it), he produced a silver whistle from his coat and sounded a blast. A coach and pair lurched into view at the end of the lane, wheels and hooves raising a clatter. At that distance, rendered featureless and distorted by the fog, it posed an indistinct black mass against the diffuse yellow light, and the coachman's bulky figure, established in vague silhouette, seemed a projection of that blackness, the crude semblance of half a man. I climbed into the coach with no little trepidation, its aspect having brought to mind a Turner seascape I had long admired, not as regards its particulars, but relating to the sinister mood suggested by its depiction of a numinous fiery light smothered beneath lowering grim clouds.

—

To reach St. Nichol it was first necessary to cross Bethnal Green, scarcely a fashionable neighborhood itself; but nothing in Bethnal Green prepared me for either the foul stench of St. Nichol's muddy byways or the view of human dereliction I had through the fluttering curtains of the coach. On the verge of the slum, in the ghastly greenish-yellow light that spilled from the door of a gin shop wherein anonymous figures staggered and shrieked and capered, perhaps dancing to the scrape of a fiddle, a man lurched toward the coach with open arms, as if in welcome, his round face red with drink, almost purplish and so bloated I imagined it would burst and release a spew of fluids. The fog thinned sufficiently to permit closer observation as we drew near Richmond's home in Rose Street. I saw an elderly man on a stoop, his toothless grin expressing lustful anticipation, gutting the flayed carcass of an animal the size of a Sheltie. I saw two prodigiously fat whores rolling in the muck, tearing each other's clothing, their pale flesh smeared with ordure. I saw what appeared to be a man's body lying in an alley mouth, a rat sniffing at its bootless feet and, hard by Richmond's house, I saw a tattered child with limbs like sticks being whipped by a creature with a shaven head, wearing a frock coat that failed to cover its womanly breasts and no trousers to hide hairy, scab-covered legs. All this grotesque misery and more hemmed in by crumbling, soot-blackened brick tenements that towered into the fog, making of the streets a canyon bottom such as might have wound through one of Hell's outlying precincts. I had not been long in London and, with the exception of the odd visit to Bedlam and Broadmoor, my experience of the city had been limited to its decorous quarters. Though I had heard tales of the poverty and horrid excess that ruled in St. Nichol, their harrowing reality affected me more profoundly than had the most shocking of those anecdotes...and this, I understood, was merely the surface of the place, the skin beneath which lay greater pathologies yet.

Iron shutters protected the windows of Richmond's house—a tenement no less soot-blackened than the rest, yet in better repair—and iron bands secured the planking of the front door. I heard a rumbling from above, as of the operation of machinery, but was unable to determine the source. Within, a demure young woman, quite fetching, her lustrous brown hair worn in a bun, clad Oriental fashion in a loose-fitting tunic and trousers of plum-colored silk, escorted us into a salon and there served us a restorative. The room had a cloying smell of sandalwood incense and was larger than some lecture halls, furnished with velvet armchairs and sofas, and divans of a Middle Eastern design, all arranged in groupings as if to encourage half-a-dozen separate conversations, these groups divided one from the other by statuettes and teak tables inlaid by ornate patterns of nacre and standing vases filled with flowering reeds and peacock feathers. It appeared to have been decorated by a sybarite, the walls hung with tapestries and paintings depicting beautiful women in various states of undress, gold candlesticks in the shape of nudes, everywhere bits of gaud and glamour—it seemed at odds with the character of the man who, having removed his greatcoat, sat drab as a beetle in his brown tweed suit, sipping a brandy. Yet I knew many other men who disguised a salacious nature behind a proper façade, and I harkened back to those rumors of Richmond's corruption circulated by the members of the Inventors' Club.

Richmond drained his brandy glass and said, "I'm afraid I have been less than forthcoming as to the reason I require your services. I did not think you would believe me were I to reveal myself prematurely. I hope that now you will forgive the actions of a desperate man and hear me out."

"It appears I have little choice in the matter," I said. "Unless I choose to take a long walk through Saint Nichol."

"On the contrary. I will have my man convey you to your rooms straightaway if that is your desire…though it is not mine."

"You have my full attention."

"And you my gratitude." Richmond settled himself more comfortably in his chair. "Following the death of my sister Christine three years ago, I moved into her house. This house. But for…"

I was incredulous. "Your sister lived in Saint Nichol? Surely not."

"Yes. For seven years, until the moment of her death. May I continue?"

"Of course. Forgive my interruption."

"I intended to gather her effects and sell the place," Richmond said. "But the longer I remained, the more reluctant I was to leave. I felt drawn to the house, and I also became obsessed with the idea of learning what had happened to her. She died alone, unattended, from a blow to the temple, yet it could not be determined whether her injuries were caused by murder or misadventure. I am, as you may know, unmarried. My flat did double duty as my office and workplace, and there were few demands on my time. Eventually I moved into the house and made it my home." He glanced about the room. "Except for some improvements to the exterior and my study, and a renovation of the uppermost floor, little has been changed since she died. This room, for instance, is exactly as she left it."

"It scarcely seems the décor a young lady would have chosen," I said.

"No, I suppose not. But then Christine could not be considered young. She was thirty-four when she died. And though she was gentle and kindly to a fault, I doubt that she would have been thought of as a lady by other than the most generous of souls. The house, you see, was a brothel that catered to the upper classes and my sister, by every account, both owned and served in it."

Attempting to address this revelation with delicacy, I said, "I realize that among the wealthy there are those who derive titillation from visiting squalid locales. Yet I should think even they might find regular visits to Saint Nichol to be something of a risk."

Bitterness invaded his tone. "Who can fathom these people, unless one is to the manor born?" He left a pause. "I suspect it was such a man who financed Christine. She had a modest income from my mother's estate, but not enough to fund an enterprise of this magnitude."

"I meant to ask how your sister became involved in this business," I said. "Am I to take it that you are not privy to that information?"

"I haven't a clue. It came as a shock to me that she was in London. Her letters bore an address on the Continent—in Toulouse, to be precise—and in them she spoke with enthusiasm about her life there. She must have had someone post them for her. When I visited her, and I did so twice a year, we met at the seaside, and whenever she had occasion to visit me, she would arrive by train. She concealed this portion of her life from everyone excepting her clientele. I cannot imagine how she sank to this abysmal state, nor have I encountered anyone who can enlighten me."

A second young woman entered the room and whispered in Richmond's ear. Though taller and more statuesque, more refined of feature, she might have been sister to the first and was clad in the same fashion.

"Very well, Jane," Richmond said. "We will be along directly."

Once she had exited I remarked on the women's resemblance to one another. His response skirted the issue.

"I offered money to the girls who worked here in order that they could start life anew," Richmond said. "Most accepted my offer, but Jane and Dorothea elected to stay with me. They have become my family, assisting me in my work and ministering to my every need."

A touch of defiance in his speech told me all I might wish to know about the extent of their ministrations.

"I will return to the subject of my sister," he went on, "but I must now, for the sake of brevity, tell you something about my work. Six months prior to Christine's death I began construction of a machine that would cleanse the air of London. It was my hope to reduce the incidence of respiratory diseases. After the shock of Christine's death had passed, after I had accepted the fact that she had debased herself, I once again took up my work."

He stood and, beckoning me to join him, crossed to a table whereon lay a leather folio that proved to contain architectural drawings and blueprints. I did not gain much from the majority of them, save that they were precisely executed and described complex machinery. However, the last drawing made a certain fantastic sense—it was an overview of central London to which had been added eight mountainous conical structures (the cones formed by concentric silver rings, separated by gaps through which one could make out intricate labyrinths of glass and metal) that dwarfed the buildings beneath, standing, I would estimate, five or six times the height of Big Ben.

"Atop the house I have installed four machines like these, only much smaller," said Richmond. "They are each of a variant design—I sought to learn which of them was the most efficient. The basic process is not one of extraction per se, but of attraction. That is, the machines do not wash the air, rather they attract particulates. In effect, they lure the particles into chambers on the sixth floor and these are then vaporized. I call the machines 'attractors'. I'm not altogether happy with that name, but..." He made a gesture of helplessness. "As time permits, if you wish, I will explain the process further, although I don't believe an explanation is relevant to your purpose. But to continue, I completed installation of the last machine two and a half months ago and..."

"This is astonishing!" I said. "Have you succeeded? If so, my God! Might I see the machines?"

"Not at present. The atmosphere on the roof is poisonous and the visibility poor due to the concentration of coal dust. When I shut the machines down for repairs, I'll take you to the roof. As to my success..." He closed the folio. "You may have noticed that the fog in the vicinity of the house is thinner than it was in Bethnal Green. This is due to the operation of my machines. So yes, I have succeeded to a degree. However, to contrive a practical application of the process will be the work of decades. As things stand now, machines of the requisite size would deafen the population of London. Until I am able to perfect a method of noise reduction, one that does not require buildings several times larger than those in the drawing, installations of an appropriate size will be out of the question. And there are other problems that must be overcome before I can start work on the project, not least among them the problem I wish you to address."

"You may have come to the wrong man," I said. "I know next to nothing about this particular branch of science."

He grunted in amusement and said, "Nor, apparently, do I. Come."

—

We ascended to the sixth and topmost floor in a cramped elevator and, as we inched upward, Richmond informed me that one of the machines had incurred minor damage during its installation—this had altered the settings of certain instruments. To effect repairs would have required several months and thus he had completed the installation, thinking to determine what result the changed settings might achieve, all the while going forward with the fabrication of a machine that would replace it. By the time we reached the sixth floor, scarcely two minutes had elapsed, yet his mood had darkened appreciably. He snapped off his words, as if impatient with me, and would no longer meet my eye.

The sixth floor reeked of machine oil and coal, and—though it had been rendered as silent as possible by doubled walls and other architectural devices designed to muffle sound—the rumbling overhead made it necessary to raise one's voice. A corridor had once run the length of the floor and the rooms along one side had been obliterated to create a dusty space of raw boards and roof beams that was now occupied by wooden benches, each laden with a clutter of tools and schematics. Those on the opposite side had been replaced by chambers with black iron walls, each having an oblong aperture that, when slid open, permitted the sampling of the air within. A gray canvas curtain hid a fourth chamber. Jane, the taller of the women I had earlier seen, waited beside the curtain—she put her mouth to Richmond's ear, imparted a message I could not hear and walked toward the elevator. After hesitating a moment, Richmond drew back the curtain to reveal a glass wall of surpassing clarity secured by ornamental iron mounts. A brown-haired woman stood within, clad in plum-colored tunic and trousers. I thought this to be Richmond's other assistant, for she greatly resembled the woman who had just left us, but Richmond flattened his palm against the glass and said, "Christine." I realized then that she was not the woman I had seen earlier, being older by a decade or thereabouts, her face and figure less full. Judging by their longing looks (looks, I noticed, that did not quite mesh—her eyes were angled to the right of Richmond), you would have thought they were lovers kept apart by an impenetrable barrier. I felt twice the fool for having submitted to this charade and was about to voice my reaction when the woman vanished. No show of any sort preceded this event, no disturbance of the surrounding air, no rush of sound. She simply winked out of existence. I started back from the glass, tripped and fell heavily on my backside. Once again I made to speak and the woman reappeared in a far corner of the chamber, dressed in a chemise with a lace collar, her head held at a crooked angle, hair loose about her shoulders, except where it was matted against her temple by a welter of blood. She moved haltingly, aimlessly, as though disoriented.

Richmond helped me to regain my feet. "Strange, is it not?" he said. "To think that when one walks about in the London fog, the gauzy stuff of other lives drapes itself over one's coat or cloak, even slips into our eyes and mouth? That all around us drift shades and phantoms, beings who cling to the bonds of the flesh, old friends and enemies who yet wish us well or ill?"

"Are you suggesting that this is your sister's ghost? You have no proof."

"Proof?" He made a derisive noise. "If her presence alone is insufficient proof, watch a while. You will see a veritable host of proofs. Ghosts old and new, the ghosts of men and women, and that of a creature to which I dare not give a name, all unwilling to abandon this plane."

He started to close the curtain.

"Wait!" I said.

"I cannot bear to watch her in torment. Once she reaches this state, she is mostly in whatever world she travels to and cannot or will not see what occurs in this one. She will remain like this a minute more and then vanish. She never stays long and is often absent half the day. But she will return and…" He pointed out a grille mounted in the glass. "You may be able to speak with her."

"Ridiculous!"

Richmond shut the curtain.

"Do you believe me so gullible? It's a medium's trick!" I said. "Some type of illusion."

"I invite you to prove your thesis," said Richmond. "Perhaps after you have failed to do so, you can then concentrate on solving my problem."

I sought to hold up logic as a shield against the fact that what I had witnessed overthrew all my notions concerning the composition of reality; but despite my protestations, as I adjusted to this reordering of the world, I was inclined to accept that the woman had been neither flesh nor the projection of a magic lantern. Her body had not been a wavering image on a backlit screen—it had been sharply etched upon the air, a vital presence edged by an almost imperceptible aura, an outline as thin as a knife-edge. I knew that I had seen Christine Richmond, her shade, the colored shadow of the person she once had been in life.

"Can you define your problem with more precision?" I asked once my nerves had settled. "You wish me observe, to counsel, but I think you have a more complicated task in mind."

"I have devised a machine whose function it is to remove coal dust from air. Instead, for reasons I do not claim to understand, it attracts ghosts, some essence of those who have gone before. One of these is my sister, who manifests regularly within the chamber and is sometimes seen in other rooms, albeit infrequently. I wish to know how she came to own the brothel and who provided the money for her venture? Is that stated precisely enough?"

His tone had been that of a teacher lecturing the dunce of the class, but I ignored this lack of civility and said, "Extracting information from a ghost may prove more difficult than removing coal dust from the air. Should it be possible, well…if it were I, my first priority would be to identify her murderer."

"It is not certain that she was murdered. She may have suffered a fall and struck her head. But if it was murder, yes, I should like to know his name as well."

"She can speak, or so you say. Why not ask her yourself?"

"She will not speak to me. Twice she has spoken my name, but no more. Why this is, I can only guess. We were close as children, closer than most brothers and sisters, though we grew apart. Perhaps she feels shame whenever she sees me."

"Shame related to what she became in life?"

"You need not mince words. She was a whore and died a whore's death."

"Shame is a predictable human reaction, not at all what I'd expect of a ghost."

"I told you it was a guess. Whether or not it is correct…" He spread his hands. "However, do not think that she is other than human, that she holds some supernatural charge. A ghost is but a human relic, a shred of the soul torn, caught and left to flutter upon a metaphysical nail. Nor should you hope to communicate with her. You may be able to stimulate a verbal response, but that is a twitch, a reflex, nothing more. It is my hope, a faint one, that your presence here will stimulate a response that will provide me with a clue."

Feeling overtaxed, I sat at one of the benches. I closed my eyes and took a deep breath in order to still my mind—a thought occurred to me. "You joined the Inventors' Club three years ago, did you not? Would I be wrong in assuming that you applied for membership shortly after your sister's demise?"

He glowered at me, but said nothing.

"Might the two events be connected?" I asked. "Did you suspect one of our fellows prior to the appearance of Christine's ghost?"

He withdrew a pocket watch and flicked open the case. "I prefer not to color your opinion with my own."

I objected to this, saying I needed every bit of information he had gathered in order to carry out an exacting investigation, but he deflected my arguments.

"It's late and I am weary," he said. "Let us go down. If you wish I can offer you a bed and all the amenities. That prospect may have greater appeal than does a lengthy coach ride."

—

My room on the second floor was staid by contrast to the salon, having sensible oak furniture, a bed with a carved headboard and pineapple posts, logs in the fireplace, and only a pair of erotic lithographs on the wall to remind of the house's former occupation. Recalling Richmond's assertion that little had been changed, this led me to hypothesize that while Englishmen might relish an exotic façade, most preferred to take their pleasure in an atmosphere redolent of hearth and home. I had no means of lighting a fire, but just when it seemed I would have to sleep in a cold bed, there came a tapping at the door and Jane entered bearing a small bundle of kindling. Speaking in a northern accent partially scrubbed away by life in London, she said that she had been sent to prepare my room. Once the fire was going, filling the air with the aromatic scent of burning cedar, throwing shadows onto the wall, lending the room the atmosphere of a cozy cave, I sat by the hearth and watched her turn down the sheets, puzzling over the resemblance she and Richmond's other assistant bore to Christine. This likeness, I realized, was not limited to her face, but extended to her body as well—long of limb, lissome yet full-breasted. Once she had finished with the bedding, she began to unbutton her tunic, doing so as though it were the most ordinary and expectable of actions. She had the garment halfway off before I regained my equilibrium and told her forcefully to desist. She covered herself and, with an air of bewilderment, asked if I would prefer that she send up Dorothea to entertain me.

"Entertainment of any sort will not be necessary," I said. "But I should like a few words with you, if you please."

She sat primly in the chair facing mine, hands clasped in her lap.

"My name is Samuel Prothero," I said. "Your employer has asked that I assist him in an inquiry regarding the death of his sister."

"So he told us."

The fire popped and she gave a start.

"Prior to Christine's death, how long were you in the house?"

"Roughly four years. I had my sixteenth birthday shortly after I arrived."

"You knew her well, then?"

"As well as any. She was always lovely to us girls. Honest and kind. She had her peculiar ways, though. And her secrets."

"I'm sure you learned some of them, didn't you?"

"I did."

"Well…?"

"They were private matters. The sorts of things you might confide in a friend, but would never tell your mother."

"And Mister Richmond? Does he also have secrets?"

"Everyone has secrets, Mister Prothero. I'm certain you have yours."

"Why would you say that?"

"You're not the first colleague of Mister Richmond's to visit the house, but you are the first to reject my hospitality." She tipped her head to the side, as if to see me more clearly. "You have a touch of the prude in you, but I believe your rejection was based on something else. Perhaps some tenet of your beliefs was involved…though not, I think, a religious principle."

"You're clever, aren't you, Jane?"

"I know men," she said. "Whether or not that demands cleverness is a topic for debate."

"These men Richmond compelled you to sleep with, were…"

"I was not compelled. He asked me if I would lie with them. I could have refused."

"Why didn't you?"

"He needed my assistance."

"How so?"

"I'll let Mister Richmond decide whether or not to tell you about that."

Fascinated by her poise and her obvious intelligence, I let a few moments slip past.

"You're very loyal to Richmond," I said. "Why is that?"

"I was loyal to Christine because she saved my life. She used me, it's true, but then every human relationship is founded upon a bargain of some sort, and had she not taken me in, I would surely have come to a bad end. I'm loyal to Jeffrey, Mister Richmond, because I am now in his employ, and because I wish to help with his investigation."

"And so, in order to gain information about them, you slept with men whom he believed might be guilty of the crime?"

She laughed. "You've found me out. Yes, for all the good it did." After a pause, her voice acquired an edge, "I would have preferred to have been brought up in a decent home and lived an exemplary life, but though I regret my past I am not ashamed of it. I've done what I have in order to survive."

I wondered why she bothered to explain herself. "Were these men members of the Inventors' Club?" I asked.

"Some, yes. Perhaps all of them were. I'm not certain."

The idea that the men had availed themselves of illicit pleasure at Richmond's invitation and then reviled him for it—it conformed to my notions of upper class duplicity.

"And tonight," I said. "Did he ask you to help with me?"

Her lips thinned. "I think you have pried deeply enough into the subject."

I stirred the fire with a poker. "How would you explain the resemblance between you and Christine…and Dorothea?"

"Christine was ever on the lookout for girls who took after her. When Dorothea happened along she was delighted—that was the year before she died. She had a client who favored our type. Sometimes he'd have the two of us together…and sometimes he'd pay for Christine to join us, though she came dear."

"Who was this client?"

She shook her head. "I never knew his name. He wore a mask that covered his head from brow to chin, except for his eyes and mouth. Not even

Christine knew him. He had money and came highly recommended—that was enough for her."

"Recommended by whom?"

"Another client, I believe. That's all I know."

"Did he bear any marks on his body that might distinguish him."

"I don't recall anything in particular." She suppressed a smile.

"What is it?" I said. "If you remember a wart, a mole, some aberrant behavior or character trait, anything at all, it could be of immense value."

"Well, he did like tipping the velvet. He never prigged me proper until he was sure I was satisfied."

I may have blushed, for she shot me a mischievous look. Flustered, I told her that I thought it time for me to retire. As she crossed to the door, another question sprang to mind, but I had been unsettled by her boldness.

"I trust you will be available tomorrow?" I said.

"I have errands to accomplish during the day." She put a hand on the doorknob and smiled sweetly. "In the evening, however, I will be here to serve you however I can."

—

I slept fitfully, inflamed by Jane's bold manner and the glimpse I'd had of her breasts, and troubled by dreams of which I could recall mere fragments. When I woke it was half-ten and I realized that I had missed my one scheduled appointment for the day. Folded atop the dresser was a change of clothing and fresh linens. I also found a note from Richmond stating that he would be gone until late that evening and perhaps overnight, doing some work at his factory. Dorothea would serve me breakfast in the kitchen and arrange for transportation whenever I decided to return home. If I chose to begin my researches immediately, and this was his hope, I was to consider the house my own.

Dorothea proved to be a bright, saucy Londoner, born and bred in St. Nichol, much more indelicate in her speech than Jane and coarser of feature, more like Christine in this regard, though her eyes were cornflower blue, not hazel. She cooked me a sturdy breakfast that I ate at the counter in the drafty, dingy kitchen, a room with a high ceiling, gray walls, an iron stove crouching on clawed feet, and a chimney covered in plaster. While she tidied up I asked her essentially the same questions I had asked of Jane. Her answers shed no new light on Christine's death, but when I pressed her she disclosed that Christine had tutored her in the art of pleasing a man, with particular attention paid to the pleasing of one man, the mysterious masked client.

"I think she fancied him," Dorothea said. "Which was odd considering she was a bit of a Tom."

"Christine was a lesbian?"

"She had her lady friends, let's say, but now and again a man would catch her eye. And him with the mask—she'd ride him to Bristol and back if given the chance. When he paid for the three of us, often as not Jane and I did nothing more than lie about and coo in his ear for all the attention she paid him. Why I recall this one…"

"I don't think it necessary to explore specifics," I said. "Why did you choose to remain in the house after her death?"

"Money," she said, leaning on her broom. "What else? Mister Richmond sacked the rest of the girls, but he made Jane and I a most generous offer to stay. The work is easy—a few men and mostly none at all. I feel like a regular toffer and not some dollymop in a bordello. Of course…" She winked at me. "Now there's you."

"I doubt I shall be long in residence," I said. "Certainly not long enough to establish the kind of relationship you imagine."

"Oh, la!" She laughed and danced her broom around. "It don't take that long to establish, believe me. And it's not me who's doing the imagining. It's Jane. She fancies you, she does."

"Indeed? Jane?"

"Yes, sir! She told me so herself."

I pooh-poohed the notion.

"You'll see," she said. "Jane will be polishing your trinkets before you know they're out in the air. You've heard what they say about girls from the north?"

"I don't believe I have."

"Give them an inch and they'll take the whole yard."

I felt myself blushing. "What do you know about Jane?"

"Oh, she's nice enough. Very caring, she is. She was always looking out for the other girls."

"I mean before she came to the house."

"She never talks much about her past." Dorothea idly swiped at the floor with her broom. "She did tell me that when she was a child, she and her sisters were the support of her family up in Newcastle. They worked in the theater, playing imps and angels and the like. Her father dosed them regular with gin, hoping to keep them small. So they could still do the job, you understand. But Jane sprouted up and he threw her out of the house when she were but nine. I'd have put a blade in his neck." Dorothea swatted at a spider web that spanned between the stove and the wall. "Jane loves the theater. She and Christine would talk about it 'til all hours. I reckon that's why they formed a stronger bond than what I did with her. Me, she trained for the bedroom, but with Jane she went the extra mile. She taught her etiquette, how to dress elegant and speak nice."

"What about you?" I asked. "Was your childhood similar to Jane's?"

"My mother whored, so you might say I was born to the trade. But thieving was my specialty...before my bubbies came in, that is. I'd dress as a boy and wander the streets between here and Bethnal Green. There wasn't a pocket watch or a wallet safe from me." She waggled her fingers and grinned. "These very fingers plucked the Duke of Buckingham's watch."

"What in the world was the Duke of Buckingham doing in Saint Nichol?"

"Inspecting his property. He must own half the houses on Boundary Road. Him and Sir Charles Mellor and some other toffs was strolling about, looking at this house and that house."

Charles Mellor was a charter member of the Inventors' Club—I asked Dorothea if she was certain it had been him.

"Oh, it was Charlie, all right. We'd see him down here right frequent. There must have been half-a-hundred children swarming around with their hands out, begging for pennies. So I sneaked in amongst them and nicked the duke's watch. Didn't get nothing for it, though. My mother took it to a pawn shop and got swindled proper."

"Where is your mother now?" I asked.

"I don't know." She began sweeping in earnest, as if suddenly called to the task.

I left Dorothea to her chores and made my way to the sixth floor and pulled up a chair in front of the glass-walled chamber. Christine was nowhere in evidence, but from time to time a revenant would manifest in the chamber. In the main they were relics of the lower classes, those whose living cousins could be seen in the streets of St. Nichol, a few dressed in the garments of another era; but there were also richly dressed men and well appointed ladies. Many were in sharp focus, visible for a span ranging from scant seconds to a minute or two, and others were frayed and tattered like rotten lace, all but worn away—these last brought to mind the phantasmagorias I had delighted in as a boy, yet they exhibited a lifelike quality, a dimensionality, that those illusions had not. They neither spoke nor acknowledged my presence, though they came close enough to touch had there been no glass. Once something dark and whirling, a dervish shadow twice the mass of man that looked to be acquiring human form, materialized in the chamber and I heard above the noise of the machines a faint roaring, as from a distant crowd. This so alarmed me that I scrambled back from the glass, knocking over my chair. The figure was headless and armless, or else its head was tucked close in against its chest, giving the impression that it was surmounted by a massive torso and set of shoulders. It looked rather like a living pencil sketch, a black core encaged within a complexity of slightly less black lines that whirled rapidly about the central darkness, making it appear that the whole of the thing was in motion. Soon this apparition lapsed and I reclaimed my seat.

What that most astonished me about the things I saw that day (and other days as well) was my reaction to them…or rather the lack thereof. I would not have believed that I could easily adapt to such a drastic shift in the way I perceived the world; yet there I sat, scribbling down observations concerning a subject whose existence I would have decried the day before, and doing so with a reasonable amount of aplomb. I mentioned this to Dorothea once and she replied that human beings were more resilient than most gave them credit for, putting this sentiment in the vernacular. "When a bloke tries to jam tackle the size of a cricket bat up your lolly, you're afraid it's never going to fit," she said. "But once it's in, it's surprising how quickly you adjust to the situation." She went on to say that ghosts no longer troubled her, even when they manifested outside of the chamber, in other portions of the house. I inquired of her about these manifestations and she told me that before Richmond had come to dwell in the house, she and others had encountered presences on the upper floors, notably an elderly woman who dragged her left leg as she walked; but Dorothea had not seen the old woman since Christine had died—it was as though she been evicted and Christine had taken her place.

At quarter past four that first afternoon, Christine appeared within the chamber. I was writing in my notebook and did not witness her entrance, but when I looked up from the page she was standing next to the glass, hands on hips, wearing undergarments obviously intended to arouse: a corset (of Parisian design, I believe) sheathed in emerald green silk and lace that constricted her waist and exposed the plump upper curves of her breasts; and pantaloons of a filmy material that clung to her hips and thighs. Her hair was a complexity of curls piled high atop her head and framing her face, and her smile had a touch of disdain. She walked away from the glass, displaying her long legs and shapely derriere, glancing over her shoulder—a dram of poison had been added to her smile. I had the thought that she was replaying a scene from her life, showing herself to someone she despised, someone who could no longer afford her charms.

Placing my mouth close to the grille, I called out, not expecting an answer. In truth, I was uncertain whether she had the ability to hear—I had no idea how she perceived the world. After ten or fifteen seconds, as though my outcry had taken an inordinate amount of time to carry across the distance between us, she came toward the glass and pinned me with a stare so fierce and hostile, I had the urge to bolt. Despite

Dorothea's acclimation to the company of spirits, I was an interloper and placed no faith in their benevolent disposition. I spoke her name again and laid my palm flat on the glass, as Richmond had done. A confusion of emotions crossed her face. Her eyes grew teary and she became distraught, plucking at her hair, touching her face…and suddenly she was gone. I stood beside the chamber a while, waiting for her to reappear. At last I turned to the bench upon which I had left my notebook and let out a squawk—Christine stood less than an arm's length away. Not the high whore (the toffer, as Dorothea would have said) in her French frillies, but bloody Christine in her chemise, pallid and dead of eye. A distinct emanation of cold proceeded from her. She gave no sign that she saw me, but shuffled off to my right and back again. It seemed she felt some sort of attraction to the spot and yet had not the consciousness to understand it, but muddled about like a chicken habituated to being fed in one particular section of the barnyard. My heart racing, I slipped past her and reclaimed my notebook. She turned, but instead of facing me, she took a step or two toward the end of the corridor. I surmised that in this guise her perceptions might be clouded, her reactions to stimuli uncertain, more so, at any rate, than when appearing in her other aspects. She exhibited a terrible slowness and sluggishness, her fingers knotting in the folds of the chemise. Her irises looked to be revolving a few degrees backward and forward like clockworks, an uncanny thing to see. I wished that I could will her from the world, because while I had no real attachment to her, one could not see her so drained of life, possessed of that eerie glamour, and remain unmoved.

—

I drew the curtain after she had gone and sat at the bench writing until late in the evening, recording a detailed account of what I had seen and felt and thought during the day. On returning to my room I discovered a fire crackling in the hearth and half a roast chicken on a plate covered by a linen cloth, along with bread, cheese, water, and a bottle of Edradour. Apparently Jane had come and gone. I sat by the hearth, sipping the whiskey, made despondent by the dreary prospect that not seeing her presented, not in the least because Dorothea had said that she fancied me, but also because I had been immersed in death and its products for many hours, and I had been anticipating a visit, however perfunctory, from someone alive and vital. As a result I drank more than I should have in an attempt to ameliorate the morbid effects of dealing with Christine. If I felt this way after a day in her company, I wondered how much drink I would need after a week? A month? I had no doubt that the investigation would last at least that long. Truth be told, I thought I could make a career of this single case. Here was a ghost who could be counted upon to appear again and again with regularity—the light that she might shed on the nature of the physical universe, on the nature of life itself, was incalculable. I pictured myself gone gray and creaky, the author of a library of books about Christine Richmond, imprisoned by obsession, incapable of discussing any other topic.

The fire burned low and I lit a lamp. A knock. Unsteadily, I went to the door and flung it open, expecting to find Richmond in the corridor. I was prepared to tell him that I did not have the stomach for this work and would be unable to satisfy his requirements; but it was Jane come to turn down my bed, wearing a crinoline night bonnet and a flannel dressing gown that covered her from neck to ankle. For all her matronly attire, she was no less beautiful than ever and I watched her intently, enlivened by the swell of a breast, the shape of a thigh as she bent to her task. However modestly dressed, her every movement was an article of seduction. She asked if there were anything further she might do for me and I bade her sit, saying that I had more questions. Yet I had none. Fuddled by drink, by the idea that I could have her, my mind emptied and, though I racked my brain, I managed to stammer a few phrases by way of preamble, yet nothing more. Once again I had the apprehension that she understood my predicament and was amused. At last I succeeded in dredging up a question that had not occurred to me before that moment…or if it had, I had pushed it to the back of my mental shelf.

"Christine's resemblance to both you and Dorothea," I said. "What part do you think it played in Richmond's desire that you remain in the house?"

She seemed to withdraw from me. "He wanted us near to remind him of her."

"I don't doubt that, but there must be more to it. He makes love to you, does he not? To women who remind him of his sister?"

"It's been more than two years since he last touched either of us. He…he changed. Our relationship changed. He became more like a cousin, an uncle. He cares for us now, and we for him. That is all."

I was immoderately pleased to learn she had no current involvement with Richmond.

"That begs the issue," I said. "He did make love to you. And he kept you here for that purpose. That he has since stopped this practice conjures other questions, but the fact remains that he chose two women who closely resemble his sister to serve as his concubines. Does this not seem a symptom of some tragic family circumstance?"

Jane frowned and spread her fingers on her knees, appearing to examine them for defect. "Dorothea has spoken to you about this?"

"I had a conversation with her earlier."

"I…" She sighed and pressed the heel of one hand to her brow. "I will not speak ill of him."

"Jane," I said. "Men and women are often driven to extremes of behavior by emotional distress. In this life we are all at fault. None of us is simon-pure, no matter how deeply we may wish it. Society may judge Richmond, but I make no judgments. If I am to determine what is going on, you must be straightforward with me. Anything you tell me will be kept in the strictest confidence."

She searched my face and then lowered her eyes. "On occasion, with me and with Dorothea, he used her name instead of ours."

"In passionate address?"

"Yes." A plaintive quality expressed itself in her face and voice. "But as I said, it's over two years since he last took either of us to bed."

After an interval I asked, "What do you make of his use of Christine's name in these instances?"

"I am not the doctor here," she said firmly. "You will have to draw your own conclusions."

"And I will. But my conclusions will be formed in large part by what you tell me."

"Dorothea believes that…" She left the thought unfinished and, after an obvious internal struggle, she stood. "I'm sorry. I have chores to attend before I sleep."

Had I not been drinking, I might have let that end the conversation, but I, too, stood, blocking her exit, and said, "I would like you to stay, Jane. We need speak no more about Richmond, but please…stay awhile with me."

A blank mask aligned with her features and she put a hand to the sash of her dressing gown.

"I want you to stay, not because you feel compelled to do so," I said. "But because it is your choice. Because…"

I began to sputter, blurting out the history of my day, the oppressive mood engendered by my encounter with Christine. I suggested that Jane stay until I fell asleep and that nothing more need happen—I did not want to take advantage of her. A lie. I wanted to take complete advantage, but I didn't want her to believe that was my aim…and I may have told her as much. So eager was I to have her good opinion that honesty seemed the only course, unprecedented honesty, honesty divested of the slightest hint of subterfuge. Fortunately I do not recall every idiotic thing I said. While I was speaking she went to the bed, removed her dressing gown and bonnet, shook out her hair and climbed beneath the covers, clad in her chemise. I made no immediate move to join her, immobilized by desire in conflict with an assortment of anxieties, amongst them the fear of looking more the fool than I already had. I might have stood there forever, but she released me from the thrall of my anxieties with the perfect counter-spell.

"If you please," she said, turning on her side, facing away from me. "Leave the lamp on when you come to bed."

—

ROSE STREET ATTRACTORS

In the morning I went to stand in the entranceway of the house to take the air, cold and noxious though it was, perfumed by the ripe scents of Rose Street. A cart passed me by, raising a clatter like an enormous sack of bones and pulled by a moribund horse, its ribs showing through its loose skin, urged along by a driver so muffled in rags that I saw of him nothing apart from steaming breath and reddened cheeks and tufted white eyebrows. Urchins screeched and squealed and whistled to one another, running pell-mell, their flights as erratic as those of birds frightened from their roosts. Ungainly wives lumbered from doorways to empty basins of slops into the gray, gluey mud of the street, disappearing back into the many-eyed oblivions of their black brick homes. Yet all this was given a gloss by the glorious night I had spent with Jane and had for me the quaint charm of a scene from one of Mr. Dickens' gentler tales. I allowed myself to entertain fantasies about a life with Jane, imagining a cottage on the sea, a child or two who would appear only after a ten-year honeymoon, sojourns in the Italian Alps and the like.

Giddy with these delusions, I headed to the kitchen, intending to cut a slab of cheese and some bread to take upstairs with me, and discovered Richmond eating his breakfast. His face was drawn, the lines around his eyes deepened by fatigue. I wished him a good morning—he gave a curt nod, muttered something I could not make out and attacked his eggs and sausage with ferocity.

"How goes your work," I said, dragging up a stool. "Well, I hope."

He swallowed, nodded.

"May I inquire what it is that you are working on?"

He sucked at a particle of food trapped between his teeth—his poor table manners were often made the butt of jokes at the Inventors' Club.

"I am completing a fifth machine," he said. "I intend to install it soon."

I started to speak but he held up a hand to stay me.

"I recognize that your investigation will be of some duration," he said. "I do not plan to replace the machine that summons Christine. Not yet. If I finish before your work is done, I will forbear replacing it or else replace another machine." He wiped his mouth on the back of his hand. "I have left you a check with Dorothea that should suffice for your immediate expenses. Let me know if you need more. I will be busy at the factory for two weeks—I doubt we will see much of one another during that time. If you have business elsewhere, patients to treat, the coach will be at your disposal. And, of course, the house is yours to use as you see fit."

I must admit that this discomfited me—it seemed an abdication of responsibility, implying that he did not actually care about Christine and that whatever concern he felt was perfunctory and had been satisfied by the act of hiring an alienist.

"Would you care to learn what progress I have made?" I asked.

He looked at me, expectant, chewing a mouthful of food.

"Progress may be too optimistic a word," I said. "But I have a theory regarding your sister's…promiscuity."

He swallowed. "Yes?"

"I believe she may have been interfered with while still a child."

I had thought he would display some adverse reaction, but he did not. He had a bite of sausage, chewed, and said, "Hmm."

"An incident of the sort I envision often leads the child to have an unhealthy view of sexuality. She might, for instance, be prone to use sex as a means of gaining approval."

He continued eating.

"It might be helpful if I could speak to your father," I said. "He may recall…"

"That would be pointless. These days he is like an infant who must be dressed and diapered. His memory is nearly gone and when frustrated he comes easily to anger. It would be an unnecessary trial for the both of you."

"Is there anyone else with whom I might speak? A nanny, or another relative."

"Only myself," said Richmond. "I am occupied today and will be, I anticipate, for the remainder of the week. Next week I can spare a few minutes, though I can't think it will be helpful. Christine and I were brought up more-or-less separately. Summers I traveled the length and breadth of England and Wales with my father, assisting him with one or another of his engineering projects. The remainder of the year I was away at school. All the while Christine stayed home. We had the occasion to spend time together, of course, but our relationship was based on holidays and a weekend here and there. We were more cousins than brother and sister."

I found this a telling disclaimer and was inclined to press him on the matter; yet I did not think it was the moment to reveal that I suspected him of having had an incestuous encounter with Christine—it would have seemed accusatory and my purpose was to define the problem, not to cast aspersions. I thought to tell him about Christine's masked client, wanting to learn whether or not it would elicit a strong reaction, for I believed that Richmond was capable of such a deception; but I decided that this, too, would have been premature. I made a packet of bread and cheese, wished him good day, and went about my business.

The weeks that followed saw me make little progress. I had a lengthy conversation with Richmond concerning Christine, but it was, as he had promised, unrewarding. My observations of her shade yielded nothing new, though she manifested for longer periods of time, as if she were becoming accustomed to my presence. Isolated with her for up to an hour, sitting for hours more beside the chamber, cataloguing the motley spirits that materialized in her absence, I imagined that I was being watched, studied by a malefic spirit, and I took to carrying a crucifix for protection. Other suspicions plagued me, prominent among them the idea that this practice brought me closer to death each day. Every so often, that dark, dervish creature appeared in the chamber. Although I had become used to it popping in from the afterlife and announcing itself with a distant, many-voiced roar, I came to assign it a demonic value; yet I did not fear it as much as I feared for my mental stability.

Then one morning as I sat at the bench fronting the chamber, searching my pockets for a pen, Christine appeared beside me wearing her plum pajamas (this had been uniform of the house during its heyday) and asked in a wispy, genteel voice, one rendered nearly inaudible by the rumbling of the machines, if I would care for a glass of wine.

"No, thank you," I said upon recovering my poise. "Your company is more than sufficient stimulation."

A handful of seconds elapsed before she spoke again, looking off to my right and at a point above my shoulder. "Shall I call the ladies in for your inspection?"

"I think not," I said. "I would prefer to spend my time with you."

After another brief delay, she let out a peal of laughter, as though delighted by my response; but she said nothing more, only continued looking above me and to the right. I wondered if she could hear me—judging by her attentive expression, she might have been listening to another voice.

"My name is Samuel," I said. "Samuel Prothero."

The delay again and then she said, "Yes! Of course! I know your father."

My father, as far as I knew, had never been to London and was so conservative in nature that the idea of visiting St. Nichol would have given him palpitations. I began to doubt that Christine was responding to me. Yet if, as Richmond suggested, a ghost was a scrap of life left behind after death, a fragment caught on a metaphysical nail, and not a faded version of the person entire, these oblique statements might be the only responses of which she was capable and she could be trying to communicate, unable to express herself more fluently than would be a tourist in a foreign land armed with phrases from a guidebook. I decided to risk a direct approach.

"Christine," I said. "Tell me about the night you were murdered."

Following an interval of twenty or thirty seconds during which she appeared to be frozen, she vanished. Soon thereafter I apprehended a chill presence behind me. I did not want to see her in that bloody guise and kept my head lowered until the feeling of cold dissipated.

That night Jane came to my room with an excellent bottle of Pinot Noir and as we sat by the fire, which had gone to embers, I asked her to tell me more about Christine. What had she been like in her unguarded moments? Did she maintain any friendships outside the brothel? Did she spend much time away from it? If so, how did she spend that time?

"I wouldn't know about friends outside the house," said Jane. "She couldn't have had many…if any at all. What time she didn't spend here, she was at one music hall or another, or at the theater. She'd tell us about what she saw, all the people and what the ladies wore and such, but she never mentioned anyone specific. And I think she would have. We were her employees, but we were also her confidantes. Like us, she was trapped here, unhappy and on the lookout for something that would make her happy. If she found it, I don't believe she could have kept it to herself."

Light from the hearth ruddied her pale skin. She leaned forward to caress my cheek.

"You'll see her again soon enough," she said. "Stop thinking about her."

"I know. It's just…"

"Tell me."

"I'm beginning to feel that my efforts are wasted here."

"But you said you had broken through to her."

"I did, but in retrospect it was the kind of moment that persuades me that what I'm doing here is worthless. I don't believe I will ever be able to communicate with her."

She mulled this over. "Dorothea says that Christine seems to enjoy her singing."

"Dorothea's singing?"

"Yes."

"What does she sing?"

"Popular tunes. 'Pretty Polly Perkins From Paddington Green' and that sort of thing. She says they seem to make her happy. It causes her to hang about longer, she says, but she's not so horrid-looking." Jane held up her glass so that the fire added ruby highlights to the wine. "It makes me nervous, her hanging about, so I pretend not to see her and let nature take its course."

"Was 'Pretty Polly Perkins' her favorite song?"

"I don't know as she had a favorite. Oh, wait now! She used to go larking about here singing snatches from 'Champagne Charlie'. If she had a favorite, I reckon that was it."

She had a sip of wine, the voluptuous, vaguely predatory curve of her upper lip kissing the glass. Though she was of Christine's type, her features were so delicate and fine that I no longer thought of Christine when I looked at her, but saw a beauty entirely her own. And it was not just her beauty that moved me. During our time together she had told me of her life, less a life than an escape route, a flight from one brutal circumstance to another. Despite this, some central essence had come through undamaged, a core of strength and sweetness unaffected by this maltreatment. She had a temper and when something she held dear was threatened, she would defend it with an unladylike ferocity; but these storms passed swiftly.

"You know," I said. "If it were not for you, I would have given up weeks ago."

"I'm glad I can be a comfort for you."

"You're more than a comfort, Jane. Without you to shore me up, I would have been overwhelmed by the morbidity of this enterprise. I can only hope my presence here has meant something to you."

"I think…" She bit her lip and fixed her gaze on the hearth.

"Please! Tell me!"

She sighed and, without lifting her eyes from the hearth, said in a small voice, "I think you know my heart. I think you have always known it."

I took her hand and the warmth of the fire, her warmth, went all through me—it was as though our physical contact had created a bubble of time and space apart from the world. I wanted to say more, but was at a loss for words, not knowing what there was to say. Our stations in life were at such a great remove one from the other, it was unlikely we could ever have a lasting connection.

She withdrew her hand from mine and, as though she knew my thoughts, said, "It might be best not to invest too hastily in our relationship…or too deeply. I care for you, Samuel, but the situation is difficult. I have divided loyalties, you see. And you, well…you have your own difficulties to overcome."

Despite the irresolution of that night, or rather because, irresolute or not, that singular moment had moved our relationship forward, I set about my work with renewed energy. Predicated upon our conversation,

I began singing "Champagne Charlie" whenever Christine materialized. As Jane had said, her mood became genial and there were times when she did not revert to her bloody, chemise-clad state prior to vanishing. Initially those were the only changes I observed, but before long I noticed that when I sang a particular verse, allowing for the apparent delay between my singing and her reaction to the song, she grew more aggressive in her behavior, coming close to me, staring intently (although her stares were not always directed toward me), and betraying signs of anxiety. The verse went as follows:

> "The way I gained my title is by a hobby
> which I've got
> Of never letting others pay no matter how long the shot.
> Whoever drinks with me are treated all the same,
> From Dukes and Lords and Cabmen down, I make them
> drink champagne."

By the time I finished the chorus ("Oh, Champagne Charlie is my name…etc."), she would have returned to normal, but for the span of perhaps half-a-minute her eyes widened, her bosom rose and fell as though her breathing had quickened, and on one occasion she laid her hand on my forearm. I was stunned, stricken. Rather than jumping back, I held perfectly still, imprisoned by that slight weight upon my shirtsleeve. I was startled to find that her hand had any weight whatsoever, and she, too, may have been startled, for she snatched her hand away and disappeared. I retreated to the elevator and thence to my room, and tried to understand what had happened. Her touch had been light, yet no lighter than the casual caress of a real woman, and there had been no spectral association, no chill. Upon regaining my composure, I ascended once again to the sixth floor. Christine was nowhere to be seen and did not return for the better part of a day; but from that point on she contrived to brush against me whenever possible—I imagined that these intimacies were reminiscent of her vital days and gave her pleasure. For my part, I experienced a mild anxiety, less than I might have when a strange cat unexpectedly rubbed against my leg, and thus I permitted the touches to continue.

I made an exhaustive report to Richmond on my findings, noting that of all the spirits who passed through the chamber, Christine was the only one who appeared in more than one guise. I postulated that because she was last to die within the confines of the house, her manifestation was correspondingly more complex. I said that her conversation might be random, yet I half-believed that she was attempting to communicate, her capacity for speech limited by her fragmented state. In support of this, I told him what Jane had related about "Champagne Charlie" and how Christine had vanished when asked about her murder. Further, I told him about our recent physical interactions. This piece of news seemed to anger him.

We were sitting at a bench on the sixth floor and when, at the end of my report, I brought the question of my finances to his attention, he pulled out his wallet, slapped it against the bench and demanded to know how much I wanted. I replied that he had mentioned twice my usual fee and named a figure. He extracted a sheaf of banknotes in excess of the figure I had named and flung them at me.

"I am nearly two months along in this investigation," I said. "I've reduced my commitment to my other patients and I have bills. I don't think it is unreasonable to ask for payment. But this…" I indicated the banknotes. "It's too much."

"When dealing with whores," he said, "it's my habit to pay more than the going rate. It inspires them to perform their duty with a certain brio."

"Listen to me, Richmond," I said evenly. "Christine's case is a remarkable one and if my financial position allowed it I would work for nothing. But should you address me again in that fashion, I will quit your employ and have nothing more to do with this investigation. Is that understood?"

He snorted, pocketed his wallet and strode off toward the elevator, leaving me to puzzle over his extreme behavior.

—

It was several weeks later, on a Ladies' Night at the Inventors' Club, that I came to terms with the fact that I had fallen in love with Jane, though I should have reached this conclusion long before—I had found it increasingly difficult to concentrate on my work, thinking of her to the point of distraction. I had tried to convince myself that the subject of that work, Christine, so resembled Jane that the waters had been muddied, and that my feelings were mere sexual infatuation complicated by psychological stress. That evening, however, I was forced to admit that a more base consideration—one of which I was aware but had shunted aside, not wishing to see myself in its light—was to blame.

On Ladies' Night the membership were encouraged to bring their unwed daughters (and their spouses, but this was a secondary consideration) to the club in order that they meet the unwed, younger members, the objective being to spark romance and subsequently create the bloodline that would produce the Great Inventor...at least this was my jaundiced view of the proceeding. For probationary members such as myself attendance was mandatory. I told Jane not to expect me back until the wee hours and that I would likely not see her until the following day. The club's banquet hall had been cleared of its long oak table for the event and was decorated after the fashion of a gala, with floral displays everywhere, a champagne bar, and a string orchestra whose insipid strains had induced several dozen couples in evening dress to dance. Shortly after arriving I was pinned into a corner by Constance Mellor, the youngest spawn of Sir Charles Mellor, an officer of the club whose work on the London underground and the electric tram had earned him the accolade, and Preshea Liddle, the daughter of Archibald Liddle, whose advances in non-flammable dry cleaning solvents had made him wealthy. Whether either of these ladies could be considered beautiful was a matter of conjecture—their appearance was artificially enhanced to such an extent, they might have been refugees from the cast of The Mikado, and they were both strapped into corsets so cruelly tight, they were forced to speak in gasps. They fluttered and fussed with their gowns, cutting their eyes this way and that, tittering and giggling, exclaiming, as Constance did at one point, "Oh, do look, Presh! Isn't Margaret's gown the absolute be-all and end-all?" She glanced coyly at me and asked what I thought. I replied on cue that no gown, however gilded, could improve on the lilies I had to hand, causing them to blush and quiver and pant breathlessly, gazing at me with painted eyes that seemed as empty as their heads. I was disposed to believe that a pair of enormous parakeets disguised as women were holding me captive. Telling them I would fetch more champagne, I pushed my way through the dancers to the bar, ducked out a side door, hurried along a corridor and entered the library, a dim, cavernous space in which a mighty crystal chandelier glittered like a far-off galaxy, throwing glints from the gilt-lettered volumes lining its walls, and there I sat in a leather chair, turning things over in my mind, eventually concluding that I had been an ass. Jane was the loveliest, most admirable, most intriguing woman of my acquaintance. I loved her and had denied the fact purely on the basis of social concerns. This revelation did not bring a song to my heart, because those social concerns were far from illusory. If we were to marry, I would have to surrender all thought of a career in London. Exposed to the scrutiny of the circles in which I hoped to travel, her past would be ferreted out and we would be disgraced. If I stayed in London and kept her as a mistress, I would have to endure a Constance or a Preshea. It was not a happy choice, but I made it happily and was about to rush home and announce myself to Jane, when the imposing figure of Sir Charles Mellor hove into view.

"Ah, young Prothero!" He eyed me with disfavor. "There you are."

I started to stand, but his hand fell upon my shoulder and I sank back into the chair.

Sir Charles sat down, crossed his legs, and adjusted the hang of his trouser cuff. I have said he was imposing, yet he was not an especially large man; his intimidating effect was produced by a fierce, bearded countenance, a cold, clinical and composed manner, and a penetrating black stare before which his subordinates were wont to quail. The stare was on full display that evening, more conspicuous than the diamond studs on his starched shirt and the massive gold signet upon his left hand.

"Apparently," he said, "you have made quite the impression on my daughter."

"And she upon me." I racked my brain for a suitable compliment. "She is utterly charming."

"Charming. Yes, I suppose." He made a church-and-steeple of his fingers, tapping the tips together. "Beautiful, I should say as well."

I hastened to agree on this point.

"Witty?" he suggested. "Intelligent?"

"Without a doubt."

"And yet here you are, lost in thought, while Constance waits in the banquet hall, devastated by your abandonment of her."

"I intended no abandonment," I said. "I felt…"

"Your intent does not concern me. Or rather it concerns me only as regards your interest or lack thereof in my daughter."

"Sir Charles, I assure you that I meant no insult. I felt ill and came into the library in order to recover."

"Constance is an imbecile," he said. "A shallow, silly young woman. But I will not permit her to be trifled with."

"Sir," I said, summoning all the righteous indignation that a short career in theatricals at Cambridge allowed me to access. "Far be it from me to dictate to you, but I am compelled to say that I thoroughly resent your characterization. I have, I admit, only a passing acquaintance with your daughter, but she seems altogether a splendid girl, a lady of pristine breeding and rare quality."

He studied me a moment longer and then made a noise that I took for a symptom of satisfaction.

"How are you feeling now?" he asked. "Better, I trust."

"Somewhat."

"I will sit with you until you are able to return to the banquet hall."

A silence ensued, alleviated by distant music, after which he said, "I have not seen you at the club lately."

"I have a patient who commands a great deal of attention."

"I see. A troublesome case, is it?"

"Most troublesome."

"I hope you're being paid and that this is not charitable work in Saint Giles…or Saint Nichol."

Recalling that Sir Charles was one of Richmond's chief detractors, I attempted to mute my reaction. His statement did not require an answer, so I offered none.

"Charity is an irresponsible act," he said. "So I judge it. No less reprehensible than the act of murder. However profoundly we may regret the pitiable state of the poor, we cannot let their plight distract us from the path of progress, lest we be dragged down to their level."

"You may rest assured that I am being compensated," I said firmly. "As to the larger issue you have raised, I believe true progress to be defined by the resolution of poverty, not its continuance in the service of furthering outmoded concepts of class and empire."

I refused to wilt under his stare.

"The sentiments of an upright young man. An idealist not yet sullied by life's exigencies. I would expect no less." He leaned forward and patted my knee. "Your spirits seem restored. You must be feeling better."

"Immeasurably," I said.

"Then let's go in, shall we? The ladies are waiting."

After several hours passed flirting with Constance under the menace of Sir Charles' unrelenting scrutiny, I returned to St. Nichol exhausted by the experience, my mind abuzz with trite observances and banalities. Only a few coals remained glowing in the hearth, but I was too weary to kindle another fire and flung myself beneath the covers. I slid down the precipice of sleep, imagining Constance's annoying voice going on and on about some inane topic, but soft hands and a kiss prevented me from completing the descent. Muzzy-headed, I made a sound of complaint. Within moments, however, I was enthusiastically engaged with her. I must have fallen asleep directly afterward, for I recall nothing more of the event apart from its intensity.

The next morning I happened upon Jane in the corridor outside Richmond's study, which was situated not far from the kitchen, and made a jocular comment about her early morning visit. Her smile hardened and she pushed past me. I went after her, blocked her path, and asked what I had done to anger her.

"I slept straight through the night!" she said. "Whoever you tupped, it wasn't me!"

She tried to elude me, but I caught her by the wrist.

"Jane," I said. "If this is true…"

"Of course it's true! You bastard!"

"I was half-asleep and there was no light. I thought it was you."

She struggled against me. "When have you known me not to want the lights on?"

"It was late—I was tired, I didn't think."

"Too right, you didn't!"

"Why would I mention it otherwise? I thought it was you."

She made a half-hearted attempt to break my grip, but her anger had, I thought, diminished.

"It's the God's honest truth, Jane. On my honor."

Her lips thinned. "Let me go."

She seemed calmer—I released her.

"Don't you understand I want only you?" I said. "Haven't I made that clear?"

She darted toward the kitchen.

I stood there bewildered, seeking to consolidate my memories of the previous night. My recollection was hazy and full of gaps, but whoever the woman in my bed had been, she had displayed the full range of Jane's passionate idiosyncrasies. I wondered if she might be a somnambulist.

A shriek, a clangor as of pots and pans falling—I raced for the kitchen and saw Jane swinging a broom at Dorothea, who cowered in a corner beside the stove, crouched down and shielding her head. I managed to interpose my body and ripped the broom from Jane's grasp. Dorothea seized the opportunity to reach across my shoulder and clutch at Jane's hair, snagging it with her fingers, and Jane did the same, yanking Dorothea's hair, provoking a scream of rage and pain. As I separated them, I heard Richmond say behind me, "This is intolerable! Stop it at once!"

Their hair and clothing in disarray, the women fell back. We all looked to Richmond, who came forward into the room and stood with his hands on hips, scowling. "Will someone tell me what is going on? I could hear you in my study."

"She..." Dorothea wiped spittle from her lips. "She accused me of lying with him! I told her I had the curse, but she wouldn't hear it."

"Who was it, then?" Jane pushed toward Dorothea, but I held her back.

"Perhaps he brought someone home," said Dorothea. "How should I know who it was? And me curled up with a rag stuffed between my nethers. Why don't you inspect his bed sheets? I was bleeding so profusely, there's bound to be evidence."

"Enough!" An expression of distaste stamped Richmond's features. "Did you bring a woman home with you?" he asked me. "I have given you the run of my house, but my hospitality does not extend to your guests."

"The only woman I was with last night was Constance Mellor," I said. "And she went home in the company of her father."

"Who is this Constance?" Jane asked sharply.

"Jesus, God!" I lifted my eyes to the ceiling.

"An aberration," Richmond said to Jane. "The daughter of an abomination. You need not be jealous of her sort." He turned to me and indicated the door. "A word, if you will." Then to the women: "You will cease your bickering and attend to your duties. If there is an issue between you, and I do not believe there is, we will discuss it later. Is that understood?"

The women muttered their assent, but on exiting the kitchen Jane cast an embittered glance at Dorothea that promised further unpleasantness.

—

The prevailing odor of Richmond's study, a long L-shaped room into which I had never ventured until that morning, put me in mind of my great aunt's house in Bridgend, the air heavy with a cachet of spice and heather, the perfume of mummified refinement and Georgian depression—but there all similarity stopped. Iron shutters prevented the ingress of natural light and at one end, tucked into the bottom stroke of the L, a reading lamp with a green glass shade, the sole source of illumination, created an island of emerald radiance about a carved oak desk that had the look of an ancient monument, its walls configured by intricate bas relief. Two chairs sat on opposite sides of the desk. Hundreds of leather-bound books lined the shelves, breathing out musty vibrations. An atmosphere of gloom and hermetic solitude held sway—this was heightened by a wide, unexploited, uncarpeted space upon which pentagrams might be sketched and half-ton entities invoked. Something had once occupied that space, for there were grooves and notches in the wood, marking the passage of a great weight. I suspected the room might have served as Richmond's workplace prior to his renovation of the sixth floor. Considering this room in context of the others, I thought that if the house was in more-or-less the same condition Christine had left it, then she must have had the sensibilities of a jackdaw, for no decorative theme was carried out—the interior design might have been the work of several women, not one.

I seated myself and apologized for my part in the disturbance, but Richmond, standing by the desk, dismissed my apology and asked which of the women did I think was lying.

"Dorothea," I said. "Yet I would have sworn it was Jane with me last night."

"Do not forget that they were both schooled in the ways of men by Christine," he said. "To distinguish between them in the dark is no easy thing."

I did not like this intimation of his former relationship with Jane. "Jane had no reason to lie," I said.

"Whores need no reason. Lying is second nature to them. They invent reasons that might not appear reasonable to you or me, yet touch upon their innermost secrets."

Bridling at this, I said, "If such is to be the tenor of our conversation, let us end it now. I have no wish to hear you speak crudely of Jane."

"Did you find that statement crude? I thought I was being a realist." Richmond took a seat behind the desk. "Samuel, you're a young man. Younger than your years, I'd say. You are perceptive and, I believe, quite intuitive. But it's obvious that you are in love and love can blind one to a great many painful truths."

"Jane loves me as well."

"Has she said as much?"

"I have made no declaration, nor has she, but I know it to be true."

"Well, though it may be that Jane is in love, I can assure you of one thing. She is not blinded by it. She may be several years your junior, but she has a wide experience of the world. That she has changed since we were involved, I have no doubt—but she has not grown more foolish or less discerning."

"I don't understand how this is relevant. My connection with Jane is my concern, and hers. If you have something to say about Dorothea's lie or upon another subject, I will gladly listen. Otherwise there is no point to continuing."

Richmond cleared his throat and then said, "Is it lost on you that there is a third woman in the house?"

I floundered for a moment. "Are you speaking of Christine?"

"I have watched you with her these last weeks. I've..."

"I haven't seen you on the sixth floor since I began my study."

"I drilled a hole that permits observation if one stands in the space between the inner and outer walls. But that is not of moment."

"Oh, no? I find it unbelievably offensive. Are there peepholes elsewhere? In my bedroom, perhaps?"

"Bear with me, I beg you. Hear me out and then I will accept the full brunt of your outrage." Richmond clasped his head in his hands, staring down at the fawn-colored blotter. "I have never spoken of these events to any man, but I believe you have sniffed out a portion of my story. That makes it no easier to disclose, but now...now I find disclosure to be necessary."

He sighed and looked up from the desk. "I was sixteen when my mother died. Christine was less than two years younger. My mother fell ill in the spring of the year and my father brought the family to our country estate near Caerphilly in hopes she might recover there. Within the week he was called away to the Continent on business, leaving my mother to be cared for by servants. He remained absent until a few days prior to her death. Why he did this..." He shook his head. "His motives were hidden from me and he has never talked about that summer. At the time I chose to believe he loved her and that his absence was due to an inability to watch her suffer. But now I think he became disinterested in her when she could no longer play the part of wife, and went off to find a new one in Europe. Which, ultimately, he did.

"My mother's decline was swift. After a month in Caerphilly she barely recognized us. The doctor told us she had weeks to live, no more, yet she lingered all that summer. Bedridden, racked by fevers, in pain and heavily drugged. We did what we could, Christine and I, but the servants kept us from her, fearing the sight of our mother in her delirium and torment would damage our tender souls—they failed to comprehend that seeing her only rarely and then for a few minutes was a torment to us. I wrote my father, pleading with him to return, but he would not respond. And so Christine and I were virtually alone, with no authority to guide us but an elderly nanny whom we no longer heeded. I would read to her and she played the piano for me, but these pursuits soon bored us and we began to wander the estate, taking a picnic lunch and passing entire days in the woods and fields, talking about this and that. Prior to that summer we had been apart so much of the time, and now, thrown together in such a powerful emotional setting, relying upon each other for support, for conversation, for all else…it was an unhealthy situation. On occasion I would notice some feature of her beauty, and I would catch her looking at me, instances that caused her to blush and avert her eyes. I repressed these moments—I thrust them aside and refused to acknowledge what they portended."

Richmond gazed at the iron shutters. "There was a pond on the property, large enough to think of as a small lake. We often ate beside it. One afternoon in early June, feeling torpid following lunch, I fell asleep. When I awoke, Christine was gone. I heard a splashing from the direction of the pond and made my way through the bushes that grew alongside the bank. Christine stood in the shallows, completely unclothed, sluicing water over her body. I thought her the most beautiful thing in all of Creation. She saw me as well. Instead of covering herself, she turned full toward me, clasped her hands behind her head and lifted her face to the sun. I raced back to the house, pierced by shame, but I had remained there long enough to imprint her image on my brain and shame would not wash it away. That night she came into my bed. I was half-asleep, yet I could have resisted her."

He wore such a morose expression, I felt sympathy for him and said, "You are not the first man to have made such an error in judgment."

"Oh, it was hardly that!" He laughed bitterly. "We were in love and love accepts no judgments. Our affair continued for months, even after my father's return, and did not end until I returned to Eaton. Christine was always more aggressive than I. She forced the issue, yet I was equally culpable."

He pressed his hands together, the tips of his fingers touching his chin—a prayerful attitude. "Years later our nanny informed me that Christine had become pregnant and a stable boy let go. She had accused him in order to deflect blame from me. I don't know what became of him…or the child."

"Christine never said anything?"

"Not a word. I wrote to her, of course. I asked what had happened. She answered my letters, but not my questions. She had been sent away…to school, my father said. In France. I didn't see her again for years. She married a gentleman farmer, or so she claimed. In one of her letters she enclosed a wedding photograph that showed her with a man with oiled hair and a little mustache. A charade, I suppose. I never had a word from him, neither then nor following her death.

"A year after her purported marriage, she asked me to meet her in Torquay. We spent a few days together and whenever I brought up our personal history, she insisted that we not dwell upon the past. Over the years we met in Margate, Ilfracombe, Ryde, Cardiff, Llandudno…in every benighted resort in Britain. Days, we strolled on the esplanade, we laughed and teased one another, we watched the Punch and Judy shows, rode donkeys on the beach and attended concerts. Only once did she offer affection of the kind I desired. It must have been shortly after she moved to Saint Nichol. She melted into an embrace and kissed me, but apologized immediately and said the kiss was a mistake. I went to sleep that night as I had on all the previous nights, alone and frustrated. You see, I still held in mind the image of her face lit to white gold by the sun, the water beaded on her flesh. I hold it still." His aggrieved expression and slumped posture gave evidence of a defeated attitude. "I hope you understand now why I have been so beastly toward you."

I allowed that, No, I did not.

"Because I'm jealous," he said. "She is returning to us and it is you with whom she speaks, with whom she flirts as she once did with me. She holds me in contempt. She blames me for everything that happened. And now she has come to you exactly as she came to me when we became lovers."

I had been about to suggest that he was reading far too much into the situation, but his last statement left me speechless. My shock must have been discernable, for he said, "Can you not see it? Jane has no reason to lie, as you say, and Dorothea's complaint is easily verified, if you have the stomach for it. Unless Constance Mellor followed you to Saint Nichol, who could it have been but Christine?"

Disordered by this outburst, I took a moment in order to marshal a response. "Firstly, we do not know that Christine is, as you put it, returning. Her behavior and the quality of her materializations reflect a shift in amplitude, but there is nothing to indicate..."

"If you were working on a jigsaw puzzle and, having completed it save for two or three pieces, you saw that it constituted the picture of a lion, do you believe that adding those few pieces would transform it into the picture of a giraffe?"

"To use your metaphor, this particular puzzle is missing many more than two or three pieces. We can make no reasonable assumption based on what is known."

"As a scientist you must know that the making of assumptions, the construction of hypotheses, is essential to progress. Take, for example, Christine's reaction to the song, 'Champagne Charlie.' Are you aware that Christine had a client who wore a mask and whose identity she claimed not to know?"

"Jane told me. What of it?"

"When you referred to Constance Mellor in the kitchen, I thought instantly of Charles Mellor. When he was young he had the reputation of being just such a man as the song describes. He enjoyed gadding about the slums, whoring and drinking in the gin shops of Saint Nichol. It's possible that he was the masked client and, further, that he funded Christine's purchase of this house. A sizeable portion of his income is derived from the ownership of slum properties. This house may once have belonged to him. I intend to look into the matter. My assumption may be erroneous, but property issues, the change of titles and so forth... it should be easy enough to prove. Now that..." He sat up straight, the movement appearing to reflect a sudden and unexpected reinvigoration. "That is merely an assumption. What we have in Christine's case rises to the level of theory, wouldn't you say?"

"No, I would not. The leap one would have to make between an apparition and a revivification, even a temporary one, seems much more extensive than that between your assumption regarding Mellor and his actual guilt. As to that, I trust you will not act precipitately."

"When one takes into account your chosen field of study, you seem a strangely conservative thinker," Richmond said, gazing at me with a ruminative air. "I find it dismaying that you are unable to reach for a height without availing yourself of a stepladder, so to speak."

I had no desire to engage in a running metaphorical battle with him and so I let the comment pass.

"Well," he said pertly. "You have been warned."

"Warned? As to what?"

"Why...Christine." He seemed baffled by my failure to grasp the obvious. "It is clear that she has designs on you and that you are in danger. I cannot but think that her ghost is in a perpetual state of torment. How can it be otherwise? Life calls to her and she feels the pull of old desires, yet she cannot answer that call. Now, presented with an opportunity to re-inhabit the world of the senses, she must be desperate to taste and touch and feel. Christine was ever prone to abrupt shifts in mood and subject to whims and cravings. As they were when she was in love with me, these tendencies have become exaggerated since she made a connection with you. I foresee a time when those whims evolve into wild and erratic impulse, those cravings into compulsion, and she will let nothing stand in the way of her desires."

—

Although it strained credulity, had anyone aside from Richmond warned me against Christine, I might have taken the warning to heart; but I had detected in him an unsound quality and our conversation had done nothing to ease my mind on that score. Then, too, I had a more enjoyable and distracting business to complete. The following afternoon I had Richmond's coachman, Henry Bladge, a sturdy, balding fellow with pork chop whiskers and a round face as unremarkable as a muffin top, convey Jane and myself to a tea room on the edge of Bethnal Green, an establishment with a small garden at the rear that sought to counterfeit a pleasance, offering an air of relative seclusion amidst shrubbery, several young trees, and a pair of stone benches—yet it lay close enough to a gin shop that we could hear the squabbling of that establishment's poorer patrons who, unable to afford a mug of their poison, stood at the door, holding gin-soaked handkerchiefs to their faces and inhaling the fumes. Snatches of music on occasion drowned out their clamor, testifying to the passage of street musicians. After tea we sat out on a sun-dappled bench, shaded by a thickly leaved elm, and there I told her (more bluntly than I had planned, for I was anxious) that I wished to marry her and make a home with her in Wales. She looked every inch the creature of fashion—under her cashmere shawl, she wore a dress cut from a tartan fabric of brown and green that complimented her eyes and hair, and also matched her sober mien. She did not give me her answer at once, but asked if I intended to complete my investigation.

"I will do my best for Richmond," I said, "if that is your concern."

"My concern is not only for him, but for Christine."

"I have no authority over the spirit world. Were I to promise a satisfactory conclusion in that regard, you would be within your rights to question my veracity."

She maintained her reserve. "I doubt myself, Samuel. I wonder if I can make you a suitable wife. Although Christine taught me how to play the lady, that veneer is thin, as you witnessed the other morning.

I understand why you would wish to return to Wales with me. Here in London I would be no asset to your career."

I objected to this, but she took my hand and said, "Please, Samuel! We must be forthright with one another."

"It is true," I said. "I was initially fearful that my career would be damaged by our union, but as my thoughts on the subject evolved, I feared mainly for you. I did not want you to suffer the scorn that would be heaped upon you by the doyennes of polite society should your past be revealed. Now that we have reached this pass, however, I realize your strength is sufficient to withstand such treatment. You have endured far worse. And I must not allow the course of my career to be dependent on the views of people who belong to a world that is fast disappearing. If you wish to remain in London, remain we shall."

"Perhaps that can be a subject for later discussion?"

"Of course."

She glanced up into the elm leaves, as though attracted by some movement there. "Do you think you know me, Samuel? I have been honest with you concerning my past, but I have a great capacity for self-deception. I may have painted myself too much the victim so as to draw you in."

"No one is immune to self-deception," I said. "I doubt the human race would survive without it. As for knowing you, I cannot imagine that any two people at this stage of their lives know one another completely. They can only anticipate learning about the woman or the man they love."

"I have one last question," she said. "I know that your politics predisposes you to have an affection for the underprivileged. Am I to be, then, a kind of political proof, living evidence of that predisposition? A token of your political views, as it were?"

"Were I a creature of the type who populates the rolls of the Inventors' Club, I would never have looked at you as other than an object of lust," I said. "To that extent, politics has played a part in this—it has assisted me in perceiving you for the woman you are. But I swear, that is the only part it played."

She drew a breath and released it slowly. "Then I will gladly be your wife, in London or in Wales. That is, if you still want me after all these quibbles and qualifications."

We embraced, albeit not for long—prying eyes peered at us through the rear windows of the tea room—and then left that place, that bench and its overshadowing elm. I told Henry Bladge to drive us round Hyde Park. It was a rare lovely day, a high, blue day accented by puffs of cloud, and warm for the first week in March, with flights of swallows banking above Kensington Gardens and people taking their ease on the green lawns; but Jane and I hid ourselves behind the curtains of the coach, kissing and conjuring a future together that, for all its optimism and halcyon vision, had not the slightest chance of coming true.

—

Richmond began to install his new machine several days later and, as the two machines that cleansed the air had been shut down (the one that summoned Christine was not, its operation signaled by a throbbing hum, not the louder, steady rumbling of the others), I took the opportunity to climb up to the roof through a trapdoor accessible by means of a ladder and located in the ceiling close to the elevator. From my vantage on the western side of the roof, standing in a thick carpet of black dust, it seemed I was at the center of a choppy sea contrived of roof peaks and chimneys from which darkling smokes trickled upward to commingle with an overcast of much the same color. Four cylindrical sections had been cut out from the eastern side of the roof and the machines had been set down in the holes thus created, approximately a third of their height hidden from the view of whoever might peer at them from the adjoining houses. The concentric silver rings (I say, silver, but that word refers merely to their color—I never ascertained the name of the metal from which they had been fashioned) that constituted their exterior rose some fifteen feet above the roof and were pitted and discolored; but the new machine was shiny and taller by half. Altogether they resembled Christmas trees of a futuristic design, three stubby and one attenuated, and appeared quite alien in contrast to the blackened bricks and tiles of their surround. I wondered why this bizarre construction atop Richmond's house had not been paid more notice by the residents of St. Nichol, especially considering the noise it produced; but then I recognized that most had little interest as to what happened in the heavens, their eyes being fixed upon the ground, their ears attuned to baser sounds.

Crouched amidst a clutter of tools (awls, hammers, and so on), Richmond and several workmen were busy bolting down the new machine to an iron plate—I could see the tops of their heads from the edge of the hole. The machine itself differed from the other three not only in height, but also in that various dials and switches occupied the interstices between certain of the concentric rings. I poked around the rooftop for a few minutes more, finding nothing to hold my interest and then, as I prepared to go back down through the trapdoor, I caught sight of an opaque, oblong shape, roughly the size of a man, hovering close by the fourth machine. It trembled, fluttering as would a leaf in a strong wind, and subsequently was drawn out into a thinner, scarf-like shape that clung to one of the concentric rings, gliding along it, fitting itself to the ring as though it were a sleeve...and then it vanished. I had grown accustomed to ghosts during my stay at Richmond's house, even to the point of being on speaking terms with one, and their formal apparitions, the images, fragmentary and otherwise, of the men and women they had been in life had almost no affect upon me; but this glimpse of the raw stuff of the spirit—that was how I countenanced it—left me petrified, my heart squeezed and stilled for an instant by cold, steely fingers, and made me full aware of the depths of the pit into which I had lowered myself.

—

My work with Christine had reached an impasse. What I had seen on the roof made me reluctant to engage her and I spent less time with her than I had, dallying with Jane instead. Richmond remained concentrated on the installation and, though I saw him each and every day, he spoke only in monosyllables and then in passing. He was oblivious to everything but the matter at hand and seemed to have lost interest in talking further about Christine. For once I was happy to accommodate him. However, on the day after the new machine had been activated, he invited me into his study and notified me that he had turned off the fourth machine and from now on, for the duration of my visit, the new machine would be the only one functioning.

"You must do as you see fit," I said. "But this is certain to impede my work."

"On the contrary, my dear Samuel," he said with gleeful satisfaction. "It will assist your work no end. Tomorrow or the next day, a window will be installed in the chamber beneath the new machine."

I absorbed this. "So the purpose of this machine is not to purify the atmosphere?"

"It is intended to restore Christine. Not entirely—I don't believe that is possible, though my notion of what is possible changes day by day. But by using the damaged settings on the fourth machine as a starting point, I have devised a means of strengthening her effect. At least that is my hope. This may serve to quicken her perceptions, broaden her range of interactions with our plane of existence, and thus enable her to assist materially in bringing her murderer to justice."

"Materially? Are you suggesting that she may be able to give us conscious, clearly reasoned assistance?"

"That is a distinct possibility."

"Yet when you say 'strengthening her effect', I have the impression that what you have done is to create an amplification of effect and not a broadening."

"As you yourself have said, you know nothing about this branch of science."

"If you recall, I was speaking at the time about cleansing the air. The creation of the machine that enhanced Christine's presence happened by accident and I cannot think that you have a complete understanding of the process. Now you are certainly more proficient than I with regard to the technical aspects of your machine, but I have studied your sister for several months and I would hazard that you know less than I about her condition. You are playing a dangerous game, Richmond."

"I'm not playing at anything!" he said. "I am desperate to gain Christine's ear. I must know that she forgives me."

"Is that truly the sum of your desires?" I asked. "At first you told me that you wanted know who financed the brothel, and then it was a clue to the identity of Christine's murderer. Now it is her forgiveness you want...and her restoration to a state of being similar to that she had in life. I infer from this progression that you may never be satisfied and will continue to elevate your expectations."

He gave me an oddly bright look, the sort of look one observes on the faces of certain mental patients, seemingly alert yet too fixed to signal actual alertness.

"I would be remiss if I failed to warn you that you have embarked on a self-destructive course," I said.

He was silent for such a long while that I began to worry.

"Richmond?" I said.

His head twitched. "I still haven't been able to come up with a better name for the machines than 'attractors'. Do you have any thoughts on the subject?"

"Did you hear what I said?"

"About my self-destructive course? Yes, I heard you. And I have moved on." He leafed through some papers that had been lying on his desk. "Having witnessed the machines in operation, perhaps you can suggest a suitable name?"

Unsettled by this abrupt conversational shift, I told him that "attractors" struck me as eminently suitable, but that I would set my mind to the task. He appeared indifferent to my concerns, so I excused myself and went in search of Jane.

In the kitchen I found Dorothea seated at the counter, popping grapes into her mouth and gazing at the wall. I asked if she had encountered Jane that day.

"She was about earlier." She winked at me. "Have you looked under your sheets?"

I sank onto a stool beside her and let my head hang.

"Well, I can tell you're in a fine fettle," Dorothea said.

"I'm worn out."

"Perhaps you need a tonic."

"Perhaps."

She chucked. "I'd rub your shoulders, but I don't care to risk another beating."

I sat mute and discouraged, and at length said, "I'm not physically fatigued. My weakness is purely spiritual."

"I was having you on, referring to Jane taking after me with the broom the other morning."

"Oh…right."

She offered me the bunch of grapes and I took one.

"I think Richmond may be mad," I said.

"Wouldn't surprise me. We're all a bit mad 'round here."

"I wasn't speaking in jest."

"Nor was I. Living in Saint Nichol is enough to put a few twists in your noggin, and sharing your home with a ghostie…" She gave her head a violent shake. "Our ghostie has been at me all morning."

"Christine?"

"If I've seen her once, I've seen her half-a-dozen times. She must have important business with someone."

Richmond's newest attractor, I thought. Doing its job.

"She's not in a cheery mood," Dorothea said.

"How do you mean? Was she wearing her chemise, all bloody?"

"No, but she wasn't the least bit happy, even when I sang for her."

I got to my feet, undecided whether or not to notify Richmond of this sudden increase in Christine's manifestations.

"You might want to wait," said Dorothea. "She'll be dropping in again any minute."

"I'm going up to the sixth," I said. "Tell Jane where I'll be, won't you?"

"What about Miss Christine?" Dorothea asked as I went out. "Have you a message for her?"

—

The sixth floor was deserted, silent except for the oscillating hum of the new attractor. Workmen had not yet come to replace the iron wall of the chamber beneath it with glass. Curious, I opened the sampling aperture and heard from within a far-off roaring like that made by the shadowy creature. I detected movement in the corner of my eye and saw Christine pacing in front of the fourth chamber, wearing her emerald green corset. I approached her cautiously (Richmond's admonition about her had not gone unheeded) and spoke as I might to a horse that required gentling. This tactic had no good effect, for she vanished before I could reach her. Turning back toward the elevator, I saw something that froze my blood. I had left the sampling aperture open and from it there projected a well-defined beam of black energy or light or some other immateriality I could not name. It was as though a black sun were contained within the chamber and its radiant stuff had shot forth from the aperture to touch the wall opposite... and upon that wall an irregular patch of darkness grew, developing into a vaguely anthropomorphic figure that had the shape and size of a small headless child. The roaring had increased in volume and it was this, the implication that somehow a monstrous, whirling shadow was being beamed onto our earthly plane...that spurred me to act. I sprang to the aperture and shut it, cutting off the beam. The dark shape on the wall began to dissolve in much the way a puddle of water evaporates under strong sunlight, albeit far more quickly. Once it had gone I sat at one of the benches and sought to analyze what had occurred, but the phenomenon beggared analysis and I was too rattled to think. After ten minutes of fruitless deliberation, it struck me that urgency was called for. Eschewing the elevator, I pelted down the stairs to the second floor, intending to collect my notes and alert the others. Upon entering my bedroom I found Jane standing by the fireplace, gazing at the dead coals, wearing the tartan dress she wore on the day I asked for her hand. I was eager to tell her all that had happened and caught her by the arm. She looked up at me with Christine's eyes, the hazel irises revolving a fraction of a turn and back again. Seen this close, they no longer reminded me of clockworks, but had the agitated motion of the tiny creatures I had studied under a microscope at university.

I stumbled back and sat down heavily on the bed, staring at her in disbelief. I had no doubt the woman before me was Jane. She had Jane's height and delicacy of feature, yet her stony expression seemed less at home on her face than it had on Christine's. And those eyes… I tried to picture the pattern of darks and brights in Jane's hazel irises, but could not bring them to mind. She came toward me, paused a foot away and uttered a peculiar fluting cry. It seemed that she had difficulty breathing, though in retrospect I believe that the fleshly mechanisms of speech were difficult to master for the spirit who had possessed my fiancée.

She opened her mouth again and this time, with considerable effort and in a voice that fluctuated between Jane's firm contralto and Christine's higher, frailer tones, she said, "Have you come to frolic? It is much too early. We risk being interrupted at our play."

This brief speech so horrified me that I remained half-lying on the bed, propped up on my elbows, incapable of answering her.

"Yet risk may add spice to our pleasure. Was that your thought? Naughty Jeffkins!" She turned her back and lifted her hair away from the nape of her neck. "Won't you help me with my buttons?"

I came to my feet and turned her to face me. "Jane!" I said, and shook her. "Jane!"

She fought against me, but I shook her again and again, each time more violently, and continued to call her name. Suddenly she went limp and would have fallen to the floor in a swoon had I not supported her. I laid her down on the bed and patted her cheeks until her eyes fluttered open—her eyes, devoid of unnatural movement, and not Christine's. She was at first confused, then angry when I told her about Christine, refusing to accept my version of events.

"Do you remember me entering the room?" I asked her. "Or anything that was said."

"I…" She put a hand to her temple. "No, but…"

"What is the last thing you recall?"

"I was..." A look of consternation cut a line across her brow. "I was in my room. Reading, I think."

"You never wear this dress in the house. Not to my knowledge. Were you wearing it while reading?"

She examined a fold of fabric that she pinched between her thumb and forefinger. "I had not finished dressing. I thought of a quotation—from Jane Austen—and I recall opening my book to search for it."

"Can we assume your lapse of memory encompassed a span of, say, ten minutes or thereabouts?"

"I'm not sure. Everything's cloudy."

She started up from the bed, but I held her down.

"We must tell Jeffrey," she said.

"Do you feel up to it?"

"I'm fine."

"All right. But you must promise that no matter how he reacts, you'll leave with me at once."

"He may need our assistance."

"If you remain in the house, you will be at risk. This may not be the first time that Christine has possessed you."

"What do you mean?"

"I think you may owe Dorothea an apology."

After a moment she said, "Oh, God! Is that possible?"

We went downstairs, collected Dorothea and bearded Richmond in his study, where I explained things to the best of my ability.

"Well now. That should remove the sting from Samuel's infidelity," he said to Jane, bemused. "It would appear that he was unfaithful to you with you."

"I see no humor in this," I said.

"No?" His smile broadened. "Let it be noted that you are a particularly humorless young man."

"I can't speak for Dorothea," I said. "But Jane and I intend to leave before a tragedy occurs."

"Oh, you have my permission to speak for me," Dorothea said. "I'm half out the door."

I leaned down to Richmond, resting my fists on his desk. "If you insist upon staying, a tragedy is inevitable. You are in grave danger."

"Nonsense! Christine is indifferent to me."

"Yet less than an hour ago, in a tone of voice I would describe as playfully seductive, she referred to you as 'Naughty Jeffkins.' Does that strike a chord?"

"Did she say that? But this is wonderful, don't you see?"

"Damn it, Richmond! She's confused me with you. Can you have forgotten what you told me? That she is a mad fraction of her former self with whom true communication was impossible?"

"I may have been in error," he said.

"Jeffrey, please!" Jane laid a hand on his shoulder. "You must leave."

"All you have done is to strengthen that fraction," I said. "And what of that shadowy creature? It seems you have strengthened it as well. Do you have any understanding of its potential?"

"No, I do not," Richmond said. "Nor do you. And because you do not understand, you are afraid."

"It's conceivable that the entity is harmless...or inimical in a trifling way, like the ghost of a demonic house pet. But when dealing with something of so menacing an aspect, yes, I deem it wise to practice caution. As would any responsible person."

"Go then!" Enraged, Richmond jumped to his feet and pointed to the door. "Go and practice caution! Be responsible! Leave me to my researches."

"You've done no research! You built your machines and left the research to me. Research, I might add, that would be much farther along had you been open with me from the outset."

I held out my hand to Jane, but she looked to Richmond instead. "Do you want us to stay, Jeffrey?"

"I cannot ask it of you," he said. "But yes, of course. A resolution is at hand and I would hope that you see me through it."

"Jane," I said.

"How long will this resolution take?" she asked.

"Perhaps a few hours. A single night. Now that she is stronger, I doubt things will go unresolved for long. Yet I cannot be precise."

"I'll be pushing along," Dorothea said. "I've given you my all, as it were, Mister Richmond. All this talk of possession, though…it's not a dance I care to do."

Jane turned to her. "We can spare him one more night, can't we?"

Dorothea said flatly, "I'm sorry."

"I won't leave without you, Jane," I said.

"I swear to you, Samuel." Richmond came out from behind his desk. "I will shut down the machine in the morning, whether or not…"

"Why should we believe anything you have to say?" I stepped away as he made to approach me. "You've done nothing but lie and dissemble since the beginning. If a resolution of the problems between you and Christine is what you actually seek, how will our presence assist in that? It will achieve nothing other than placing us in peril."

"You're right," he said. "I'm frightened. I'm afraid of being alone with her. If you feel you must leave, I understand."

Judging by the sympathetic expression on Jane's face, I recognized there was little hope of countering Richmond's self-serving statement; but I tried nevertheless.

"You are afraid, yet you wish us to stay," I said. "And you care so little about our well-being, you expect us to join you in this dangerous folly. How noble!"

Jane shot me a reproving look.

"He's manipulating you," I said.

"He's right," said Richmond with a hangdog expression. "You should leave."

"Good Christ!" I slammed the flat of my hand against the desk, making a loud report. "Now he's feigning weakness to rouse your sympathy. Can't you see?"

Both Jane and Richmond regarded me sadly, as if they were aware of some nuance, some shading of the truth that I had yet to comprehend.

—

Scientific curiosity may have played a part in my decision to remain in the house. I was genuinely anxious for Jane and I wanted to keep an eye on Richmond—I insisted that we wait out the night together, thinking that should Richmond begin to behave erratically or Christine attempt to possess Jane once again, I would take decisive action. But as we sat at a bench on the sixth floor, speaking minimally or not at all, I came to ponder my missed opportunities. Had I not become involved with Jane and focused the bulk of my attention on the ghosts that passed through the chamber, I might have arrived at some firm conclusions about the spirit world. As things stood I could make only the most general of suppositions. I vowed to devote myself henceforth to uncovering material proofs pertaining to everything I had observed.

Not until that night did I realize how unseemly a perdition the sixth floor was. With its mouse droppings, dusty spaces and raw boards, its gray canvas curtain, iron walls and benches laden with machine parts, and with its ghosts and the vibration of the attractor, it had an ambiance that was part futuristic charnel house, part wizardly lair. I could not wait to relegate it to memory. My dislike for the place was augmented by Dorothea's absence. Her pragmatism and humor had been necessary to the sustenance of the unusual family we had become during the past months, and I felt a corresponding disunity. Jane leafed through a book of poems, occasionally offering me a nervous smile. Now and then Richmond glanced at the ceiling. He may have been alerted by some aberrance in pitch of the attractor, though I detected none. During the initial hour of our vigil, Christine materialized in her several guises on fourteen separate occasions, never for more than seconds, but made no effort to possess Jane or to do anything other than look morose. After that she appeared no more. I was nonplussed by her withdrawal and Richmond's manner grew funereal, sitting with his hands clasped and eyes downcast. Every so often he would blurt out a question such as "Where do you think she is?" or "Do you think we should move downstairs?" Our response to these and other questions was essentially the same: I don't know. Another two hours passed in this fashion. Finally, during the fourth hour, he told us that he was going up to the roof.

"For what purpose?" I asked.

He drew himself up to his full height, presenting a stern pose. "I will not answer to you in my own house."

I blocked his way to the trapdoor. "In this instance, one in which our safety is at issue, I'm afraid you must."

"Are you threatening me, sir?"

"I am attempting to ensure that you not place us in greater danger than you already have."

"I need to inspect the machine," said Richmond. "Something may be wrong."

"It seems to be running smoothly."

"Idiot! You can't tell by listening to it! I have…"

"Yet you were listening to it earlier, were you not?"

Richmond hissed in frustration. "One cannot make such a judgment merely by listening. I have to see the instruments."

Jane closed her book. "We should allow him to do what he needs."

"I don't trust him on his own," I said. "And I will not leave you alone down here."

Richmond tried to force his way past me and I shoved him back.

"I'll go with you," said Jane. "It may well be that something has gone wrong. We'd be foolish not to let him attend to it."

I argued that venturing up onto the roof would be incautious, but with Richmond attacking me verbally and Jane supporting his basic argument, I relented. I insisted, however, on taking the lead. Nothing out of the ordinary met my eye when I cracked the trapdoor, yet when I threw it open I saw that something had gone very wrong, indeed.

Streamers of fog trailed across the rooftop at eye level, but above the house a bank of thicker fog lowered; though actual fog was not its sole constituent. Its uppermost reaches stretched across half the sky and, depending from its bottom, a funnel had developed, extending downward toward the tip of the new attractor, itself visible above the roof peak, its silver rings glowing with a bilious, yellow-green radiance. At first glance the bank was like a great cloud whose bottom was cobbled with faces, but I saw on its underside a myriad images of not only disembodied faces, but torsos and limbs as well—they roiled up for an instant and were subsumed into the fog, replaced by the other revenants. Rags of filmy, opaque material were disgorged from the mouth of the funnel and these battened onto the attractor, fitted themselves to one or another of the rings, and slid down out of view. Whenever this occurred, and it occurred with increasing frequency, a silent discharge of yellowish green energy shot upward from the attractor, spreading through the bank like heat lightning, permitting me to see shapes deeper within the fog. I thought that some of the shapes so illuminated were inhuman, yet they passed from sight so quickly that I could not swear to it.

Urged on by Richmond, I clambered up onto the roof, still partly in shock, dismayed by the sight, and by the silence as well. Oh, there was the omnipresent humming, loud and variable, but this apocalyptic scene, that of the ghosts of St. Nichol, the relics of the damaged and the poor lured by the attractor, perhaps to their doom, for God only knew what Richmond's improvements had wrought...it should have been accompanied by an explosive music, the final pyrotechnic symphony of a mad Russian who had devoted his life to its creation and then, having awakened to the worthlessness of his work, of all creative labor, had chosen self-slaughter over the ignominy of existence. Jane came up beside me and Richmond scrambled to the roof peak and stood, one hand on the chimney for balance, his hair feathering, superimposed against that insane sky. He let out an agonized shout and pointed—filmy bits were being torn away from the fog, spinning down away from the attractor.

I climbed toward the roof peak, Jane at my heels, and reached it just as Richmond disappeared into the hole into which the new attractor had been set. At the edge of the roof stood the demon, the shadowy, headless thing—I could make out no more of its features or form than I had previously, yet I noticed that its dark substance whirled more slowly, perhaps because it was feeding, absorbing the opaque scraps that were ripped from the underbelly of the bank. That was my interpretation of its actions, that it must also be an attractor, albeit of a vastly different and less potent variety, a living version of Richmond's machine. Some credence was given this viewpoint by Christine, who stood on the slant of the roof fifteen or twenty feet distant, her figure elongating, bending sideways at the waist and seeming to flow partway toward the shadow before snapping back to true, as though she were made of an elastic material and barely able to resist its pull.

We climbed down the slope of the roof toward the hole so as to learn what could be done to help Richmond. I saw him below, his hands busy with the switches on a brass box situated between two of the rings. He shouted and beckoned for me to join him. Whatever hesitancy I felt was erased by the garishly lit fogbank, lowered to within a few feet of the attractor, spewing forth its ghostly issue—the moil of limbs and faces over our heads was supremely grotesque, Dantean in scope, yet the multiplicity of forms also put me in mind of the rococo ornamentation I had seen on the walls of a temple in Udaipur, only in this instance the ornaments were animated by some occult principle. Bursts of yellow-green light now flickered across the breadth of the sky.

I lowered Jane into the hole and jumped down after her. Communicating with shouts and gestures, Richmond demonstrated that the switches no longer functioned—we would have to break the rings in order to stop the machine. There proved to be insufficient room in the hole to swing the long-handled hammers with which he equipped us, and we were forced to climb back onto the roof, leaving Jane to do whatever she could with a smaller hammer.

We stood side-by-side, Richmond and I, and each blow we delivered against the rings of the attractor sent a huge bloom of radiance into the fogbank. The humming rose in pitch and melded with the roaring of the shadowy creature to create a singing rush. Our blows scarcely dented the metal, however, and so we concentrated our efforts on a single ring. I lost track of Christine, unable to spare her a glance, and swung the hammer until my shoulders and arms ached with strain. I had given up hope that our assault would produce a result, when without warning the attractor crumpled all along its length, as if squeezed by an enormous fist. I cried out in exultation—I had the urge to embrace Richmond and turned to him, but was enveloped in a burst of light and lifted up...lifted, I say, and not flung.

If this were an explosion, it was a most peculiar one. There was no concussion, no heat, no sound, and I felt buoyed up in that flickering, yellow-green space. On every side were the fragmentary beings I had formerly seen from beneath. Ghastly, semi-translucent faces bobbled and drifted away from me, some with ragged, immaterial bodies in tow, and it seemed I was passing among them, pushing upward through their closely massed numbers. They did not appear to register my intrusion. A profound calm blanketed my fear and I thought that I had become a ghost and that this calmness must be a natural protection that attended my sudden transition into the afterlife, a kind of emotional shield. Believing that I shared their fate, I studied the spirits nearest me, searching for signs of agony or distress. They were haggard and bore signs of ill-usage and disease, yet their expressions were uniformly neutral, conveying the idea that they had come to terms with death, something that fresher ghosts like Christine had not. I derived little comfort from this, speculating that I might spend decades in a desolate condition before achieving even a negligible measure of peace, and I clutched at the hope that I might still be alive and that my deathly surround was an illusion, a dream I was having as I lay unconscious atop the roof; but all that served was to rouse my discontent, causing me to struggle, to jostle the spirits around me, creating gaps amongst them. Through one such gap I spotted a dark shape that swiftly grew in size and definition—the shadowy creature, heading straight toward me. My capacity for fright had been suppressed and I did not panic, but I did renew my struggles and discovered the yellow-green radiance to have a viscous consistency that hampered movement. Yet the shadow moved through it easily, as if born to that medium...though its movement may not have been so facile. I saw that it was spinning ass-over-teakettle—slowly, mind you, with an ease and grace that caused me to think it had done this many times before. I estimated, judging by its path, that it might miss me, but it did not. As the thing tumbled by, a portion of it grazed my hip, or better said, passed through my hip. It failed to disrupt my course in the least—there was no painful collision—but I felt numbness spread from my hip down my left leg to the knee, and I had an overwhelming sense of joy that may have been the residue of that brief contact. Not a meat joy, not an emotion bred by pleasure or by appetites fulfilled, but a blissful feeling, an ecstasy I would associate with purity, the sort of thing saints claim to experience when communing with God. The joy soon dissipated, however, and with it went my calm. Terrified, I thrashed about, attempting to break free from whatever held me fast. I continued to struggle until the light abruptly dimmed to the ordinary darkness of a London rooftop and I fell.

When I regained consciousness, the fog had thinned to a mist through which I could see a salting of dim stars. Jane kneeled beside me, her face smeared with coal dust, streaked with tears. She could not tell me what had happened, having been down in the hole the entire time, but according to her everything I had experienced had taken place in a matter of seconds. At length she helped me to stand. My leg was still numb and I had aches and pain resulting from the fall, though I could not have fallen far, because nothing was broken. All of the attractors were twisted and crumpled, like shriveled silver weeds—since most of them had been shut down, I guessed that a wash of energy from the one we destroyed had resonated with some core element in the machinery of the other three. Richmond lay facedown in the dust a dozen feet away. I hobbled over to him, dropped to my hands and knees, and asked if he was all right. He stirred and made a feeble sound.

"Are you able to stand?" I asked.

He turned his head so that I could see his face—his eyes were closed, blood trickled from his nostrils, but his color was good, his pulse strong. I encouraged him, telling him that we had succeeded, but received no reply.

"Tell me what to do," I said. "Should I fetch Bladge to help me carry you?"

He yielded a throaty squeak and opened his eyes. They were Christine's eyes, hazel irises alive with agitated motion, twitching to the left, then to the right, like the dial of a combination lock that had jammed. All the muscles of his face were taut with strain, the tendons of his neck cabled. He sought to speak once again, making a horrid, guttering noise.

I recoiled, as did Jane, who had been peering over my shoulder. Richmond stared, though not at me—he was looking to my left at something that no longer existed in this world.

"Help him!" Jane reached out a hand to him, but withheld her touch. "Can you not help him as you helped me?"

I was loathe to shake him, afraid that whatever injuries he had suffered might be affected; but I felt I had to try, although I knew in my soul that Christine had finally recognized her brother, and now that they were reunited, for better or worse, they would never be parted again.

—

A week after the events I have related, the body of Sir Charles Mellor was discovered on a mud flat alongside the Thames. The corpse was badly decomposed and this made it impossible to determine the date of death; but it was obvious that he had been dead for quite some time and there can be no doubt whatsoever as to the cause: seventeen stab wounds to his neck and torso. His murderer has never been brought to the bar, but I am persuaded to believe that Richmond, half mad and desperate to avenge Christine, acted upon the information I provided, woefully insufficient though it was. I imagine anyone of Mellor's class and character would have suited his purpose and assuaged his guilt.

Shortly before I abandoned the house on Rose Street and returned to Wales, I visited Richmond in Broadmoor, where he was being held preparatory to his transfer to a private facility—the costs of this transfer and all subsequent costs to be assumed by Jane and Dorothea, the chief beneficiaries of his will. An orderly led him into the office where I waited, one belonging to a Dr. Theodore McGuigan, a harried, portly man with a Glaswegian accent, wearing a white smock and braces. When the door opened to admit Richmond I heard demented laughter and shouts and a scream from off along the corridor. He stood blinking and disheveled, unmindful of my presence…of any presence, it appeared. His condition, as far as I could tell, was unchanged, except that his beard was untrimmed and food stains decorated his shirtfront. I asked McGuigan if I might have a moment alone with Richmond and, once the door closed behind him, I perched on the edge of his desk. Richmond stood downcast at the center of the room, his eyes lidded, one hand plucking fitfully at his trouser leg.

"I've had a while to think about things," I said. "Had I been less self-involved, I might have understood what happened long before now. But I believe I've finally pieced it together."

Richmond's mouth worked, making a glutinous noise.

"That first night when you said that you wanted to learn who funded Christine…that was all you wanted to know, wasn't it? You knew who had murdered her. You were simply looking for a way to shift the blame for her death onto the shoulders of another guilty soul."

He rubbed the knuckle of his forefinger against his hip.

"You were the masked client. That's why Christine responded to him as she did to no other man. She may have had some instinctual knowledge that you were the client. And then one night the mask slipped, or else you revealed yourself. What happened next? Did she reject you? Did she threaten you? You've told me she was the aggressor, but you've lied about so much, I wonder if that was just another lie."

He shifted his weight from one leg to the other.

"Everything you did, all your attempts to bring her back…they were by way of expiation. She did something to infuriate you and you killed her."

He remained unresponsive.

"Isn't that right, Christine?"

With a laborious movement, he lifted his head and stared at me with those strangely animated eyes, eyes alive with dartings and glints of light—it was like looking through a crystal into the depths of an inferno and I tried to imagine what he felt trapped in that terrible place. I had thought I would have no pity for him, but I was wrong. His facial muscles strained, his lips trembled, and a feeble fluting of indrawn breath issued from his throat. Then his head drooped and once again he appeared oblivious to his surround.

That, I realized, was likely as close to an answer as I would receive and, seeing no point in prolonging this one-sided dialogue, I called in the orderly who led him back to his cell, there to continue an internal dialogue with his sister.

As he escorted me to the entrance, a short walk attended by the cries and pleadings of the deranged, Dr. McGuigan said, "I'm told that Richmond was engaged in important work."

"Indeed, he was. But I fear it may never be recreated," I said. "His machines were destroyed and his notes have gone missing."

"What a pity. He was a brilliant man."

We went a few paces in silence and then McGuigan said, "You were there, weren't you? On the night he was stricken. Can you enlighten me as to what happened?"

"I was in another portion of the house."

We approached the door and McGuigan spoke again. "Tell me," he said. "What do you think caused the abnormalities in his eyes?"

"I can be of no assistance to you there," I said. "I know nothing about them."

—

I did not lie to Dr. McGuigan—I know nothing except that I know nothing. It may be that I am like all men in this, yet it seems they are unaware of their condition and thus act with an authority of which I am no longer capable. Everything in my story is subject to doubt, to words such as "perhaps" and "likely," and since that story is central to my life, I have grown to doubt most of the certainties of my existence.

Jane and I were married in May of the year and that same summer I opened a clinic in Swansea where I treat the disadvantaged; yet I do so absent the enthusiasm that once I had for the task. I doubt the worth of charity and justice, those values that underscore the work, and find it difficult to reconcile the conviction needed to perform my duties with my loss of faith in the good.

Over the ensuing six years I have taken to writing fiction. Using details gathered during my months on Rose Street, I have gained a wide readership for my ghost stories, which are written with an excess of detachment yet are often praised for their passionate expression. However, the true function of these fictions is self-examination, the same as when I peer into mirrors, looking for shadows in my eyes, afraid that my encounter with that darkness in the cloud of ghosts has infected me and is—despite its apparent state of bliss—responsible for my despairing outlook. Sometimes I remove Richmond's notebooks from the hidden drawer in my desk and go through page after page of equations and technical gibberish, as indecipherable as hieroglyphs, hoping they will magically spark some insight into the essence of that darkness. The feeling of joy it transmitted when I brushed against it, so at odds with its terrible aspect...Was joy its natural state? Was that emotion a tool of the divine? Did it signal the opening of a portal into heaven or was it the lure of a devil? Did it offer a sweet oblivion to the revenants of St. Nichol, a state counterfeited by Richmond's attractors, which instead acted to destroy them? That might explain why they flocked to the rooftop, and it might explain as well why Christine did not hide from it—I may have misinterpreted her presence on the roof. I suspect if I could fathom that mystery, I would understand everything. Perhaps we are all of us either attractors searching for ghosts upon which to feed, or ghosts seeking oblivion. And perhaps the salient difference between the spirit world and this one is that here we can be both.

Jane is the single truth in my life, its sole constant. I have no reason to mistrust her affections, yet I often construct scenarios that paint our marriage as the endgame of an elaborate hoax. When I tell her about them (I tell her everything), she is amused and chides me for being so dismal. For instance, the other day, a sunny day with a salt breeze, as we walked in the green hills above the beach at Pwll Du, she responded to my latest fabrication by saying, "I had to labor at it, else you might have escaped my clutches." She glanced at me with mischief in her eyes and said, "Seducing you was no easy task."

"As I remember, it was I who seduced you."

"Oh, please!" She gave me a pitying look. "After you rejected me that first night, we stayed up all hours, Dorothea and I, plotting your downfall."

"You consulted with Dorothea?"

"It was her idea that I dress as I did on the following night. She thought if I wore matronly bedclothes it might put you at ease. And she lent me her robe. You may recall that it fit me rather snugly."

"The crinoline bonnet," I said. "That almost put me off."

"Yes, I suppose that was a bit much. We debated whether or not to employ it."

"Why did you…?" I left the question unstated, but she finished it for me.

"Why did I seduce you?"

I nodded.

"Because you were beautiful," she said. "Because you were sweet… and kind."

"Beautiful, perhaps," I said, and smiled. "But these days I don't feel especially kind or sweet."

"You're still the man I fell in love with."

"Not so naïve as that man, perhaps."

She blocked my path, preventing me from walking onward. "You're getting better, Samuel. You may not recognize it, but…"

"I don't," I said.

"I wish I'd undergone what you did on the rooftop that night. If I could understand what you went through, I might be able to help you more efficiently."

"I can't understand it myself. It didn't seem like much of anything… at least in retrospect. A few seconds of fear, a few seconds when I was unafraid. But it's been six years and everywhere I put my eyes, I see disease, poverty, corruption, things I once wanted to remedy, but now I no longer can…I don't know."

"The world is not a happy place. That won't change. But you can. You have! You are getting better."

We started walking again.

"You're more vigorous, you're working longer hours." She worried her lower lip. "I think you should give Jeffrey's notebooks to someone. It can't be beneficial to pore over them night after night."

"If I could decipher them and remove the material relating to the attraction of ghosts, I would. That information would surely be exploited."

"Burn them, then. Or give them to me. I'll put them somewhere safe. You need to divest yourself of the past…that portion of it, anyway."

We had reached a spot overlooking a strip of white beach guarded at both ends by enormous boulders. The blue sea stretched, tranquil and vast to the horizon, and the cloudless sky, a lighter blue, empty of birds, echoed that tranquility. Nothing seemed to move, yet I felt a vibration in the earth and air that signaled the movement of all things, the flux of atoms and the drift of unknown spheres. An emotion swelled in my breast, nourished by that fundamental vista, and I felt, as I had not in years, capable of belief, of hope, of seeing beyond myself. Jane linked her arm through mine and rested her head against my shoulder, and whispered something that the wind bore away. And for that moment, for those minutes atop the hill, we were as happy as the unhappiness of the world permits.